GW00535929

Also by Antoine Vanner:

The Dawlish Chronicles

Britannia's Innocent
February – May 1864

Britannia's Guile
January – August 1877

Britannia's Wolf
September 1877 - February 1878

Britannia's Reach
November 1879 - April 1880

Britannia's Shark
April – September 1881

Britannia's Spartan
June 1859 and April - August 1882

Britannia's Amazon
April – August 1882
(Includes bonus short story *Britannia's Eye*)

Britannia's Mission
August 1883 – February 1884

Britannia's Gamble
March 1884 – February 1885

Britannia's Morass
September – December 1884
(Includes bonus short story *Britannia's Collector*)

Being events in the lives of:

Nicholas Dawlish R.N.
Born: Shrewsbury 16.12.1845
Died: Zeebrugge 23.04.1918

and

Florence Dawlish, née Morton
Born: Northampton 17.06.1855
Died: Portsmouth 12.05.1946

Britannia's Guile

The Dawlish Chronicles
January - August 1877

By

Antoine Vanner

Library of Congress Cataloguing-in-Publication Data:

Antoine Vanner 1945 -

Britannia's Guile / Antoine Vanner.

Hard Copy ISBN: 978-1-943404-38-4

Kindle: ISBN: 978-1-943404-36-0

Cover design by Sara Lee Paterson

Published by Old Salt Press

Old Salt Press, LLC is based in Jersey City, New Jersey with an affiliate in New Zealand

For more information about our titles go to: www.oldsaltpress.com

To learn more about the Dawlish Chronicles go to: www.dawlishchronicles.com

Britannia's Guile

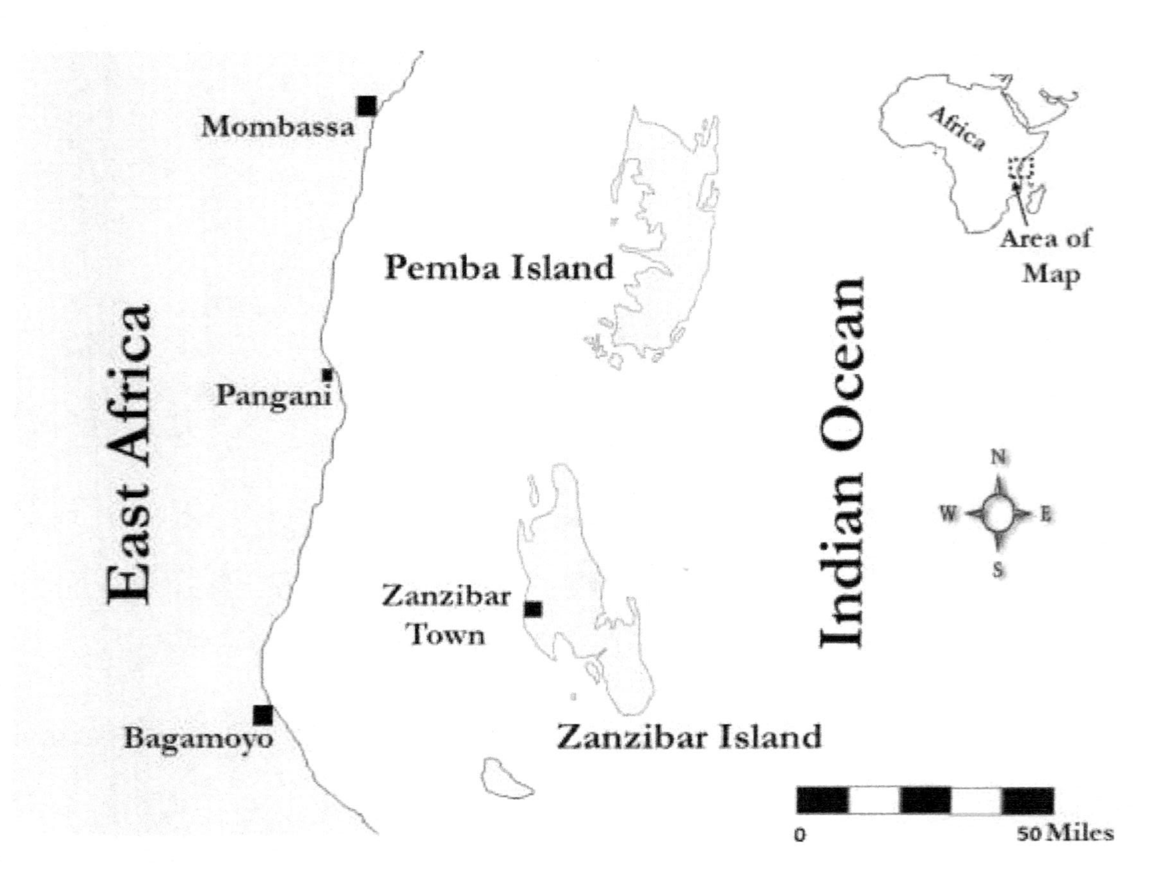
East Africa
Mombassa
Pangani
Bagamoyo
Pemba Island
Zanzibar Town
Zanzibar Island
Indian Ocean
Africa
Area of Map
N
W
E
S
0
50 Miles

Chapter 1

Pemba, East Africa, New Year's Day 1877

The cutter grounded soon after midnight and Lieutenant Nicholas Dawlish waded ashore through the tepid water. Eight others followed. Lighter now, and pulled by the ebbing tide, the cutter moved seawards again under Midshipman Baxter's direction. The sound of the oars was already lost in the lapping of the waves on the beach when the group reached the scrub that extended almost to the high-tide mark. Eastwards, over the island, the moon was full.

Dawlish caught the smell of cloves on the warm air as he fell in with his men behind Musa, the Zanzibari interpreter. They skirted the low brush along the beach until the point where a track emerged. It was little wider than a man. They followed it, more tense now that their range of vision was restricted to a few yards of overgrown and twisting path. The sand underfoot deadened the tread of their canvas shoes and the chatter of the night insects emphasised their own grim silence.

The track broadened after ten minutes into a small clearing bordered by three huts. They flitted across this space one by one, each allowing a short pause before the next followed. No dog barked, no goat bleated. Another ten minutes and the growth about them was thinning. Then the track forked.

Musa, tall and wraithlike in his white kanzu, halted and turned to Dawlish. His teeth flashed as he gestured leftwards. There was the creek. And to the right, the shamba, the plantation, of Abdul bin Ibrahim.

Now the party must split.

"Be ready to cover us, Plummer," Dawlish said. The bosun would take two seamen, Jones and Yates, down to the creek. The lives of the whole party would depend on their success there. "We may be followed when we arrive."

"Aye, aye, sir." Plummer saluted. His rolled-up duck trousers, woollen jersey and sennet hat made him look a sailor in an operetta. The holstered revolver strapped round his waist, the cutlass stuffed in his belt and the Snider rifle grasped in his left hand did not.

Dawlish, similarly armed, watched the three disappear. He felt perhaps more confidence in the bushy-bearded twenty-year veteran, than he did in himself.

"Lead on, you heathen." He pushed Musa forward. His own small group followed him down the right-hand track.

Five more stealthy minutes brought them undetected to the first fields of the shamba and their man-high clove bushes. A little further on, the main buildings, long and low, were separated from the field boundaries by a haphazard scattering of mud and palm-thatch hovels. More cultivation beyond – millet, vegetables, cloves. The party took cover in the bushes to the side of the track, eyes straining for signs of guards. All seemed tranquil and unguarded.

Musa pointed to another track that led away from the left of the buildings through plots of straggling millet. Wide enough to take an ox-cart, it would be the line of retreat to the creek. Plummer's party should have reached there by now. A dog barked in the distance, then fell silent.

Time now to determine whether the birds had not flown deeper into the island's interior. If so, then the mission could be abandoned now without loss.

"Musa!"

Dawlish caught his eye and nodded. Go ahead now.

The interpreter slipped from cover and sauntered towards the buildings. He seemed at once a natural part of the scene, a late home comer perhaps. He knew the place, had posed as a peddler of amulets when he had investigated it the day before. Soon he was lost to sight among the huts. The others waited in silence for his return, nervously fingering their weapons.

The darkness had a velvety warmth. Dawlish, heart pounding, mouth dry, checked the breech of his Snider and opened his holster flap. The butt of his Tranter revolver had a reassuring feel. He toyed with his cutlass, testing its balance. He knew he might die in the coming hour. The knowledge brought the same mix of fear and excitement which he had first known when, still a child, he had crouched in a stagnant ditch before the Taku forts, waiting for the assault signal. The same feeling had often been with him during eighteen months with the Navy's Anti-Slavery Patrol off the East African coast. Short spasms of violence had punctuated months of boredom and discomfort, of endless three-week patrols in open boats, of sun-scorched days, of cramped and aching sleep beneath the thwarts, of glare-dazzled eyes, of half-cooked food and of skin rubbed raw by wet clothing. Alone in the immensity of the Indian Ocean, men and officers alike ate, slept and relieved themselves in close proximity through endless days and nights, longing for, yet fearing, the lookout's call that would hurl them into a headlong chase.

And yet he had craved that elation, would wish to be nowhere else. The massive ironclads of the Channel and Mediterranean Fleets might awe the world but only on distant stations could the peace-time navy offer ambitious officers the chance of action and independent decision.

This patrol had started like a dozen before. HMS *Briton* had worked north towards Mombasa, dropping off a chain of small open craft to intercept Arab slavers. Some would be heading north for the distant and lucrative markets of Muscat and the Gulf, but it was to block any traders aiming to satisfy more local demand that Dawlish's two cutters had taken station off the Pemba coast. Little smaller than Zanzibar, fifty miles to its south, the island was hungry for slaves. Cloves were the foundation of its wealth and the great Arab-owned plantations that grew them devoured labour. The profits were high, high enough to justify the risk of running slaves by the dhow-load past the naval patrols. Powerful Arab raiding parties penetrated hundreds of miles into the African mainland, looting villages of their inhabitants, driving the strongest towards the coast in shackled misery, marking the progress of their shuffling caravans with the corpses of the oldest and the youngest, of the weak and the infirm.

Zealous reformers might thunder from British pulpits about the iniquity of the trade but the actual work of suppression fell to a handful of seamen in open boats. They laboured under one overwhelming disadvantage – slave cargoes intercepted at sea could be liberated but once landed on the Sultan of Zanzibar's territory, which included Pemba, they were legally untouchable. Trading, not possession, constituted the crime in International Law. Three years before, Britain had persuaded the reluctant Sultan Barghash to end the trade, and to permit the Navy to use Zanzibar as a base, but his sovereignty must otherwise be respected. That sovereignty allowed slaves to be held legally on his territory, including Pemba. Slaves could be liberated at sea. Once ashore they were private property.

He glanced about him, saw the men crouched in the shadows, knew from a half-dozen earlier skirmishes and boardings that he could rely on them. But the dangers this time were higher. Had he taken his craft only slightly further south the night before, deeper into the forty-mile channel dividing the island from the mainland, no substantial living cargo could have slipped across.

But this had been his worst luck ever on this coast.

A cutter had landed Musa early the previous morning. His task was routine, to prowl Pemba's markets with ears open for news of expected shipments. The cutter had stood out again after dropping him. It rendezvoused with its consort and loitered over the horizon through daylight. Towards dusk both cutters had sighted a dhow and gave chase northwards. It was midnight before they boarded and found it empty of slaves.

The return southwards was a series of slow tacks so that it was almost daybreak, four hours behind schedule, when they had again picked up Musa. His excitement had made his pidgin almost incomprehensible.

A large dhow had crossed during the night from Pangani, on the mainland, laden with over eighty slaves. It lay now in a creek close to the plantation of Abdul bin Ibrahim. His legal business was as a clove-planter but he was reputed to have bought before from slavers. The dhow's cargo had already been transferred to barracks ashore, at rest at last after their shackled march to the coast and their nightmare sea crossing.

Dawlish had sickened at the news.

Eighty slaves!

On each the Admiralty would have paid a bounty of five pounds sterling, to be divided among all attached to HMS *London*, the depot ship at Zanzibar. A negligible reward, but its loss enough to earn the reproachful glance of every seaman who would feel cheated. And enough also to dent that reputation for success and resolute action that Dawlish had built up on the Patrol and which might yet lead to longed-for promotion. He knew at once that he must land and take those slaves.

He watched the silent, moonlit buildings, waiting with impatience for Musa's return, checking his weapons yet again and ignoring the quiet, logical, internal voice reminding him that he might already have been too hasty, that retreat without detection was still possible. Only action mattered now, he told himself. A landing on Pemba was a clear violation of the Sultan's sovereignty, but that would count for little if he returned with eighty slaves. The legalistic excuse of 'Hot Pursuit' could cover a multitude of sins. The Nelsonian blind-eye would ignore everything except failure. But failure – which would end his career and perhaps result in criminal prosecution – was a very real possibility.

Musa ambled back a quarter-hour later. He was beaming.

"All well, bwana!"

His news was good, when Dawlish extracted it in whispers in the shadows, slowing him so that there was no ambiguity in his mix of Arabic, English and Swahili.

The dhow's crew was sleeping at the shamba, exhausted after feasting and drinking and haggling with Abdul over price.

How many in the house?

Many.

What was many? Ten, twenty?

Musa didn't know. Just many.

And guarding the slaves?

No more than four. The male and female slaves held in separate barracks, two guards to each. Musa had seen them just now, nodding in half-sleep.

And bad news also.

Thirty slaves gone already, all male, purchased by Abdul's cousin, marched to his plantation at Msuka, further north.

One hundred and fifty pounds lost. And yet perhaps a blessing. Fewer now to be dragooned into escape.

Were the slaves chained in the barracks?

Only the men. Rightly so, Musa said. They were wicked people, very savage, M'yeos from Nyasa country. But the women and children were loose within their barracks.

Dawlish had heard enough. He turned to his men. He had explained each role in detail before landing. Now he repeated them.

"Egdean, Strachan – cover the house! I'll join you as soon as I can."

The two Snider and cutlass-armed seamen padded forward in the ragged shadows of the banana clumps fringing the track. Egdean, barrel-chested, tall and powerful, moved like a cat despite his bulk. In long years on the Patrol he had come to know every landmark on the coasts from Kilwa to Lamu and he bore the scars of a dozen or more close encounters with armed slavers. His comrades endured his strong Temperance convictions with amused exasperation.

Strachan followed, a dark and reserved Irishman, a marksman who had picked off the steersman of a fleeing dhow at half a cable as he had balanced in the bows of a pitching cutter. Even in the enforced intimacy of the open boats nobody alluded to his habit of wearing his sleeves long, though all knew of the tattoo high on the right arm. Blotched by a clumsy attempt at removal, the Fenian symbol was still discernible. Dawlish had questioned him about it once. Once had been enough.

"It's why I've been ten years on foreign stations, sir," Strachan's answer had been grudging. "If I went back, me own gang would as soon cut me throat. And your people might have a score to settle also."

But the only answer Dawlish cared about was Strachan's cold reliability in repeated boardings and coastal raids and the quiet, bitter satisfaction he took in his skill.

Now the two seamen headed for Abdul bin Ibrahim's white two-storied house. It stood to the right of the slave quarters, overlooking the plantation. They disappeared into the cluster of huts occupied by the overseers and the older, trusted, slaves who were free to move about unchained.

Dawlish followed Musa. Dutton and Ransford, both seasoned men, were at his heels. They flitted from shadow to shadow, fearful of a wakeful dog, weapons at the ready. Musa brought them to a crouching halt behind a low wall. Beyond it were the long wattle and daub palm-thatched buildings that housed the slaves, the second some twenty yards beyond the first and half-obscured by bushes.

Two guards slouched on stools in half-wakefulness at the doors of the women's barracks. They died in silence when Dutton and Ransford crept up behind them and smashed cutlass hilts into their temples. One needed a second blow.

While Dawlish's hands probed the bodies' warm, sour-smelling robes, searching for keys, Dutton and Ransford headed towards the men's barracks. One of the guards there was slumped backwards in sleep with his rifle across his knees, mouth open. The other was leaning forward in a stupor, supporting himself on a Brown Bess. Dutton repeated his cutlass-hilt trick on this man but as the body pitched forward the musket clattered to the ground. Ransford was poised to strike the other Arab but the noise jolted him into consciousness. He reacted immediately, flinging himself forward so that Ransford's blow brushed harmlessly past him. He opened his mouth to yell but Dutton was on him, one hand locking on his throat while the other drove the cutlass in a brutal body-thrust. Musa accepted the Arab's rifle from his relaxing fingers as he dropped to the ground.

Dutton, Ransford and Musa re-joined Dawlish at the women's barracks.

Dawlish had found the keys by now. This was the critical moment. Success depended now on the slaves' co-operation. He selected a key and tried it in the lock. Beyond the door somebody snored and a child whimpered.

Four keys tried before the door creaked open. A hot stench hit them, foetid and sickening. Musa entered. Dutton and Ransford crouched by the door with rifles at the ready. Dawlish looked in and his eyes accustomed to the gloom. He could just discern the individual forms sleeping on the three tiers of shelves along the sides. Others lay in the floor between. No movement. Sleep must be an almost forgotten luxury for wretches who had shuffled in manacles for weeks towards the coast.

Musa selected an older woman near the door. He locked his hand on her mouth to silence her and shook her awake. Her eyes stared in terror, frightened less by the blade he held to her throat than by the sight of the seamen silhouetted in the doorway. She listened nonetheless to his Swahili and indicated co-operation by head-movements. Musa's hand eased and she whispered something to him. He came back. It was the old story. The captives had never seen a European and the slavers had terrified them with stories of white devils who would roast and eat them.

"Show her Dutton," Dawlish said.

Musa led him to the woman. He lifted her trembling hand and ran it over the seaman's arm and against his thick blond beard.

"Never fear, mother. Never fear." Pity in Dutton's voice.

She could not understand him but it seemed to reassure her nonetheless. He was not a devil.

"Now hurry, Musa," Dutton said. "Time's a-going."

Calmer now, the woman listened to the Zanzibari's instructions. She should waken the older women and explain that they would be taken to freedom. They must control the others during evacuation to the creek. She could understand Musa's dialect only with difficulty and he had to repeat himself.

"What's the problem?" Dawlish said.

She was agitated by fear that she would be loaded on the dhow again. Incarceration in that rolling dungeon had been the most novel and most terrible experience of all since death and whips and shackles had come to her village. Musa wheedled and pleaded. She seemed reassured at last and began to rouse the other women.

Now pandemonium erupted.

Dutton helped the woman drag sleepers to their feet and hunt them towards the entrance. It could not be long before the alarm was raised by this bedlam of wailing women and howling children.

"Send them to the creek, Musa!" Dawlish fought to contain his excitement.

Terrified and bewildered, the women began to hurry down the track, dragging their children. Dawlish and the others chased the remainder from the barracks until the entire building was emptied, then rushed back with Musa and the first woman to the male barracks. The slaves inside it, awakened by the din, were already beating on the door. The woman shouted explanations above the noise of hammering fists and rattling chains while Musa searched for the correct key to liberate them.

It was time for Dawlish to join the rear-guard.

"Dutton! Ransford!" His voice was urgent. "I'm leaving you now! You know your orders. Drive as many of the men as you can down the track, but don't wait for stragglers!"

Musa found the key and the door was swinging open as Dawlish turned away and began to run to join Egdean and Strachan in the thicket opposite Abdul's white two-storied house.

The sleep-befuddled occupants had not yet been woken by the increasing din. Strachan's hissed directions guided Dawlish through the light foliage to where he and Egdean lay close to the edge of the bush, obscured by the growth, rifles trained on the building. The main door emerged on to a verandah. The windows were unglazed, the shutters open for ventilation. A twenty-yard patch of beaten earth lay between the house and the low bushes sheltering the seamen. Dawlish lay down between them, five yards from each, almost in line with the door.

Yelling continued from the barracks. It could be only moments before the alarm was raised. Dawlish, hand trembling, took ten rounds of ammunition from his pouch and laid them in a row in easy reach to his right, ready to feed the breech of his single-shot Snider. He forced himself to take deep breaths and waited for his hands to calm.

The cacophony at the barracks reached a climax.

And then, at last, a white-clad figure appeared at an upper window and leaned out in curiosity. Dawlish stiffened, heard an intake of breath from Egdean, to his right.

"I have him," he whispered as he raised his Snider and held the unsuspecting target in his sights.

Twenty yards. Almost point blank.

Then the Arab was turning, was shouting into the room behind him. Dawlish squeezed his trigger. The heavy bullet caught its victim in the side and spun him back, screaming, into the darkness.

The house came alive with shouting and flickering lights.

Dawlish ejected, reached for the next round, pushed it into the smoking breech. His heart was racing but he forced himself to perform the routine with slow deliberation. Another figure appeared at a window, dark against the glow behind. This time Egdean fired, without result.

The lights died, the windows became black voids again. Silence engulfed the house. There must be confusion within, frantic scuttling below window level, urgent grasping for weapons. The noise from the barracks told that the slaves were on the move.

The main door burst open and Dawlish instinctively shifted his aim towards it. Nobody emerged and he realised too late that the action had been to divert attention from the figure leaping from the window to the right. He arced the Snider across and fired as the sights caught the crouched and running shape. The smoke obscured his view for an instant but he knew he had missed. Strachan's weapon blasted from his right and, as the cloud cleared, and as his own trained hands ejected and reloaded like independent beings, Dawlish saw the Arab pitching forward, a dark crater gouged in his midriff. He shifted his aim back to the still-swinging door. Strachan's prey was dragging himself back towards the house, moaning.

A ball tearing through the bushes to Dawlish's left told him that his position was betrayed by his muzzle flash and gunsmoke. Before he could shift himself, a volley of unaimed fire crashed from the upper floor, and lashed the foliage around him. He flinched but the shooting was only diversionary for, with the reports, the lower windows and door disgorged a pack of shouting men. He fired at the first to come bounding towards him, saw him crumple, was already reloading as Egdean's shot flung another to the ground. Strachan brought down a third. The others hesitated – one bolted back – and then came on again, howling.

Dawlish rose on one knee and fired, dropping the sword-wielding Arab charging straight at him. Egdean's shot took another, hit in the leg. Strachan was on his feet, head and torso exposed, firing, reloading, firing again, missing a crouching figure rushing towards him with a musket but smashing him down with his next shot.

His breech was open and smoking but Dawlish realised he would have no time to reload. Two powerful-looking men were almost upon him, both armed with viciously curved swords. He scrambled to his feet and grasped his rifle by the barrel with both hands. The leading Arab leaped towards him, swinging the sword downwards towards his head. Dawlish flung the rifle up and the blade thudded into the stock. The impact almost knocked him over. For a split second the attacker was off balance and Dawlish had the advantage. His right foot kicked up into the Arab's groin. The man doubled up with a cry and dropped his blade.

The second Arab was a yard away, his sword drawn back across his shoulder for a sweeping cut. Dawlish sidestepped its hissing swing and swung his rifle like a club at his assailant. The butt smashed into his temple and he sank to his knees. Dawlish rushed in on him, beating the butt twice more into the bloody head until the man lay still. He was remotely aware that Egdean and Strachan were still shooting. In front of the house several Arabs seemed to be in retreat. It was time to break off the action.

"Fall back, Lads!" Dawlish yelled, "To the –"

He pitched forward as the first Arab, winded but not immobilised, impacted into his back. Two hands fastened on his neck from behind and probed for his windpipe. He began to choke and he dropped his rifle so as to prise the fingers free. Gasping, tongue protruding, he knew he was about to black out. With his last reserves of strength, he flung himself backwards and took his attacker crashing to the ground beneath him. The man gasped in pain and his grip relaxed for a moment. Dawlish twisted free. The Arab was already wriggling towards the sword that he had dropped earlier.

Dawlish reached for his holster but the attacker was on his feet again and coming at him, sword scything for his neck. He ducked and the blade swished over his head. His revolver butt was in his grasp now and he was pulling it out but he realised that he could not be in time. He saw the blazing hatred on his enemy's contorted face, the arm drawn back for the death stroke. This was the end, he recognised, almost with calm. He tensed to take the blow.

Egdean was standing ten feet to the right. Even at that range he steadied his pistol on his forearm, taking careful aim. His shot blasted the Arab's face open just as the sword commenced its swing.

Deliverance.

Chapter 2

Plummer's group had arrived at the creek to find the small landing stage unguarded. The Pangani dhow swung at anchor in deeper water, twenty yards out. There was no sign of life. Several dugout canoes lay moored at the jetty. Yates stood watch while Plummer and Jones paddled out and boarded. Plummer satisfied himself that a few blows of a cutlass would sever the cable and then paddled back, leaving Jones on board. The tide had turned and was now breaking in a ripple against the vessel's bows.

They heard the shooting long before the shouts of the slaves fleeing towards them. Then a living torrent came pouring down the dark track, bodies glistening in the moonlight, first the women, some dragging or carrying children, then the men, tripping and falling, hobbled by their chains. Behind them came Dutton and Ransford, here hauling a fallen slave to his feet, there beating onwards a woman who had sunk in exhaustion. They turned every few paces, rifles ready, alert for pursuit.

A knot of panting women was first at the jetty. Plummer and Yates pointed to the canoes but the women refused to board, shrinking from the dhow that nudged the current in midstream and from its cargo of memories. The confusion continued until Musa arrived, dragging the woman he had first chosen as his interpreter. Exhausted, retching, she collapsed on all fours while Musa yelled that she must persuade the others to enter the canoes. Precious minutes passed before she regained her breath and yet more before the first laden canoes splashed towards the dhow. But now the slaves seemed to sense deliverance. A few men were reunited with their families and began to help stroke the canoes back and forth to the vessel.

Dutton and Ransford took up positions fifty yards up the track while Plummer counted off the slaves. He reached thirty-seven. Another dozen or so to go. He wondered how far away was Baxter's cutter. It should have been in the creek by now to cover the retreat.

And sounds of spasmodic shooting was still coming from the shamba.

*

Dawlish's throat still burned from his near-throttling as he darted with Egdean and Strachan towards the men's barracks. They paused there, glancing back to see their pursuers milling after them.

"Slow them!" Dawlish fought to regain his breath.

Strachan turned, raised his Snider, took aim and fired, reloaded, fired again, five rounds in quick succession. He dropped one Arab and scattered the rest into cover before Dawlish pulled him away.

They pounded past the now empty barracks, down the winding track. On either side the ground was covered with waist-high millet and isolated stands of bananas. Around a bend – the track ahead was straight for eighty yards or more. They were panting now and shots were crashing out behind them, but the balls sped wide. Then a welcome curve blocked them once more from their enraged hunters. Dawlish's muscles screamed. Each breath was a rasping agony. Egdean hammered on just ahead of him, Strachan to his side.

Now they could smell the creek and hear the excited din there, even the welcome roar of Plummer's voice. The sounds of pursuit were close but the jetty was in sight and the track ran die-straight towards it. They were going to make it.

A hundred yards, ninety . . .

Dutton's was yelling: "It's Mr. Dawlish! And Jem Strachan! And Jerry Eg –"

The cry was drowned by a musket report. Egdean crashed down, blood erupting through his white trouser leg. There was no time to sidestep and Dawlish collided with Egdean's fallen bulk and his rifle dropped from his hand. He struggled to his feet, glanced back. A knot of pursuers at the bend were dropping to their knees to take aim. Egdean was already crawling towards the dry ditch beside the track.

"Get down, sir!" He pulled Dawlish down with him into the trench.

Strachan jumped down beside them. "I've only two rounds left." he said.

Dawlish groped in his own pouch and passed his remaining six Snider cartridges to Strachan. A search of Egdean's stock yielded five more. Strachan took them, scrambled along the shallow trench, found a position that offered both cover and a clear view of the bend. He ducked as a ragged volley screamed overhead.

Even in the moonlight Dawlish could see the colour draining from Egdean's face. The seaman pushed him away. "Save yourselves, sir." His voice was weak already.

"Hold your tongue, Egdean," Dawlish said. "You're coming!"

Strachan was firing with deliberation, ejecting, reloading and aiming again as calmly as he might on a shooting range. From the jetty Plummer and the others had joined his fire to prevent the Arabs advancing down the track, then driving them into cover. Egdean sighed with pain as the initial shock wore off. His right calf was a soaking mess of torn flesh and cloth. Dawlish felt it. The bone seemed intact but the blood spurting between his fingers told of a ruptured artery. With every pulsation the seaman's life was draining away. He groped for Egdean's belt, loosened it, then passed it round the leg just above the knee and dragged it tight.

""I'll hold it, sir". Egdean's voice was hoarse. "Don't let them pagans surround us. It's what they'll try."

Both their rifles lay where they had dropped them on the track. Dawlish was damned if he would leave them as trophies. He darted out, crouching, and scooped them up, and a ball howled close overhead as he dived again for the ditch's cover. He pulled out his revolver and glanced up the track. It was deserted now. The firing had died away.

Plummer's foghorn voice roared. "We're ready to cast off, sir! Do you need help?"

Low and not too-distant rustling broke the silence that followed. Dawlish realised with horrible certainty that the Arabs were creeping through the crop and outflanking him. He dared not answer Plummer lest he betray his presence.

Strachan looked back and gestured towards the millet. He too had heard that terrifying rattling of the stalks. Dawlish signalled him to join them. Strachan began to creep bac down the ditch, turning every few paces to scan for movement.

"We're moving now, Egdean." Dawlish pushed one of the Sniders into his hand and swung the other on his own shoulder. "Hold that belt tight! Hang on me and support yourself on that rifle as best you can. Ready now?"

"I'll do my best, sir." Face paper-white.

Dawlish dragged the heavy seaman upright, felt him stiffen with agony as he passed an arm around him for support. They waded into the millet. Dawlish tried to stay stooped but doing so made progress impossible. He straightened up and found they both towered over the half-grown crop. Egdean groaned with every step, only his last reserves of will sustaining him against the pain. Shots rang out left and right as they crashed forward. Strachan followed a few yards behind, ducking and weaving through the growth, bobbing up to blast towards any indication of movement left or right or behind.

Plummer bellowed, "Cut the cable, Jones! Let her drift! We'll follow in a canoe." And then, like some succouring angel, "We're coming for you, Mr Dawlish!"

The pursuers were close. Dawlish could hear their yells but he stumbled on, his strength at its limit, for Egdean was almost a dead weight by now. His heart leapt as Plummer and Yates came plunging towards him through the millet, firing past him as they came.

And then a scream, long, dreadful, rent the air behind. Dawlish turned to see a confused scuffling of crouched bodies and two swords slicing downwards in the moonlight. He saw Strachan stagger to his feet, hands clasped across his cloven head and face, then crumple under another murderous blow. Yates pushed forward towards the fracas, firing as he did, but too late to save his shipmate or to hit either of his killers as they scuttled back into cover. He stooped for a moment, appalled by the hacked and crimsoned remains, then sprinted back towards Dawlish.

Now the pursuers seemed to be on all sides, screaming hatred, flushed by prospect of vengeance. Their shots lashed through the millet, flaying fragments from the stalks. The air was thick and acrid with drifting smoke. Musket-fire from the direction of the creek told Dawlish with sickening certainty that his small party was outflanked and its escape cut off. He lowered Egdean to the ground as gently as he could, then stooped by him, drawing his own pistol, taking the seaman's also. A small, cold, inner voice told him to count his shots as he fired. Two rounds must remain at the end, one for Egdean, one for himself.

They formed a rough triangle in the trodden crop as they made their stand. Plummer was blasting with his revolver at any close movement. Five yards away, Yates, winded by his run and out of ammunition, had drawn his cutlass to withstand the inevitable final charge. Dawlish crouched over the groaning and now only semi-conscious Egdean, four cartridges remaining in his Tranter's cylinder, knowing that they were pinned down without hope, trapped by the white-clad figures that bobbed from the yard-high millet to blaze at them. Death was but minutes away and all knew it, Dawlish most bitterly of all, conscious that his pride and recklessness that had brought them to this.

It was at this moment, when the dhow was drifting down the creek under Jones's command, its cable severed, the slaves huddled in its hold, and when Dawlish's group was trapped in the millet like cattle in a shambles, that Baxter and the remainder of the patrol arrived in the second cutter.

Delayed by a grounding, it now swept up the creek, oars beating rhythmically. Baxter was crouched in the bows by the launching tube for 24-pound Hales rockets, a slow match glowing in his hand. The cutter shaved past the dhow and already the tube was being swivelled and elevated, for Baxter had spotted the dark knot and the drifting smoke among the millet. He raised the elevation still further and held the match against the fuse. The rocket sizzled, then blasted from the tube, showering sparks over cutter and dhow alike.

Dawlish heard its whoosh as it blazed overhead like a long-tailed comet. It lit his and his men's upturned faces as they looked up and saw it like some portent of deliverance. Their attackers looked up too, but in horror, at its fiery progress. Even before it fell in the millet some hundred yards beyond, blasting a crater and shaking the ground, Baxter and his men were manhandling another rocket into the tube.

The first missile harmed nobody, even though it panicked Abdul bin Ibrahim's men into headlong retreat, but the second fell among them, killing three and maiming several more.

And so Dawlish and his group survived.

They turned their backs on the smoking crater and the fragments of scorched flesh, away from the flames that now crackled though the dry crop and shed crimson light on the carnage. Plummer plodded towards the creek, an unconscious Egdean hoisted on his huge shoulders. Dawlish and Yates followed, dragging what was left of Strachan, their progress marked by a bloody streak of trampled millet. A shredded sleeve flapped open to reveal a tattooed harp and three indecipherable letters, not that it mattered any more.

Out in the creek, forty-seven terrified slaves cowered in the dhow, unaware as yet of what their liberation into an uncertain future signified.

Had the price paid been too high? Dawlish closed his mind to doubt. He had done what he had come to do.

And that counted as success.

Chapter 3

White-clad figures moved aside as Dawlish guided his mount through the foetid streets flanking Zanzibar's main market. It was just after eight, and he had set off on his ride through the outlying plantations in the cool before sun-up, but now he was no less sweat-soaked than the horse he had borrowed from the Sultan's stables. He needed a long drink more than food. He heaved himself from the saddle before a thick-walled Arab house, passed the reins to the groom who had followed him on horseback and threw him a coin. The man bowed and turned away. He would return the beast to the stables and meet Dawlish here again early the following morning. It was a daily ritual during shore leave between patrols.

Servants rushed forward to hand Dawlish a basin, towel and a glass of sherbet, and to take his hat and whip.

He mopped his face. "Bwana Robert, is he back?".

And yes, Bob Sinclair, the Scots clove trader of his own age with whom he lodged when ashore, had returned for breakfast after starting work in the first light of dawn. Dawlish dropped his sodden shirt to the ground, sponged his torso with water from the basin, then pulled on the gown held ready for him, and moved into the house's shadowy cool.

Six weeks had passed since his Pemba exploit had swelled the bounty fund by two hundred and thirty-five pounds. He had been the hero of HMS *London's* wardroom for all of a week. The station commander had brushed aside the Sultan's complaint about violated sovereignty. The familiar hot-pursuit excuse was offered with a straight face and accepted after ritual protests. Midshipman Baxter, intoxicated by the havoc wrought by his streaking rockets, and hopeful of promotion for the affair, had sent off an account of the raid to a London journal under the penname of 'Heart of Oak'. Strachan had been interred at Zanzibar with full honours, Egdean's leg had been saved and Dawlish had completed another patrol, this time uneventful. He returned from it to find the Pemba affair already forgotten.

Sinclair set down a creased newspaper on the table and pushed a bowl of fruit towards Dawlish. "I don't know why you want to ride in this bloody climate, Nick." He was stout and florid, sweat glistening on his face even here in the shade. "I find it enough just walking to and from the counting house."

A stack of other newspapers on the table caught Dawlish's eye. Sinclair's sister regularly sent him bundles of months-outdated British newspapers and journals.

"So the *Amelia's* docked, has she?" Dawlish said. The vessel had been overdue from Aden, occasioning Sinclair's mounting concern.

"She took a battering five days back A heavy squall off Malindi, but she's here now." Sinclair spoke without looking up, engrossed in his reading. The subject had to be interesting to distract his attention from the arrival of a vessel which he had fretted over for a week while waiting for business letters. There was talk of a telegraph cable to link Aden, Zanzibar and ports further south, but investors were as yet holding back. Arrival of mail was still a longed-for event.

Dawlish skimmed through a succession of month-old copies of *The Times*, eager for the latest news of the conflict simmering in Bulgaria. War threatened there and promised a perhaps-wider European conflict. And prospects of action, glory and promotion. He raced over news that was predictable – agrarian outrages in Ireland, frontier disturbances in India, a rail disaster in the United States, a financial scandal in France. Rumours that Gainsborough's portrait of the Duchess of Devonshire, spirited away from a London gallery in May, had been located in a German baron's schloss had proved unfounded.

Across the table Sinclair had fallen silent, apparently shocked, but fascinated, by what he was reading.

Naval news had distracted Dawlish from Bulgaria. The findings of the enquiry into the sinking of HMS *Vanguard*, rammed by her sister *Iron Duke* in a fog off Dublin Bay were depressing. A boiler explosion on HMS *Thunderer* had caused forty deaths. An item from early January indicated hope abandoned for a French-constructed Russian ironclad en-route from the builder's yard to St. Petersburg. She had put in at Vigo for coaling and had not been seen since. *The Times'* naval correspondent speculated that the *Alexander Nevski* had been overtaken by a disaster similar to that which had befallen HMS *Captain* in the Bay of Biscay six years earlier. Heavy guns mounted too high in a full-rigged ship had capsized her in a squall. It brought back memories to Dawlish of two contemporaries who had gone down with her.

He lit a cigar, picked up another paper, was soon deep in the Balkan crisis. Bulgarian Christians, oppressed beyond endurance, had revolted the previous year. They had not anticipated the savagery with which their Ottoman Turkish overlords would respond. Murderous irregulars, Bashi

Bazooks, had been unleashed to massacre whole communities in atrocious reprisals. Russia, posing as champion of Orthodox Christendom, was threatening intervention to stop the persecution.

And that could be a spark to set off the European powder keg.

"What would a war do for the price of your cloves, Bob?" Dawlish called across the table. "The Russians seem set at taking on the Turks again."

For war, he knew, might not stop at Bulgaria. Almost a quarter of a century before, Britain had come to Turkey's aid in the Crimean bloodbath to resist Russian pressure. There would be every incentive for her to do so again. Barbarous the Turks might be, but their oppressed territories in the Balkans represented the only sure obstacle to Russian expansion to the Mediterranean.

"You're a cold devil, Nick," Sinclair threw his paper down in disgust. "You'd love it, wouldn't you? Action, glory, promotion. And never a tuppeny damn for the poor wretches the same Bashi Bazooks you'd be defending would be free to slaughter."

"I'm no politician," Dawlish said. "If their Lordships show me an enemy and tell me to fight him, then that's what I'll do."

For war, if it came, would mean death and mutilation for many, but for the lucky few in the Royal Navy it would signify opportunities and promotions impossible in peacetime. Without a major war, an ambitious officer could only seek advancement through assignments to dangerous, small-scale operations like the Anti-Slavery Patrol, and hope to draw attention by dash and enterprise. The dangers could be mortal and, all too often, recognition did not follow, the reports filed away and forgotten in some Admiralty pigeonhole.

"Hold your cynicism until you've read that." Sinclair passed over a copy of the *Daily News*. "There!" He stabbed at a lengthy article.

Dawlish liked his friend too much to argue. He read at first from courtesy but, as he continued, the writing gripped him. He had seen enough action before now to sense the raw truth of an eyewitness's outraged account of Ottoman atrocities perpetrated on Bulgarian peasants. They went beyond the most insane mind's imagination. He wanted to believe that there must be exaggeration. The number of dead, fifteen thousand, seemed impossible, the cruelties too lurid.

And yet there was a dreadful sense of truth about the reporting. It troubled him but he did not want to admit it. Lieutenant Nicholas Dawlish had an image of cold ruthlessness to maintain.

"No correspondent ever made his name by understatement," he said. "The fact that the fellow's name is MacGahan may explain a lot. He sounds like an Irishman. They're notoriously unreliable."

"You're cold, cynical and mercenary, Nick!" Exasperation, but no malice, in Sinclair's voice. He shook his head and plunged into another paper.

"And you're a canting hypocrite, Bob," Dawlish tried to make a joke of it. "Never a damn about where the labour comes from to till your precious cloves, but a psalm on your lips every Sunday and an ebony Venus in the back quarters for the rest of the week!"

Sinclair threw a date at him in mock anger. Such insults were an established part of their relationship. But as he resumed his reading, he could see that Dawlish was again absorbed in MacGahan's catalogue of evil, his face troubled.

*

HMS *Dryad*, a screw sloop, arrived from Port Said three days later. A parcel of books was among the mail for Dawlish, forwarded by a London bookseller. They were his one major extravagance. And *Dryad* also brought news of his future. He found himself summoned to the station commander's cabin on *London* two hours after the sloop's arrival.

"It looks as if your time with the Patrol is up, Dawlish" he said. "I've no doubt the station will be the duller without you."

"Any details of my next ship, sir?"

"Report to their Lordships on arrival at the Admiralty, nothing more. You could be heading anywhere. But if you take my advice, you'll try for the Mediterranean."

"Do you think there'll be war, sir?" Dawlish guessed that *Dryad* had carried despatches.

"The Lord knows. Nobody else! It seems there's a conference of the powers at Constantinople. Mollify the Russians, maintain the balance of power, that sort of thing. You won't be surprised to hear that the Turks are offering guarantees of Christian rights. Maybe the Russians will be fool enough to trust 'em. I wouldn't."

HMS *London's* wardroom drank that night to the damnation of the peacemakers in general and to failure of Lord Salisbury, Britain's delegate at the Constantinople conference, in particular. There were also toasts, many tinged with envy, for Dawlish's next assignment. The prospect of endless chases of dhows off Zanzibar seemed less alluring now when there were chances of fleet action off Odessa or Sebastopol.

Dryad departed for Malta in late-February. Dawlish joined her, wondering whether advancement was in the offing. At thirty-one, after two years on the Anti-Slavery Patrol, a record of meritorious service before that and a succession of mainly favourable reports, independent command was just possible. A small gunboat perhaps. The first grey was streaking the dark of his temples and close-cropped beard. It would go well with command. He hankered after more than the excitement of the Patrol and the carefree bachelor establishment shared with Bob Sinclair.

He paid one debt of honour before *Dryad* departed. He knew that Egdean had not seen relatives or homeland for almost a decade. *London's* surgeon was easily cajoled into recommending Egdean for sick leave and convalescence in Britain.

When he brought the news to Egdean in the sick-bay, he saw a Bible on the small shelf next to him. It must have seen years of service, for its leather cover was scuffed and discoloured. He knew the seaman to be a Good Templar, steadfast and loyal to the temperance pledge taken years before. Now he was studying a copy of *Ashore and Afloat*, the Evangelical magazine for seamen that seemed to reach every station, however remote. A Miss Agnes Weston published it. She was a lady who had taken the cause of seamen's welfare and temperance as her own, was respected by upper and lower decks alike.

Dawlish remarked on it.

"My reading's been a comfort, sir, while I've been here." Egdean said.

Yet, to Dawlish's surprise, he seemed hesitant at the mention of home leave.

"It ain't that I wouldn't want to see my brother and sister, sir," he said. "But there was a spot of trouble before I enlisted." He looked uncomfortable as he said it, the memory of some old shame still obviously fresh.

"Something with the law?" Dawlish smiled, tried to make light of it. "If it's anything short of murder we could put a good word in. Or even a woman?"

"No, sir. Not murder. And … and not a woman neither. But I'd dearly like to see my family, sir."

"If there's a problem you can call on me for a reference. You'll have a good one." Dawlish scribbled his father's address on a scrap of paper.

"This will find me during my leave. And now I need your brother's name."

It was not Egdean.

Like so many, the seaman had enlisted under an alias.

"It's just a place nearby my home," Egdean said.

But, at last, he was reassured enough to give his brother's address. Before *Dryad* weighed anchor to head north, he hobbled on board and slung his hammock in the forecastle.

A virtual passenger, Dawlish's duties were minimal, to assist with navigation and stand relief watches when needed. For the rest he haunted the engine and boiler rooms, much to the amusement of *Dryad's* officers, familiarising himself with the machinery, satisfying a passion denied on the Anti-Slavery patrol. He also struggled with Mr. Darwin's newly arrived *Descent of Man.*

Aden, as always, was like an oven but it had one major advantage compared with Zanzibar – the telegraph linked it to Europe and fed recent information to the single newspaper published there. The peace conference was still sitting in Constantinople, the Bulgars were still suffering, the Russians were still threatening, the Ottomans were still unrepentant and intransigent. Lord Beaconsfield, Britain's prime minister, the recently ennobled Benjamin Disraeli, was still pleading for understanding for the Sick Man of Europe. And his opponent, the Liberal Mr. Gladstone, had returned from retirement to denounce the Ottomans with righteous indignation and scathing oratory.

Dryad ploughed northwards though the steam bath of the Red Sea and on through the Suez Canal. At Port Said the international situation was unchanged, but the newspapers purchased there told of an increased level of military and naval preparedness – even uneasiness – among the great powers. The presence at the canal's portal of Britain's *Rupert* and *Tenedos*, a French ironclad and an Austrian-Hungarian cruiser moored close by, told its own story of tense anticipation.

Dawlish's hopes for action were rising as *Dryad* battered her way westwards though stormy seas. His heart rose as she slipped into the Grand Harbour at Malta and found it pregnant with naval might. The ironclads of the Mediterranean Fleet lay there, proud names – *Sultan*, *Agincourt*, *Temeraire*, *Hotspur*, *Swiftsure* – splendid with their white hulls and buff masts and funnels, brightwork gleaming, lesser craft clustered about them like chicks around a flock of hens. Should war come, it was with this force that he longed to serve. It thrilled him to imagine this fleet pressing through the Dardanelles and Marmara and Bosporus, and into the Black Sea, to harry the Russians' flank, destroy their shipping and blast their bases into rubble. Here was history on the eve of birth. Here lay advancement.

But first he must report at London. He gained leave at Malta to proceed at his own expense rather than wait for naval transport. He first ensured that Egdean was lodged in comfort at the Naval Hospital. The earnest seaman was almost fully recovered and would be proceeding to Britain by the next naval vessel to depart.

"You've become quite famous, Egdean."

Dawlish showed him an account of the Pemba affair in a London-published illustrated journal. Heart of Oak's overblown narrative was overshadowed by the engraving that accompanied it. A band of resolute tars on an open beach blazed at hordes of attackers, whose losses were already in dozens. A wounded giant – Egdean himself – lay on the ground, his head cushioned by a shipmate and his eyes cast heavenwards. He clasped his breast with one hand and with the other gestured to the Union flag that a noble-looking officer steadied while as he thrust his cutlass into an attacking Arab. Over his left shoulder the cutter surged to the rescue, a huge rocket rising from it in a torrent of sparks.

"It's beautiful, sir." Egdean's voice was hushed in solemn respect. "It ain't exactly how it was, but 'tis close." His eyes filled. "If only my mother had lived to see this, sir. She would have framed it, sir, she surely would. And my brother, he'll treasure it too."

Dawlish pressed a sovereign on him, shook his hand, hoped that he would encounter him again and departed the next day to Marseilles by commercial steamer. Mr. Trollope's latest, *The Prime Minister*, shortened the passage. His civilian attire, tailored at short notice in Malta, felt strange and inappropriate.

Misfortune struck at Marseilles. A bout of his recurrent malaria, the heritage of his Ashanti service, delayed him for a week of alternating fever, teeth-chattering chill and blinding headaches. Quinine brought relief but he was weak and exhausted when he travelled onwards by rail to Paris. He spent three days there but fatigue frustrated his attempts to enjoy the sights of a city that had already forgotten the horrors of siege and civil war six years before. Then he journeyed on to London.

He arrived at Victoria Station on Tuesday the 24th of April. There was a commotion outside the building, the newsboys were proclaiming a 'Stop-Press.' He pushed through the excited crowd, threw down a copper, picked up the single-page broadsheet and scanned it.

His heart soared. Russia had declared war on Turkey. Her forces had crossed the Rumanian frontier and were heading for the Danube.

Opportunity.

Chapter 4

Dawlish telegraphed his father of his arrival and went by hansom to put up at the Charing Cross Hotel, conveniently located near the Admiralty. He reported there the following morning. Its corridors were thronged with command-hungry officers, all conscious that it could only be a matter of time, should the war scare continue, before vessels were recommissioned from reserve. Names of half-forgotten ships that had swung at anchor in backwaters for half a decade, decaying and rusting, were now bandied about as if their refurbishment was essential to national survival. The staff looked harried and impatient. Messengers hurried from office to office with armfuls of files.

He sat in a succession of anterooms and learned that he was nobody's priority. It took a day to secure a medical examination and another two for some inconclusive meetings with impatient middle-ranking officials. He might have waited longer than the week he did for the interview he sought with the Second Naval Lord, responsible for matters of personnel, had he not served as a midshipman with this demi-god's secretary. He was out of the office again after three minutes, wondering if he had damaged his chances for good by pushing for the meeting. His Lordship did not hide his impatience and neither the Anti-Slavery Patrol nor Pemba were mentioned. He noted with irritation Dawlish's desire for immediate employment and reminded him that there were dozens of other young lieutenants, no less well qualified, who were also soliciting appointments. Dawlish had already been accorded three months leave, had he not? He would just have to wait and see. The rest would no doubt be good for him - he had a damn sickly-looking pallor about him. Malaria, did he say? Damn careless – he was expected to take his quinine wine daily and set an example to the men. Then he was wished a curt 'Good Morning' and he found himself in the anteroom again.

Seven other officers were waiting their patient turns as he left, four in their early thirties, doing their obvious best to give an impression of eagerness and efficiency, the others middle-aged men probably eking out a life of shabby respectability on half-pay. He walked out into the sunlight. Now, at last, he was going home.

His father stood waiting on the station platform at Shrewsbury, tall and erect in his mid-sixties, a quarter-century widower, ruddy-faced and fit from hunting two days each week through the season.

"You're looking pale, Nicholas. I thought you had sun in Zanzibar." He greeted Dawlish with a strong handshake while William, the groom, loaded the trunks into the waiting dogcart.

"It was malaria, Father. I had a touch in Marseilles."

"Nothing a few days in the saddle won't put right then. I'll see you well mounted."

They rattled through the streets towards the rambling house on the town's outskirts.

"You should have been here last week, Nicholas," his father said. "You missed a damn exciting day! The Richardson case came to court. I hope you got the details?"

Dawlish nodded in resignation. He had read only the first and last pages of the bulky letter that had reached him in London. This was the start, he knew, and soon he would hear more than once of every disputed will, of every petty action for damages, of every disagreement over rights-of-way that had busied his father's solicitor's practice since his last visit.

But, as always, there was another presence in the cart, unmentioned but powerful. His elder brother was dead for half a decade. Had James not shown aptitude to follow in his father's footsteps, and a talent for detail and routine, Dawlish himself might never have been permitted to enter the Navy. While he himself had gone on to risk and survive death in a dozen forms on most oceans and continents, James, a market-town solicitor, had died with a broken neck during a fox hunt when his gelding failed to clear a five-barred gate.

The homecoming was like every other in the last nineteen years. Mrs. Gore, his former nurse, now the housekeeper, clasped him and wept and laughed in turn, blessing God for bringing Master Nicky safely home from the blackamoor heathens. Other servants, less familiar, hovered in the background, bowing and curtsying their welcomes.

His trunks were lugged upstairs and unpacked in the room that had stayed unchanged since he had left for the Navy at thirteen. The shelf above his bed still held his childish books, the same chipped ewer stood on the washstand beneath the sampler embroidered by his mother that stated that God is Love. He reached out, touched it, was sad that he could not remember how she had looked. The single sepia photograph taken of her showed her stiff and unsmiling for the camera's long exposure. It had nothing of her warmth that he half-remembered. She had died in childbirth when he was four but the wound of loss had never healed. The elm outside was in leaf and a branch still brushed across the window in the breeze, as it had always done. It seemed unreal to him that he should have come once again to this safe haven, as if the hardships and dangers of the Indian Ocean had never been.

Mrs. Gore had conducted a reign of terror in the kitchen to ensure that Master Nicky's favourite roast leg of lamb, laced with mint sauce, was on the table that night. His father washed all down with more claret than was good for him. Two years' pent-up stories were rushing out now, epics of codicils and affidavits, uncertain boundaries and dubious testaments.

"Perhaps you read in the newspapers about the Patrol's successes?" Dawlish tried again. "Not just at Pemba, further north too, all along the coast and …"

His father might have heard him – or he might have been rehearsing in his mind the next story of his own legal acumen – but he had neither question nor observation about his son's proud anecdotes. It had ever been thus, two men who loved each other, who longed for each other's company when separated, but who talked past each other when reunited.

And then, at last, as so often before, the familiar suggestion, half-pleading, half-embarrassed. That he should resign from the Navy, take articles, join his father in the practice.

"You'd like this work, Nicholas. You really would."

"I wouldn't, Father."

"You would, Nick. It's not too late. A few months' study. That's all it would take. You're a clever chap, God knows, and I'd be there to assist you. And we could hunt together, twice a week in the season, sometimes even thrice. You'd like that, wouldn't you?"

Dawlish tried to make light of it. "I'm too old a salt, Father. I'd miss the sea. And besides, the Navy suits me."

The moment passed. His father began to speak of the details of a complicated marriage settlement and he feigned interest. Yet he knew the question would come back. It would lie like a barrier between them and would grow until the inevitable outburst came, with recriminations and harsh words, just before he left again. And in some moment of danger in the uncertain future, he knew he would regret those words and long back with love and contrition to live again this evening of affectionate boredom.

They rode together the next morning, calling on families Dawlish had known since childhood. He was a passing focus of interest for neighbours, friends and clients, displayed with pride by his father to eligible daughters and calculating mothers. In the following days he visited his farms in the south of the county that an agent managed for him. They were his own, not his father's, inherited from his mother's brother. They brought in little, in some years barely enough to cover the cost of his uniforms. He discussed possible improvements with the agent. He always did, and now, as always, they agreed that only a few could not be afforded. On other days he spent long hours on one of his father's two hunters, picking his way through country lanes, eating a simple lunch at some wayside inn and revelling in the spring landscape he had so often recalled during steaming tropical watches. Those evenings on which he could avoid invitations to neighbours and the scrutinies of judicious parents he spent reading.

Pleasant though this time was, an uneasiness, bordering on depression, haunted him. Seeing that farms had brought back memories of the uncle who had bequeathed them to him. Ralph Page had been a naval officer too, one driven from the navy by consumption. The hope of recovery offered by Pau, the spa-town in the Pyrenees, had proved futile. Dawlish had spent the final months with him. Even at twelve years old he could sense the infinite sadness of a man dying unfulfilled.

And that prospect could be his also.

His visit to the Admiralty had reminded him that he was just one of a host of officers qualified to command a gunboat. There would be, in due course, appointments for all who did not make this step. They would be essential but mundane posts, would never bring exposure to the sort of opportunities that made careers in major wars. An exploit like that at Pemba was not unusual and too soon forgotten. Great names were made in battle with powerful foes. Without the French, Nelson's career might have passed in worthy obscurity. It was not the French this time, but the Russians, and the present opportunities might never come again.

Six weeks passed and only the arrivals of each day's *Times* and *Morning Post* were reminders that Europe tottered on the edge of general war. The Russians built up their forces in Rumania, their intent of forcing the Danube line obvious. Ottoman Turkish vessels dominated its waters. South of it, Turkish army units moved into defensive positions. The miracle of the telegraph brought the newspapers long, graphic reports from correspondents with both armies. The Russian colossus was pushing ever-greater numbers into Rumania and correspondents predicted imminent Turkish rout. Britain and the other powers still held aloof, watchful for advantage, intent on recognising the critical moment.

Dawlish fretted for the Admiralty telegram that would recall him to duty. He was wearying now of his father's relentless returns to his favourite subject.

"I'm getting old, Nicholas," he said one evening as they drew on cigars while dusk gathered in the garden. "It's normal for a man to want his son to succeed him. You'd be happy here. You'd like the work after a little while. You could even find yourself a wife."

And Dawlish tried to laugh it off. "The Navy's wife enough for now, Father."

It was true, might perhaps be ever so. A disappointment a decade before had let him untrusting of women.

"That daughter of Squire Emery for instance," his father said. "Rowena. The old chap worships her. She's worth five thousand, maybe six, if she's worth a penny. She'd have you in a flash, Nicholas. I saw her eyeing you on Wednesday evening."

"That was just her fetching natural squint, Father. And she's fourteen stone if she's an ounce! That wretched mare of hers has gone bow-legged under her."

"You're a fool, Nick, a damned fool!"

"Then marry her yourself, Father. You're spry enough. Why, you still take fences that men half your age balk at! And I'd have no objection to a half-brother or sister if it came to that."

The old man blushed and protested. But he was pleased.

A dinner invitation came from Squire Emery the following day. A week later another, and then a reciprocal invitation, and so a predictable sequence was established. And Miss Rowena Emery, supported with no great subtlety by her father, had obvious matrimonial ambitions.

There was no other escape for Dawlish but to head to Lancashire to visit his sister Susan and her mill-owner husband Adolphus Harkness. They were living well in a small mansion in its own grounds a few miles outside Preston, far from its smoking factory chimneys. He kissed Susan, admired both family additions who had appeared in his absence, and praised the growth of her other children. He had all but lost count of them and another was due soon. It troubled him that the fresh-faced joyful girl who had comforted him as a motherless younger brother and lighted up their home, was now slow and bloated from repeated childbearing.

He toured Adolphus's mill, commented on the latest machinery and endured four endless days of him holding forth on the price of cotton, the relative merits of Egyptian, Alabaman and Yazoo, and the ingratitude of his workforce. Balding, overweight and red-faced, over-partial to his drink, Adolphus did not now seem quite the catch he had been when Susan had first entranced him during an Isle of Man holiday. An endless dinner with him and four like-minded cotton-magnates at Preston's Arkwright Club was the last straw and Dawlish headed, with gratitude, back to Shrewsbury the next day.

June 21st.

He did not know it yet, but his peace was at an end

Chapter 5

Dawlish was engrossed in an account in the *Daily News* of the destruction of two monitors of the Turkish Danube Flotilla. The Russians had transported spar-torpedo craft overland from the north and launched them in the river. What followed had been near-suicidal. Explosive charges at the end of long poles extending from the attacking vessels' bows had been pushed against the Turkish hulls before exploding them. The Russians did not lack nerve.

A maid entered with a telegram on a silver tray. He tore it open, hoping for mention of a new appointment, even a command, but saw nothing more than an order to report at the Admiralty at half-past nine next morning. To see a Captain Rich. He had not heard the name before but Rich must be some assistant to the Second Lord.

Two other words, unexpected. Civilian dress.

He had time enough to pack, not just enough for a stay of a few nights, but his uniforms and other kit as well. With luck, he would not be returning to Shrewsbury from London. And yet there was guilt in leaving, in awareness that he was hoping for an opportunity that would smash that harmless dream of a father-and-son partnership that would last into a dull, comfortable and predictable future. When the time came to depart, the old man hugged him tightly, then turned away to hide his emotion. William brought the dogcart to the door and loaded the baggage. Mrs. Gore flung her apron over her head and wept, a ritual that caused no distress as it had been repeated at his every departure for the last two decades. But he turned to look back as the cart went spanking out the gate. The ivy and honeysuckle- wreathed house, with the mallows in luxurious pink bloom before it, had never seemed more beautiful. He wondered if he would ever see it again.

In London, he put up, as before, at the Charing Cross Hotel.

A five-minute walk brought him to the Admiralty next morning. There were even more comings and goings than when he was here last time. The Navy was readying for war, even if Britain was still standing aloof. For now.

He asked directions for Captain Rich's office. The porter asked his name. He told him.

"Aah, Lieutenant Dawlish. Captain Rich left a letter here for you, sir." An envelope was extracted from a pigeon hole.

It was marked 'Urgent' and its flap sealed with red wax.

Dawlish slit it open with his pen knife.

A single page of headed Admiralty paper. The address of a club on Pall Mall. Eleven o'clock. Ask for Captain Rich on arrival.

The signature was an indecipherable scrawl.

*

The club was half-way up Pall Mall on the southern side. It was not as grandiose as the Atheneum or the Reform but the unadorned Georgian façade indicated quiet dignity and discretion within.

A man of his own age emerged as Dawlish mounted the steps to the entrance. He blundered past, uttered the curtest of apologies as he brushed Dawlish's sleeve. Seen for seconds only, his face seemed vaguely familiar. Then recognition dawned. He was John Cordwainer, a fellow midshipman in HMS *Nile*, not met since. Dawlish had heard that he had spent time at HMS *Vernon*, the navy's mine and torpedo establishment and, more recently, of him serving in a gunvessel on the East Indies Station. He was apparently well thought of.

Dawlish entered, asked for Captain Rich.

"Captain Rich? Of course, sir." A hint of amusement in the porter's tone. "He's waiting for you in the library. Haven't been here before, sir? No? Then young Perkins will show you the way."

Dawlish followed the page along a corridor lined with portraits of past members, many of them instantly recognisable, statesmen, soldiers, renowned explorers. A glimpse through open doors into what the boy identified as the coffee room yielded an impression of men confident in their worth in decorous relaxation. It felt like another world than the Admiralty. It was difficult to imagine naval business being conducted here.

The library was empty but for a single occupant in dark civilian clothing seated in wing chair in a far corner, books and papers on a small table between it and another opposite. He stood up and extended his hand.

"Lieutenant Dawlish? Good of you to come." No warmth in his tone. He was older than Dawlish had expected, late fifties perhaps, face thin, even cadaverous, piercing blue eyes above a close-trimmed iron-grey beard. He made no mention of his position but waved towards the empty chair.

Dawlish saw a stack of three or four manila files on the table. Rich lifted that topmost and flicked it open.

"Two years on the Indian Ocean Patrol, I see," he said. "You found it useful, I trust?"

"Very valuable experience. I enjoyed it, sir."

A repeat of the opening of the fruitless interview with the Second Sea Lord that had led nowhere. But now there was a sense of genuine, if impersonal, interest.

"I've read your report on that business of yours on Pemba. Did it worry you that it was illegal and that there would have been serious diplomatic consequences had it failed?"

Stand your ground. Don't apologise.

"I didn't intend for it to fail, sir. And it didn't."

"Not the first instance of rashness, was it, lieutenant? You enlisted in that farce in Denmark, didn't you? Even at eighteen most young men would have been more careful."

I'm being tested now. On my discretion, on my ability to forget.

"I don't know anything about Denmark, sir, farcical or otherwise."

He had been sworn to secrecy about it, rewarded with a hundred and fifty guineas and packed off to the obscurity of the Pacific Station. Powerful people had not wanted to be reminded of that affair. He had understood that all records related to it had been destroyed.

"I must be misinformed then." A chill smile on Rich's lips, his eyes gleaming like a reptile's. He lifted another document from the file. "You didn't do yourself much good in Ashanti, did you, lieutenant? The thanks of the Army are well enough, but Sir Garnet's and Sir Evelyn's endorsements don't count for much if you antagonise your naval superior. And you did, didn't you?"

Dawlish recognised the document now in Rich's hand as a flimsy, the dreaded confidential assessment written each year on every officer.

Rich read the words. "Courageous but reckless, destined for an early grave unless he learns moderation."

Even worse than Dawlish could have imagined, for he had never seen the report, though he had guessed that it had been less than favourable. The memory was bitter. The naval-brigade's bluejackets had worked shoulder to shoulder with Sir Garnet Wolseley's army units in hacking a track through the dense Gold Coast bush. Visibility was yards only and every yard advanced brought danger of yet another ambush. Dawlish had carried a wounded Sir Evelyn Wood to safety after such an attack. But his direct naval superior had felt slighted by the credit given Dawlish for his role in the final reckoning at Kumasi, the more so since he had exceeded timorous orders.

Don't explain.

"Captain Hawes is a fine officer," Dawlish said. "I've no doubt that he regarded that assessment as a fair one."

"And you don't, lieutenant?"

"There was some truth in it, sir."

"Recklessness – dash, if we more charitably term it – is sometimes tolerated in a junior officer." Rich paused, then said, "but only in a junior officer."

He was leafing through the file again.

"The *Oberon* trials. You were secretary to the committee investigating Mr. Whitehead's invention. I read your reports. Nothing rash in your assessments then, lieutenant. No rush to judgement. Impressive, systemic work, I might say."

Dawlish had witnessed the entire series of launchings of Whitehead fish-torpedoes from HMS *Oberon*. They were a new weapon then, self-propelled, unlike anything conceived before. The weary succession of tests in the Medway in 1870 had culminated, after countless adjustments to the steering mechanism, in the sinking of an old coal hulk. He himself had suggested several modifications, later accepted. He had machined replacement components and it helped that he had learned to operate a lathe during leisure hours on overseas stations, much to the amusement of other officers. It was a widely held opinion that real sailors depended on sail, not steam, and held men tending engines and furnaces and boilers in barely concealed contempt.

"Are you familiar with torpedo developments since, lieutenant?"

"Only as much as I'm entitled to know at present."

It was the right, and cautious, answer. Dawlish had seen nothing on the topic since those tests and their aftermath. Torpedoes' details were still considered so secret that officers were initiated into the mysteries of their mechanisms behind closed doors guarded by Marine sentries.

Rich didn't comment, but said, "I gather the Ashanti expedition left you seriously ill."

"Malaria, sir."

It had nearly killed him. And jaundice afterwards. It might lurk within him forever, raging at random intervals with fresh malevolence.

"East Africa's rotten with it," Rich said. "Deadlier than any Arab slaver. And yet you volunteered for the Anti-Slavery Patrol afterwards. Why, lieutenant?"

Best to say it, admit the ambition.

"I wanted another opportunity to get my name known. There are few enough of them in peacetime."

"You're aiming high, lieutenant?"

"I'm aiming very high, sir."

High for a market-town solicitor's son without friends or influence. But the only fulfilment that I want.

"So you're ready to run risks that others wouldn't. Does advancement mean that much to you, Dawlish?"

"Is that reprehensible, sir?" The words slipped out, insubordinate, regretted at once.

Rich did not rise to them. Instead, he said, "You're wondering why we're meeting here, and not at the Admiralty, are you not?"

"I assume that there's a good reason, sir."

"Then let's come to business, lieutenant. A certain high functionary has empowered me to offer a chance to perform a service. One for which both your character and your experience fit you. I can give no details other than to say that it will be hazardous, even deadly. But vital alike to the interests of your country and your own career."

"You said 'offer', sir. Not an appointment?"

"You must choose, lieutenant. If you refuse you'll hear no more of it. You'll forget this conversation. Your present prospects will be neither bettered nor worsened. There'll be no black mark in your record."

Dawlish felt his heart thumping, feared that it was audible. He understood now why Cordwainer had been here before him, why he had left in such agitation. Put to the test, his ambition had been lower than he'd thought. He had chosen safety.

Rich was silent for a full minute. Then he leaned forward. "Should you accept, Lieutenant Dawlish – and should you succeed – you'll receive no formal recognition other than, perhaps, early promotion. Your record will show a period of half-pay to explain your absence. But you'll know that in the future you can rely on the sympathy, indeed the active interest, of several highly placed persons. Do I make myself plain? Do you understand me?"

Dawlish's answer was a hoarse whisper. "I do," he said, "I do indeed."

This happened before. When I was tempted to Denmark. And no good came to me of it. And yet …

An image flashed unbidden in his mind. Pizarro, confronted by his mutinous followers, scraping a line in the sand with his sword. On one side Darien, safety and poverty. On the other Peru, hazard, wealth and glory. Rich was tracing just such a line for him and he must choose whether to cross it. He knew there would never be a second offer.

"Perhaps you need some time to consider?" Rich said. "There are books enough here to allure me for ten minutes."

But there could be but one decision, Dawlish realised, not if he were to avoid years of futile mediocrity in the Navy or of dreary routine as a partner in his father's office. The carefully-planned fury of that night on Pemba had bought this one opportunity to escape those fates. And this time the promise might – might – be fulfilled.

"There's no need, sir," he said. "I'll undertake any service."

"I hoped for no other answer."

"You'll hear more tonight. Where are you lodging?"

Dawlish told him.

"You've brought evening clothing?"

He had, luckily.

"Good. A gentleman who'll introduce himself as Corry will collect you at seven o'clock."

Rich stood. The interview was at an end.

"And one final point, lieutenant. My name isn't Rich, though it's convenient to use at times. It's Topcliffe."

*

Dawlish knew the name. By the time he had joined the Navy in the late fifties, legends had already gathered around Captain Richard Topcliffe. The Crimean War had earned him one of the earliest Victoria Crosses. The Sea of Azov was too shallow for even the smallest gunboats to operate in safety, but Topcliffe had improvised batteries on rafts of spars and barrels and brought them there through the Straits of Kerch to harry Russian supply lines.

When mutiny had engulfed India, his ship's company had transported her great 68-pounders up the Ganges on barges for the bloody reckoning at Cawnpore and had manhandled them cross-country afterwards to blast a path for the Army's relief of Lucknow. No obstacle had deterred Topcliffe. Respected rather than liked, but matchless in efficiency, he was spoken of as a coming man, a future First Naval Lord.

And afterwards a fading.

His was a name that had drifted into obscurity after successful command of an ironclad in the Mediterranean, appointment as deputy to the commander of the Channel Fleet and then some obscure appointment in the Admiralty itself. Predictions for rise to the highest levels forgotten, transferred to other officers of outstanding promise.

Dawlish had not heard Topcliffe's name mentioned for years, had assumed that ill-health or even death had intervened. But he was alive, and active, with an air of confidence and authority in whatever position he now occupied.

What that now was, Dawlish would learn this evening.

Chapter 6

A liveried coachman stood waiting outside the hotel when Dawlish emerged at one minute before seven.

He tipped his hat. "Mr Dawlish? Good. Mr. Corry is waiting for you, sir."

The blinds on the windows of the waiting brougham were closed. The door carried a crest but the coachman opened it too rapidly for Dawlish to see the details. He entered.

"Lieutenant Dawlish, I presume?"

In the shadows he saw a handsome, black-bearded man of about his own age.

"I'm delighted to meet you, sir." he said. "My name is Corry. Montague Corry ".

Dawlish shook the smooth hand reached out to him. The name was familiar. He had come across it somewhere in the newspapers in recent days but he could not place it. He settled on the rich upholstery as the step was raised and the door shut.

"Only a short distance, lieutenant," Corry said. "To Lord Kegworth's place." He spoke as if Dawlish should know it. His tone, though friendly, indicated no desire for conversation.

The journey was short, noises from without indicating crowded streets. Only a few sharp turns and then a straight run of some four minutes. Dawlish guessed the general direction as westwards. Then another turn, a halt, the sound of gates swinging open, closing again after the brougham moved forward and swung to a halt.

The door opened to reveal a footman bearing a branched candlestick. Beyond him, marble steps led upwards beneath an elegant Palladian portico. Dawlish glanced back, saw the trees of Green Park on the far side of the street. This was Piccadilly, the western end, and the mansion was set back from the pavement by a cobbled courtyard.

Another footman must have been sent to announce their arrival, for as they mounted the steps a balding, portly man in evening dress, red-faced and bewhiskered, came out to meet them. He seemed pleased and eager as he grasped Corry's hand and looked towards Dawlish.

"And this gentleman is?"

"Lieutenant Dawlish, My Lord."

Dawlish wondered if this was one of those highly placed persons with whose sympathy and interest Topcliffe had tempted him. He shook Lord Kegworth's hand.

"Aah, good, Dawlish. Your fame precedes you and you're welcome here." It sounded both friendly and sincere. Kegworth turned to Corry and dropped his tone. "Our friend's waiting in the library," he said. "He doesn't look well tonight."

"The asthma has been mild of late. But the gout –" Corry shook his head. The unfinished sentence spoke volumes.

Liveried servants took their cloaks. Kegworth led the way. The house blazed with gaslight. Dawlish marvelled at the richness as they ascended the main staircase – the ceiling's delicate plasterwork, the classical nudes shrinking coyly in niches, the life-sized portrait of some contemporary of Marlborough's, periwigged, aquiline and contemptuous, the Peninsular battle-piece on the landing, the sound-deadening carpet, the great sparking chandelier.

"And the ladies, My Lord?" Corry asked.

"At the Northampton estate," Kegworth said.

He brought them to a door flanked by two men in cheap civilian suits. Both powerful-looking, hard, one with half an ear missing. Not footmen, not domestic servants. Kegworth tapped the door, opened it himself and then stood aside to allow his guests to enter.

Topcliffe was standing at one side of the book-lined room. He was talking to a benevolent-looking gentleman, bespectacled and with luxuriant white hair and beard, with something of the cleric about him. But it was on the wizened figure in an easy chair by the fireside, an ageing dandy arrested in the act of raising a glass to his lips, that locked Dawlish's gaze. There could be no mistaking him.

Benjamin Disraeli, Lord Beaconsfield, the Prime Minister.

Dawlish felt his pulse racing, his mouth dry. He could never have anticipated this.

Topcliffe came across, took Dawlish's left elbow and brought him forward as Beaconsfield extended his right hand. It was limp and weak, the veins raised like knotted cords across its back, almost the hand of an invalid, its gout-tortured fellow swaddled in flannel. But for all its age and wrinkles, the face that rose above the goatee beard had the vitality of a younger man and the eyes sparkled with life and energy. When he spoke, his words were slow and careful.

"Your presence indicates acceptance of a certain proposition, Lieutenant Dawlish."

"You sent a very convincing emissary, My Lord," Dawlish was aware of the tremor in his own voice. He was standing before a legend and he knew now that he had been selected to serve him. There could be no retreating now.

"I sent a trusted emissary to summon you to a nest of conspirators, lieutenant!" Beaconsfield said. "All honourable men, but conspirators nonetheless, gathered for a meeting that none will concede ever happened."

Something like that was said about the Denmark venture also. And afterwards, promises disowned.

"Lord Kegworth's an old friend," Beaconsfield said. "My trusted adviser, even though he holds no official post in government. He's been kind enough to place his house at our disposal this evening. And Mr. Corry, my private secretary, you've already met."

The clerical-looking gentleman proved to be Mr. Nathaniel Barnaby.

Dawlish knew of him. Every officer did. The Director of Naval Construction had overseen the perfection of the central-battery ironclad concept, had designed the *Inflexible*, the revolutionary turret-armed battleship now under construction. It was said that he was already talking of replacing an iron navy by a steel one.

"And you're already acquainted with Admiral Sir Richard Topcliffe," Beaconsfield said.

The name might have faded from memory, yet here he now stood, the confidant of the most powerful man in Britain. Admiral. Full admiral, no Rear or Vice.

"You're no doubt unaware of the nature of the admiral's duties," Beaconsfield's face puckered in amusement, "and indeed it wouldn't do to define them with any too great exactitude. You agree, Sir Richard?"

"Admirably expressed, My Lord."

"How should we put it then for Lieutenant Dawlish? Let's say that Sir Richard's task is to keep under surveillance anything, anything whatsoever, that might be detrimental to the interests of the Crown. He's answerable to the holder of my office, and to him alone. The task may at times demand somewhat undiplomatic measures. Britain has enemies, many of them undeclared. Sir Richard's been known to frustrate their knavish tricks ..."

". . . and confound their politics." Topcliffe completed the quotation. "This is just such an occasion, Dawlish."

Beaconsfield rose unsteadily, supporting himself on an ebony cane. Dawlish saw that one gout-swollen foot was enclosed by a silken slipper. He moved, wincing with pain, to the long table in the centre of the room, illuminated by two low-slung gas-chandeliers. Corry pulled back a chair for him at its head and assisted him, as a son might, to take his seat.

"Lieutenant Dawlish, you will sit by me." Beaconsfield gestured to the chair on his left. "And Sir Richard, here to my right, if you please."

Kegworth tugged the bell-pull. A servant entered in silence, refilled glasses and then glided out. The others seated themselves around the table. A sheaf of large papers lay before Beaconsfield, the uppermost a map of Eastern Europe. He leaned forward, suddenly looking younger, more alert, and swept a hand across it.

"We live in dramatic times, Lieutenant Dawlish." He paused, as if relishing the moment of drama. "Europe teeters on the brink of a chasm and the Muscovite horde presses ever onwards. Enlighten us, Admiral!"

Topcliffe traced the line of the Lower Danube with his finger.

"The river's no longer an obstacle to the Russian advance," he said. "Not since those two Turkish monitors were sunk. And the remainder of their flotilla is trapped by mines that the Russians have laid up and downstream of the sinking – here, and here."

"And the latest intelligence, admiral?" Beaconsfield said.

"A report just received of a Russian crossing here – at Galatz," Topcliffe pointed. "The Turks are falling back before it. It may only be a feint, but I doubt it. We know of pontoons being brought forward by rail, so a bridging operation's probably imminent. If so, then it can be only days before the last vestige of Turkish resistance collapses along the entire Danube line."

Beaconsfield must know this already, Dawlish thought. The words sounded as if they had been rehearsed with himself in mind.

"Thereafter, lieutenant, the Turks can hope for no more than a delaying action." Beaconsfield was toying with his glass as he spoke, swirling a weak mixture of brandy and water. "Their Christian subjects will welcome the Russians as liberators. The Muscovite armies will sweep across Bulgaria and Thrace. It can be but little time before they arrive before Constantinople. And, once they invest it, there is no reason why it should not fall."

He was speaking to Dawlish now as if there were no others present.

"At that moment Russia will achieve the goal that has so long obsessed her autocrats – a gateway to the Levant. The Third Rome will possess the Second and the Czar will celebrate his triumph in a reconsecrated Hagia Sophia. Then he can perhaps dream of matching the conquests of Justinian and Belisarius." Beaconsfield's voice had dropped, as if both fascinated and appalled by the images he evoked.

"The other European powers will accept such a Russian victory." Beaconsfield's tone was suddenly cold and analytical again. "Sir Richard has evidence that the Austrians have been secretly bribed into neutrality with the promise of the territories of Bosnia and Herzegovina. In Berlin, Chancellor Bismarck will welcome any diversion of the Czar's attention from their shared frontier. And as always, worst of all, the French. We can rely on them to remain neutral until the very moment when the situation is most disadvantageous to Britain. At that moment they may well ally themselves with St. Petersburg."

Silence around the table, a sense of a powerful and pragmatic men peering into an abyss. Britain had been drawn into a European war just once since the fall of Napoleon. The empty victory in the Crimean war, won at excessive price in lives and wealth, had been a disaster for Britain.

Now something far larger, far more dangerous, was in prospect.

"Russia today isn't the ineffective giant we faced in the fifties." Topcliffe broke the silence. "Internal reforms, modest as they are, have made her the world's greatest land power. In General Skobelev, who's now dazzling in the Balkans as he has already done in Asia, she has a commander of genius. His campaigns against Samarkand and Bokhara and Khiva brought Russia's armies to the frontiers of Afghanistan. The Czar's agents subvert that wretched place's rulers and it's conceivable that they might accept Russia as a protecting power."

Beaconsfield's voice had passion in it now. "Russia's every action in the region threatens those Indian territories over which our gracious Sovereign Lady has been so lately proclaimed Empress. I've long aimed at securing our tenure in India in perpetuity and at guaranteeing our communications to it. It was to that end, that I secured our financial interest in the Suez Canal. Without it we cannot hold India."

He wiped his brow with a silk handkerchief.

"Mr. Gladstone does me an injustice when he implies that I don't recognise Turkish rule as an affront to civilisation. I've known that since I travelled their domains in my youth. But the Canal must come before all else! At this moment, nothing but the Ottoman Turkish Empire, corrupt, degenerate and barbarous though it may be, stands between Russian greed and our lifeline to India. Let but Constantinople fall, let but the Straits pass into Russian hands and then the entire Levant may be closed to us. In such circumstances we could not hope to reinforce India soon enough against any Russian onslaught through the passes from Afghanistan."

Beaconsfield stopped to let his words sink in. His old-man's face was flushed, his emotion palpable. When he spoke again it was in a quieter voice and Dawlish felt drawn to him by the conviction and strength of personality that somehow did not seem inappropriate to the frail body.

"Make no mistake, Lieutenant Dawlish. If Constantinople is threatened, then Britain must fight Russia, and France too if need be. The Royal Navy must defend the Bosporus. The Russians know this full well. And they've taken measures to ensure that, if we do concentrate our forces at the Straits, it will be at a cost terrible to our overseas trade and fatal to our prestige."

This man is talking to me alone. About what lies for me beyond Pizarro's line.

"I don't understand, My Lord" Dawlish found himself half-amazed at his own temerity. "Russia may be a great land power, My Lord, but her fleet's inferior to our own."

Beaconsfield leaned back in his chair, as if weary. He gestured to Topcliffe to continue.

"You've heard of the *Alexander Nevski*, lieutenant?".

"The ironclad that foundered in the Bay of Biscay some while ago?"

Topcliffe's answer was to push aside the map of the Balkans to reveal a large technical drawing on flimsy paper. A separate white sheet had been placed beneath to reveal the plan and elevation of a large warship.

"The *Nevski* was built in the La Seyne dockyard at Toulon for the Czarist Navy," Topcliffe said. "She was intended to serve as a model for three identical ships to be constructed in Russian yards. We know she's formidable, very formidable, and these tracings confirm it. Our price for them was enough to set up a traitorous French naval draughtsman in comfortable retirement. I'll ask Mr. Barnaby to give us a professional assessment. Would you be so kind, sir?"

The Director of Naval Construction rose and stood between Dawlish and the Prime Minister. He leaned over the drawing with obvious enthusiasm, no longer the benign cleric but the designer of fighting machines, impressed by a skill equal to his own.

"We see her as completed a few months ago," he said. "She's all but identical to the *Admiral Duperré,* which the French are now building for their own navy. Until my own – forgive me, My Lord, rather Her Majesty's own – *Inflexible* is commissioned, the *Alexander Nevski* will be the most powerful warship afloat."

Dawlish found himself fascinated by the leviathan's proportions, by the sweeping ram bow, by the overall sense of power and menace, as Barnaby pointed to the principal features with a pencil.

"She's steam-propelled but she carries sufficient canvas to make her independent of coaling stations for extended periods. And here, carried high, her main armament."

Two open-top barbettes – great iron cylinders – positioned between the fore and main masts, just ahead of two side-by-side funnels. Sponsoned out to port and starboard, the single gun barrels extending above each barbette top and shrouded with protective hoods, could cover an arc from dead ahead to dead astern. And two more such barbettes, one between the main and mizzen masts, covering a wide arc on either beam, and another abaft the mizzen which must have a twenty-four points field of fire.

"Forty-six ton breech-loaders. Thirteen and a half-inch calibre. On most headings three can be brought to bear on any target," Barnaby said. "Twelve inches of barbette-armour and here, along her waterline, the armoured belt's up to a full twenty-two inch thickness."

"Eleven thousand tons, Dawlish," Topcliffe spoke almost with reverence. "Over seven thousand horsepower. Fourteen knots at full power. And we know that one of her main weapons penetrated over nineteen inches of armour on the testing range."

"How might our most powerful ships compare, sir?" Dawlish had already guessed, and feared, the answer.

"At this moment should the *Nevski* still be afloat, we've but four vessels capable of facing her. Facing her, mark you, and little more. *Alexandra* and *Temeraire* have at least the armour to confront her but their guns are too light to inflict anything but minor damage. *Thunderer* and *Devastation* might make some impression, but their freeboards are so low as to make them useless outside the Mediterranean. Without *Inflexible,* and it'll be a year or more before she'll be commissioned, we've nothing capable of matching the *Nevski* on the world's oceans."

"You must be thinking, Lieutenant Dawlish," Beaconsfield said, "that it was a little too convenient for us that the *Alexander Nevski* was lost on her maiden voyage. That she foundered in the stormy Bay of Biscay."

"It was, without doubt, a blow for Czar Alexander." Topcliffe was smiling. "His heart bled so much for it that he attended the service in St. Isaac's Cathedral in Petersburg to pray that she might yet survive. It's been announced that he'll make a personal donation of a million roubles to a fund for the widows and orphans once the loss is confirmed beyond doubt."

"It was the second painful loss the Czar suffered in the space of a few months," Beaconsfield said. "Are you familiar with the name of *Grigori Orlov*, lieutenant?"

Dawlish's mind dredged up an identity from long-past reading. "A gentleman on terms of some intimacy with the Empress Catherine? Besides being one of her chief ministers."

"Quite so," Topcliffe said, "but it's also the name of an armoured corvette of the *General Admiral* class. She's a powerful vessel in her own right and designed specifically for commerce raiding. The *Orlov* left the Russian Pacific Coast late last December, en route for St. Petersburg. We know that she put in at Batavia but that she didn't pass through the Suez Canal. Reports reached me that she took on coal, food and water in secret at Nossi-Bé in Madagascar, with the full connivance of the French. That was in February. And there's been nothing of her since – no report of her in any port in Europe, Africa or the Americas. She hasn't passed into the Baltic or entered any Russian harbour and the Imperial Government has made no further reference to her disappearance. It might of course be argued that the authorities would not wish to publish news of a second major naval loss during wartime."

"Surely a reasonable assumption, sir?" Dawlish said.

"Aah yes, lieutenant. But consider the situation if neither ship were in fact sunk. If they were skulking intact, awaiting a declaration of war to fall on Britain's shipping like wolves on a sheepfold? They're economical steamers and as they carry a full sailing rig they could be independent of coal supplies for long periods. Captured colliers would satisfy their modest needs, or some underhand arrangement with our French neighbours might also secure coal supplies. Imagine the forces we would need to track them down, assuming that we did even have a ship to match the *Nevski*."

Beaconsfield interrupted, his tone urgent. "In the late American War, a single Confederate raider, the *Alabama*, caused immeasurable damage to the Union's commerce on the high seas. It needed a major diversion of naval power from the main theatre to hunt her down. That's the Russians' inspiration. But now, however, we don't speak of a single lightly armed corsair but of two of the most powerful men o' war afloat. Let us but send our fleet to defend Constantinople and these iron Cossacks will be free to sweep our commerce from the seas."

His voice sunk to a whisper.

"You see now, Dawlish, why the Imperial Russian Government might wish to lie about the fate of the *Nevski* and keep the whereabouts of the *Orlov* obscure." He sighed, seemed again the infirm old man he was. "And we've another weakness. This war already splits my cabinet. Derby, my old and trusted friend, is for peace at any price. Salisbury thinks that the progress of Russia is the progress of religion and civilisation. Carnarvon welcomes the prospect of Christian services being held again in Hagia Sophia." Beaconsfield fixed Dawlish with terrible intensity, passion glinting even in the right eye across which the lid drooped. "They're decent men, Lieutenant Dawlish, too well-intentioned to see that the Russians will be satisfied with nothing less than India itself. They're not conspirators, not like this group before you tonight. They, and all others of my cabinet, would deplore what we intend. They must know nothing of it."

An uncomfortable silence. Dawlish broke it.

"But this might just be surmise, My Lord," he said. "Is there any concrete evidence that these ironclads do still exist?"

Topcliffe who answered. "Evidence enough, and from an unimpeachable source, an eyewitness. Our one consolation is that we know exactly where they lurk".

Dawlish guessed what was coming even before Beaconsfield told him.

"You, Lieutenant Dawlish," he said very quietly, "will penetrate that place of concealment. You will find those warships and you will sink them at their moorings. That is the mission for which you have made yourself available".

Dawlish's stomach tightened. His mouth was dry.

"It will be of the utmost secrecy," Beaconsfield said. "An act of undeclared war that we shall quite brazenly disown if you're unsuccessful."

"An act of piracy?"

"An act of raison d'état."

A reason of state. The justification used by every pitiless ruler since Richelieu had coined the term two centuries since. National interest sanctioned any action, regardless of moral or legal considerations.

"If you succeed, lieutenant, it's probable that the Russians will make no public recognition of the incident. The Czar's prestige will not permit the deception to be unmasked so ignominiously. And we'd also prefer it like that."

Dawlish felt alone, more alone than ever in his life, no less overwhelmed by the enormity of the responsibility than by the personal danger. He glanced around the table and read a mixture of concern and pity on those faces turned towards him – those that were not looking away with expressions of embarrassment and unease. He realised that these men believed that he was going to his death.

"Where?" His voice was hoarse.

"Sir Richard will explain the details to you, lieutenant." Corry said. He had caught the admiral's eye, was making the slightest shake of his head. The message was clear. Beaconsfield was fatigued.

The Prime Minister had caught his secretary's intent also. He tottered to his feet with the aid of his cane. The decisive personality of moments before was replaced by a near invalid. Corry hovered behind, ready to steady him if needed.

"Enough of business, gentlemen," he said. "Lord Kegworth's hospitality must be trespassed upon no longer His always excellent table awaits us"

He turned away, taking Dawlish by the right arm and leaning on it.

"Success is the child of audacity, lieutenant," he said, "and you seem to have enough of that."

Then they moved towards the library door.

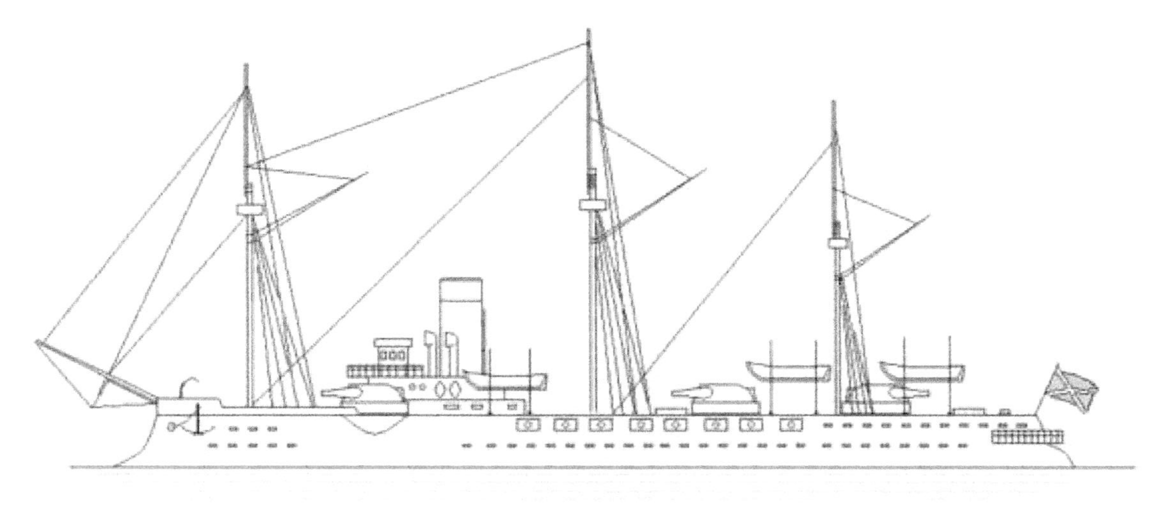

Alexander Nevski

Builder: La Seyne shipyard, Toulon. France
Completed: October 1876
Displacement: 11,030 tons
Length: 319 feet along waterline
Beam: 66 feet
Armour: Belt 10 in. – 22 in.
Barbettes 12 in.
Gun shields (partly open): 2 in.

Machinery: 7300 Horsepower, Twin Screws
Speed: 14 Knots (Max.)
10 Knots (Cruising)
Note: Twin funnels, side by side
Armament: 4 X 13.4 in. Rifled breech -loaders
8 X 5.5 in, 16 5-poundrs (Ports & deck)
6 X 1-in. 4 bbl. Nordenvelts (Tops & deck)
Complement: 660 (as designed)

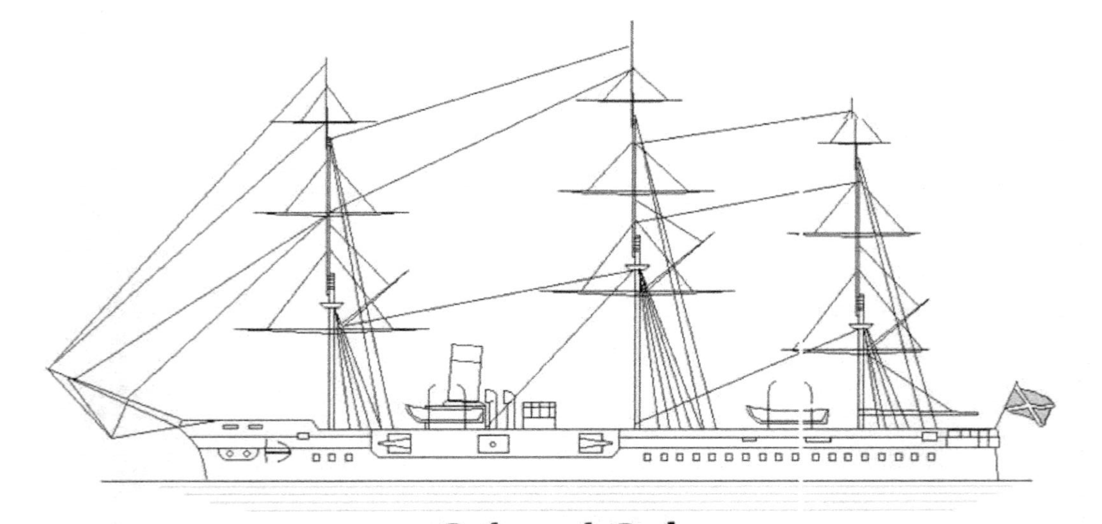

Grigori Orlov

Builder: Baltic Shipyard, St. Petersburg
Completed: August 1874
Displacement: 4,850 tons
Length: 285 feet along waterline
Beam: 48 feet
Armour: Belt 5 in. – 6 in.
Complement: 480 (as designed)

Machinery: 4470 Horsepower, Single Screw
Speed: 14 Knots (Max.)
10 Knots (Cruising)
Armament: 6 X 8 in. Rifled breech-loaders
6 X 5.5 in. Rifled breech-loaders
6 X 1-in. 4 bbl. Nordenvelts (Tops & deck)

Chapter 7

It would be a continent away, and in circumstances so desperate that any confidence might pass without hesitation between officer and enlisted man, that Dawlish would hear Egdean tell how he had spent his first night in years with his own kindred.

While Dawlish was waiting in the hotel lobby to be collected by Mr. Corry, Able Seaman Jeremiah Egdean was hesitating in the Sussex lane leading to his brother's cottage. There was still time to retreat, he told himself, time to return to the anonymity in which the Navy had clothed him for so long.

He had landed at Portsmouth the previous day, had been granted his leave, his pay, a night's rest in the naval barracks and a rail warrant that carried him to Pulborough station next morning. From there he set out to trudge westwards along a dusty road, uncomfortably conspicuous in his uniform and with his kit bag slung on his shoulder. He had thought the limp he had carried from Pemba was almost imperceptible but it was enough to spur a sympathetic but inquisitive carter into offering a lift.

Did he know these parts?

Egdean evaded the question and turned the conversation to his foreign service. The carter was uncomprehending. Zanzibar then – was it like London? He had heard tell that it was a powerful heathen place too. He was disappointed when Egdean refused to enter a tavern with him when he set him down, but thankful for the threepenny bit he slipped to him.

The early evening was still warm. Insects droned and the lowing of cattle being driven towards milking carried across the fields. Down the lane, half-hidden by the foliage of the flanking hedges, Egdean could see the creeper-clad gamekeeper's cottage. He had grown up there, and on their father's death his brother had succeeded to it, and to stewardship of the game on a small estate that flanked the huge walled demesne of Petworth Park. But he himself had been long departed by then, lost under the name of a hamlet close to this place. He stood now in an agony of indecision, longing to advance, yet fearing what discovery might bring, knowing too that it could be only minutes before some homeward-bound labourer queried the presence of a bronzed seaman in this leafy backwater.

And then the decision was made for him.

"Are you my uncle?"

It was a child's voice. A girl of five or six was looking up at him, her face full of trust.

"Father said you would come someday." The features were unmistakable.

"Yes, child," he said. "I'm your uncle." Tears were starting to his eyes.

The girl slipped her hand into his and led him towards the cottage.

It was awkward at first. He had never met his sister-in-law and she seemed unsure of him, though several children clustered round him in delight. An older boy was sent to fetch Egdean's brother. The man who entered ten minutes later, excited, flushed from running, might have been his father a quarter century before. Nothing was said. They fell upon each other, embracing, weeping. Now he knew the answer to the fear that had so often nagged him, whether the cold London arches that sheltered so many a maimed veteran must be his home should he ever return a legless cripple.

The night was a long one. An occasional letter, slowly and painfully written, had been the only contact for many years but now the passage of time took on life and colour. His younger sister Mary was married to a grocer in Midhurst, close enough to visit. The business was doing well and she had five children. His brother Stephen had taken the skills learned as a shepherd on the South Downs to New South Wales a decade before and he was doing famously. And a recent blow. His youngest brother had died in a steel-mill accident in Pittsburgh six months before. Egdean could barely remember him. Tom had been no more than a baby when he himself had enlisted. For an instant the image floated before him of a puny, bare-foot infant. He was glad that there were no details of the manner of his death.

One by one, nephews and nieces, delighted by this exotic presence, departed with reluctance for bed. And this, Egdean saw, with envy, was a happy home and the framed photographs, curtained windows and blooming garden were witness to modest prosperity. The family was secure and respected. His eldest niece was a parlour maid at Petworth House, where her brother was an apprentice coachman. Another nephew was assistant to his father on the nearby Lensbury estate.

His sister-in-law, thawed towards him now, was last to excuse herself, kissing him on the cheek as she left for bed. He was alone now with his brother. Neither spoke until at last he proposed a final pipe.

The soft warm silence of the night engulfed them when they went into the garden. Egdean glanced back to the house then moved yet further from it. He passed his pouch. They filled their pipes in silence, lit up and drew. Long minutes passed, each reluctant to broach the subject that could not be avoided.

It was his brother who spoke at last.

"He's dead," he said.

"You're sure?" Egdean felt his heart leap.

"I heard it at a shoot. Just after Christmas, it was. From one the guests' men. And then I checked, discreet like, and it seemed it were so. Then Sir Reginald Heyford was here for the shooting a few months back. He's one of the same sort. His man knew all about it."

"How did he die?"

"As he deserved. He just rotted in some private asylum. In Paris it was, in France."

Egdean had dreamed of this moment for years, with anger, shame and bitterness. Now there was no satisfaction, just relief.

"It's over, Jerry. You could come home. Nobody will follow it up now."

The finished their pipes in silence but as he turned for the cottage, and the bed made up for him in the parlour, Egdean felt a sense of rebirth. He was little over thirty. There could yet be another life.

It was already late when he awoke. His brother had gone to tend hatchlings and, but for the two youngest, the children had departed for the school that the nearby village now boasted. His sister-in-law brewed tea and he toasted bread before the kitchen fire.

The windows were open and the scent of flowers wafted in. The sky was clear, the sun bright. Three solid weeks of freedom stretched before him. His brother would escort him with pride today through the estate's coppices and coverts and later he would walk into Petworth to buy sweets for the children. Tonight, he would display that illustrated paper's drawing of the battle on Pemba. He could already hear the children's gasps of horrified glee as he told of the struggle and he could imagine his brother's pride. Later in the week he would visit Mary and her family in Midhurst and he would take the picture with him and have it framed for his brother's parlour, like those photographs he had so admired.

And he would take the time to think about his future.

He had almost five pounds in his pocket and another hundred and twenty-seven lodged in the Dockyard Bank, the proud result of years of steady remittances and unremitting sobriety. He had served long enough for discharge to be in sight. A Coastguard appointment might be a possibility. Lieutenant Dawlish would speak up for him, he was sure of that. With it might come a cottage, not unlike his brother's, near some comfortable South Coast fishing-hamlet. The baby sat on his knee, laughing and happily tugging at his beard as he sipped his tea and fed it small pieces broken off the sugar-loaf.

It was Milly, the niece who had first welcomed him, who broke his reverie.

"There's a policeman coming up the lane, Mother!" she called as she bounded in. "He asked me if there was a sailor-man here! And now he's coming to see Uncle!"

Egdean rose, suddenly pale and shaking. Fear chilled him, blood pounded in his head. For one wild moment he thought of flight, but already it was too late and the constable's bulky figure was filling the doorway, affably greeting his sister-in-law. Yes, she was saying, they did indeed have a visitor, and very welcome he was too. Egdean set the baby down and advanced towards the intruder. He had already resolved to go without protest.

"I'm sorry to disturb you on your first day here." The constable's tone was apologetic. "You're Able-Seaman Jeremiah Egdean?"

Egdean nodded.

"I'll need to see your paybook to confirm it. No offence, you'll understand. Just regulations."

A quick rummage and it was produced, but scarcely glanced at.

"Unusual, this," the policeman said, taking out an envelope. "I can't think why it wasn't sent the normal way, but it seems powerful important. It came to the station, with special instructions for it to be delivered by a constable." He seemed flattered by the errand.

Egdean's hand was trembling as he tore the cover open and read the pasted strips. The first sentence requested immediate safe-hand delivery to Able Seaman Jeremiah Egdean, whose further movements were to be facilitated by all means necessary. The second ordered him to proceed with all despatch to Devonport and there report to Lieutenant Nicholas Dawlish on board HMS *Nomad*. The costs of his train travel, third-class, would be reimbursed.

Egdean did not know it yet, but his peace, like Dawlish's, was at an end.

Chapter 8

At Topcliffe's direction, Dawlish sent a telegram to his father. He was being posted to the West Indies about an urgent matter. He might not be able to write for some time. The old man would accept the story without questioning. And if it came to it, neither would he question any later message about a death from sudden fever, of a burial at sea.

And Dawlish still knew nothing of the location of the Russian vessels when he accompanied Topcliffe to HMS *Nomad*.

"A narrow anchorage," was all the admiral had said. "Very narrow, perhaps little over a hundred yards."

"And defended?"

"Probably. But we don't know the details."

"Where is it, sir?"

"You'll be informed in due course, lieutenant."

The tone indicated no desire to impart more at this time.

But Dawlish did know now that it was his knowledge of Whitehead torpedoes that had ensured his selection. No other weapon would be capable of destroying large warships in such an anchorage and even the thickest armoured was still vulnerable to damage below the waterline. Sharing a closed compartment with Topcliffe on the train from London, he had immersed himself in drawings entrusted to him of the latest fish torpedoes. The technical improvements since he last worked with them were minor.

"You'll have new craft for launching them," Topcliffe said. "Three of 'em. Fast, like nothing else we have." He produced a general arrangement drawing from his briefcase. "This will give you some idea. You'll see the real thing when we arrive."

Dawlish studied it in silence, was impressed but intimidated, most of all by the information block in one corner that detailed performance. It would take long exercising before daring to venture with them into a narrow anchorage. He asked Topcliffe how much time was available.

"Three days. We can't afford more. Our friends can put out to sea at any time."

Too little. But I can't say that.

"Where will we train, sir?"

"Arrangements are in hand."

Said in a tone that invited no further questioning.

*

Nomad lay at anchor in the Hamoaze River, just west of Plymouth and the Devonport naval dockyard. Dawlish knew of her by repute, a steam corvette that had entered service just a year before. She and her sister *Rover* were now the Navy's fastest vessels of their size, their machinery proven capable of maintaining fifteen knots even in heavy seas. She had swung out a loading boom to lift three long tarpaulin-shrouded objects from the lighter secured alongside.

"You'll have no contact with *Nomad's* officers," Topcliffe told Dawlish before they boarded. "You'll have a cabin to yourself. You'll take your meals there too."

"And Day and Talbot?"

Dawlish hadn't yet met the two lieutenants who would report to him. He had seen their files. Topcliffe had selected them and both had experience of torpedoes.

"They'll bunk together. *Nomad's* captain understands that his officers must keep their distance from you three. You'll talk to nobody but me."

The crews, twenty-seven men in total, would sling their hammocks in a screened off section of the main deck. They too would live in an isolation enforced by posting of marine guards. Like the lieutenants, they were yet to board.

Topcliffe received the honours due his rank when he climbed to *Nomad's* entry port. The captain conducted him aft without introducing his officers. Topcliffe's seniority was enough to protect his remoteness. A midshipman, embarrassed by the silence imposed on him, brought Dawlish to his cabin. It was comfortable and well appointed, vacated by the third officer.

He joined Topcliffe to watch the loading.

Stripping of the tarpaulins revealed three slim mahogany-coloured hulls with a minimum of superstructure. The taper towards the sharp, vertical, stem was long and pronounced. Dawlish had already familiarised himself with their drawings and knew their dimensions. Ninety feet long, their greatest beam little over eleven feet. Products of the renowned White's yard at Cowes.

Seamen passed broad leather-cushioned slings beneath the first of the chock-supported hulls and positioned them to lift between the white stripes painted on the sides. The craft was now at its most vulnerable –

incorrectly positioned supports could break its back under the weight of its boiler and engine. Further adjustments of the slings, and then the steam winch panted and rattled, the cables tautened and the boat rose from the deck.

To reveal its full beauty.

The main deck sloped gently from bow to stern. The forecastle was turtle-decked and the hull's graceful curves were marred only by the what looked like hollow elephant-tusks on either side of the knife-sharp stem.

"It's a new launching method." Topcliffe had noticed Dawlish's surprise. "It's been tried and it works. It makes for better aiming than with dropping gear."

"How, sir?"

"The torpedoes are carried in tubes. Compressed air blasts them out."

The bridge was no more than a raised platform sheltered by an iron shield. It was open to the rear and carried the helmsman's wheel and a simple telegraph. The rear closures of the torpedo tubes were below it.

Just ahead of the bridge, wrought-iron sponsons, light structures of rail and grating, protruded beyond each side at deck level and carried pedestal mounts for Gatlings. The raised boiler casing and engine-room roof occupied much of the craft's length abaft the bridge. Two funnels, the after flanked by large air-scoops, protruded from the casing to carry the furnace exhaust.

"The engine's like a locomotive's," Topcliffe said. "There's no condenser. Spent steam exhausts up the funnels to increase draught. It saves weight, but it costs endurance."

Right aft, a mounting for a third Gatling. The decks and all that rose above had been painted matt black but the wooden hull was left in its natural colour, varnished and polished. To reduce skin friction, Topcliffe said.

The craft looked exactly what she was, a burnished and slender rapier, honed to kill.

But as vulnerable as an eggshell. The only hope of survival would lie in speed and surprise. And the crews had not yet trained on them. No other crews in the Navy had done so either.

"We've been lucky, Dawlish, damn lucky," Topcliffe said. "Three of the four ordered were ready just in time – quite fortuitously, I assure you. We had thought of them as experiments. Now they might be the most important vessels in the entire Navy."

The craft was dangling above now, dropping inch by inch towards the cradle between *Nomad's* main and mizzen, revealing the full sub-waterline contours.

"Mr. White outdid himself," Topcliffe said. "Can you guess how he came to those lines?"

"Trial and error, sir?" The basis of the art of ship-design for centuries.

Topcliffe shook his head. "It's a new world, Dawlish. A scientific world. White's working with an engineer called Froude. You've heard of him? Good! I've seen the long test tank he has in in Torquay. He tows wax models through it and measures resistance. He helped White try out models with different hull lines until they got it right. Maximum speed for minimum resistance. It's the way of the future. With his tank and his dynamometer and his formulae, Froude will put us a decade ahead of any other navy."

"The screw does look strange, sir." The positioning of the single large bronze propeller looked as if its blade tips would protrude above the waterline.

"It concerned me too when I first went to Cowes to see the tests," Topcliffe said. "But once she gets under way the stern digs in. The bows lift and the keel's exposed for several feet at top speed. White contracted for seventeen and a half knots, but each of these made at least a knot more on the Solent during acceptance trials. I saw them myself. Few craft afloat could catch them."

It took the best part of ten minutes to lower the hull, with as much care as if it were a piece of porcelain, into its padded cradle. Time had been short to modify *Nomad* to carry the three boats and the hoisting arrangements left much to be desired.

Topcliffe moved close to hull.

"Touch it," he said.

Dawlish stroked the surface. It was as hard and smooth as a mirror, a thing of beauty.

"Slippery as an eel and built like a racing shell, Dawlish. Strong and light. Four thin layers of wood, each of 'em laid at right angles to the one beneath. Not up to a buffeting in a seaway for long, admittedly, but ideal on sheltered waters."

"How are the boiler and the engine secured, sir?" It had looked complex on the drawings.

"Iron tie-rods to spread the load. A damn ingenious cat's cradle. You'll be impressed, lieutenant, and by a lot more than that besides!"

The second craft was ready for lifting.

"Have they names?" Dawlish asked. They were important. British seamen liked to call themselves by their ships' names and rallied to them in action.

"I'll leave it to you, lieutenant. But neutral. You'll be flying no ensign. Her Majesty will be making no claim of ownership."

Dawlish's mind raced. X, Y and Z would inspire nobody, numbers even less. Tom, Dick and Harry – too British. And the crews wouldn't like Athos, Aramis and Porthos – too French. Marius, Sulla and Julius – too pretentious.

And then they came to him.

"*Alpha*, *Beta* and *Gamma*, sir." Neutral, but with something of the mysterious about them.

"Not bad," Topcliffe said. "Not bad at all. *Alpha*, *Beta* and *Gamma* they'll be."

He left Dawlish to watch the loading of the two other boats. A pinnace arrived from shore soon after and Day and Talbot came on board. Dawlish had two and three years' seniority over them respectively. Formal introductions and then viewing of the boats, conversation only technical. He could sense their excitement, but their mystification also and their expectation that he might have something to tell about their destination. He saw that they were evaluating him, just as he was them, both eager for clues about his character and temperament. He had decided his own stance towards them already. He would be their commander, not their friend, slightly aloof, leading, supporting and encouraging, but demanding and tolerating nothing less than excellence. And given that they, or any member of the crews, might well die because of his orders, he wanted no close attachment that might deter cold resolution.

The crews arrived in late-afternoon, with one man still to come. Dawlish left it to Day and Talbot to see them settled in their isolated berthing and reinforce the warnings they had received already as to secrecy. They too had been offered an inducement for being bound to secrecy. How much? £100 a man, maybe £150? Either would be a fortune in a service that paid an able seaman £27 per year. But a cheap price for a life.

He decided that it was better to wait a night before addressing them. Topcliffe himself had approved the selection made by some unknown officer at the Admiralty. He had passed the lists to Dawlish, brief notes on each man, shorter than the reports on the two officers, just curt summaries of service and skills. An evening's work lay ahead to decide allocation of duties between them. And, after that, just days to weld them into teams and master handling of the fragile craft at some yet undisclosed location.

Egdean was the last to board. Dawlish had asked Topcliffe if he could have him, was glad to see him, a man he knew he could trust to the death. The pinnace that brought him from shore also carried five bales of clothing.

Old clothing, civilian. Seamen's gear, oilskins, jerseys, trousers, shirts. All different, all second or third hand, much of it threadbare, patched or ragged, needing washing. All purchased that day in Plymouth slop-shops.

Clothing to fight – and die – in.

Nomad dropped seawards just before midnight, swung south-westwards as her revolutions climbed, ran parallel to the coast. It was a course that might take her anywhere in the western hemisphere. Only now was Topcliffe confiding the immediate destination to her captain.

And then the navigating officer would have a busy half-hour before him.

*

Dawlish would command on, and from, *Alpha*. He told Day that he would have *Beta*, Talbot *Gamma*. He presumed that Topcliffe had dangled the same inducements to them as to himself, but the topic was unmentionable. Their records, besides some acquaintance with torpedoes, looked impressive. Charles Day, slim, fair-haired and boyish-looking, the more cheerful of the two, had experience of piracy-suppression on the China Coast. The short, dark and taciturn Roger Talbot had served in anti-blackbirding operations on the Australia Station. They had as little experience of fast craft as he had himself. That could not be held against them. These vessels were of a new breed.

"It's going to be Kronstadt, isn't it?" Day said. The prospect of venturing into the Russians' fortified naval base outside St. Petersburg seemed to elate rather than awe him. "Maybe even before war's declared. A new Copenhagen!"

"We won't speculate, Mr. Day." Dawlish made his tone icy. "We'll know when we need to know. That's enough for us."

He ran through his list of crew allocations, explained his reasons, invited comments. Day had none but Talbot had a few pertinent criticisms. Dawlish listened, saw merit in a few of them, thanked Talbot and modified the list accordingly. It was clear that the lieutenant had a talent for organisation and could be entrusted to sort out the crews in the coming hours.

*

Nomad had given Land's End a wide berth late in the morning watch and was now ploughing into the Atlantic swell under a clear sky on a course that Dawlish judged as north-west by west. He guessed the destination now as Bantry Bay on Ireland's south-west coast. He had been there before. A broad channel between a hilly island and the mountainous mainland provided a secure fleet anchorage, one protected by shore batteries. He remembered the channel's outer entrance being as narrow as two cables. It would be an ideal location to practise a torpedo attack in close waters. Pleased with his own acumen, he went to inspect the torpedoes.

Topcliffe must have expected damage or losses during training, for twelve of the expensive weapons had been shipped. Dawlish went through the dedicated logs provided with every one, records of repeated test launchings, adjustments of rudder trim after each to endure straight running. It was a weary, repetitive process, one that all too often ended in frustration when some fault prevented the torpedoes rising to the surface for recovery after the compressed air that drove them was exhausted. Young officers dreaded the prospect of such costly losses, of reprimands in personal files that would hang over them for years. Each torpedo had its own unique characteristics, imposed by the tiniest imperfections of cross-sections. Even a record of successive die-straight runs was no guarantee. Variations in water salinity, collisions with shoals of fish, the profile of the wave encountered as the torpedo bored beneath the surface, could all impose deflection from the intended track.

There was but one solution, potentially suicidal.

Launch at the shortest possible range.

*

Talbot had the crews ready for inspection that afternoon.

An officer in command of each boat and responsible for her torpedoes. A senior rating to act as quartermaster and maintain discipline, a gunner and a loader for each Gatling position, an engineer and a stoker. Talbot identified each man by name as Dawlish moved along the ranks, stopping now and then to refer to the man's prior service. It was the oldest trick of leadership, file details memorised in advance and flattering when recalled.

Lowe, *Beta's* helmsman, his face scarred, had served on the Ashanti expedition. Dawlish made no comment and passed on, then paused as if recognition had dawned. He came back.

"You were at Kumasi, weren't you, Mr. Lowe?" He couldn't recall having seen him there, but it didn't matter.

"Aye, aye, sir. With the old *Decoy's* contingent, sir." He stopped, as if wondering if speaking was presumptuous, then noticed Talbot's slight nod. "I saw you there, sir."

"And damn good work all you *Decoys* did then," Dawlish said. He moved on.

Maxwell, one of *Alpha's* gunners, had taken control of a thirty-two pounder and continued to serve it on *Euryalus* at Kagoshima, after most of the gun crew had been killed or wounded.

"CGM, wasn't it?" Dawlish said.

"Yes, sir." Justifiable pride. Conspicuous Gallantry Medals were dearly bought.

Stothert, one of *Beta's* loaders. had been first into a Maori pah a dozen years before.

"With the *Esk's* brigade, weren't you?" Dawlish said. "With Lieutenant Ford?" He knew him, had been together as midshipman on *Nile*, had not seen him since but had heard that he'd done well in New Zealand.

"A fine and gallant gentleman, sir." Stothert was beaming.

"Not just Lieutenant Ford. Gallant the lot of you, he told me."

He congratulated Egdean, for whom the honour of personal selection seemed to have cancelled out his broken leave.

And then the engineers and stokers. Dawlish asked them enough about boilers and the compound engines to let them know that he was more familiar with technicalities than most officers.

At last, he stood them easy. He could feel their curiosity about the unfamiliar commander whose decisions could mean life or death to them. Moments like this were always uncomfortable, necessary exhortations that could so easily fall flat.

"I can't tell you where we're going, lads." He raised his voice just enough to carry, and with the tone of confidence that he must always use with crew, no matter what his internal qualms. "But I can assure you it'll be hot. Damned hot. And I'm not talking about the climate either."

A ripple of uneasy smiles. Egdean was nudging a companion and nodding ever so slightly. Just as he'd predicted, there'd be no pleasure cruise with Dawlish.

"We're going to fight the Queen's enemies, and until then we'll be a closed family on this ship, with not a word beyond ourselves about our business. And our enemies won't know what we're about until we're sending them to kingdom come."

Shuffling, sidelong glances shot from man to man. They had been uncertain until this, but now action was a certainty.

"You've seen our vessels, lads. Beauties, all three of 'em. Now you're going to know them better than you know your wives and sweethearts! We'll have only a short time to learn how to turn them inside out. And no matter how they bounce on the wave-crests, Mr. Maxwell will show us how to write our names in Gatling fire. And you know what these boats did on test? Eighteen and a half knots! And that won't be good enough, not where we're going. Mr. Hickley and Mr. Bradford and Mr. Lloyd and their shovelers are going to give us a full nineteen on their boats, or they'll drop of heat-stroke in the attempt."

Uneasy smiles, yet somehow also a dawning of shared resolution.

"I'm promising you one thing at this moment. It's that you'll have little rest between now and the moment we hurl ourselves on the enemy like the wrath of God, because we're going to train with every weapon at our disposal, and that includes our bare hands. And I'm making an offer from my own pocket – a sovereign, here it is – for the first of you to best me in cutlass practice. Have I got takers?"

A few nods, uneasy smiles, eye contact lost with others. Nothing like the cheers inevitable in patriotic fiction.

Just an awareness that the business was serous. Deadly serious.

Parade dismissed.

*

It wouldn't be Bantry Bay, for in the sun's dying light, *Nomad* had swung on to a northern heading. Ireland must lie over the horizon on the starboard beam. Topcliffe had selected some location for training that was yet further removed from witnesses.

Even those on British warships at Bantry, or manning its shore defences.

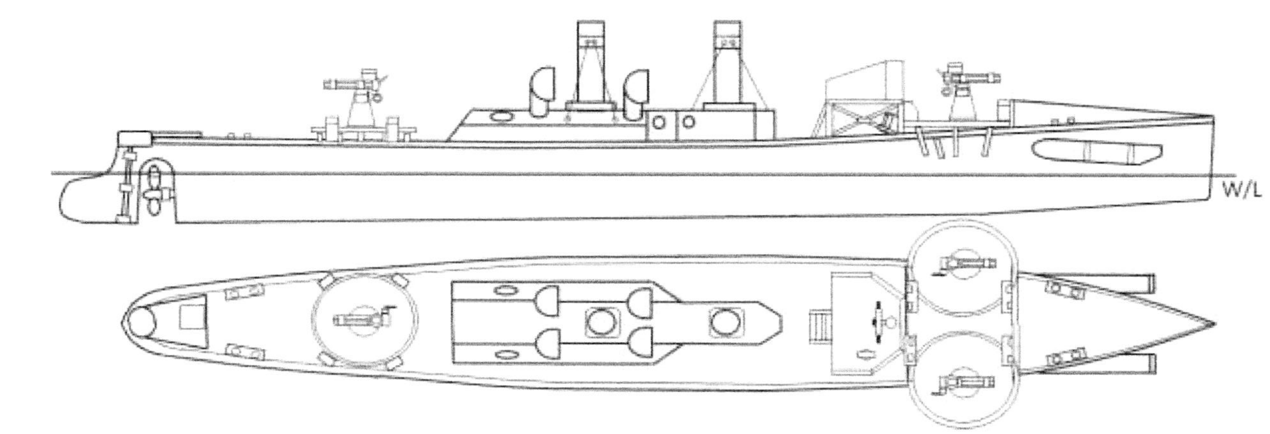

Alpha, Beta and Gamma, 1877

Research indicates that no Admiralty or yard drawings of these craft remain, probably since their existence was never officially recognised or recorded. This drawing has been reconstructed on the basis of a sketch and notes found in Admiral Sir Nicholas's private papers. He appears to have made them in retirement in 1911 and he described them as "based on memory". Sir Nicholas indicted length as "about 90 feet". Armament two 14" Whitehead torpedoes and three .65" Gatlings

Chapter 9

Dawlish came on deck at dawn. The three boats' crews were already mustered and Day and Talbot set them to preparations for dropping the torpedo boats once *Nomad* had moored. She was at half-revolutions, advancing eastwards with caution. He saw Topcliffe on the portside bridge wing, standing apart from the officers and quartermaster at the helm and studying the coast ahead through a telescope. Topcliffe noticed him, beckoned him to join him. A long chain of mountains lay ahead, dark against the lightening sky, still hiding the rising sun. Two large islands lay two miles or so off either beam, smaller ones to north and south.

"That's Inishbofin," Topcliffe gestured to the island to starboard and handed him his glass, "and that's Inishturk to port."

The light breeze from the southwest was throwing up surf on their rocky shores. Stone walls bordered a few tiny fields and grey peat smoke was drifting above a scattering of tiny thatched cabins. It must be a brutal life there.

Off the starboard bow white scatters of surf identified half-submerged reefs and skerries. Ringing from the bridge telegraph told of revolutions being reduced yet further.

"You know these waters, sir?" Dawlish said.

"In my youth." It was hard to imagine this cold, almost reptilian, man ever having been young. He pointed ahead. "There, that's the mouth of Killary Harbour."

It was hard to pick it out, for the mountain barrier seemed all but unbroken. Dawlish knew of the place by reputation, knew too that it was the 'harbour' designation was misleading. This was a fjord, a long, deep, narrow channel that ran eight miles eastward between high mountains.

"Is that where we're to exercise, sir?"

"No better place. The other vessels needed are there already."

Nomad crept forward through a wide semi-circular bay. Strips of green fields on the lower slopes of the heather-covered mountains to the south, a few wretched cottages, more stone walls. Through the telescope Dawlish saw three figures leading a donkey along a yellow beach to the north, the beast's creels laden with kelp. Even at this distance he sensed hopeless resignation.

Now Killary's entrance, less than two cables wide, brown and green clad mountains to the north and south dropping steeply to the water's edge, no sign of habitation. It was impossible to imagine any Czarist agent observing activities here. The channel was running south-eastwards now, broadening to four of five cables. *Nomad* crawled on some four miles. Then a slight turn – a few squalid cabins to the south here – carried her eastwards. Narrow again over the next two miles, then widening into a broad triangle of open water almost as long. The mountain slopes were less steep here, levelling out to stone-walled fields and a few cottages clustered on the south-eastern side

And at the furthest apex, two gunboats at anchor, all but blocking the narrow gap beyond them.

"*Frolic* and *Rifleman*," Topcliffe said.

"They're to be the practice targets, sir?"

"Oh no, lieutenant. That would be too easy. Your target is beyond."

And not yet visible.

*

Alpha was already moored alongside *Nomad*, and *Beta* was being hoisted from her cradle when Dawlish returned with Topcliffe. *Nomad's* steam launch had carried them through the half-cable wide channel beyond the two gunboats that led to the head of the inlet. There, in a wide hammerhead strewn with green islets, the target lay. A coal hulk, the *Dromedary*, towed there by *Rifleman* and moored eighty yards from shore. But practice attacks on her must wait until handling of the torpedo craft was mastered.

And now the first run, *Alpha* unburdened for now by torpedoes and Gatlings. Day had overseen her preparations and he reported that she was ready when Dawlish boarded. He went below into the tiny space between the large locomotive-style boiler, the engine and the anthracite hoppers. Hickley, the engineer, and Barrow, the stoker, somehow found room for him. Both were stripped to the waist. The atmosphere was already like a Turkish bath even before the full blast of heat from the glowing furnace hit him.

"The safety valve's just lifting, sir." Pride on Hickley's sweat-streaked face.

"Ninety-three minutes." Dawlish snapped his steel watch closed. Day had told him the time when *Alpha* had rested in the water. "Good, Mr. Hickley, damned good. And just what I expected of you."

He took the bridge with Egdean, selected as helmsman because it was easy to imagine him holding an attack course, regardless of defensive fire.

Mooring lines cast off. At quarter-revolutions, *Alpha* pushed away from *Nomad's* flank and nudged into open water. Dawlish fought down the awareness that Topcliffe was looking down from the ship above. The deck beneath his feet shuddered as the screw bit. *Alpha's* bows swung over to track the centre of the fjord seawards. Half-revolutions now, rung to the engine room from the tiny telegraph next to the helm behind the bridge-screen. The stern dug in, as predicted, and the bows rose. The speed built, then levelled at what Dawlish estimated might be thirteen knots. He ordered Egdean to hold it there for the next ten minutes, only the slightest movements of the wheel needed to maintain the course die-straight.

Satisfied so far, he reached for the telegraph and pulled the handle back to demand full speed. The prow rose yet higher and the bow-wave began to stream from a point well abaft the stem. In this long trench, sheltered between the flanking mountains, the water was smooth and vibration was negligible. The speed built further, reached a maximum, stayed there. Dawlish had not streamed a log but judged that this must be close to eighteen knots.

The channel had broadened to its widest now. It was time to reduce speed, nudge over towards the south, then sweep into a gentle turn to starboard, keeping it for a full circle. The craft held steady, bringing the promise of stability at higher speeds in tighter turns. A series of them now, to port and starboard, each sharper, each faster, than before. Dawlish sensed that Egdean was gaining confidence with each creaming, slewing turn. He wanted that confidence for himself also.

He took the helm, half-revolutions and straight running until he sensed that he had the feel of it, then throwing the craft into sharp turns, snapping out of them until he trusted himself with full revolutions. Now he ran towards the fjord's narrow entrance. The islands and skerries outside had sapped the strength of the Atlantic swell but, even so, the water here was ruffled. Only now did *Alpha* lose something of her steadiness. Even the slightest ripple made the hull all but leap from the water and the tight turns were terrifying, the vessel heaving and jolting as she heeled.

Yet Dawlish soon felt familiar with his new command, doubling back to fling her again and again across her own wake, bounding over rather than ploughing through. Satisfied, he handed the helm to Egdean again and ordered a turn back towards the head of the inlet. He went to the engine room hatch and shouted down to Hickley.

"How much coal left for maintaining full speed?"

"About a half-hour's, sir. Maybe a little more."

He decided to chance it, to risk the prospect of a humiliating tow back, powerless. *Alpha* streaked onwards, rounded the channel's turn to the east. *Nomad* came in view and on her bridge Topcliffe must see the white bone in the torpedo craft's teeth, a triumphant justification of his confidence in her design. On she ran, past the corvette's flank at a half-cable's separation, her bow-wave rocking the *Beta* and *Gamma* moored alongside, raising a cheer from the men on their decks.

Dawlish pointed to the two gunboats ahead. Little over a half-cable separated them.

"Through that gap," he told Egdean. "Helm hard to starboard once we pass. But wait for my word!"

He felt fear – physical fear, knotted stomach, pounding heart – for the first time since he had accepted this assignment. A manoeuvre like would be all but suicidal. The separation might be wider if *Nevski* and *Orlov* lay like this, but sharp-eyed lookouts would have seen the oncoming craft by now, and alerted officers would be calling for defensive fire from the fighting tops. Speed alone could save the eggshell hull at such a moment, speed too high for aimers to swing their weapons to track it.

The gap ahead looked narrower by the second. *Alpha* was racing past *Rifleman's* bowsprit now and *Frolic's* a little beyond. Nobody on board seemed to have anticipated this, for heads were appearing along the bulwarks and officers were scrambling to the bridges. Ahead, through the narrow channel leading to the inlet's head, Dawlish glimpsed *Dromedary's* black hull. The gunboats' flanks were slipping past and he could sense Egdean's tension as he waited for the command to turn.

Now past *Rifleman's* stern.

"Starboard, hard over!"

Alpha creamed over under the gunboat's counter.

"Hold the turn!"

Almost sixteen points, until heading westwards. Dawlish called for Egdean to straighten the course, run back towards *Nomad.* He reached for the telegraph, rang for quarter-revolutions.

Better to return with something still left in the coal bunkers.

*

Day and *Beta* had performed well also. Now, in early afternoon, a racing arrow of white water marked Talbot's testing of *Gamma*.

Nomad was lowering *Alpha's* Gatlings to their mountings. Hickley and Barrow – still unsteady from the heat exhaustion suffered in the morning's test – were overseeing emptying of sacks of best anthracite into the depleted bunkers. It was the amount of fresh water exhausted through the funnels during the runs that concerned Dawlish most. The tanks were almost dry, the level in the boiler at the danger mark, when he had rung 'Finished with Engines' on *Alpha's* telegraph. Water rather than fuel would determine endurance. It had to be fresh. *Nomad's* evaporator was supplying it now and topping up the tanks through a hose was easy. It might be less so at the still undisclosed location where the torpedo boats must operate.

Dawlish watched as one of the six yellow-painted torpedoes that now lay on cradles on the corvette's deck was hoisted. He already knew them, and the spares, as intimately as a lover. On passage from Devonport, he and Day and Talbot had supervised their complete disassembly, the checking of their every component, their reassembly and the charging of their air-tanks. They lacked only their explosive charges, for which ballast substituted during exercises. Now the first fish-shaped, sharp-nosed, torpedo was swung outboard and lowered to the *Alpha* to be manhandled with extreme care into the port tube beneath the bridge. The second would follow. *Beta* and *Gamma* would load theirs, and their Gatlings too. With weapons and ammunition on board, the crafts' trim and handling would now be at battle conditions.

Dawlish accompanied Topcliffe below to discuss the night's trials. The possibility that the Russian ships might already be putting to sea hung over them like a shadow and was forcing the pace. Just two full days more could be allowed for familiarisation before the *Nomad* must depart. The coming work would concentrate on approaches in the dark. Actual torpedo practice would commence on the morrow.

*

There was no moon but the sky was clear and starlit above the blackness of the inlet's steep walls. Though fearful of some submerged rock, Dawlish was still keeping *Alpha* as close to the southern shore as he dared. He was alone with Egdean on *Alpha's* steering platform and she was crawling eastwards at little over three knots. The two-man crews in the Gatling positions on either beam were also straining their eyes to detect the *Nomad's* bulk. She must surely loom up soon. Despite the darkness, Dawlish was apprehensive of betrayal by the slight bow-wave or by starlight caught in the grey steam-filled coal smoke spilling from the funnels. A cable-length astern, and slightly to port, *Beta* too was stalking up the inlet. Only the briefest glimpses of her smoke confirmed that *Gamma* was keeping pace close to the northern shore. Dawlish had judged during the day's exercises that Talbot and his crew had performed better than Day and his own. The margin was narrow, but enough for trusting Talbot with more independence should it prove necessary.

This would be the last chance of success before steam and fuel ran out. Three earlier attempts to surprise *Nomad* had ended in detection when the attacking craft were still far outside torpedo range.

"Two points off the starboard bow, sir!" A sudden hiss from the port gun-position.

And there was *Nomad*, her black bulk separating from the dark land-mass behind and her masts and yards standing out against the sky. She had weathercocked a little since last sighted and now she lay diagonal to the channel's axis, a cable off the southern shore.

"Hold her steady, Egdean!"

Dawlish reached for the covered red lantern on the rail behind him. He raised and lowered the shutter twice, flashing astern to Day. There was no response from the *Beta* but seconds later Dawlish could just make out the tiny bow wave edging to port for better clearance of *Alpha's* wake when she built speed. He pointed the lamp towards *Gamma* and flashed three times. From this moment on, all three boat commanders must make their own decisions.

He whispered a course correction to Egdean to bring the *Alpha* towards the centre of the channel, far enough over that a swing to starboard would expose *Nomad* beam on, the best approach for successful torpedo launching. He glanced astern, saw that *Beta* was still close inshore. He could see nothing of *Gamma*.

The range was closing. Twelve hundred yards, he guessed. *Alpha* needed a quarter of that to accelerate to full speed.

Minutes passed. Still undetected.

Then it was time. Dawlish reached for the telegraph and pulled it back. Down in the engine room it was shrilling to tell Hickley to open the throttle. Long seconds and then the screw threshed faster. *Alpha* surged forward, bow wave building. She was at the centre of the channel now and in seconds a slew to starboard would bring her target dead ahead.

An arc-light sparked into life on *Nomad's* foretop. Its cold white shaft stabbed into the darkness to starboard. Dawlish hoped for a moment that it might be seeking *Beta* but instead it came sweeping over towards his own craft. Still he held her course, even as the beam found her, transfixing her in icy, dazzling brilliance. He yelled to Egdean to throw the helm over. Half-blinded by the light, he knew that *Nomad's* long flank was now dead ahead.

Two hundred yards.

Dawlish knew that if this had been a real attack he would at this moment, in the split second before the target's defensive weapons showered ruin, be throwing forward the twin torpedo-firing levers, hurling destruction towards the corvette. Success but suicide. He would be dead in seconds more, but his torpedoes would almost certainly score hits. Now however he yelled to Egdean for full helm to port, to run parallel to *Nomad's* flank, then skid into the tightest possible turn to come into the blind spot below her counter. The searchlight operator had reacted already, had recognised the impossibility of tracking *Alpha*, was sweeping again, then finding and holding *Beta.* In seconds more, a real target's defensive weapons would be beating her to matchwood.

Alpha was swinging around *Nomad's* stern when something shot past her in the opposite direction, avoiding collision by feet only. Talbot, still undetected, had hugged the northern shore before sweeping back in a wide turn to approach *Nomad* on her opposite side. She would have delivered her missiles successfully, and would possibly have escaped unharmed even had *Alpha* failed.

Dawlish signalled for half-revolutions to the engine room and ordered Egdean to take the boat back alongside the *Nomad* for mooring. It was a not unsatisfactory end to his first day's acquaintance with his new attacking force.

And five hours of needed rest ahead.

Chapter 10

It was the turn of the Gatling crews next morning. Each of the gunners and loaders, capable of exchanging duties in an emergency, already had experience with such weapons. These six-barrelled, .65 inch, versions were more powerful than the rifle-calibre Gatlings used on land. Larger warships carried them in their fighting tops for close-defence.

Nomad's steam pinnace and steam launch set off down the fjord. They were towing target rafts far astern that carried wattle targets painted with red and white chequerboards. The three torpedo boats took turns to overtake them at full speed, opening fire as they ran at a cable's separation alongside with the weapon in one of the forward sponsons and that mounted aft. They tore on, past the targets and their tugs, then heeled into a wide turn far ahead, then ran back to repeat the manoeuvre on the opposite beam.

The first results were disappointing. Even in smooth water, the torpedo boats' slight heave and roll at high speed challenged accuracy. The gunners swung their weapons to hold the targets in their sights as long as possible, blasting great holes in the targets with the huge rounds when lucky, boiling the waters around with misses if not. The loaders scorched their hands on the hot barrels as they transferred ammunition from the storage lockers into the insatiable feed-hoppers above the breeches. Despite orders to restrict each burst of fire to five rounds, jams were still frequent – as always with these weapons – and clearing them took enough time for the targets to slip past unscathed.

But, with each run, the gunners grew more accustomed to the motion of the boats and their effectiveness improved. Each raft carried a stack of wattle targets to replace those shattered. Erecting them gave time for Gatling barrels to cool, for their crews to rest.

By mid-morning, Dawlish was satisfied that accuracy of broadside firing had reached an adequate level. He would have wished for better, but time was short. The challenge now was to attain a comparable standard with the weapons in the sponsons firing ahead. This was the most important capability of all, that needed in attack. The boat must be driving straight towards her prey, both weapons blasting to suppress defending fire, until the very moment that the torpedoes would leap from their tubes. Then helm hard over, turning, racing away, with the stern Gatling now unmasked and pouring fire in the seconds before the torpedoes struck home. It was the vision of success that Dawlish carried with him, one that he must believe in however much a small cold voice within him reminded that it needed – demanded – more luck than he could reasonably hope for.

Now the renewed attacks, *Alpha* and Betta and *Gamma* racing bow-on in turn towards the targets, sometimes, but not always, tearing them to splinters, slewing away to port or starboard eighty yards or less from the rafts. It was in such a manoeuvre that the enterprise suffered its first casualty, *Beta's* stoker flung against a furnace door as she turned away, burning his torso and breaking his arm. Neither injury was mortal and the man was more indignant at being eliminated from the craft's crew than concerned by his own pain as *Beta* carried him back to *Nomad* for treatment.

No more time available for further gunnery exercises.

What mattered now were the torpedoes.

*

The daylight torpedo tests would confirm the straight running ability of each weapon. *Nomad* served as the target, vertical white stripes painted on her starboard flank at twenty-feet separations, and numbered, on either side of the yard-wide red column amidships that was the aiming mark.

Now the first run.

Alpha drove up the centre of the channel, building speed, *Nomad* off her starboard bow. Helm over then at Dawlish's command, and into a tight turn, straightening out as Egdean spun his wheel, held the turn too far, corrected course to hold the corvette dead ahead and *Alpha's* stem pointed to the red mark. To his right, Dawlish had braced himself against the low metal shield, each hand grasping the torpedo-launching handles. He could see men from *Beta's* and *Gamma's* crews perched along *Nomad's* bulwarks, one over each white stripe, to look for the trail of bubbles that would betray the torpedoes' tracks and detect the point of impact.

He launched at what he guessed was two cable's length, saw the torpedoes shooting from their tubes. Even as they hit the water he was telegraphing for dead-slow ahead and Egdean was carrying the craft to port and killing speed. Dawlish sought, but could not find, the bubble trails. He fought down the fear that, as sometimes happened, the shock of hitting the water's surface had impaired depth-keeping. Delicate bellows-operated mechanisms, which sensed pressure, acted on the horizontal rudders to keep the running torpedo at a set depth – today twelve feet. In a worst case, damage to these items could send the weapons driving towards the seabed. But there was no way of assuring maintenance of direction, none except accuracy of launch and pre-adjustment of the vertical rudders. He was counting the seconds and impact must be imminent.

And then a seaman on *Nomad's* bulwark was flourishing a semaphore flag above the second white stripe to the right of the red target. The yellow torpedo was breaking surface and bobbing there, air exhausted. Even at this separation, the flattening and denting of its nose was obvious. It had hit, and hit hard. Between the red stripe and the white directly to its left, another seaman was semaphoring success as the second torpedo also rose into sight.

One all but dead-on target. Some slight out-of-roundness of the other's casing had carried it forty feet off. A slight adjustment of the vertical rudders would correct that.

Measures were set in hand to hoist the spent torpedoes from the water. *Alpha* moored against the corvette's opposite flank to take on coal and water. Part of her crew would observe and signal from the bulwarks, replacing *Beta's* men.

For it was her turn now.

Steam was already raised and in her engine room a broad-shouldered volunteer from the *Nomad's* boiler-room named Winstanley had replaced her injured stoker. Tempted by the promised bounty, he had been sworn to the same secrecy as the other crew members.

The launchings continued into early evening, each torpedo tested twice, their dented nose cones replaced after each hit, their rudders adjusted, then loaded again into their tubes. One of *Gamma's* weapons did not resurface and one of *Alpha's* was so badly damaged by impact as to be unsuited for further use. All the spares ran tests and two of them replaced those lost.

Darkness ended the exercises. Bunkers filled, water tanks topped up, Gatling ammunition loaded, engines checked, a gasket replaced on one craft, a leaking flange tightened on another, all three boats were loaded to their operational waterlines.

And a torpedo lay snug in each tube, its weight essential for ballasting the craft at attack-draught, but with the firing pistol removed.

When next launched, it should be in anger – and armed.

*

The last day at Killary, devoted until mid-afternoon to perfecting boat-handling and thereafter to readying the craft for the night's exercise and snatching a few hours' sleep before it. Topcliffe had specified the objective as delivering a mock attack on the *Dromedary*. The approach should begin five miles seaward of *Nomad's* current mooring. Dawlish had sole responsibility for deciding the tactics.

"May I reconnoitre the anchorage first, sir?"

On arrival, he had seen the hammerhead closure at the inlet's eastern end and had worried since about the islets there.

"Before you attack the Russians, you'll have to reconnoitre also," Topcliffe said. "We know nothing of the specific anchorage, only its general location. So yes, it's reasonable that you examine *Dromedary* in daylight. I'll see to it that you have *Nomad's* launch."

Dawlish took Day and Talbot with him, up through the narrow channel outside which *Frolic* and *Rifleman* stood guard. The moored hulk lay just eastwards of the point at which the channel, like a haft, lodged in the hammerhead. The small islands, rocky green-clad outcrops, lay to the north-west. Changes of surface colour to their east indicated shallow water. A semi-circular space lay south of the *Dromedary* and less than a cable's length across.

"Limited manoeuvre room, sir." Day stated the obvious.

Difficult to navigate at any significant speed in daylight. And damn near impossible in the dark without detection.

"We won't let that stop us, Mr. Day" Dawlish hoped he sounded more confident to the others than he felt himself. "Let's go out to the gunboats and come in again. Note every feature this time."

For there must be a way.

Nearing *Nomad* again, they saw three horsemen approaching the shore across the steep moorland to the south. A whaler was stroking across to meet them at the water's edge. Black uniforms, spiked helmets, carbines slung across their backs. Dawlish had seen them before, during visits to Bantry. The Royal Irish Constabulary was a semi-military force, hated by a population that simmered in resentment that often turned to violence. One of the them was handing something over. Then the whaler was turning back to *Nomad* and the riders were heading south again.

One likelihood.

A despatch for Topcliffe.

*

Dawlish opened the dark lantern, checked his watch. A half-hour past midnight. It was time.

The slight sliver of waxing moon threw sufficient light from a clear sky to distinguish land from water, nothing more. The three boats had hovered in the shadows here since sundown, just seawards of the bend that hid them from *Nomad.* All Gatling crews were in place but their weapons were unloaded and the air reservoirs for launching the torpedoes were depressurised. Topcliffe had given Dawlish discretion as to when to begin his advance. He had waited, hoping that the lookouts on the defending vessels would have grown bored and less attentive.

Brief red flashes to *Beta*, close astern, to *Gamma*, unseen against the dark wall of the northern bank. Answering signals.

"My compliments to Mr. Hickley," Dawlish said to Scanlon, loader in the port sponson. "Dead slow ahead."

Scanlon moved aft, called down in a low voice into the engine room. Only in an emergency would the telegraphs transmit orders this night, for the sound of their bells could carry far over smooth water.

Slow advance now, all three boats hugging the shadows. Around the channel's bend. A mile and a half eastward, *Nomad's* masts were just visible against the sky. Speed little over walking pace, too slow to break the bow waves into white, the gurgle of the waters slipping alongside louder than the engine's low panting or the slow churning of the screw. Dawlish could see nothing of the other boats. With luck, they might, all three, pass *Nomad* undetected.

Then, shocking, heart-chilling, a rocket soaring from the steep slope to the south, soaring with a fiery tail, reaching high above the channel's centre before exploding. A brief flash, reflected in the still waters below, illuminated for a second the shores to either side. In that instant Dawlish saw *Gamma* silhouetted against the cliff beyond her. He had not expected this, but from what he already knew of Topcliffe, he realised that he should have. Observers looking down from the hills had a better chance of spotting movement in the channel than those in *Nomad's* tops. Another rocket was rising now, showering sparks, and Dawlish realised that at this instant the operators in *Nomad's* foretop must be swinging the knife-switch closed to ignite the arc light. The rocket burst, once more revealing *Gamma.*

No option now.

None but to flash the agreed signal from the dark lantern – the shutter flipped four times – first to *Gamma*, then *Beta*.

"Full speed!"

Scanlon scuttled to relay the command to the engine room. Egdean edged the bows out into the channel. Revolutions building, the screw bit and *Alpha* lunged forward. *Nomad's* searchlight was blazing into life, its cold beam lancing through the darkness, wandering for a moment before steadying. It began to sweep back and forth across the channel three hundred yards ahead.

Alpha's speed was building – near maximum now – and she was close to the centre of the fjord, racing towards the illuminated ellipse on the water's surface that now crept slowly from shore to shore, reversed, then crept back. Glances to port and astern revealed ghostly white bow waves. The two other craft had also swung out from the shorelines so that all three were racing ahead in arrowhead formation, *Alpha* in the lead, the others a hundred yards behind and fifty to port and starboard of her wake.

The searching beam was passing northwards ahead. Elevation of a few degrees would have transfixed *Alpha* but Dawlish was calling for Egdean to throw the helm over. The boat slewed to port, straightened, ran behind the moving beam.

And was through.

Nomad was a hundred yards off the starboard bow, close enough for lookouts to spot the racing *Alpha* in the near-darkness and to shout alarms. And too close for the searchlight to track her. Dawlish glanced astern, saw that the beam now held *Beta.* Violent turns shook her free for moments and lost her in darkness until the tenacious beam caught her again and yet another turn liberated her. Yet, all the while, her sinuous course was sustaining her advance. And *Gamma*, undetected, must still be forging on at full speed.

Alpha had run past *Nomad* now and the outlines of the two gunboats ahead were just discernible.

"The light's out, sir!" A cry from the Gatling mounting at the stern.

Darkness shrouded *Beta* as she ran past the corvette. Dawlish knew that arc lights, so recent an introduction to the Navy, were prodigal in consumption of the carbon rods between which the spark trembled. *Nomad's* had burned away in how long? Three minutes? Four? And how long to replace them? Knowledge that might save the situation in an actual attack, for the Russians too must surely have such lights.

A mile to reach *Frolic* and *Rifleman*. Dawlish flashed the recognition signal off the port quarter and a red glow winking in return confirmed *Gamma's* presence. Another signal confirmed that *Beta* was running in *Alpha's* wake.

The gunboats' profiles were sharper now and, through the space between their flanks, Dawlish could just make out the narrow channel beyond, grey in the faint starlight. Time for decision now. Discussion of tactics that afternoon had identified three options for driving through this obstacle. Topcliffe had approved all three.

"You'll decide which, depending on circumstances," he had told Dawlish.

"And if it's the wrong decision, sir?"

"It'll be my responsibility, Lieutenant Dawlish. I'll back your choice."

Now, knowing that speed had had been the best protection so far, and that surprise would reinforce it, he made that choice.

Six flips of the lanterns shutter, the signal for tactic number two.

And acknowledgements.

Rockets rising from the gunboats, four in immediate succession. Their bursts cast enough brief scarlet light for Dawlish to spot *Gamma* still off *Alpha's* port quarter, bow wave frothing, and to see that *Beta* had nudged across to starboard, the arrowhead formation resumed.

Course steady now, *Alpha's* bows headed for the centre of the gap between the gunboats. At this moment, were it real action, she would be the sacrificial decoy, depending for survival on the sponson Gatlings blazing at any searchlights and raking fighting tops, her mission to divert attention from the two other torpedo boats speeding towards the gunboats' outer flanks.

Dawlish was reaching for the torpedo-launching handles as his boat forged into the gauntlet, *Frolic* to port and *Rifleman* to starboard. He was conscious of figures on the bulwarks, of shouts, of lanterns there, close enough that small arms fire could have lashed his decks despite the defensive fury of his Gatlings. Dead ahead he saw the land to north and south side funnelling into the hundred-yards wide entrance to the hammerhead.

Alpha was through, the gunboats dropping fast astern. A glance astern told that *Gamma* and *Beta* were past them too, on their outer flanks, helms over now to enter the channel. More rockets from the gunboats burst high overhead, their falling sparks reflected in the narrow, dead-calm, slot ahead and lighting a few stone-walled fields to either side and peat smoke rising from cabins. A long white blur was the first sight of *Dromedary*, the long stripe along her mastless black hull. A thousand yards to go and the approach-course angle ideal. A rocket rising from *Dromedary* told that the party on board her had detected *Alpha's* onrush, so also perhaps *Gamma*, and *Beta* astern of her, and well inside the channel.

Five hundred yards, four, three, *Dromedary's* flank like a wall dead ahead, Dawlish's hands locked on the launching handles, Egdean holding steady course. Now bursting into the hammerhead, an islet just to port, range under two hundred.

Dawlish pushed the handles forward, could imagine, could all but feel, how the torpedoes would have been hurled from their tubes as he shouted "Hard over!" to Egdean and rang the telegraph for half-speed. *Alpha* almost collided with the hulk but, with momentum lessening, she circled around her stern. Another ring – dead slow – as she passed along the target's side, was at walking pace when she reached the bows. Satisfaction flooded him as told himself that both torpedoes would have found their marks.

But . . . but only if *Alpha*, and her crew, had survived this far.

A big 'If'.

The Russians would defend with more than searchlights and rockets.

Loitering ahead of *Dromedary's* bow, Dawlish could now see *Gamma* running up the channel, her approach as faultless as *Alpha's* own and with *Beta* following close astern. Seconds later *Gamma* was speeding into the hammerhead, her helmsman giving the dreaded islets to port a wide berth, then straightening for a perfect launch. Talbot must know, as his vessel pulled to port to follow *Alpha's* manoeuvre, that his torpedoes would have smashed against the hulk. Dawlish's eyes were locked now on *Beta* as she entered the hammerhead, her run also promising success.

And then a cry from aft, from the Gatling mounting at the stern, a cry incoherent but horrified.

Dawlish spun about.

Gamma had not slowed enough, had pulled too wide around *Dromedary's* stern, was hurtling towards the rocky shore at the head of the inlet. Foam boiled at her stern as her screw beat in reverse and she was losing way. But not fast enough. She ground on the jagged bank just as *Beta*, her mock attack also a success, lurched into sight astern of the hulk. Dawlish saw that *Gamma's* back was already broken, engine and boiler exposed, the glow of furnace flames revealed, shattered wood thrown clear, the section abaft the second funnel heeling over, the stern submerging, the forward section trapped on the rocks. A single inhuman scream cut off, other shouting, men leaping into the water.

The exercise had been all too realistic.

*

Boats from *Frolic* and *Rifleman* came to help the search. Together, they pulled four men alive from the water, all shocked but uninjured, and two more with broken limbs. From the rocks they rescued three more, no worse than bruised. The only deaths were of Talbot and his helmsman, their heads smashed against the metal shield before them as *Gamma* struck.

One craft lost before even before leaving home waters.

And *Nomad* would sail as soon as *Alpha* and *Beta* could be hoisted.

No time to mourn, only to fear what was to come.

Chapter 11

Reporting failure was always bitter. Topcliffe, in *Nomad's* captain's quarters, which he occupied, listened to Dawlish in silence. He offered no reproof.

"I recognised the chance of something like this happening," he said. "But the exercise was invaluable. You know now what you'll face and how you'll handle it."

"But a pity about Talbot, sir." Dawlish was grateful now that he had decided not to form a close attachment to him or to Day.

"A pity, but he knew that the task was dangerous." Said without feigned regret.

He'll say the same of me if, maybe when, it comes to it. And I couldn't blame him. I accepted the deal.

And yet Dawlish felt a sense of desolation, of awareness now that the mission was all but hopeless, even suicidal, that more would almost certainly die.

I've staked my honour. There can be no going back.

Rifleman's captain would take care of the burials. *Nomad* would still depart as planned. The despatch brought by the mounted policemen provided good reason for haste.

"The Russians have a bridge across." Topcliffe pointed to the large map on the table. Even from feet away Dawlish could identify the Danube writhing across it like a blue snake.

"Where, sir?"

"Here – at a place called Zimnitza." Topcliffe marked it with a red pencil. "A pontoon bridge, substantial, damn well done apparently. They have a full Army Corps on the south bank already and more to come."

"And the Turks, sir?"

"Confused and out-generalled. And there's worse, a large Russian force heading for Tirnova." Topcliffe lifted a magnifier, searched, found it, "There it is! Just north of the Balkan Range. If they can take the key passes – the Hainkioi, or the Shipka, there, and there – they'll have cut off the Turkish forces in Northern Bulgaria."

Dawlish glanced at the map's scale. "And then, sir?"

"Then, lieutenant, the walls of Constantinople will seem but a stone's throw distant. And the moment of decision will be upon Her Majesty's Government. Unless …"

"... unless, sir, we've buried our torpedoes in the *Nevski* and the *Orlov* by then."

He felt embarrassed as soon as he had said it. Too trite.

"You're wondering where that will be, Dawlish? Yes? You'll hear when we're at sea. And in the meantime, you've two boats to bring aboard."

Revelation, and rest, must wait.

*

Midday, steaming south, Ireland slipping past off the port beam. *Nomad* was its own world now and the danger of a careless word somehow reaching a Czarist agent was past. Topcliffe had invited Dawlish and Day to his quarters. The curtain of secrecy was to be swept aside.

It was nothing like Dawlish had expected. Not a fortified anchorage made available by the French according to some clandestine agreement, not even a remote South American inlet that was visited seldom, if ever, by small coastal traffic.

The map delineated a fan-shaped area. Straggling radii crept outwards towards a ragged circumference. They might have been the veins and arteries of a spread hand, running from wrist to fingertips, some wide, some narrow, some like tiny capillaries.

"The Delta of the river Niger," Topcliffe said. "It's has the only remote deep-water anchorages on Africa's West Coast. It's nothing but a vast and featureless expanse of mangrove swamp, well over a hundred miles across, with hardly a foothold of dry ground". His finger moved across the sheet. "There are a few trading villages, grandiloquently known as 'Kingdoms' – Bonny and Brass and Opobo, here and here and here. A few smaller ones besides, but for the rest it's an all but uncharted wasteland."

Dawlish knew of the area, was glad that he had never been there. It was few hundred miles east of Ashanti. He had carried its malaria with him from there. But the Niger Delta could only be worse, sodden with the same dead, fever-laden heat that sapped energy and life. A place where only quinine stood between a European and his grave.

"The chart is sketchy," Topcliffe said. "It's enough though to show the principal channels of the Niger and other rivers entering the Bights of Benin and Biafra. Several of the largest are up to a mile or more wide and they're deep enough to carry even large ships far into the swamp."

"Haven't we a presence there, sir?" Day said. "A protectorate, something of that sort?"

Topcliffe shook his head. "It's an acknowledged sphere of British influence since the Royal Navy swept the slavers from it – but there's nothing more formal. A few British palm-oil traders are established in the coastal villages. I'm assured that most of them usually too drunk to venture far from them. Some of the newer trading houses, and a handful of missionaries, have been penetrating inland by the main channels. Naval launches are sometimes sent to protect such people. Our presence's minimal however. The areas outside the main trading routes are seldom, maybe never, visited by a European."

He paused and Dawlish already guessed what was coming.

"It's in just such a place the Russians are skulking. Here in fact." Topcliffe stabbed a finger at a point some fifteen miles from the coast, "West of an offshoot of the San Bartolomeo Channel, in an area under dispute between the petty Majesties of Brass and Bonny. The upshot of their quarrel was that a villainous cutthroat named Ephraim Loveday outmanoeuvred both parties and proclaimed himself king. His capital is here, at Elepa." He pointed to a dot amid a maze of convoluted creeks.

It looked as if it would never be possible to find such a place in this maze, Dawlish thought.

"At first Loveday was considered no more than an obnoxious nuisance but a few months ago he murdered two British traders and grossly insulted a lady missionary who remonstrated with him," Topcliffe said. "Our vice-consul at Bonny asked the Navy to intervene. A Lieutenant West – Arthur West, your contemporary, Dawlish, I believe that you served with him in *Nile* – was despatched with a steam launch to teach him a lesson. He expected no stiffer opposition than a few canoes armed with old slavers' swivel cannon."

It would not have mattered if it had been a squadron of ironclads, Dawlish thought. West would have faced them anyway. He had seen him as a fourteen-year-old midshipman taking on a gunroom bully twice his size. And thrashing him.

"West did meet several such canoes and he blew them from the water. But soon after he ran into two small steam craft manned by Europeans. Surprise was on their side. A massacre followed. West's craft was sunk and his surviving crew shot in the water without mercy. He was a powerful swimmer however. Though wounded, he made the cover of the mangrove."

"But he escaped?"

"He did, but what came after was a nightmare. He realised that he encountered more than mere piracy – the force and discipline he witnessed indicated the involvement of some navy. He managed to steal a canoe from a fishing village. He followed his attackers in the direction they had departed. He travelled only at night. And this is what he found."

Topcliffe lifted aside the map to reveal a crude pencil-sketch on a stained sheet of cartridge paper. Rough as it was, it showed the outlines of two fully rigged ironclads.

And unmistakable. The disposition of the barbettes was enough to identify the *Nevski.*

"Would West have known about her?" Dawlish said. "Have read about her in some technical journal perhaps?"

"No. I'm satisfied about that. The La Seyne shipyard was closely guarded during her building. It was a condition of the contract. I know that because we secured a copy."

Dawlish studied the sketch while Topcliffe spoke.

"West made the drawing after some friendly Africans who'd found him brought back to Bonny. He was more dead than alive. He'd survived on crabs and shellfish and his wound was badly infected. Gangrene had set in and it proved mortal. He'd done his duty however. A message was despatched immediately – it arrived shortly before I interviewed both of you in London. It wasn't unexpected. It could only have been a matter of time before we got some inkling of the presence of those ships close to a major trade route. We were lucky that it reached us in time to take action. *Volage* and *Druid* have left already to prepare a base of operations."

Nomad's near sister, as fast and as well capable as her of carrying extensive supplies. And a smaller corvette in company.

More was already in hand for this mission than Dawlish could have guessed.

*

The torpedo boats crews' spirit had been high at Killary. Good natured rivalry had built between them but it had plummeted after *Gamma's* loss. The hasty transfer of her crew's sea-chests to *Rifleman* before departure and the bare hammock hooks on the section of *Nomad's* gun-deck enclosed by canvas screens were stark warnings of hazards perhaps still more daunting ahead. There was but one way to restore that spirit. Training and more training, building confidence and reliance on self as well as others.

Dawlish's narrow escape on Pemba had convinced him, as so often in his career, that physical fitness and prowess in close combat could decide between life and death. Should the attack on the Russians fail, then any man of *Alpha's* or *Beta's* crews might face an ordeal as bad as West's. He devised a training regimen that left the men only marginally more exhausted than himself by each nightfall. His malaria and his spell ashore had eaten into his reserves of strength and endurance. By just how much was shown on the second day out when he arrived panting at the main-top a full nineteen seconds after the fastest of his men. He persisted in the following days, muscles aching and breath rasping, until he could swarm up the shrouds as fast as the best of them.

They spent much of each day was with cutlass and bayonet under the direction of a marine sergeant. Dawlish found it impossible at first to get past this instructor's bayonet guard and was knocked to the deck again and again by his padded rifle-butt. Days passed before he took his revenge, and that once only. With the cutlass he fared better, for since his youth he had prided himself on the hewing strength and darting skill of his right arm. Long drill sessions on the open deck, thrust, parry, stamp forward and hack, preceded one-to-one mock combats. Several men accepted his personal challenge and the first ended, sprawled against a bulwark, with Dawlish's point held to his throat. Two more accepted in the coming days, and failed. Day fared no better. In the end it was Egdean who assisted a vanquished Dawlish to his feet and who, almost apologetically, accepted his sovereign.

It helped the growing cohesion that the crew's enclosure was guarded by Marine sentries to prevent fraternisation with *Nomad's* complement.

"Is the accommodation better than on the Patrol, Egdean?"

It was the fourth day out and Dawlish was still panting from the climb to the main-top. Egdean, unwinded, had beaten him to it and was resting there.

"It's fine, sir. And the food's better too."

It had better be. Topcliffe has ordered them all be fed like fighting cocks. Fresh meat every second day. Three bullocks in the pen ahead of the foremast still unaware of their approaching fate, and four dozen laying chickens in the coop there.

"And the *Nomads*, sir, they've got a name for us."

"A name?"

"The Pariahs, sir, seein' like we're so isolated."

"And why do you think you're being isolated?"

Egdean paused, unsure if he should answer.

"Go ahead," Dawlish said. "You're allowed to think about it."

"Against the Russians, sir. The Baltic, that's what some said at first. But not anymore, sir, not since we're headed south. There's men among us who was in the Crimea an' they say 'tis either Sevastopol or Kinburn or the Kerch Straits."

Dawlish made no answer, but when Gibraltar was left far to port and the southerly course remained unchanged, wagers about destination were being lost in the wardroom as well as on the lower deck. The sea continued favourable, winds light, squalls infrequent. *Nomad* was forging west of south at little under her maximum speed, grey smoke billowing from her ochre funnel. Bunkers must be depleting fast. Dawlish asked Topcliffe about it.

"A collier will rendezvous with us off the Delta. Far out. You'll have gone ashore by then."

But the most important of all was training with the Gatlings. The Russians' massive cannon might be the weapons that would vanquish ironclad opposition and devastate trade on the high seas, but it was their fast-firing small-calibre repeaters that would stand the best chance of ripping Dawlish's boats apart before they reached torpedo range. Exercises at Killary had shown that only torrents from the stuttering Gatlings could offer any hope of blinding searchlights and silencing weapons like themselves.

Alpha's and *Beta's* Gatlings were now on temporary mountings on *Nomad's* starboard bulwark. Despite the urgency of her voyage, twice per day, in the Forenoon and First Dog watches, the corvette dropped several yellow-painted barrels, and then coursed around them in three tight turns. Informal competitions between gun crews highlighted slight differences in proficiency. Dawlish offered a prize of two sovereigns. By a narrow margin, Jarvis and Stothert of *Beta* snatched it from O'Malley, an Irishman who had no hesitation in rolling up his sleeves, and his loader Scanlon, from the *Alpha*. The other four crews finished close.

Dawlish insisted on even the engine-room personnel becoming proficient with the Gatlings. He himself, with Egdean as loader, became reasonably handy, if not particularly accurate, with this cranky and difficult weapon. The design was prone to jamming and much of the training was devoted to perfecting rapid clearance, dragging hot brass cartridges from smoking breeches with pincers.

"One distorted round at the wrong moment could be a disaster," Day said after a series of jams had left a gunner and loader swearing at their silent weapon and burned fingers, "but I'm damned if I know what to do about it."

"We'll have to hand-pick them," Dawlish said.

"Every one? But we need thousands!"

"Every last one, and then we'll set them aside."

Dawlish had one of the *Nomad's* artificers set to fashioning brass gauges. Plates with circular holes milled to a thousandth of an inch accuracy would check each round so that one with even the slightest ovality would not pass. A profile of the round's ideal linear section was cut along each plate's edge to check straightness. There had been little time for relaxation before. Now there was none, only an end to card-playing and yarning, even to Egdean's Temperance advocacy, in whatever free moments remained to the Pariahs. For long monotonous hours they were set to checking box upon box of the heavy rounds, segregating them into those that passed the gauges and those that did not. The rejects were reserved for training but the selected rounds, less than seventy percent of the total, were sealed into separate boxes marked with a red stripe. They alone would be carried into action.

Examination of *Alpha's* and *Beta's* hulls revealed bruises and gouges inflicted by collisions with *Gamma's* drifting fragments at Killary. These were filled and sanded smooth. Rudder cables were renewed. The engines were stripped down, worn bearings replaced, stuffing boxes adjusted, boilers cleaned. Dawlish worked on the torpedoes with Day, disassembling them, washing every component in fresh water, replacing any part he doubted, oiling and testing. The yellow paint that had provided visibility during training was now replaced by black. The explosive heads were mounted and only the detonating pistols remained to be fitted.

Dawlish and Day spent long hours closeted with Topcliffe, poring over a table on which blocks of wood represented the ironclads and the attacking torpedo boats. Two lengths of rope defined the meanderings of the channel in which the Russians lurked, each time different, for they knew they must simulate as many anchorage-configurations as possible. These sessions, no less than the Killary exercises, confirmed that both attacking craft must concentrate at first on the more serious threat, the *Nevski*. And yet the indications were less than hopeful.

"Elegant theoretical solutions won't help us, gentlemen." Topcliffe said. Another simulation had proved that exact knowledge of the channel's width and curvature was essential.

"I'll conduct the reconnaissance, sir," Dawlish's spirit was already shrinking from the thought. It was one thing to go speeding towards the Russian ironclads with guns blazing and torpedoes armed. It was another to follow in Arthur West's doomed footsteps. But better to volunteer before Topcliffe ordered it.

"Might I have the honour of –" Day began.

Topcliffe cut him short. "I can't risk both of you."

There was a brief silence and then the ropes were rearranged yet again and the manoeuvrings with the blocks resumed.

*

A fourteen-day passage.

Muscles hardened. Eyes and hands grew ever more familiar with their weapons. *Nomad* swung south, then east and the air grew heavier. Flying fish appeared. The air grew first warm, then moist.

And at last Africa lay like a green streak on the northern horizon.

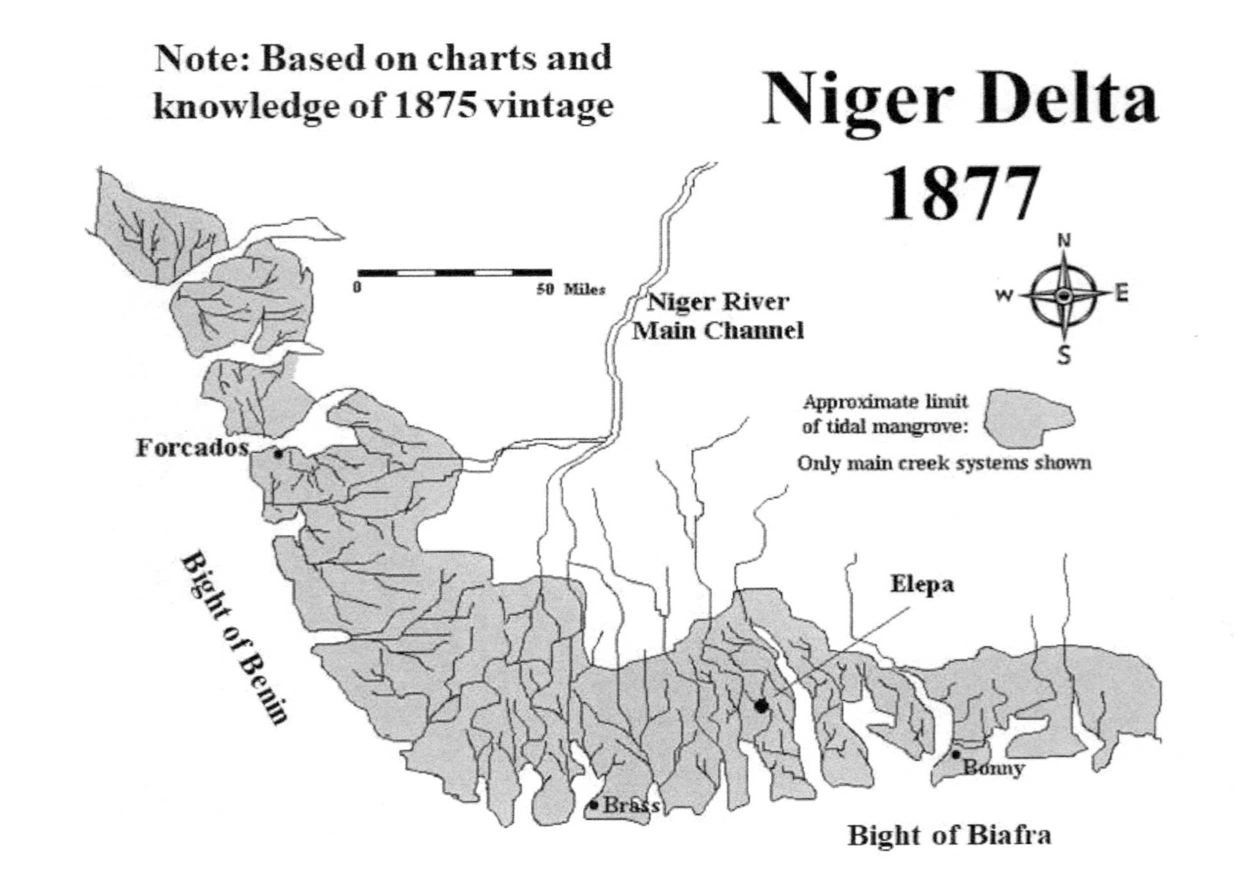

Note: Based on charts and
knowledge of 1875 vintage
Niger Delta
1877
0
50 Miles
Niger River
Main Channel
N
W
E
S
Approximate limit
of tidal mangrove:
Only main creek systems shown
Forcados
Bight of Benin
Elepa
Brass
Bonny
Bight of Biafra

Chapter 12

The rendezvous with the corvette *Volage* was just west of the point where the San Bartolomeo Channel pierces the outer periphery of the Niger Delta.

Topcliffe had been pacing the quarterdeck in anticipation since early morning. Sensing his tenseness, *Nomad's* officers had given him a wide berth. Dawlish, by his side, noticed his relief as the lookout's cry and the sight of the corvette's topmasts identified her just before noon. Even before a flurry of flag signals between the approaching craft confirmed it, *Volage's* presence on station was enough to confirm that the Russians had not yet emerged. There was no sign of *Druid*, the second vessel sent out from Britain with *Volage*. She must be standing further out to sea.

The initial exchange of signals was hardly complete before a gig bounced across from *Volage* to *Nomad*. Two officers sat in the sternsheets, sweating in formal uniforms and looking uncomfortable by comparison with the boat's stripped crew.

"The older officer's Captain Dempster of the *Volage*," Topcliffe told Dawlish. "I presume that the younger man is Lieutenant Tattersall, poor West's colleague. He's got a considerable reputation in these parts, by the way, a promising officer. Dempster carried sealed orders from Britain for him. We'll hear soon enough how well he executed them. Damn well, I'd wager, given his reputation."

Dawlish recognised in Frank Tattersall another young officer who, like himself, had sought action and advancement on a remote and dangerous station. Based with a small naval detachment at Bonny, on the eastern fringe of the Delta, he provided support to the British vice-consul there. Tattersall must be ambitious indeed if he were to endure service on a steaming coast that was a byword for discomfort and early death.

The gig bumped alongside and the two officers pulled themselves on board. Topcliffe led Dempster below after a round of introductions, leaving Tattersall on deck with Dawlish. He was a head shorter, but solidly built and exuding energy, instantly likeable.

"I've been making straight the paths for your coming, Dawlish, but I'm in ignorance about what you're going to try or how you'll go about it. You could have chosen a better time for it though." He gestured northwards, towards the coast, where dark-streaked columns were spilling torrents from a leaden sky. "The rains are on us. We'll have 'em for another five months."

"What's under those tarpaulins might interest you," Dawlish nodded towards the still swathed shapes of the torpedo craft. Only the lower hulls were visible.

Tattersall ran his hand along a gleaming flank.

"Beautiful," he said, then hesitated. "But they're long, Dawlish, damned long. They'll be devils to manoeuvre through the creeks. Most of 'em are as crooked as a ram's horn."

A summons to Topcliffe's accommodation cut their inspection short. They found him bent over a map with Dempster. It showed the Delta, with a circle drawn in red just east of the centre.

Topcliffe looked up.

"Join us, gentlemen. And Mr. Tattersall, I believe you've been busy since *Volage* brought your orders?"

"Busy indeed, sir." Tattersall moved to the chart, paused to orientate himself. "You asked me to establish a secure base on a deep channel, sir." He spoke with confidence, uninhibited by Topcliffe's rank. "I doubt if there's a better place. Here, about forty miles by my reckoning south-east of the enemy. It's a mile upstream from the coast, so access is easy. It's on a small island far enough in the swamp for the mangrove to give good cover. We've established a little clearing away from the channel for the stores."

"Well defended?"

"We landed a pair of seven-pounders and a Gatling, sir. I don't doubt we'd see off the premises any enemy boat that came nosing around. But it was a devil of a job to get those guns positioned. The whole island's a sea of mud when it rains, and that's every day."

Topcliffe swept his finger around the circle.

"You think the enemy's somewhere here?"

Judging by the map's scale, Dawlish saw that it was perhaps ten miles in diameter. Three large channels straggled through it, north to south. No marking of whatever serpentine creeks that must link them.

"As best as I could judge from West's account. He wasn't very coherent, poor fellow."

"And you've found guides who know the area?" Topcliffe said.

"It wasn't easy, sir. Ephraim Loveday, that blackguard West went against, has terrorised that part of the swamp. It's hard to find canoe-men who'll admit to knowing the area much less consent to venturing into it."

"But you did find somebody?"

Tattersall grinned. "Luckily old Jack Burnett owed me a favour. He's a common palm-oil ruffian but a damn good chap for all that. Here since God knows when, trading out of Brass for a Liverpool company. Some of the locals buy palm oil for him from villages further upstream and bring it down. They've done it for years. Jack swears by them."

"But would you, Lieutenant Tattersall?"

"Yes, sir. I would." No hesitation. "I asked Jack to select twenty Brassmen for me. They know every creek like the backs of their hands. Their headman's a chap called Tobin, not a bad sort, and he helped me before. I've offered what you authorised. They're willing."

"Where are they now?" Topcliffe asked.

"At the camp. Camp Beaconsfield, sir. The name specified in your orders."

"You're convinced the enemy doesn't suspect your presence?"

"Absolutely, sir. I followed your orders to the letter. No expeditions on my own behalf to spy out those ironclads." He hesitated, then said, "To be honest, sir, it hurt me somewhat to comply. I know the swamps and I've a score to settle on Arthur West's account."

"Your enthusiasm's admirable, lieutenant." Topcliffe said. "But this undertaking wasn't to be endangered by useless heroics. Are you sure the camp is undetected?"

Tattersall looked unmoved by the rebuff. "The only intruders so far were a pair of fishermen we grabbed last week, sir. They've proved handy for digging latrines and the like. They're terrified to death of the Brassmen. They think they'll eat them the first chance they get." He laughed. "I don't blame them. I'd be frightened myself."

"There you have it, Lieutenant Dawlish," Topcliffe said. "A secure base from which you can mount your reconnaissance and your attack. I can now adopt the role for which my age and infirmities fit me. That of spectator. You'll consider Camp Beaconsfield your base of operations and Lieutenant Tattersall will provide all the support you require."

"Thank you, sir." Dawlish could sense Tattersalls' silent hurt.

Topcliffe flipped his watch open and looked at it. "I'll leave you now, gentlemen. I'll want a schedule for your operations in precisely three and three-quarter hours."

*

As always, supplies dominated.

Tattersall listed those landed so far. Nine tons of coal, in sacks, best anthracite from *Volage's* bunkers. Six dozen barrels of water tapped from the corvette's own boiler. An adequate supply of biscuit, canned meat and other rations. All run ashore in cutters under cover of darkness.

Tattersall had followed orders, was proud of his stockpile, but Dawlish was concerned.

"We exercised the boats at Killary," he said. "They're a damn sight hungrier and thirstier than anticipated. We'll have to increase that fuel and water hoard."

Quick calculations, and then a safety margin on top. Even using *Nomad's* cutters as well those of *Volage*, three more nights of supply runs would be needed. The torpedo boats would be run inshore thereafter.

"Topcliffe's orders were to find a break in the surf," Tattersall said. "There's an almost continuous sand-bar lying off most of the Delta's coast. Surf breaking on it usually makes it bloody dangerous for small craft. Other than at Bonny and Forcados, the only really decent break is the one I suspect the Russians used to get up their channel."

"Calm?" Dawlish asked.

"Deep and calm. But we can't tempt fortune by using it. We must assume that it's being watched. But I've found another semblance of a break in the bar. It's direct, though rough enough at the best of times. You'll have to decide yourself if your two boats can manage it."

Dawlish nodded. The prospect of the fragile torpedo craft ploughing through surf was hair-raising. The boilers and engines might well break loose, even if the hulls withstood the pounding.

"I'll go in tonight with the supplies and I'll judge," he said. "In any case we'll need to bring *Alpha* and *Beta* in as light as possible. We'll already have to carry reserve coal and water on deck for the passage in, so the Gatlings and ammunition will have to go in by cutter."

A delicate point remained, unspoken and skirted around until now. Dawlish plunged in.

"You want to find the ironclads yourself, Tattersall," he said. "I can well understand that. West's memory deserves it. And you know the swamp, better than I ever can."

Tattersall nodded.

"But I'm going to carry out the reconnaissance, with this fellow Tobin you mentioned to guide me. I'll be leading the attack and it's vital that I learn every detail of the Russian anchorage beforehand. I'd be glad to have you with me but you're needed in reserve to repeat the survey, and to guide Day to the spot, if I don't return."

"I'd make the same decision." Tattersall tried to smile.

And he showed no sign of disappointment when Dawlish outlined his plans to Topcliffe that evening. Day was also present. The ship was rolling lazily and, despite the open scuttles, the heat and humidity in the captain's quarters was oppressive.

"I propose that Tattersall brings me to Camp Beaconsfield tonight," Dawlish said. "I'll take Egdean with me and I'll start the reconnaissance tomorrow."

"How long do you expect it to take?"

An impossible question.

"Three or four days."

It was a guess. A wild guess. Topcliffe must know that too, but he did not press.

"Tattersall will continue landing supplies. Day will remain in *Nomad.* He'll see to the final engine and weapons checks and supervise off-loading of the boats. Two nights from now Tattersall will come out to help Day bring *Alpha* to Camp Beaconsfield. He'll have to use *Beta's* helmsman because Egdean will be with me."

Topcliffe frowned. "Your helmsman? I saw him handle *Alpha* well at Killary. Do you want to entrust her to other hands?"

I'll stand my ground. If I'm left in a plight like West found himself in, then I want Egdean with me.

"He did well with me on Pemba, sir. He'll stand by me in any circumstance. I'd prefer to have him with me for the reconnaissance."

Topcliffe shrugged. "As you wish, Dawlish."

"Thank you, sir. Once *Alpha's* safely at Camp Beaconsfield, Day and Tattersall will return to *Nomad* and bring *Beta* in the next night."

"And after that?"

"If I come back, sir, we'll send the Russians to perdition."

He could only hope. Already he could smell – no, rather feel – the steaming Delta. The great swamp, invisible over the northern horizon, seemed to cast its miasma over *Nomad.* He hoped that it was not an omen.

*

The three cutters left their parent ships two hours after sundown. Darkness had long since fallen and gathering clouds partly obscured the moon. Tattersall foretold a wet and miserable night. Dawlish felt that his putting aside of his uniform and pulling on of washed-out duck trousers and a ragged shirt without badges of rank seemed like a monk's renunciation of the world. The sack tossed down into the waiting cutter held further reserves of anonymous clothing. He hoped he looked like some palm-oil ruffian of Tattersall's acquaintance. Egdean had already dressed the part to perfection. No member of the attacking force would wear uniform so that, in the event of failure, there would be nothing concrete to link them to the Royal Navy. Topcliffe was adamant that prisoners would be disowned and left to their fate. That knowledge had not been communicated to the crews.

Dawlish had half-expected Topcliffe to remind him of what England expected, but he was remote and formal when they shook hands. He had gone below before Dawlish dropped into the waiting cutter. The swell was considerable and Egdean steadied him as he stepped into the pitching craft. He settled in the sternsheets as the cutter pushed off from *Nomad's* side. The brisk south-westerly filled the sails and the boat lost itself in the darkness.

Dawlish could hear the bar, three miles off the coast, long before he saw the feathery white streak of breaking water in the semi-darkness. *Volage's* cutter, by now a veteran of repeated crossings, led *Nomad's* two in line astern. Dawlish, in the sternsheets, could feel the crew's apprehension in the craft that carried him. No word was spoken but several of the men were looking nervously at the coal sacks and barrels nestling between the thwarts, and assessing how easily they could be jettisoned if necessary. The moon had emerged by the time the cutters went plunging into the extended cauldron of spray and breakers. For long minutes they leaped and wallowed in the foaming spume. *Nomad's* second boat, third in line, shipped so much water as to be all but swamped but, like the others, it emerged into the calmer waters beyond at no greater cost than a ducking for the crew and the dumping of a few sacks of coal.

But could the torpedo boats make it?

Just, Dawlish surmised. With good handling and judgement. He trusted Day to abandon the attempt if the conditions were worse on the night and try again on the next.

The roar of the breakers died astern and the coast was a dark stripe that grew higher and blacker as they approached. Closer still, the lighter ribbon of a sandy beach showed gentle surf breaking against it. They bore eastwards for a mile or so and came to a break in the shore's dark mass. It revealed itself as an estuary, a hundred yards wide at the point of entry to the sea. *Volage's* boat swung over to its eastern bank and the others followed, hugging it so that their outlines were lost against the dark foliage.

The tide was still flooding and it plucked and teased at the trailing branches of the mangrove. Only the lap of the water against the hulls and the odd scream of a frightened monkey somewhere in the darkness broke the silence. The channel narrowed and split. They followed the eastern arm, first north, then east, then north again until the channel entered a series of meanderings that defied analysis. The breeze died, choked by the high walls of foliage that reduced the creek's width to less than twenty yards.

Sails yielded to oars. Dawlish was impressed that Tattersall had ordered greasing of the rowlocks to prevent squeaking. An air of uneasiness hung over the boats as they stroked forward. The rowers, no less than the lookouts, peered apprehensively into each shadow and every side channel. Dawlish shared their unease, for he knew from experience there are few environments as eerie and menacing as a mangrove swamp by night.

A single red light flashed astern from the leading cutter, the agreed signal that Camp Beaconsfield was close. The boats backed water and slid almost to a halt, carried forward now by the weak tide. A call, a poor imitation of a bird's cry, came from the darkness. *Volage's* cutter answered with one no better. Then a green light flickered ahead twice, three times. The cutters crept towards the island that now separated itself from the darkness. As they progressed it became clear that it was cradled in a wide sweep that carried the creek back on itself in yet another crazy meander. The leading craft disappeared into the mangrove to starboard and minutes later Dawlish's cutter also was swallowed up by a narrowing creek that penetrated almost to the island's centre.

A group of Africans, the Brassmen, was already at work, unloading *Volage's* boat under the energetic direction of a foul-mouthed British seaman. It began to rain heavily as Dawlish stepped ashore and he sunk to his ankles in the ooze underfoot. He had arrived at Camp Beaconsfield.

And a miserable place it was.

Chapter 13

It had stopped raining but the island looked even more desolate by daylight.

Dawlish sat with Tattersall in a tent on upturned boxes, eating a meagre breakfast, cold and damp after four hours of comfortless sleep. Another copy of the map seen earlier lay before them on other boxes. An irregular area on the eastern side, in from the coast and covering perhaps five hundred square miles, was marked with a network, hand-drawn in blue-ink, dates noted alongside various sections. A red cross near the centre identified Elepa, the capital of the latest petty tyrant of the swamps, Ephraim Loveday. If the Russians hadn't shifted their anchorage, they must be somewhere close to there.

"It isn't complete," Tattersall said. "Nor by a long chalk. But Arthur West and I built it up over the last two years. We surveyed as many as we could of the creeks linking the Niger's main channels"

"How broad are they?"

"Many of 'em are twenty or thirty yards across, others even more. But what we couldn't identify were all the yet smaller creeks that link these ones. There are thousands of them. We couldn't get even a pulling whaler up most of them. But locals, people like Tobin and his Brassmen, they know them well and use them as shortcuts in their canoes."

"So you'd mapped some of this before there was any indication of Russian presence?"

"We needed them for moving fast." Tattersall sounded enthusiastic to a degree unjustified by the surroundings. "I've been on this station for three years. Most of the time rescuing missionaries from the consequences of their own folly, running down and executing parcels of rogues who've robbed British palm-oil ruffians and patching up treaties between villages after they've had one of their nasty little squabbles. But in that time Ephraim Loveday caused more trouble than the rest of the Delta combined. If we'd had the good sense to hang him when he first came to our notice, we might have been saved all this palaver and the Russians might have ended up somewhere else."

"So you've had other dealings with this Ephraim?" The story might enliven the meal of sodden biscuit and black tea.

"Too damn much, I'm sorry to say. His career really only began soon after I got here. Poor West showed me round. He'd been here a year already. We were both detached from *Dwarf* – she's the gunboat allocated to supporting the traders and showing the flag on this stretch of coast. We were based at Bonny, with some small craft for work in the Delta and over to the east of it also. We only went into action at the British vice-consul's discretion."

"Often?"

"Often enough. My first jobs were all over in Calabar, small boat stuff, but a good introduction. In those days Ephraim Loveday was a sort of grand vizier for George Pepple, who calls himself the king of Bonny. He controls much of the palm-oil trade in the eastern Delta. Ephraim's clever and he's had some education in a mission school. He can read and write English in a fashion. But he had ideas above his station and wanted to usurp King George. He got a faction behind him and tried his luck. The upshot was that half of Bonny was burned in the scuffle."

"Many dead?"

"Lots, dozens. It's what happens when things go to the devil around here. And what made it our business was that two palm-oil storage hulks belonging to a Liverpool firm went up in flames also. Loveday fled upriver afterwards with canoe-loads of booty and half of Georgie Rex's wives and children as hostages."

"What did you do?"

"Nothing! We had to keep our bluejackets standing by during the fracas because the bloody vice-consul was hemming and hawing and consulting his standing instructions and deciding whether British property had been destroyed by accident or by design and whether the situation warranted intervention by Her Majesty's Navy. By the time he'd made up his mind the bird was well flown. The pity of it was that I could so easily have put a bullet in Ephraim's fat belly on the night of the riot."

"Did you go after him?"

"Good God, no! All of a sudden, we had too much on our plate. There was more missionary trouble and we'd to bring *Dwarf* over to bombard a village on the Cross River because they'd got up to some real beastliness there. The upshot was that Mr. Loveday was left to his own devices and had time enough to establish himself at Elepa. It wasn't too difficult since the area was already disputed between Brass and Bonny. When I finally went to Elepa it was under flag of truce, to fetch home King George's abducted harem. Half of them didn't want to leave but when Ephraim realised that we were ready to live and let live, he was glad to send 'em packing."

"You've been in Elepa then? You know the route?"

"I started this map during the journey there. I knew that if I had to go again it might have to be in a hurry. The swamp between here and there is the most astounding maze of waterways imaginable."

"Any more trouble with Loveday before the affair that brought West after him?"

"Plenty. He was established in too remote an area to be visited regularly. He charged excessive duty on palm-oil passing through his territory and he wiped out a few villages that gave him trouble. We'd have put up with that – after all it's not British territory and we're only supposed to defend the rights of British citizens. Civis Romanus Sum and all that. But then we had the affair of Annie McPherson."

"A missionary?"

"A pillar of the Kirk Militant. She'd worked around Calabar for years, was well thought of by the locals there. That made her confident enough to come across to convert Ephraim and his gang. He received her with open arms. Too open in fact. He wanted to add a white woman to his seraglio and even a fifty-year old Scots spinster would have done. She had to beat a hasty retreat – not good for British prestige that – and so he had to be taught a lesson. I was down with malaria, raving, I'm told, so Arthur West took on the job. And he got more than he bargained for. You can't imagine the state he was in when he got back."

Tatersall fell silent. His earlier good humour was gone and he stared out in glum silence into the clearing. Dawlish drained his mug of tea and stood up.

"Let's see those Brassmen of yours," he said, "I'd like to meet your Mr. Tobin."

*

The six men Tattersall had chosen as the best of the twenty strong Brass contingent were small and wiry. All spoke the peculiar West African pidgin. Dawlish found it difficult to understand. Several threw themselves on their knees before him when Tattersall identified him as the master whom they would henceforth serve.

"Don't be fooled by this humility nonsense," Tattersall said. "They'll as soon knife you as grovel before you. Isn't that so, Tobin? Get up, man! Where's your pride?"

He laughed and made as if to kick away a small ill-favoured figure who had grasped Dawlish around the calves. The man had bowed his head and was calling on God to bless his new master. He looked up, grinned and said to Tattersall, "You know us, sir!" as he struggled to his feet.

"This is Mr. Tobin," Tattersall said. "He's a villain, aren't you, Mr. Tobin? But he's a damn fine fellow for all that. None better. You can stake your life on him. He'll show you the canoe he's getting ready for you."

The dugout was hollowed from a single log, some twenty feet long by thirty inches wide. It looked both uncomfortable and unstable but Tattersall assured Dawlish that accomplished canoe-men could propel it at a respectable speed with their long, leaf-shaped paddles. It was raining again by now and the bottom of the dugout was awash. Dawlish found himself scratching his arms. His first insect bites were already livid blobs of discomfort. He returned to his tent to rest, in preparation for the night's travel.

Sleep did not come easily.

*

Tattersall had identified three wide channels in the vicinity of Elepa as the probable anchorages for the ironclads because of their widths and depths. A direct approach from Camp Beaconsfield was liable to be hazardous since the intervening creeks were probably well patrolled. Even though longer, an approach from the north would less prone to detection. The first night's paddling would therefore be the first leg of a sweeping movement that would carry Dawlish well to the north-east of Elepa, after which he would move directly westwards. With luck, and with Tobin's skill. the second night should bring him to the Russians.

He was roused, as requested, at five in the afternoon. It would be dark in little over an hour, for night would fall with the suddenness of the tropics. He ate a meal for which he had little stomach and chatted on trivial matters with Tattersall. Recognition that he might not return lay unspoken and heavy between them. He found it hard to suppress his impatience to be off. Egdean was supervising the loading of the canoe and had already earned the respect of the Brassmen with a few simple feats of strength. Food in oilskin packages and bottles of fresh water had been placed in the dugout. They checked their weapons. Dawlish, like

Egdean, had a Snider, a cutlass, a knife and a revolver and brought field glasses in addition. Tobin seemed wedded to his gas-pipe trade musket but the other canoe-men were armed with machetes only.

It began to rain as they set off, saturating them before they even emerged from the creek that penetrated the island. It blotted Camp Beaconsfield from view as they stroked northwards and almost obscured the thick banks of mangrove that shut them in to either side. Darkness fell. There was no sound other than the rain beating the water and the steady chop of the paddles.

Dawlish and Egdean sat amidships, wet and uncomfortable despite their oilskins. Before them the rain ran off the glistening bare backs of the paddlers. Tobin's white teeth flashed whenever he turned to hiss the name of some new creek into which they turned. Dawlish tried to reconcile the twists and turns with what he could remember of the sketch-map, copied from the larger map, that Tattersall had given him but which he could not take out because of the rain. Within half an hour he felt lost. He was totally in Tobin's hands.

The rain ended around midnight. Hitherto there had been halts of ten minutes every hour but now Dawlish ordered one of thirty. While the Brassmen ate some food and took snuff he tried to determine his position on Tattersall's map, using his oilskin to shield the light of a succession of flickering lucifer matches held by Egdean. By cross checking their remembrances of the twists and meanderings of the creeks so far, they managed to fix their position with what Dawlish guessed was reasonable certainty. They had travelled about twelve miles due north of Camp Beaconsfield, though the actual distance covered was far greater. Until now, the flowing tide had aided their progress but the going would be slower when the ebb commenced and gained strength in the early hours.

The journey continued. There were more signs of life now. They had left the broader channels and were moving through the narrower creeks that cross-connected them. At several points they encountered groups of canoes engaged in fishing. Earthen pots of glowing charcoal, carried amidships to give light, warned of them well in advance. The fishermen were visible, even from a distance, their bodies illuminated in red as they cast their nets and called to each other. Others had moored to fish traps, chevron-shaped wattle constructions pointing seawards, sited to catch prey with the ebbing tide. Clinging to the shadows close to the banks, the furtive canoe crept past unnoticed. Further on were several clusters of three or four huts built over the water on stilts. All were quiet but for the movements of a few fishermen tying up their crafts or bickering over the division of the night's catch.

It was more difficult now that the tide was ebbing. It raced at a knot or more against them in some of the narrower channels and the paddlers were fatigued. By five o'clock, with an hour of darkness remaining, it was time to find a spot for hiding during daylight. Dawlish ordered Tobin to take the dugout up a narrow side-channel, and then another, and then up yet another leading off that also, until they found themselves in a winding creek scarcely six feet wide and all but roofed over by the mangrove.

The falling tide had exposed high banks of malodours black mud. The canoe was almost too long for the creek's twists and once it caught and had to be manhandled free. They disturbed a crocodile, the first encountered. It was not large – six or eight feet – and it slithered across the mud and disappeared into the water ahead. Dawlish trembled. No human enemy could be worse. The creature was close and there must be others in the vicinity. A troop of monkeys screamed and chattered somewhere deeper in the mangrove but for the rest it was silent. They found at last a spot that promised to be high and dry, even at full tide, and they dragged the canoe out of the water. The Brassmen laid out their palm-mats on the mud, pulled their sodden rags about them and were instantly lost in the sleep of the exhausted.

Dawlish took the first watch while Egdean slept in the bottom of the dugout, inadequately protected by an oilskin. It had started to rain again before the sun rose on a filthy, wet and comfortless world. Camp Beaconsfield had been a paradise compared with this misery.

The day passed slowly, and in the greatest discomfort. The itching torment of insect bites, sweat and intermittent rain made sleep difficult. Oblivious of his surroundings, Egdean produced a tattered pocket Bible and frowned as he studied it, his finger moving slowly across the words. Dawlish compared progress against Tattersall's map, and was impressed with its accuracy so far and by the skill with which Tobin, with only his memory to guide him, had brought the canoe through the maze of waterways. His confidence in him had by now increased and, when he questioned him – the pidgin made a slow business of it – he found that his knowledge of the creeks round Elepa seemed to coincide closely with the map.

He had not expected to meet such nocturnal activity the night before, so many fishermen. Now he came to a reluctant decision and spoke to Egdean about it.

"None of them challenged us, last night. We were probably not even noticed. But that was luck."

"And by the grace of God, sir."

The answer would have been insubordinate at any other time. Here, dependent on each other, it did not.

"It'd be a safer in a smaller canoe," Dawlish said. "We saw a few like that. Only big enough for two. One like that would be less likely to be spotted. Easier to hide too."

"We haven't got one, sir."

"I don't think that Mr. Tobin's conscience would trouble him about taking one."

"Stealing one, sir?" Egdean looked troubled.

"That's right. Stealing one."

"And I'd go with you, sir?"

"No. I can't go on without Tobin. It'll be just him and me together. You'll wait behind. You'll get word to Mr. Tattersall if I'm not back by tomorrow night. The other Brassmen will guide you."

He could see that Egdean didn't like it but there was no help for that.

And yes, it would be safer so, Tobin agreed when he raised the subject. A theft would not be difficult but the further from Elepa it was committed the better.

They ate a cheerless meal before sundown and then began the return down to the larger channel from which they had turned off. It proved no easier than passing up it before and the canoe stuck twice. Several of the Brassmen dropped over into shin-deep water to drag it free. They did not hesitate, despite the possible proximity of crocodiles, and Dawlish was impressed that they accepted the danger as an unavoidable aspect of travelling through creeks. The moon broke through the clouds at intervals as they resumed their progress through the shadows by the creeks' sides. By nine o'clock Tobin calculated that they were sufficiently to the north-east of Elepa to allow the course to be shifted due westwards.

They encountered fishing canoes again, their positions marked by the now-familiar pots of glowing coals. Most of the fishermen were too engrossed in their labours to mark their passing. The few who did must have assumed them to be similarly employed and called out salutations. Onwards then, gliding through the shadows of the opposite bank past several tiny villages. At every one, the activity level – people moving about, canoes setting off or returning – was too high to justify the risk of thieving there. Dawlish welcomed the next downpour. It promised cover for a raid.

The opportunity came just after ten. Half a dozen canoes lay drawn up on the foreshore of a cluster of huts on slightly higher ground. The rain was keeping the occupants inside and the only signs of life were wisps of smoke seeping up through the thatch of the chimneyless roofs.

Tobin hissed something to his men and they paused in their strokes, their paddles dragging the dugout to a standstill. He looked back, his expression requesting assent. Dawlish nodded. The craft rocked as two Brassmen lowered themselves over the side into the muddy, rain-speckled waters. They struck out in silence for the village and the canoe crawled on. Dawlish watched the two dark heads bobbing towards the village. At the next bend the canoe pulled in to wait beneath the drooping mangrove.

The thieves returned in less than five minutes, grinning in triumph as they swept alongside in a small dugout, eight or nine feet long, enough for two occupants only.

The downpour continued, shrouding the two canoes as they continued up the creek.

Chapter 14

The world had contracted to an endless winding channel, walled in by high banks of mangrove. The paddling was little more than an unconscious reflex, like the stumbling of an exhausted man.

Dawlish felt himself nothing more than a passive victim of small agonies, bites and itches and cramps. He had to be able to handle the stolen canoe and so, with Tobin, changed places with the two successful thieves. The paddle was not difficult to use but he soon had an ache in his right side, brought on by the necessity of paddling to port so as to allow the more expert Tobin, at the stern, to steer as well as to stroke to starboard. The first ten minutes were the worst but he must endure until he would call the next halt on the hour. By the time the break came he had mastered the basic technique and felt a weary pride despite his aching side and blistered hands. He was, nevertheless, glad to step back into the larger canoe for the next stage. He would need all his energy later in the night.

By two o'clock they were, according to Tobin, still north-east of Elepa. He had difficulty estimating the distance to it, as he thought in terms of time travelled, but questioning narrowed it to about five miles. The indirect approach had proved its worth for, since the theft of the canoe, the passage had been through an area of narrow creeks and dense mangrove in which neither fishermen nor villages were encountered.

And it lulled them into a sense of security that almost led to disaster.

They had paused by the entrance of a side-channel.

"Here? A good place to hide?" Dawlish was uncertain if Tobin understood him, though he was nodding and grinning anyway.

Then, a sudden flurry of movement at the bend of the channel, some two hundred yards ahead. Dawlish looked up to see a creaming bow-wave sweeping into view. A large, dark hull rose above it and a plume of flame-tinted smoke billowed from the funnel, illuminating the gun crew in the bows. This was no war-canoe of Ephraim Loveday's.

Tobin moved first, his men an instant later. Before Dawlish could utter a word, they were stroking in silence into the side-channel and almost burrowing the canoes under the exposed mangrove roots.

Silence broken only by the soft beat of the approaching steam engine. Dawlish forced himself to breathe deeply as he crouched aft and watched the vessel bear down the creek. He slipped his revolver from its holster and saw that Egdean was withdrawing his Snider from its oilskin.

The steam pinnace passed so close that its wash bumped the canoes against the enveloping roots and almost swamped them. It was large, its length all of forty feet, and built heavily enough to carry a shielded weapon in the bows – it could be a three-pounder. Three Europeans in sweat-sodden white-duck uniforms stood by it, oblivious of the canoes lurking so close. Above, on the roof of the boiler-room, half-hidden its shield, was some kind of rapid-fire gun. It could be a two or three-barrelled Nordenvelt. Close to it, Dawlish recognised – and the knowledge chilled him – what could be a small, and as yet still unlit, arc-searchlight. Sparks showered from the brass funnel, lighting the high Slavonic cheekbones of the helmsman in the cockpit. Close to him a figure lounged against the deckhouse, exhaling the smoke of a cigar. The boiler-room scuttles were open and Dawlish glimpsed a perspiring shaven head, dyed crimson by the furnace's light. Another Nordenvelt stood at the stern.

For an instant the black hull and white upperworks filled the proscenium formed by the overarching mangrove. It was a sight to chill the blood, a more-than-worthy adversary not only for this scouting party but for the thin-skinned *Alpha* and *Beta* also. It ploughed on and was lost to sight.

The ripples died but Dawlish and the others remained motionless, silent, frightened. The game seemed at once more deadly. The enemy's face had been revealed and it was a daunting one.

"Now!" Dawlish's hissed command and outstretched arm directed both canoes further up the side-channel. He could sense fear around him. He turned over in his mind the implications of what he had witnessed. Arthur West must have encountered this craft, or a sister. How many such boats were there? Did they patrol fixed routes? How far from their parent ships did they venture?

The canoes turned up a succession of ever-narrowing creeks until they were shut in and roofed over by the mangrove. They dragged the larger dug-out from the water and on to a dry patch. The exhausted paddlers threw themselves down to sleep.

Dawlish checked his watch.

Three and a half hours of darkness left. Too much to waste.

One last precaution needed before embarking on the last stage. He scooped up a handful of viscous dark-grey mud. It smelled foul. He rubbed it over his clothing and then, while Egdean watched with ill-concealed mirth, ran his hands over his face and neck, wiping his whiteness away in the dark.

"You're in command now, Egdean." He handed him his watch. "You'll wait here for forty-eight hours. If I'm not back by then I'll never be back."

"I'll pray for you, sir." Egdean's voice was solemn but sincere.

"Don't wait any longer. Get back to Camp Beaconsfield and give Mr. Day and Mr. Tattersall all the information you can about the route here. They'll know what to do."

It would be another reconnaissance, in all probability like a lamb to the slaughter, with all advantage of surprise lost. He shook himself from this gloomy reverie, pushed the thought of failure from his mind. He could not afford to think longer than twenty-four hours ahead. The sight of that picket boat – solid, brutally armed – had shaken him and he knew that it could gnaw into his confidence. Caution might preserve him in the coming hours, but timidity would, without doubt, doom the entire mission.

"Come now, Tobin. I'm at your mercy." He clapped him on the shoulder.

He stepped into the small canoe and laid his now unwrapped Snider on the bottom before him. He picked up the paddle while Tobin took position at the stern and pushed off into the narrow creek.

The darkness of night and Africa closed around them as they passed beneath the overhanging foliage.

*

The first channel that had Tattersall identified as a possible anchorage proved empty, though Dawlish recognised it as having the ideal combination of width and configuration to have made an ideal lair. To reach it they had threaded their way through a maze of small waterways that cut like winding tunnels through the masses of vegetation separating the larger creeks. Tobin navigated this labyrinth with the born instinct of a swamp dweller. The sinuous ripple of a swimming snake and the odd clamour of a distant monkey were the only signs of life. Each wide creek to be crossed was an obstacle that had to be evaluated with caution from the shelter of the bank. When satisfied that neither canoes nor picket boats were in the offing, they scuttled across like a frightened water-beetle.

Twice more they saw the pinnace or, worse, an identical sister. Dawlish, cowering beneath the mangrove, strained his eyes to find some tell-tale difference but he could not be sure that the three-pounder was indeed mounted further aft than on the craft sighted earlier. His suspicion that a searchlight was carried was confirmed in a terrifying fashion on the second of these sightings when the pinnace came prowling down the creek with its arc light sweeping the banks. Dawlish and Tobin had succeeded in dragging the canoe far under the dipping mangrove branches and were grovelling in the bottom of the craft by the time the vessel reached them. They froze in mute terror as the cold, harsh glare swept over them but left them undetected. The pinnace passed close enough for Dawlish to hear the crew conversing in a language strange to him and to hear the rattle and slap of the belt driving the dynamo off the engine-shaft.

The approach to the second possible anchorage brought them skulking past the northern fringes of Elepa. It seemed to Dawlish no more than a larger version of the other villages he had seen already. There were several dozen canoes drawn up on the foreshore and many more bobbing at moorings. Several fires glowed and there was a marked degree of activity for so early in the morning hours. The sound of voices carried from the huts. They froze once more in the shadows as a very large dugout, with perhaps twenty paddlers, came beating up the creek towards the village. An antiquated muzzle-loading swivel gun was mounted in the bows and several of the non-paddlers clustered amidships looked to be armed with Brown Bess and gas-pipe muskets. The war-canoe grounded on the foreshore and the occupants waded ashore, shouting and brandishing their weapons. Dawlish and Tobin, shaken, resumed their progress unobserved.

And the second anchorage was as empty as the first.

Dawlish choked back his disappointment and reviewed his options. He estimated that it was almost five o'clock. One hour of darkness remained. He dared not strike a light to consult his sketch map but memory told him that the distance to the final potential anchorage would take about an hour's paddling. His back and sides were aching and the unfamiliar squatting position caused his legs agonies of cramp. His hands were raw, his skin itched from insect bites in a score of places and every muscle screamed for rest. One hour to go – but he was too close now to give up. He thrust his paddle into the water and pushed hard. Tobin followed suit.

A reckless determination drove him in this last hour before daybreak. He took chance after chance, breaking from cover too soon to dash across stretches of water that might well have harboured a war-canoe or Russian picket. He was forcing his luck to the limit, yet the hope that he was on the verge of discovering the enemy spurred him on. Tobin assured him that just one more block of swamp separated them from the possible location. Into this morass they headed, stroking through a succession of winding and narrowing creeks that were indistinguishable from dozens they had navigated earlier. The tide was running against them and many of the channels were reduced to rivulets with steep three-foot banks of mud.

The dugout ran aground repeatedly, each time necessitating a knee-deep plunge into the ooze to drag it into deeper water. Now the channel was narrow, tunnel-like, arched across by interlinked mangrove. Once a snake dropped into the water just feet ahead of the canoe and was still slithering – black, glistening, loathsome – up on to the muddy bank as they passed. Dawlish shuddered. It was long, just kept coming, no head or tail visible. Had it fallen a few seconds later and it would have been in the dugout. Another unspoken fear was added to that of crocodiles.

The creek petered out to a trickle. They had reached the watershed of this block of swamp. They had come too far to retrace their course and seek another route, even had they been certain of finding one. Breaths rasping, they could only accept a crawling battle forward, knee-deep in the mud, dragging the canoe to a point where they could find a watercourse running westward. The exposed, shell-encrusted mangrove roots tore at their legs, inflicting searing cuts, and the branches plucked and grasped their bodies, hindering every step. Glimpses over their shoulders revealed the first red fingers of dawn reaching into the eastern sky.

They passed the watershed somehow. A rivulet before them widened and deepened into a creek just capable of floating the canoe. Mud-smeared and aching, they hoisted themselves in and collapsed on the bottom as the weak current carried them downstream. They lay there, fighting for breath, for five or six minutes. The canoe bumped against a root and held fast. Dawlish heard the thumping of his heart subside and his breath resume its normal rhythm. Only the dull ache of exhaustion was left. He closed his eyes and allowed his muscles to relax. He began to count, promising himself that he would move again at two hundred. On reaching it he somehow pushed himself into a sitting position and groped for the paddle. Tobin struggled weakly to his knees and together they freed the craft, strength all but exhausted, and began to stroke again.

It was now full daylight.

Chapter 15

There was no delight, no joy, in discovering the Russians. Exhaustion had robbed them of any other feeling.

Dawlish crouched in the little dugout and peered dull-eyed through the shielding foliage at the dark hulls and towering masts that rose over the tendrils of morning mist. Figures moved on deck and scraps of unintelligible conversation carried with surprising clarity across the intervening water. He saw three heavy steam pinnaces, and no less than four hand-pulled craft, returning to their mother ships and yet he had barely enough energy to absorb this much. There was no sense of achievement for him now, only the ache of a body pushed to its limits. His brain told him that this was not the time to observe. He must withdraw, rest and return refreshed to spy out each detail of his enemies with care and deliberation. His hour of madness was past and the time for caution had returned.

They retreated into the mangrove, following the meanderings of a small channel to an overgrown spot just above water level. They dragged the canoe under the foliage and huddled in the bottom. Dawlish slept at once.

It was early afternoon when deluging rain awoke him. There must have been rain earlier, for the canoe was already half-full, but he had not noticed. Neither had Tobin, who still lay sleeping on his back with the water streaming over his face. Uncontrollable shivers racked Dawlish and he was cold and stiff. He opened the oilskin pack that contained his meagre provisions and allowed himself a mouthful of brandy. Its warmth coursed through him and he began to satisfy himself with ship's biscuit, made marginally more palatable by bites at an over-ripe banana. But as he ate, a feeling of satisfaction began to permeate him. The ironclads were here and, mighty as they were, he had them at his mercy. Cold and wretched as he might at this moment be, but he held their secret in his grasp.

And he would use it to destroy them.

Despite his fatigue, the prospect of the journey back to Camp Beaconsfield seemed as nothing to him now. For the first time since that night at Lord Kegworth's Piccadilly mansion he felt hopeful of success. A myriad of questions about the details of the anchorage were crowding on him and making further inaction intolerable. He shook Tobin into grudging wakefulness and thrust the brandy flask between his teeth. The liquor brought some life into him and he fell thankfully on the biscuit. Watching him, Dawlish felt respect for him and for his uncanny accuracy of guidance. Poor and illiterate Tobin might be, but he was a man as good as himself, a man worthy of admiration.

The downpour was raining itself out. With caution, pausing between short advances, they dragged the dugout from cover and pushed it into the little creek.

*

It was four hours to nightfall.

They lay motionless in the canoe, peering out from cover to view the great black ships swinging bow-on to the quickening tide. Little over four hundred yards, two cables, lay between them and the ironclads. The channel was half that wide.

Thankful for the overcast sky that cancelled the risk of sunlight flashing on lenses, Dawlish studied the vessels through his field glasses. Patches of rust mottled the vessels' flanks and fungus-patched canvas awnings screened their decks from the intermittent downpour. Every port and scuttle had been thrown open to admit some breath of ventilation to the stifling interiors. The masts and yards rose massively above the awnings and the thick bowsprit jutting over the largest vessel's curving ram lent a sinister and aggressive aspect. No flag or ensign interrupted the grim monotony of black and grey. Wisps of smoke drifting from the funnels confirmed that the furnaces were being kept warm, even if no great head of steam was being maintained.

If seen in isolation, the smaller and closer of the two ironclads, the *Orlov*, would have been daunting enough. She caused Dawlish no great surprise for she was similar enough in appearance to counterparts in the Royal Navy, such as *Raleigh* or *Shah*. It was her consort, the gigantic *Nevski*, unlike any other ship previously launched, that impressed for her bulk and might.

The drawings spread before Beaconsfield had given but a faint impression of the power of this monster. Her towering sides fell inwards above the clearly visible armour belt at the waterline, rising to the deck in a pronounced S-shaped tumblehome. Just ahead of the main mast the hull flared out into the overhanging sponsons that carried the forward barbettes, one to either side. The other two barbettes, on the centreline, were somewhat hidden by the awnings but above each iron breastwork

Dawlish could discern the muzzles of the thirteen and a half-inch breech loaders that constituted the main armament. Except for dead ahead, there was no direction in which this floating mountain could be approached without coming in the sights of three of the most powerful guns afloat. Almost invulnerable behind the twelve-inch barbette armour, the crews serving these weapons could face any existing ship, from any navy, with total confidence. And he remembered Barnaby's warning that until the *Inflexible* was available, Britain would have no ship capable of challenging this Russian brute.

Yet it was not the main armament that concerned Dawlish most. The forty-six ton guns could never be a threat to his rapid torpedo crafts in these confined waters. More dangerous was the row of light weapons, probably quick-firing breech-loaders, that grinned from ports along the flank and the individual Nordenvelts, quintuple-barrelled by the look of them, that perched in the fighting tops. Guided by the great arc-searchlights visible in the fore and mizzen tops, these spitting demons could rip his frail racing shells apart in seconds, hurling a hot rain of death down on, and through, their flimsy decks. From the evilly curving ram at the bow to the graceful gallery at the stern, this ship exuded menace.

In any other company than the *Nevski*, the *Orlov* would have inspired awe for the sense of purpose so apparent in her design. Long and slim, she looked what she was, a lean, deadly corsair, a hunter and destroyer of merchant shipping, swift enough to outrun any vessel more heavily armed, powerful enough to engage, and probably destroy, any fast enough to run her down. Unleashed alone against Britain's commercial shipping, she could wreak untold havoc. Operating in concert with the *Nevski* she might aspire to ravaging trading ports as well as terrorising trade lanes. The three eight-inch weapons mounted amidships on either side in their armoured box-battery could inflict mortal damage on any comparable British ship while the six-inch bow chasers could butcher any fleeing merchantman at long range. A menacing row of rapid-firing three and five-pounders jutted from a row of ports. Each fighting top carried a Nordenvelt.

But *Nevski* and *Orlov* were not alone.

Four other vessels, all seemingly unarmed, lay at anchor further up the channel that curved towards the north-east. Their grimy appearance identified three of them as colliers. They would no doubt shadow the warships and their cargoes would be more than sufficient to double their action radius. The bunkers of captured ships would have to supply fuel once the collier's reserves had been eaten up. But the fourth vessel was a surprise, a long, sleek clipper-bowed steam yacht. Even at this distance, the graceful white hull – it could not be shorter than two-hundred feet – and ochre funnel and masts told of expense and luxury.

There was little activity on the colliers but Dawlish saw, with professional admiration, efforts in hand to keep the men-of-war shipshape even in these steaming conditions. Several dozen men were chipping and painting hulls from cradles suspended over the sides and three pinnaces alongside were being readied for another night's patrols. Canoes laden with fresh fruit clustered about the ships. He could make out bananas, pineapples and mangoes, which must have been brought from further inland. That needed local assistance. Ephraim Loveday and his underlings must be helping the Russians to avoid scurvy.

Dawlish now considered his attack.

The Russians lay in the crook of a long and gentle bend of a channel a cable wide, though it did appear to narrow both upstream and down. There was no break in the foliage on either bank. He studied the downstream sweep, straining for signs of guns having been landed to command the approaches. He saw no obvious indication, but this did not mean that a palm-log redoubt might not shelter a battery in the mangrove.

Another hazard, a more serious one, was all too obvious some three cables seawards of the ships. There a double row of linked tree trunks stretched across the channel from one bank to the other, the log-tops awash and glistening. Upstream, beyond the yacht, a dark line showed a similar obstacle. Here and there an orange patch stood out against the black of the wood to identify the rusty chain on which the logs were strung like beads on a necklace.

Both of these crude but effective booms seemed anchored in the mangrove of the banks. They were the types of obstacle Dawlish had most feared encountering, all but invisible at night and strong enough to shear the bottom off a light craft hitting them at speed. They were well in range of the ironclads' defensive fire but they must be broken if there was any chance for a torpedo attack. The challenge was terrifying.

A sound issuing from the *Nevski's* deck drew his attention from the booms.

A parade of white-shirted seamen was forming up on deck. The sound grew in volume, low and reverberating and incongruous in the present surroundings. Only when the group parted for a black-capped, white-bearded priest to emerge in stiff brocade robes, swinging a censer, did Dawlish realise that he was hearing an Orthodox chant and witnessing a funeral. The sound swelled and a rectangular object shrouded in an Imperial ensign began its stately progress along the deck. One of the steam pinnaces was drawn up alongside to receive this grim cargo and the canoes and their occupants had been driven off to a respectful distance. The crew stood to attention as the sad procession descended to the smaller craft.

The Delta had claimed another victim. Dawlish wondered how many other wretches had already succumbed here to malaria or blackwater fever.

The chanting continued as the pinnace drew away from the *Nevski's* side and headed slowly upstream with the draped coffin at the stern and the priest's straggling white hair waving behind him. The *Orlov's* crew had lined up, heads uncovered, and officers stood at the salute and her ensign dropped as the pinnace crawled past, then on along the colliers and yacht. The craft maintained a steady, stately, course until it was almost at the floating barrier. Then it slowed yet further and swung sharply to starboard. It was now steaming parallel to the boom and heading straight for the bank. Only when it was within some thirty yards of the mangrove did it turn tightly to port, as if it was going to ram the boom head on. It continued to swing however, completing a full sixteen-point turn, and only straightened out when it was heading transversely across the channel.

Between the parallel lines of floating logs.

Now Dawlish understood the significance of the double row. Each of the two lines of logs was anchored well inside the mangrove at one bank but their other extremities were moored to piles some twenty or thirty yards from the far side. At opposite ends, passages led into the space between the parallel barriers. A small craft, at low speed, could thread its way between these booms. It would demand careful manoeuvring, but it was feasible. His interpretation was confirmed when the funeral pinnace, now almost at the other shore, swung to starboard, rounded the extremity of the upstream log-row and emerged into the open water beyond.

Dawlish felt a flush of triumph. This was no impassable boom but an obstacle that would slow down, but not block, the passage of any competent helmsman who knew the secret. He tried to imagine the distance between the two rows. Ten or fifteen yards perhaps to allow comfortable passage for the pinnace and probably not more. But enough for his torpedo boats to manoeuvre into, though it would have to be at dead-slow speed. The greatest concern was the depth of water close to the banks where the deep-biting screws would be at risk. The one way to minimise the hazard would be to time the attack for high-water. He nudged Tobin and pointed to the upstream boom.

"Can you bring me to this place, again? Beyond that barrier?"

It took several attempts to explain it in halting pidgin.

"And through a wider creek than we've come through?"

Tobin understood at last. He nodded and answered in a whisper that conveyed his awe of the ironclads. There was indeed such a channel, narrow, he thought, but passable. And it avoided Elepa.

Dawlish smiled. His plan was forming.

*

The struggle back to Camp Beaconsfield commenced soon after sundown. The Russian steam-pinnaces and pulling-cutters had departed on their night patrols, the funeral barge of earlier having reverted to its more usual role. Dawlish and Tobin faced back into the mass of vegetation from which they had observed the warships, striking northwards to find the creek that Tobin believed branched from the anchorage channel further upstream. It represented not only the best approach for the torpedo boats, but the first step on the journey back to camp. The rising tide aided their efforts, yet even so it still proved necessary to manhandle the dugout over a small watershed, tiring them even before the travel was well-started.

A thunderstorm broke in fury as they reached the channel that they sought. Saturated, with water streaming over their faces and bodies, they paddled eastwards through this winding creek. Every ten minutes they stopped to bail out the rainwater sloshing ankle-deep around their feet. The downpour reduced visibility was to a few yards and without the lightning they could not have seen where they were going. Their discomfort was compensated for by the lack of patrols, either by the Russians or by Loveday's people. Dawlish noted as they stroked on that though the creek was winding it was nowhere narrower than twenty yards. Negotiation of the sharper bends by the torpedo craft would be tricky, but not impossible.

The storm still raged when they reached the end of the tortuous creek and emerged on one of the wide channels that they had crossed the previous night. It ran approximately north-south and, according to Tobin, curved over towards Elepa. They crossed it during almost continuous lightning. Each prolonged flash illuminated the waters boiling about them under the beating of vertical torrents of rain. A million tiny hammers pounded their heads and shoulders to rawness until they lost all sensation. The opposite bank loomed ahead at last, dark and impenetrable. They cowered under the mangrove there for fifteen minutes, bailed out the canoe again and swallowed a mouthful of brandy each.

Then time, all too soon, to push off from their shelter and to crouch over their paddles, let the accelerating tide carry them northwards along the channel. Soon afterwards, Tobin sensed in the murk an intersection with a creek running in from their right. He turned the dugout towards it and Dawlish fell in with the rhythm of his stroke. They paddled on through the rain and darkness so that by the time the storm had spent itself they were close to the spot where Egdean and the Brassmen awaited their return. The moon emerged through the clearing shreds of cloud and lit their progress. By the time they reached the point at which they had first encountered a Russian pinnace on the previous night, there was enough light to distinguish this waterway from a dozen others they had passed.

Another hour, then Tobin began to emit a series of sharp, piercing screams, similar to those of a frightened monkey. No answer. Dawlish forced from his mind the terrifying image of discovery and massacre that rose in it, but he reached nonetheless for his rifle.

They advanced two hundred yards up the narrowing creek. Tobin yelled intermittently. Still no answer. Dawlish stiffened as he half-heard, half-sensed, a movement in the foliage behind him on the left bank. He swung around, raising his Snider, as Tobin stroked the dugout towards the opposite bank and under the foliage. He was still trying to identify a target when an answering monkey-call rent the air. He almost sobbed with relief when a familiar voice behind him broke the ensuing silence.

"You're welcome, sir, though you're a bit earlier than we expected." It was Egdean. "Thank God you're back."

He emerged from the shadows, edging his weight out across the overhanging branch on which he sat, legs dangling and his rifle cradled in his arms. Tobin manoeuvred the canoe under him and he dropped into it.

"You seem to be adapting well to this infernal place," Dawlish said. "You could have blown the back off my head without me knowing you were there".

Egdean's teeth were bright in the darkness. "It isn't the rifle I'd have used, sir. It would have wakened the whole swamp. The cutlass is your man on these occasions".

"It's neither the cutlass or the rifle we need now." Dawlish felt elation at being able to confide his discovery to a fellow Englishman, even if only a common seaman. "We'll need the Whiteheads for the job before us."

"They're there, sir?" Egdean's voice was hushed.

"Two of 'em. The finest ships you'll ever see." Dawlish found awe creeping into his voice as he remembered them. "Think of the mightiest ships in the Queen's Navy, Egdean. *Alexandra* or the *Temeraire* perhaps. Imagine a ship that dwarfs them both. That's what the *Nevski's* like, a floating mountain! And her consort, the *Orlov*, there's a ship any man would be proud to sail in, sleek and powerful and beautiful! They're up there all right, lying between double booms in a broad channel."

The larger dugout emerged from the darkness ahead, its crew breaking into a low chatter of pleasure at the sight of Tobin. When it bumped alongside, Dawlish transferred gratefully, vowing inwardly that he would never again pick up a paddle. He had stroked and dragged and waded enough for a lifetime. He sank to the canoe bottom and wolfed down the meagre food and drink that Egdean laid before him.

*

They abandoned the smaller canoe and left the hiding place. The Brassmen could now sense food, rest and security ahead and established a steady paddling rhythm. Dawlish half-dozed but the itch of his innumerable bites, the stinging of the cuts and scrapes on his shins and calves, the chafing of his sodden clothes and the hardness of the dugout bottom kept him from deeper slumber. The sky had cleared enough for moonlight to make negotiation of the larger creeks nerve-racking. It was not difficult to imagine a Russian pinnace come creaming around the next bend and catching them in open water. They pushed on, negotiating an endless succession of seemingly identical waterways, with only

Tobin's instinctive feel keeping them on course, as surely as a Cockney's sense for the warrens of Whitechapel.

No Russian detected them, but the enemy they blundered into about one o'clock was no less menacing.

They were beating down a broad channel, closer to one shadowy bank than the other, and emerging from a shallow bend, when they ran all but head-on into three large canoes coming flailing towards them. Egdean shook Dawlish and gestured silently towards the approaching craft. He emerged from an uneasy sleep into a waking nightmare.

The canoes were big, big enough to carry a small brass muzzle-loader in the bows, and at least twenty men propelled each one. A row of glistening paddles, flashing silver in the moonlight, rose and fell with precision. Torches brandished aloft threw a flickering light over the clustered occupants. They came on with no sound other than the paddles' chop.

The Brassmen froze. There was no time for retreat, not even for a spurt to the shadows. Their paddles trailed in the water and dragged the dugout to a halt. Panic-stricken faces turned to Tobin and Dawlish at the stern and implored directions. Dawlish's heart raced as he reached for his rifle. He felt himself like two separate beings, one coldly determined to make every shot tell, the other almost howling in despair that, though he would die fighting, he would die a failure.

The canoes had almost reached them now. There was yelling, for the men standing amidships among the paddlers had spotted them and were waving Brown Bess muskets. Egdean was ahead of Dawlish in the canoe and was starting to draw a bead with his Snider. Disaster was a split second away when Tobin shoved Dawlish forward on his face and hissed in his ear.

"Make you lie down! I call for Ephraim!"

A chance, however slim, worth taking.

Dawlish pushed Egdean down and whispered to him to hold his fire. He pulled his revolver from its wrapping and laid it close to his own rifle. The canoes must be almost on top of them, but he dared not lift his face to see.

Tobin rose to a standing position and began to wave his paddle over his head, shouting something as he did. The other Brassmen, following his cue, joined him.

It must be a common salutation, an admission of subjection, a recognition of power and might, for many in the war canoes called acknowledgements as they passed. Curiosity mastered Dawlish, though cowering in the canoe bottom, and he peered over its bulwark.

The nearest dugout was eight yards away and its flaming torches illuminated a scene of barbaric splendour – the paddlers with their gleaming bodies, straining to maintain the rhythm, the gaudily decorated warriors in their shreds of cast-off European finery brandishing muskets and machetes, the knot of terrified prisoners chattering with fear, the victims of a nocturnal raid on a sleeping village.

But the tableau at the stern was more bizarre than any opium eater's nightmare. A gilt armchair with red plush upholstery, which would not have looked out of place in the palace of a German princeling, was lashed down there with coir rope. A obese albino was slumped in it, his flesh light cream and his hair a fuzz of orange. His eyes glittered between folds of facial fat and reflected the light of the torches. A British officer's scarlet tunic hung open over his vast belly and a battered silk hat was canted on his head. He acknowledged Tobin's salute with a lazy wave as his craft sliced past.

But stranger than all else was what reclined at his feet, resting against his knees, a thin, slatternly white woman in a bedraggled muslin dress, her long blond hair matted and her eyes bloodshot and empty. Her head was thrown back as she drained the last drops from a squareface Dutch Gin bottle.

Ephraim Loveday, monarch of the swamp, had somehow acquired the white addition to his harem that he had so long desired. And she was clearly not the Scots missionary of whom Tattersall had spoken.

The flame-lit flotilla disappeared around the bend and the sound died. Dawlish and Egdean raised themselves to their knees, incredulous that they still lived. Dawlish found himself unable to control his trembling hands. To have fought would have been less terrifying than lying immobile, expecting discovery at every moment. And the sight of the white woman distressed him. She must have fallen far to end like this, and he could do nothing for her.

Tobin gave a word of command and the canoe moved forward again into the night.

*

They reached Camp Beaconsfield at four in the afternoon. Darkness had carried them beyond the region under Loveday's control and progress in daylight had been fast. They had passed the smoking ruins of the village from which they had stolen the small canoe. Thieves far more ruthless had visited it in the meantime. A few charred poles were all that remained of the huts and corpses littered the foreshore. The stench of burned flesh stayed in Dawlish's nostrils long after the pathetic ruins were left far behind. He remembered the prisoners in Loveday's canoe and tried not to visualise their fate.

A Welsh voice sang out a challenge as they approached the green mass of the island base. It was a welcome sound. Minutes later they were slipping up the narrow creek that led to the camp itself. They rounded the final bend and saw before them, as out of place against the dank mangrove as Loveday's gilt throne, the elegant forms of *Alpha* and *Beta*. They had survived their passage of the bar.

The next phase of the mission could begin.

Chapter 16

Day and Tattersall crowded around, eager for details. Dawlish was standing under a shower improvised from a perforated zinc bucket, kept topped up by a seaman, and sluicing away caked mud. He refused to give them more than the barest details, or discuss next actions, until after he had washed, slept and eaten. He knew himself well enough to distrust his own powers of recollection when at this stage of fatigue.

"They're up there, no doubt of it." He was trying to lather with carbolic soap but the brackish water frustrated him. "Seeing them on a plan's nothing to the reality – Hurry up there, man! More water! – but they're as vulnerable as any canal barge below the waterline. Once we get in range for the torpedoes, they're as good as sunk."

"It's getting there that worries me, sir," Day said. "This damned swamp it looks like a labyrinth."

"You forget the estimable Mr. Tobin", Dawlish said. "A poor and ignorant heathen perhaps, but he's a guide of genius. A damn fine man too. I'll swear he knew where he was during every twist and turn of the way."

He hoped they were taken in by his show of jauntiness, for here, back at Camp Beaconsfield, the difficulties involved seemed to assume gigantic proportions. It was not the ironclads themselves, nor their protective booms, that worried him most but rather those armed pinnaces chugging resolutely through the creeks. He would not mention them yet. He waved aside the seaman who stood ready with another bucket of rainwater and began to towel himself dry. The scrapes on his legs would need treatment with antiseptic. He had seen smaller wounds mortify and kill.

"We'll depart tomorrow evening," he said. "Just over twenty-four hours and I'll sleep for ten of them. The boat crews must be well rested too before muster. I trust the engines and weapons have been checked after arrival, Mr. Day?"

Day summarised the work in progress while Dawlish stropped his razor. His beard felt prickly and uncomfortable. It needed trimming on cheeks and neck. He adjusted his shaving mirror and an unkempt, hollow-eyed tramp looked back at him from a face lumpy with livid mosquito bites.

"How did the boats cope with the bar?"

"Better than we could have hoped. Calmer than when you came over," Tattersall said.

"And the hulls?"

"No signs of strain," Day said. "But I was concerned about one of *Beta's* boiler ties. We've tightened the bottle-screw. It seems fine now."

"Fuel consumption? Water?"

"Heavy, higher than at Killary. The bunkers were almost empty and the boilers were damn-near dry when we got here."

"We'll need to be careful then to conserve supplies on the approach."

Tattersall had less to report. The vicinity of the camp remained undisturbed by intruders. Though two more men were down with fever he did not consider the defences undermanned. Dawlish thanked them, regarded with satisfaction the neater visage now returning his gaze, tended his myriad abrasions and savoured the luxury of fresh clothing. He drank one cup of tea and then collapsed on the cot in his tent.

*

Heavy rain was drumming on the tent's roof when Egdean shook Dawlish awake, as requested, at six the next morning. It felt as if his rest had lasted for minutes only. Water had dripped through the canvas roof, and through the mosquito net, and it had half-saturated him. He had been too tired to notice. It would be full daylight in a few minutes but he ordered the lamp lit, more for the illusion of warmth than for its light.

He sent for Tattersall and Day to join him for breakfast for he had a desire to start at once. Afterwards, he sent for Tobin. Roused from sleep, a long cloth knotted around him, he stood behind Dawlish, not comfortable, shifting from foot to foot. Egdean, summoned also, looked little more at ease when Dawlish beckoned him to sit at the same rough plank table as the two officers. The oil lamp cast a yellow glow over their faces. A solitary mosquito winged over the lamp chimney and disappeared in a tiny puff of smoke.

Dawlish took his time to tell the story of the reconnaissance. He missed no detail and encouraged Egdean to supplement his own story with points he might have overlooked. Then he invited questions from Day and Tattersall.

"Those Russian pickets worry me." Day looked sobered. "If they catch us unawares, they'll tear us apart."

Dawlish didn't minimise the intensive nature of the pinnaces' patrolling. He also admitted that the negotiation of the booms, though feasible in theory, would not be easy.

He ended by telling of the meeting with Loveday's war party.

"So Ephraim's up to his old tricks again," Tattersall said. "Massacring innocents, burning villages. I'll look forward to settling his hash when all this is over."

"But all credit for our deliverance must go to Mr. Tobin," Dawlish said. "If he hadn't been so quick-witted, Egdean and I would have been providing Ephraim's dinner tonight.".

Then he remembered Loveday's companion.

"Here's something else that will interest you, Tattersall. Ephraim seems to have acquired a white wife after all. She's a bedraggled-looking slut, and well able to down a bottle of squareface, but she's white nonetheless."

Tattersall's low whistle of surprise was a stronger reaction than Dawlish had elicited by his mention of the devastated village and its captured inhabitants

"A woman? And white? You're sure of that?"

Dawlish nodded. "Any idea of who she can be?"

"I'm damned if I know. I can't imagine she's Russian. And she doesn't sound like some blushing damsel who's just fallen among thieves by accident."

But now to fix the plan of attack.

Using the rough chart, by now rain-soaked and discoloured, and by eliciting details of the route from Tobin, Dawlish sketched the approach to the anchorage. Egdean's memories complemented his own for the first section. To calculate fuel and water requirements, they estimated the distance, adding a twenty-five percent contingency for unforeseen detours. The greater part of the passage would be at low speed but, even so, *Alpha* and *Beta* had insufficient coal and water capacity to bring them there and back. They must therefore set out not only with topped-up bunkers and boilers but with their decks loaded with yet more sacks and barrels. Each would tow a coal and water-laden cutter to a point two-thirds of the way. Deck-loaded supplies would be the first consumed. Whatever had been drawn from the crafts' bunkers and tanks would be replaced from the cutters just before these would be secreted up a side-creek. *Alpha* and *Beta* would go into action with clear decks.

For the last time, two short lengths of rope snaked across a box lid to delineate the banks of the anchorage. Wooden chips represented the Russian ships. Lines of lucifer matches – four lines, two upstream, two downstream of the moored vessels – marked the booms. *Alpha* and *Beta* were the smallest chips of all.

The growing light did little to lift the sombre mood. The experience at Killary proved invaluable when they considered manoeuvre options, dismissed them, considered others, modified them, rejected them too and began again. All aimed at the one objective – bringing *Alpha* within a half-cable of the *Nevski's* flank, and her sister within similar range of the *Orlov*.

And, at last, the plan.

Approach via the northern booms. Slow negotiation of those obstacles, perhaps while illuminated and under fire. Dawlish sensed, and shared, Day's grim recognition of the risk involved. Only beyond the booms, in the anchorage itself, could speed be protection, that and the brief shielding offered by the moored yacht and colliers. The optimum outcome would see both the *Nevski* and the *Orlov* attacked but should either torpedo craft be damaged – Dawlish hesitated to use a stronger word – then the other should concentrate on the larger warship alone.

He looked around. Tattersall's hearty confidence stilled for once. Day taciturn, studying with terrible concentration the scraps of rope and wood before him. Egdean still uncomfortable in the close presence of officers but his whole bearing a mute assurance of dogged, perhaps hopeless, loyalty.

A terrible voice within him, cold and merciless, told Dawlish that two of these men expected to die, and that the third mourned them already. Their listless discussion of the details of the withdrawal confirmed that. Only Tobin, sniffing snuff, was oblivious of the significance of the moment. Yet beyond their grim acceptance, Dawlish recognised the sort of resolution that he had first encountered it in a muddy Chinese ditch, that he had shared in the thick bush in Ashanti, that he had felt when he had stood with that encircled but undefeated group in the millet on Pemba. He could rely on these men, and he was satisfied.

There was nothing more to say. He dismissed the group. Tobin shuffled off though the rain to his hut, a sack clutched over his shoulders. Watching his bedraggled figure, it was hard to believe that the whole venture's success rested on his piloting.

*

The morning was busy.

The rain died soon after nine, easing the task of stripping the guns and torpedoes, then cleaning and reassembling them for the last time. The Gatlings were mounted, oiled and covered with tarpaulins. Their feed-hoppers were loaded and more ammunition transferred to the ready-use lockers. In the engine rooms each flange was once more tightened, each packing readjusted, each oil-cup on the bearings refilled. Dawlish left Day to oversee the work on the engines and Tattersall to supervise the distribution of the coal and water loads while he himself concentrated on the torpedoes.

The most critical components, the 'Whitehead Secrets', proved to be in good working order. These were the balance chambers that regulated the depths at which the torpedoes would run. Each consisted of a flexible diaphragm exposed to water pressure and a system of levers that magnified this movement and acted on the horizontal rudders to maintain constant running depth. Dawlish set two of the mechanisms to ten feet and two to fifteen. Each boat would carry one of each setting. Either would guarantee impact on the hulls of the ironclads but he hoped that near-simultaneous strikes at different depths would have marked disruptive effects on the internal hull structures. Satisfied at last with these items, he turned to the air reservoirs. A glance at the gauges told him that they had maintained pressure since being topped up in *Nomad.* He turned the propulsion screws by hand. The pneumatic motor and the gearing rotated smoothly but he regreased them to be on the safe side.

One last task remained, the checking of the firing pistols, dangerous and best performed far from bystanders. He unlocked the nuts that secured them in their respective warheads and carried them on a piece of canvas into the undergrowth. The disassembly was hazardous but he had to be confident of satisfactory functioning. He checked that the pistol-arming fan would spin free once the torpedoes were travelling forward through the water. Once the fan had dropped away, only a thin shear-pin would hold the striker away from the detonator. Impact on the target would break the pin and cause detonation, setting off in turn the warhead's main charge. He reassembled the pistols, then carried them back to the torpedoes and restored them to the weapons. Nothing remained then but to watch over their cautious manhandling into the tubes in *Alpha's* and *Beta's* bows

The crews had a meal at midday. In the final inspection that followed, all men stood at their assigned stations on the boats. Dawlish made his rounds, first over Day's craft and then his own. There was little, indeed nothing, to find fault with. The crews had entered into the spirit of the enterprise and the boats showed it.

Until now, other than Egdean, none of the men knew the exact nature of the mission. Dawlish had agonised long over how to explain it. Patriotic exhortations were never effective, he knew. At the moment of crisis, these men would be fighting for each other, not for crown or country. He should appeal to that and tell them only the bare facts.

He ordered the crews ashore after the inspection, had them drawn up in two facing lines. They looked a ragged and cut-throat group in their tattered civilian slops yet there was a smartness about their rank-dressing that showed them to be picked men, proud of their skills and pleased that their efforts had passed muster. He stood them easy.

"Tonight, lads, we're going to do what we came here for," he said. "We're going to attack and destroy two powerful warships. One has the guns to tear great holes in any ship you've ever served in. The other has the speed to run down and destroy any British merchantman."

He had their attention, saw puzzlement on their faces.

"Who are they, you wonder? They're ships of an undeclared enemy of the Queen. They're skulking in a creek not thirty miles from here. I've seen them myself."

The men were electric with anticipation now, glancing sidelong to each other. Bets were being settled mutely at this moment.

"It's better that you don't know who these enemies are. But you have my word that they're lurking there for no good intent towards us."

He waited, let the words sink in.

"They're not honourable foes. We'll treat them for what they are, pirates outside the law." He paused. "And we'll sink them at their moorings in the way we rehearsed at Killary."

Apprehension, doubt, suppressed fear on their faces. Every man questioned his own courage at a moment like this.

"Gather round me, lads, and I'll tell you how it is."

He spread out an old chart, face-down, on a box and, as they crowded around, he outlined the general location of the *Nevski* and *Orlov* with quick pencil strokes.

"It's going to be slow, careful work getting there," he said. "The creeks twist and wind. Don't they, Egdean?"

"Indeed they do, sir."

"And I know you'll be itching for full revolutions, Lowe." *Beta's* helmsman was nodding. "But you'll be following *Alpha's* course and speed. We'll be holding our horses until we get into the anchorage."

Then, in larger scale, he sketched the creek where the ironclads lay, showing the bend in the channel, the yacht and colliers and the double booms.

"The last stage will be bloody difficult. We'll have manoeuvre each boat at low speed between those double rows of logs. We might be illuminated and under fire from our targets. Blinding the searchlights comes before all else! You hear that, Gatling crews? You'll be showing us how, won't you Maxwell? And those cartridge hoppers will be emptying damn fast but I'll want them filled as carefully as if you were on the range. So no jams, that's right, Stothert, isn't it? If you're still unsure I've no doubt that Browning will tell you how it's done, won't you, Browning?"

A ripple of uncomfortable laughter.

Dawlish dropped his voice. "It might be damn unpleasant there at the booms and we can't hurry, no matter what they throw at us." He swept his gaze over the crews, looked each man in the eyes in turn while he continued. "At that moment, our lives and our success will depend on your coolness in carrying out your orders. Once the boom is passed – and I've have no doubt it will be passed – your skill and steadiness will help us sink two of the most powerful ships afloat."

He paused, and his last words were heartfelt.

"At that moment I will be confident, as every British officer is always confident, that every man will do his duty".

Nothing further to be said, no cheers for the Queen, none for England, Home and Beauty.

Nothing but to break up in silence, each man with his own thoughts, to snatch a last few hours of rest.

Chapter 17

The two torpedo boats headed into the swamp, before nightfall, at a steady six knots. The cutters straining on towropes astern, heavily burdened with coal and fresh water, precluded any higher speed. Dawlish stood on *Alpha's* tiny bridge with Egdean and Tobin. From his earlier journey he recognised many of the twists and bends they now negotiated but he knew that without the Tobin's guidance he would have been incapable of retracing this course.

Daylight faded. Scattered clouds drifted across the moon, gathering for the night's downpour. The small sternwards-pointing lantern at the rear of *Alpha's* bridge served as a guide for *Beta*, following some fifty yards astern. They encountered random groups of fishing canoes, each with its glowing pot of charcoal, as on the earlier journey. There was no need for evasion now and the torpedo craft ploughed past, leaving the fishermen gaping in their wakes.

Dawlish and Egdean took successive turns at the helm, responding to Tobin's instructions – "Turn'm for left! Small, small – eh heh! Make you turn'm straight!"

The gunners and their loaders stood by their Gatlings, straining their eyes to detect the slightest movement in this world of dark shadows and shimmering water. The engines were running at quarter-revolutions.

They reached the northernmost point of their course by ten o'clock and could start the westwards swing. Their track would now lie across the north-south grain of the main creeks and through the narrow and twisting watercourses that interconnected them. It was time to transfer the necessary coal and water from the cutters and to leave them behind in hiding.

The *Beta* advanced two hundred yards and drew in against the shadows of the mangrove to stand sentinel. *Alpha* hung back, sought the bank and brought the cutter alongside. Her engine had already used up the coal and water carried on deck and had drawn down a third of the stocks in her bunkers and tanks. The sweating engine room crew came on deck for air while the men in the cutter transferred sufficient fuel and water to replace usage. *Alpha*, her deck now clear, proceeded upstream a quarter mile to take her turn as picket while *Beta* replenished also. The cutters stayed behind with six of Tattersall's seamen and four Brassmen in each. They would pull up a side-channel and hide until the torpedo craft returned. Should they not appear after two days, then the cutters would return to Camp Beaconsfield.

Clouds were gathering, deepening the darkness and obscuring the moon for minutes at a time, but the sky still just bright enough for the torpedo boats, now unencumbered, to increase speed. Dawlish had taken *Alpha's* helm to relieve Egdean. They had progressed little more than a mile however when a flash lit up the whole creek, followed in less than a second by the crash of thunder and the first lash of the night's rainstorm. The bridge-screen offered no protection. Dawlish, instantly soaked, and confronted by an impenetrable wall of cascading water, rang to the engine-room for lower revolutions. He hoped that *Beta*, forging in his wake, would follow suit and not come crashing into the stern. He glanced over his shoulder and saw the black bulk of the other craft emerge briefly from the grey curtain of rain, illuminated for an instant by another lightning flash, then drop back into the murk. Day, good seaman that he was, had followed suit.

The gun crews, devoid of protection, huddled in misery over their weapons. Dawlish noted with satisfaction, though not surprise, that they had thrown the canvas covers over the breech mechanisms and loading hoppers. The rain might scourge the crews themselves but their precious guns were protected. Tobin crouched over the top of the bridge shield and peered into the rain ahead, somehow picking out in the lightning each twist and bend of the creek and relaying instructions. Progress was maintained, crawling forward at less than two knots. But it was at least progress.

Then Tobin stiffened, grabbed Dawlish's arm and gesticulated ahead. His face was a mask of horror.

"Make you look there!" he said. "Make you stop 'em!"

Dawlish didn't hesitate, his trust in Tobin by now total. He did not want to risk the sound of the telegraph's ring – it could carry far – and he sent Browning, the starboard sponson's Gatling loader, scurrying to the engine room with the order to stop the engine.

"Take over. Egdean! Bring her into the shadows."

Egdean took the wheel as Dawlish peered over the shield with Tobin. The craft was already losing way and it nudged against the bank, the trailing mangrove branches dragging her to a halt.

A long chain of lightning illuminated the creek and Dawlish did not need Tobin's pointing finger to show him the Russian pinnace, half-lost in the cascading rain and nuzzled, stationary, against the port bank a hundred yards ahead. But worse, for as the cold light died, he was left with the image on his retinas of a white-clad figure, certainly a lookout, scampering aft to rouse the remainder of the crew from their dry shelters. Both British and Russians had sighted each other at the same instant.

Dawlish's mind raced. Only manned action-stations favoured the frail torpedo boat against the sturdier pinnace, yet with every second that advantage was evaporating as the Russians scrambled for their gun positions. He could not risk a gunnery duel – the picket boat had the advantage in weight of metal and solidity of hull. He must get under her lee before the three-pounder in her bows tore *Alpha* apart.

He reached for the telegraph, rang for full speed, and yelled to Egdean, "Take us alongside! We're boarding!".

His right hand snapped down to loosen his holster flap and he drew his revolver and cocked it as *Alpha* leaped forward. The gun crews had also spotted the Russian and were stripping the covers from the Gatlings.

Dawlish shouted their orders: "Port gunner! Engage enemy ahead! Short bursts over the deck! Starboard and stern crews! Join me on the bridge with cutlasses! Prepare to board!"

At that instant the pinnace's small searchlight burst into life, half-blinding him. He shielded his eyes. It could be only seconds before they were alongside. A flash ahead, a stab of orange flame, then billowing smoke obscuring the searchlight's beam. Then an explosion in the mangrove somewhere to starboard. It had been close. And the next round would be aimed lower.

O'Malley, the port gunner, ground his weapon into life before the next lightning flash, raking the pinnace's upperworks, seeking and finding the searchlight, blinding it. Smithson and Webb, from the Gatling position aft, were pulling themselves past the bridge platform, cutlasses in hand, to join Maxwell and Browning at the starboard sponson. Dawlish followed and swung himself down over the bridge-shield. With the port Gatling still hammering in short bursts to his left, he crouched with the others, grasping at any handhold for steadiness as the torpedo boat shuddered forward.

Now the pinnace was looming up ahead. *Alpha* grated alongside, her forward momentum killed by the revolutions astern for which Egdean signalled just before the two vessels touched. Dawlish and the others froze, not daring to jump, as the port Gatling stuttered into action again and blasted past them. It caught two bounding white figures in its hail and collapsed them before they could reach their midships Nordenvelt.

Dawlish glanced towards the bows. The three-pounder's crew there were swinging it over and depressing it to blast *Alpha* at point-blank range. The Gatling's fire died in sudden silence.

"Boarders away!" he shouted. "Head for the mounting at the stern!"

He leaped upwards on to the pinnace's deck, a foot above the torpedo boat's low bows. He landed, skidded on the wet surface but kept his feet. Behind him the gun crews swarmed aboard and raced sternwards towards the Nordenvelt there, cutlasses raised. He ducked behind the boiler casing. O'Malley's Gatling in the *Alpha's* port sponson could not bear on the three-pounder and he had reserved it for himself. He could just make out its outline in the darkness, could hear a voice yelling in Russian and the clang of the three-pounder's closing breechblock. There was a fresh shell in the weapon and the gunner must be reaching for the firing lever. Seconds counted now.

He rocketed to his feet and threw himself horizontally on top of the boiler casing with his revolver outstretched before him. He sprawled there, trying to pick out the gun crew's silhouettes, but his view was obscured by the Nordenvelt atop the casing and by the two bodies, one still writhing and gurgling weakly, close by it. He wriggled sideways and raised his pistol.

The three-pounder erupted in a smoke-enveloped flash as it fired into *Alpha's* stern, the only section of her on which it could bear. Then another flash, almost simultaneous with that from the gun's muzzle, as the shell struck home. The explosion's searing breath whipped Dawlish's face. He fought down the rush of anger that came with realisation that his craft might be mortally wounded.

The Russian bow chaser's breech rattled open. Now he had the gun crew at his mercy. And he had none. The empty shell case was tumbling out on the deck when he hurtled to his feet and dashed forward. Lightning filled the sky as he pounded across the slippery deck and exposed the scene in the bows. One Russian was pushing the next shell into the breech while the other held the gun aimed at *Alpha*. Dawlish was on top of them before they could react. He blasted the man with the shell backwards so that he toppled over the bows, then re-cocked. The other gunner was still turning towards him, was perhaps frozen in shock. Dawlish shoved his revolver within a foot of his face before he fired. The prolonged lightning chain died and he crouched behind the three-pounder's shield as he pushed new rounds into the revolver's empty chambers.

The noise of hand-to-hand scuffle aft, punctuated by two separate shots. Crouched, he padded towards it but paused as he passed one of the open scuttles of the engine room. It was no higher than knee level but a sudden rustling alerted him. He fired twice inside and then peered through the opening. Nothing to discern there except the red glow around the edges of the furnace door. Another shot into the darkness, avoiding the direction of the boiler. He pushed new rounds into the revolver and waited, attention fixed on the engine room companionway some eight feet to his right. It opened suddenly and somebody began to crawl through it on hands and knees, retching blood. Dawlish stepped forward and fired into the injured man's head. He crumpled and collapsed back down the ladder into the engine room.

The conflict was over. Two of the *Alpha's* men were hacking with their cutlasses at the remains of the crew of the second Nordenvelt. Sheltering below from the rainstorm, they had not reached their weapon in time. By the after-cabin Maxwell, the starboard gunner, was bent over the remaining boarder, who appeared to be injured.

Wedged between the telegraph and the wheel, the shredded corpse of the Russian helmsman showed that he too had not reached his position in time. The eyes of the man who had lain dying by the midships Nordenvelt were locked open in death. A body blocked the open-flung door of the after cabin. Dawlish turned it over with his foot. A vertical cutlass blow had almost bisected the face but the cigar clamped between the teeth still smouldered. Dawlish recognised the officer who had lounged so nonchalantly on the deck of the picket boat three nights before.

There was no further opposition.

The boarders came forward, half-dragging their injured shipmate. It was Browning, the loader from the starboard sponson. He was grasping his hands over his bloodied stomach and colour was already draining from his face.

"The poor bugger caught it in the belly, sir." Pity and anger mixed in Maxwell's voice. The bond between a gunner and a loader was a close one. "One of them bastards had a pistol and he let him have it before we could finish him".

Browning was moaning.

"Am I hurt bad, sir?" he said to Dawlish, "Am I hurt bad?"

"Only a scratch. You'll be fine." He could not but lie. "Get him over to the *Alpha* as gently as you can, lads."

Then, remembering the three-pounder's hit on the vessel's stern, he called across to Egdean. "Is she damaged? Will the helm respond?"

"It ain't too bad, sir," Egdean shouted back. "The stern Gatling's finished but the steering chains are intact. She'll answer."

"Stand by to get under way," Dawlish called. "I'll see to this craft and I'll be across directly."

He hurried forward on the pinnace, thankful to escape Browning's agonised groans. When he reached the bows he pulled aside the body of the Russian gunner, avoiding the sight of his shattered head. He found what he had been looking for, a rope-handled box of shells. It was heavy and he half-carried, half-dragged it aft along the deck towards the engine room companionway. He paused there to gain breath before lifting the box across the raised sill and pushing it with a crash into the space below. He followed after, descending with caution into the semi-darkness, guided by the flickering light from the half-closed furnace doors. As he reached the bottom, he tripped over the prone body of the man he had shot at the entrance.

He was shifting his footing to avoid stepping on the corpse when he sensed movement to his left. He turned towards it, reaching for the revolver that he had returned to his holster.

And was too slow.

Something came swishing down past his left ear and caught him a glancing blow on the shoulder, knocking him off balance and down on the deck. He rolled over and sighted the tall figure that was again raising the coal shovel that had just missed his head. A glimpse of iron piping to the right, and he scrambled towards it. He ducked beneath as the shovel descended again, clanging uselessly on the pipe that now sheltered his head. The Russian was stepping back for another swing as Dawlish brought up the revolver and fired once, twice, three times, hurling his attacker across the engine room. He heard groaning as he struggled to his feet and stood over the twisting body. Shaking from shock he emptied the remaining chambers into it. In the furnace's glow he recognised the shaven head of the stoker he had glimpsed during that first encounter with the pinnace.

Now to finish the work. He picked up the shovel that had almost been his death and used it to prise the furnace doors fully open. He plunged it in, withdrew a glowing heap of coals and strewed them against the compartment's wooden sides. He reached for another shovelful, and another, repeating until he saw the first wisps of smoke curling from the wood. Only then did he cast the shovel aside and clamber back up the ladder.

Smithson and Webb, the stern Gatling crew, now without a weapon to serve, met him on deck.

"We heard the shooting, sir, and –"

He cut them off. "Get back on board!"

His hands were trembling. and his knees weak and he let them help him across to *Alpha*. He joined Egdean on the steering platform, saw Tobin crouched below the armoured screen. *Beta* had already drawn alongside, having arrived when the action was finished. He yelled across to Day on *Beta* that all was well and that he should tail *Alpha* as before. He ordered Egdean to get underway at once. Day's craft edged into midstream and Egdean drew *Alpha* away from the doomed pinnace.

The two torpedo boats moved forward into the solid wall of rain and left the Russian craft astern with smoke billowing from her scuttles. It was already lost to their sight when they heard the three-pound shells starting to explode, one by one at first and then all together. An instant later a dull 'crump' told of the boiler's rupture tearing the hull apart.

Tobin was still huddled, eyes bulging, shaking, overcome by a horror he could never have imagined. Dawlish caught him by the shoulder, dragged him to his feet, saw that he was close to hysteria. Tobin wriggled and squirmed in his grasp, trying to regain the illusory safety of the deck. Dawlish fought down a feeling of panic – a nervous collapse by his guide was the worst that could happen at this stage.

"No trouble anymore! No trouble, you understand?" He pulled out his brandy flask and thrust it between Tobin's teeth. "You've done bloody well! Just stand there now and guide us. There's nothing more to fear!"

Tobin choked on the brandy but was soon sufficiently recovered to advise taking a turn into a creek to port. Dawlish felt a flush of respect and affection for him. He had indeed done well. The rain had lessened by now and the lightning storm had drifted eastwards.

He left Egdean at the helm and went aft to assess the damage. He paused at the bottom of the steering platform's ladder. Browning lay there on a tarpaulin and Smithson crouched by him. Webb had already been taken the wounded man's position as port loader.

"How is he?" The question was unnecessary. Browning was unconscious but breathing. Weakly.

"The poor chap's had it, sir," Smithson said. "He don't look as if he'll last much longer an' the sooner the better".

For all that it was worth, Smithson had at least managed to stop the bleeding. Dawlish handed him his brandy flask to dose the dying man, should he come round again. He moved towards the stern and surveyed the damage done by the Russian hit. The Gatling mount was wrecked and the weapon was unserviceable, but it had deflected the blast away from the rudder quadrant and steering chains. The ammunition locker had not exploded, even though it was knocked over and jammed closed.

When he came forward again, Browning was still. He felt for the pulse, found none, put his ear to the chest, heard nothing. He pulled the tarpaulin over the face.

"He were a good mate," Smithson said. "He weren't no saint an' he liked his grog, but he were a good mate."

It wasn't a bad epitaph.

Dawlish sent Smithson aft to force the jammed ammunition locker open and distribute its contents between the two remaining Gatlings. Then he returned to the bridge. The clouds were clearing from the moon's face, illuminating the creeks better than before.

The creek they now threaded was so winding that it was often necessary to slow down to a virtual standstill to inch the craft around the acute bends. Dawlish recognised this as the area where he and Egdean had hidden in the large canoe on the first night of the reconnaissance. The general trend of the journey continues across the flow of the main channels flowing towards the sea. On reaching each of these wide waterways he signalled for *Beta* to pause while *Alpha* crept forward to scout the broad expanse of water for any sign of Russian patrols. Once the 'all clear' signal was winked astern both craft went racing across together at high speed to the shadows of the opposite shore.

At twelve-thirty they reached the entrance of the final narrow channel that passed north of Elepa and towards the Russian anchorage.

The last stage of the approach now began.

Chapter 18

Dawlish stood beside Egdean on the steering platform, wet through and cold, his shoulder aching. The stars were out now and the clouds had largely cleared, giving more light than earlier for navigating the creek's meanderings. The *Beta's* slender form, a dark mass astern before, was now clearly delineated against the shimmering water. This new visibility was worrying. Conditions at the anchorage would be similar.

He looked at his watch. One o'clock. Somewhat less than half an hour to go. This creek would enter the channel in which the Russians lay at a point above the upstream booms.

Though concentrated on his task, the thought lurked in the back of his mind that he might cease to exist in the coming hour. The fact of death itself held no fear. If there was a God, and he half-doubted that there was, though he prayed to him for courage at this moment, he knew that he would be merciful. It was injury, hideous mutilation, pain beyond imagination, an agonised passage from life that frightened him. Compared with that, the death of the seaman whose body lay shrouded below the steering platform had been merciful.

Yet there was something worse than fear, an awareness that had haunted him for days that he would pass so soon, and so easily, from memory. His father would mourn him for a while, though probably less than he ever had his older son, James. His sister Susan would grieve longer and might name some future child for him, but her sorrow too would fade in time. Only Mrs. Gore, his nurse, would lament him to her grave. The Realm, the Navy, would not, could not, honour his memory. Some official document would list him as dying of illness while on some ill-defined business in the West Indies. Nobody would question it. No woman had loved him and, but for one stupid infatuation, he had loved none either. No child would remember him. His name was writ in water.

Alpha was emerging from a narrow and convoluted twist of the creek, almost a full circle. Her speed was low. It was now that the second Russian pinnace caught the torpedo boats in ambush. Dawlish's craft had passed the bend, was speeding up as it entered into the straight section of creek ahead, when the pinnace opened fire. *Beta* was thirty yards astern.

Dawlish spotted the muzzle-flash in the shadows of the port bank ahead. A half-second later, the three-pounder shell screamed over *Alpha's* bridge and exploded in the mangrove to starboard. It must be another pinnace, he realised, the second of the three he had seen at the Russian's anchorage, and it was crouching, all but invisible, under the foliage's overhang. That was the likelihood. It was still too far from the ironclads to expect a landed weapon in an emplacement. Standing out against the bright water astern, *Alpha* must be a perfect target.

Another streak of flame, another miss. The shell's explosion in the mangrove drowned his yelled orders to bear to port. It hardly mattered, for Egdean was already swinging the helm hard over to hide *Alpha's* silhouette in the shadows of the bank. The bows slid across, then straightened as the vessel glided beneath the drooping branches that came brushing and plucking against the upperworks.

"Dead slow, Egdean," Dawlish whispered. "Edge her forward".

Egdean's great hand clamped over the telegraph lever and pulled it back as Dawlish hissed his instructions to the gunners in the sponsons.

"Starboard Crew! Watch for the next muzzle-flash and give it a short burst. Short, mind you, short! Port Crew! Stand by to engage when we move into midstream again. Rake the upperworks! Go for their guns!"

Beta had come forging on in her sister's wake and now occupied the spot in midstream that she had just vacated. Her bows were already swinging over to seek the shadows of the starboard bank. Only yards separated her from their shelter when the next Russian shell found its mark in her, penetrating the side of the hull abaft the bridge, just below deck level. It exploded with a sharp crack in the bunker space ahead of the engine room. A brief flash erupted through the flimsy deck planking and sent one of the ventilating cowls toppling sideways. *Beta* shuddered, rolled slightly, and then slipped into the shadows as the Russian Nordenvelts cackled into life and boiled the waters astern of her. They coughed into silence once more as their target lost itself in the shadows.

It was a silence deeper and more ominous than Dawlish had ever experienced, but it lasted only an instant. He heard Maxwell, the starboard gunner, mutter "Just up a trifle" and grind his firing crank forward. The Gatling's multiple barrels spun for six, seven rounds, paused, spun again before stammering into the same silence that had engulfed the Russian weapon. And no indication of damage inflicted.

From across the creek however came the sound of moaning from the *Beta*, an inhuman, bestial, sound. Day's voice drowned it as he called out in the darkness.

"Lieutenant Dawlish! We've no incapacitating damage, but the port Gatling's out of action. The gunner's had it. There's no harm done to the boiler or machinery. Are we going to run for it?"

Even before Day spoke, Dawlish was churning alternatives in his mind. To stay put and engage in a sniping duel in the darkness could only end in disaster. The Russian was more stoutly built and more heavily armed. To run the gauntlet under a covering hail of Gatling fire might just offer success. But the run must be immediate.

He yelled his resolution across the creek to Day.

"I'm running in twenty seconds from now, Mister Day! Once I've cleared your line of fire, open on the enemy with all you've got. Then wait thirty seconds and follow at full speed. If I don't make it, then carry on alone!"

The crack of the Russian's three-pounder drowned Day's acknowledgement. Its shell burst in the foliage just aft of *Beta.* Then a long, piercing scream as a glowing fragment cut down an unseen crewman. Dawlish heard the cry remotely, as if from another universe, for his gaze was intent on the creek ahead as he told Egdean to signal for full revolutions.

The starboard Gatling hammered as *Alpha* leapt forward. The weapon in the port sponson joined it when the boat surged into midstream. Dawlish grasped the edge of the bridge-screen to steady himself against the acceleration. He dragged his revolver from its holster and held it straight before him, ready to add its puny contribution to supplement the Gatlings.

Now *Alpha* had cleared the line of her sister's fire and a hail lashed out from where *Beta* lurked – that must be Jarvis, the gunner who had won that sovereign so long since on *Nomad*, now seeking the enemy in the shadows.

Dawlish was counting the seconds in his mind before *Beta* would leave cover and follow astern. Nineteen and twenty, and twenty and twenty-one . . .

Then another blast of flame from the pitch blackness of the bank ahead, a rush of air above and the report of the three-pounder's discharge an instant before the shell exploded in the mangrove off the starboard quarter.

Another miss!

Dawlish's elation transformed to sick horror as a black mass detached itself from the shadows. The Russian pinnace, stout and solid, was swinging out from the bank and towards the centre of the creek. He could make out three-pounder in the bows, and beyond it the Nordenvelt and its crew. They were arcing their weapon across to bear on *Alpha.* Less than sixty yards now separated the rapidly closing craft as the Russian pulled further from the shadows and the torpedo boat raced towards her on a collision course.

Escape depended on Egdean's helmsmanship now. Dawlish held his pistol before him and pumped round after round towards the figures on the ever-closer pinnace. Remotely, as if a second personality coexisted with the frenzied being on the bridge who kicked aside Tobin, cowering at his feet, Dawlish heard the pinnace's Nordenvelt erupt, his own starboard Gatling stutter into silence and Maxwell and his mate swearing at its jamming. He heard too the lethal rattle as the torrent of Russian fire riddled *Alpha's* forward funnel and ventilators and the last, surprised, gasp of Scanlon, the port loader, as he toppled overboard with his chest torn open. Even before he was lost in the darkness, Smithson had taken his place. O'Malley, the port gunner, had lost his loader but he never slackened fire.

Somehow, like an automaton, Dawlish was still counting the seconds.

And thirty-nine and forty, and forty and . . .

Remembering why, he glanced over his shoulder to see that the *Beta* had burst from cover and was forging up the channel in his wake.

The Russian was now clear of the shadows and close to midstream. Its Nordenvelt was still firing, but its crew had momentarily missed their aim and their fire was screaming harmlessly overhead. The three-pounder blasted again, striking the *Alpha's* after funnel and carrying it overboard. By some lucky chance, the shell had not exploded.

The pinnace's searchlight burst into dazzling brilliance as *Alpha* charged at her, the separation narrowed now to forty yards. The port Gatling, the only weapon capable of bearing, was chattering but its aim was off, its crew blinded by the beam. Dawlish, dazzled, flung up his arm and buried his face in the crook of his elbow.

Egdean was also attempting to protect his eyes while continuing to steer. Now there could be but one course of action and he took it, flinging the helm over and swinging the craft to port. For one brief instant the two vessels, British and Russian, were on parallel but opposite tracks, and then Egdean was flinging the helm over again. *Alpha* went skidding under and past the Russian's stern. Only inches separated the two hulls.

The searchlight's beam was lost in the turn but the moonlight gave illumination enough for the Russian's stern Nordenvelt, swivelled by its yelling crew, to rake *Alpha*. A few rounds probed the open rear of the bridge, shaving past Dawlish and somehow sparing Egdean. But one found Tobin where he crouched in terror. He half rose, then crumpled and fell to the deck below the steering platform. The greatest weight of fire fell further aft, ploughing a splintered furrow along the deck beside the boiler casing.

Speed unimpaired, for now at least, *Alpha* was sprinting down the creek towards clear water. Dawlish turned to see the Russian craft receding rapidly astern. Elation coursed through him as he realised that the *Alpha* had survived the gauntlet, though at an as-yet undetermined cost.

And that elation turned to horror as he witnessed the tragedy that now unfolded.

Lowe, the *Beta's* helmsman, less quick-witted than Egdean, had not realised the impossibility of passing ahead of the pinnace. The torpedo boat came ploughing on towards the ever-narrowing gap between the Russian's bows and the bank ahead. Seconds before the heavy pinnace rammed the frail torpedo boat amidships, the Russian three-pounder fired once more, its explosive shell blasting through the *Beta's* boiler casing. A dull 'whumf' followed on the shell's sharp report as the boiler exploded. A billowing cloud of steam enveloped the craft's entire after-half. *Beta* staggered forward, only to be ground against the bank as the Russian's bows crashed into her already mangled side. The hammering of the small-calibre weapons reached a climax as the next twist of the channel blotted the catastrophic scene from Dawlish's view.

He was shaking all over, stunned more by the loss of *Beta* than by his own recent proximity to death. Cold, gnawing, disappointment surged through him, banishing the manic excitement of seconds earlier. With half his command eliminated, *Alpha* alone must storm the anchorage ahead.

And the survival of one at least of the Russian raiders was guaranteed.

He forced himself to ignore that awareness and concentrate of the creek ahead. It was no narrower and no worse convoluted than that left astern. He rang by telegraph for low revolutions, confident that the

Russian pinnace could never catch him up but concerned that the present speed, if maintained, could result in disaster on an acute bend or unseen snag. The noise of gunfire receded astern and then died out with a few short bursts. He had to admit to himself, with reluctance, that they were those of a Nordenvelt rather than of a Gatling.

Egdean was saying something to him and pointing down to the deck. Tobin, forgotten in the last mad minutes, lay there, motionless and bloody. Dawlish swung down from the steering platform, past the body, moved aft to survey the recent damage. A column of sparks and steam was shooting through the top of the boiler casing from the gap left by the missing after-funnel. Had the decks and upperworks not been sodden from the earlier rainstorm, they might already be at risk of fire. He could take no chances. He called for Webb to come aft from the starboard sponson.

"Fetch a bucket! Douse the casing and the decks. Look sharpish though and get back to your position as quickly as you can."

He picked his way over the debris littering the deck, the splintered planking, the riddled remains of a ventilator cowl, a torn lifebelt, the buckled ties that had failed to restrain the missing funnel. He pushed open the hatch leading to the engine room and called down his deepest fear.

"Any damage to the boiler? Any leaks?"

And there were none.

The last savage raking by the Nordenvelt had missed the boiler but the suction pipe of one of the feed pumps was all but severed. Hickley and Barrow, engineer and stoker, were crouched over it, binding it with hemp packing and securing it with a leather trouser-belt.

"It'll hold for a bit, sir", Hinkley called, "It ain't perfect, but it'll do".

They were working in the narrow space between the boiler and the hull side. The sight prompted a rapid but appalling impression of the probable end of their counterparts on *Beta*. Dawlish forced the image from his mind and returned on deck. Maxwell had cleared the jammed Gatling in the starboard sponson.

"She got too damn hot, sir," he said. "She'll be all right now that she's had a chance to cool down."

"Ammunition. How much?" Dawlish noticed that the gunner's arm was bound with a bloodstained rag, through which small globules seeped and dripped, but Maxwell made no mention of it.

"Bloody little, sir. The hopper's full and Webb's still got half a box in the locker. And that's it."

The situation was even worse in the port sponson where the loader, Scanlon, had gone overboard with a box of cartridges in his arms. Smithson, the powder-blackened replacement, had been stocking the depleted hopper. He showed Dawlish the remaining supply, just over three hundred rounds.

"It ain't much to be getting along with, sir," he said. "If there's another of them buggers up ahead, we won't have much to hit him with."

Dawlish thought to himself that if there was indeed another of them buggers up ahead then the game would be as good as up, but he did not say so. He had little comfort to give.

"Short bursts only then," he told O'Malley, the gunner. "And go for the searchlights!"

He went back towards the steering platform. Beneath it lay one duty that he did not wish to delegate. He half-lifted Tobin's body, amazed at its lightness, and pulled it to the deck-edge. A pang of respect and pity coursed through him as he looked into the shocked face, the open, sightless, eyes. Tobin had been brave and resourceful. Without him the expedition could never have come this far. He had died in terror in a situation for which his culture and experience had not prepared him. A quarrel which he could not comprehend had destroyed him. He had owned almost nothing but his life, and now even that had been taken from him. Dawlish paused, kept looking in the face and then dropped the small black shape, pathetic in its bloodied rags, over the side and saw it disappear.

And something more went with Tobin.

Knowledge of the swamp's labyrinth.

He might never find the ironclads. And even if an attack would be successful, it would be close to impossible to find the way back to Camp Beaconsfield. But that concern must be set aside for now.

Dawlish took his place on the steering platform again, could sense that the same realisation was lying heavy on his crew. It was essential now to demonstrate confidence that he did not feel.

"Hold her steady, Egdean." The creek ahead was curving over to port and broadening. He rang for half-speed. Coal and water must be conserved.

He had been here before with Tobin and recognised the wide channel that the creek now joined. But from this point on he could rely only on guesswork and luck.

Down this channel now, and it was broadening yet further, but he was almost sure that it was not that in which the Russian ironclads sheltered. A half-mile further on it forked and he gambled on following the branch leading south-west. Then it twisted, twisted again, narrowed, forked again. He chose the branch leading to the west – sooner or later a westwards course must take him into the Russians' channel.

And all the while he was fighting a panic rising in him, an awareness that he was all but lost in this maze, that fuel and water stocks were running down by the minute.

Another fork, south of west this time – and a near disaster. It narrowed to fifty yards, was still narrowing and twisting. He could not take the chance of it petering out so that *Alpha* could not turn and must retreat at dead-slow astern. There was option but to go back. Even that was difficult, even though the creek was still forty yards wide, necessitating edging the bows successively dead-slow ahead and astern, helm over alternately from starboard to port, five heart-stopping times, until she was heading back down this treacherous waterway.

Now seeking another creek westwards, finding one comfortably wide with only the broadest of turns. And no sign yet of the third Russian patrol pinnace coming bustling towards the sounds of recent action, if indeed the sounds carried so far through the moist, heavy air.

The Russian's channel could not be far ahead now. This close to it, extreme caution was needed. Dawlish ordered revolutions reduced until *Alpha* was making little over three knots. He was all but certain now that he had been here during his reconnaissance, that the curve ahead was sweeping towards the sought-for channel.

"Take her close in towards the port bank, Egdean."

The shadows on the inner side of the bend, enveloped them. But, even then, the now-diminished flight of sparks from the gap left by the lost funnel still threatened betrayal.

"O'Malley! Maxwell! We're near now. Barrels spinning freely?"

No need to ask, just an opportunity to force calm resolution into his voice and communicate it to the Gatling teams. But his heart was pounding, his throat dray, his palms sweating. He hoped that the third Russian pinnace was patrolling somewhere far to the south. But a more immediate hazard must be confronted soon.

"Watch for the floating boom, Egdean," he said. "It's so deeply awash that we could run into it before we've spotted it. The gap we need will be over to starboard."

To his anxious ears the slow hiss of the engine's pistons sounded like a pile driver and it seemed impossible that the entire swamp was not awakened by it. He forced himself to believe his fears groundless. Remembering his revolver to be empty, he reloaded. He was short of ammunition for it and the last chamber remained empty. He snapped the weapon closed and heard the sudden chatter of an alarmed monkey troop and realised, by comparison, how quiet the engine sounded.

Luck had been with him. The junction with the anchorage channel loomed ahead. The expanse of water there seemed vast and limitless compared with the creeks astern. *Alpha* swung into it, a long curve that broadened yet further as she advanced.

And there, suddenly, were the Russians, stark against the silvery water, the yacht closest and ghostly pale, then the three colliers and the long sleek *Orlov*.

Beyond them the floating fortress.

Alexander Nevski.

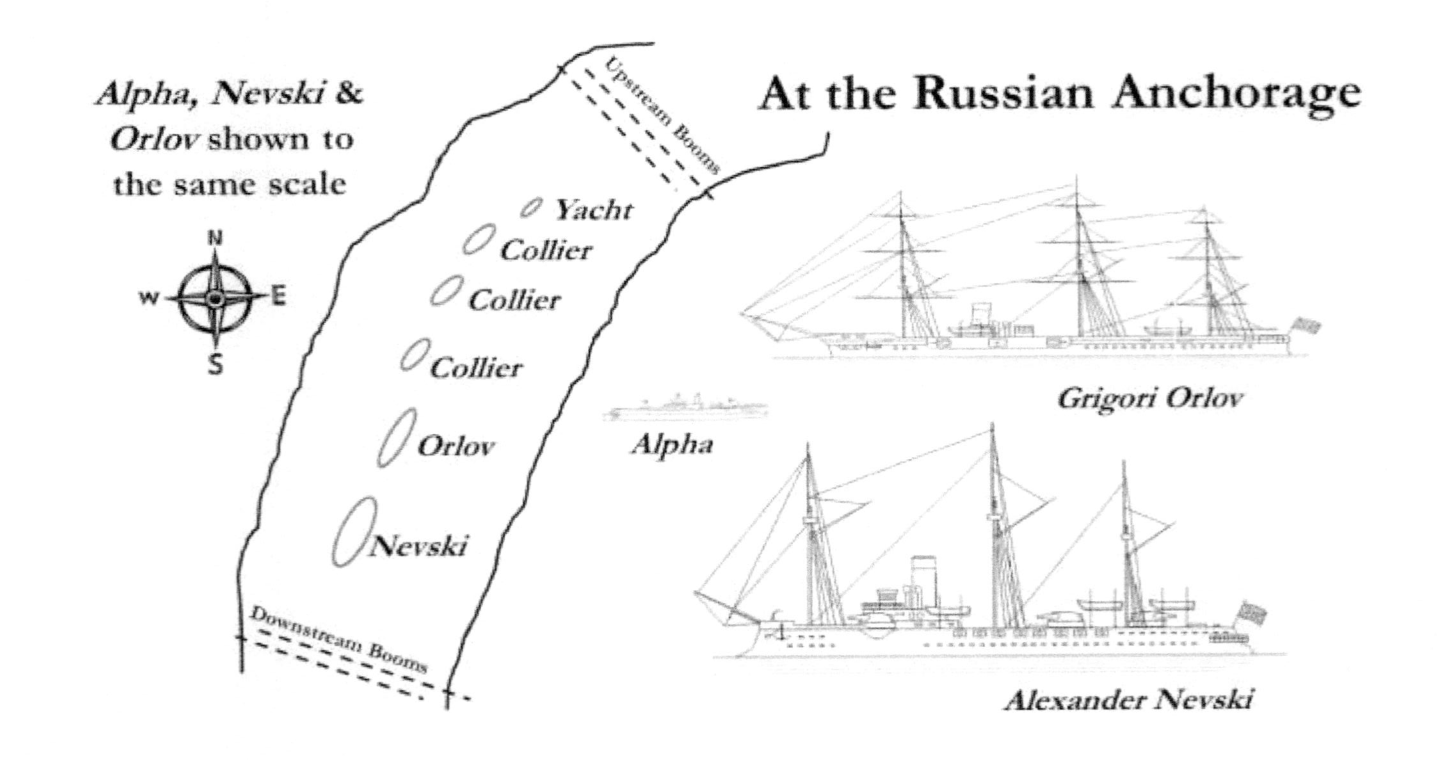

At the Russian Anchorage
Alpha, Nevski & Orlov shown to the same scale
N
W
E
S
Upstream Booms
Yacht
Collier
Collier
Collier
Orlov
Nevski
Downstream Booms
Alpha
Grigori Orlov
Alexander Nevski

Chapter 19

Dawlish heard the gun crews' sharp intake of breath and sensed their mix of awe and fear, as they glimpsed the line of ships. By his side, Egdean, who had been all but impassive through the night's carnage, whispered "Merciful God!" as he saw the *Nevski's* vast bulk and towering masts and yards. Upstream of her the *Orlov*, scarcely less intimidating. The two ironclads swung like floating fortresses in midstream, but the three colliers and the yacht lay closer to the western bank. Every bow pointed upstream to face the gently ebbing tide.

"We're going for the larger vessel, lads," Dawlish spoke loud enough for all to hear and hoped that none would detect the quaver in his voice. "She's big but she's no match for our Whiteheads."

The boom must be close ahead, awash, almost invisible. And deadly.

"Egdean! Once we're past the boom we'll run down along the far bank so the colliers will mask us. Try to approach the *Nevski* broadside on and we'll let her have it amidships. After that head downstream at top speed. And watch for the second boom."

"Aye, aye, sir."

The instructions were those agreed around that rough table at the camp. His eyes scanned the water ahead, intent on finding the boom before the bows crunched into it.

No sign of life aboard the ships ahead, though he did not doubt that lookouts were posted. No lights winked against the black hulls and, best of all, no searchlights were sweeping the anchorage. He strained his eyes to detect the boom.

"Gatlings! Hold your fire until I give the word! If there are searchlights, I want them blinded, you understand?"

"There it is, sir," Egdean said.

It was just possible to pick out the twin black barriers that stretched parallel, in shallow arcs, across the channel, undulating with each ripple. No option now but to emerge from the shadows and cross the channel to the gap in the boom close to the opposite bank. The urge to order full speed was strong but Dawlish resisted it. With luck, *Alpha's* slight mass might appear to an observer as drifting vegetation.

"We'll maintain dead slow," Dawlish's voice was hushed, "and there! There's the gap, right in near the bank."

Across the bright, open, water, crawling at walking speed. It lasted aeons.

The moonlight revealed how the booms were secured. The nearer row of logs was bound with chains to a stout pile driven into the creek-bed some thirty yards from the mangrove. The downstream row, separated from the first by twenty yards, ran out of the water and into the vegetation, where it was no doubt securely anchored. Together, the two barriers blocked any direct progress downstream.

"You can do it, Egdean. Your ship."

"Aye, aye, sir."

Egdean manoeuvred the *Alpha* into the gap between the shore and the termination of the upstream row. He waited until the bows were abreast of the pile before he swung the helm over. The low speed made the response sluggish. The turn could not be made in one smooth motion. The knife-edge stem bumped gently into the downstream barrier and the boat strained against it.

"Half-speed astern."

Webb, the appointed messenger, scurried from the starboard sponson to relay the order to Hickley in the engine room. It seemed an eternity before the screw reversed and pulled the craft slowly astern towards the mangrove. The current was weak so close to the turn of tide, but it was enough to begin to drag the vessel parallel to the booms.

"Now ahead. Dead Slow."

Alpha paused, then nosed forward, hemmed in to either side by the parallel rows of logs. Now the entire width of the channel must be traversed at a crawl. At the eastern bank another slow speed turn would be needed to get around the extremity of the downstream row and into open water. Egdean held the craft on a steady course between the logs, so deeply awash as to be scarcely visible. All other eyes were directed towards the Russian ships.

The torpedo boat was almost in midstream when a 'whoosh' sounded from the undergrowth on the shore ahead and spark-showering rocket arced into the sky. There must be a lookout post on the bank. Even as the rocket burst in a red ball, another was soaring after it.

In instant reaction to the alarm, a searchlight stabbed a brilliant finger from the *Nevski*, just missing the *Orlov* and probing the bank a hundred yards off *Alpha's* bow. It swung out from the mangrove and the ellipse it cast on the water began to crawl towards the boom.

"Hold fire!" Dawlish called to the gunners. The range, six hundred yards or more, was too long for Gatling accuracy.

A second beam joined the first, and then a third, this last from the *Orlov.* They too began to sweep upstream. Then the first found the end of the boom ahead and began moving back along it in short jumps.

The urge to increase speed was strong, to run through that icy light towards the boom's gap, but a collision with the logs at any significant velocity would rip the frail hull open. The only option was to maintain low revolutions.

"Steady as she goes, Egdean! Dead Slow!"

Dawlish's hope now was that the Russian gunners might also be inaccurate at this range. The yacht and colliers would mask *Alpha* from the *Nevski's* and the *Orlov's* fire once she had passed the boom and headed back across the channel.

But now, with eighty yards to go to reach the gap at the banh ahead, the first searchlight found *Alpha* and held her. She jolted against the downstream boom as Egdean threw up his arm to shield his face. Half-blinded, he lost control for an instant. The current held the craft against the logs. She grated forward along them for several yards before Egdean shook her free and resumed course midway between the booms. The second beam reached her now, and then the third.

The bank ahead was still distant when orange flames rippled along the *Orlov's* flank, four light-calibre guns flashing in succession into life. Two more spat from the *Nevski*, three or five-pounders by their reports.

The *Orlov's* shells fell short, but well in line – one degree more of elevation would have done for *Alpha*. Four white plumes skidded across the water in the searchlights' beams and, before they collapsed, the *Nevski's* rounds were striking closer still. The torpedo boat was still crawling forward when the next salvo fell. The gun-layers' aim was better now, for one shell landed upstream, close enough for its fountain to shower *Alpha's* deck and bridge with its falling spray.

One of the beams had tracked away, was illuminating the boom's gap at the bank ahead. Some Russian officer had realised that the best change of destroying the torpedo craft was to catch her during her slow turn there. This must be the end, Dawlish realised. Passage through that gap must be as unhurried as that at the western end if there was to be any hope of getting through. *Alpha* would be manoeuvring there for two or three minutes and the ironclads' gun layers had already found the range.

The Russians' light weapons barked into life again. Several shells screamed close overhead and others smashed into the water just yards astern. The gap was still long seconds away.

Dawlish tore his gaze from the warships. A fast dash straight ahead would bury *Alpha's* bows in the mangrove. Some of the crew might be able to scramble away into cover before the shells tore her apart. The Russians would find them, maybe capture them, but even then they might still have a chance of life. He owed his crew that.

And for me – what?

His hand was hovering over the telegraph, about to ring for full speed when he heard a sudden shout.

"Look there, sir! Look there." Maxwell was yelling from the starboard sponson and pointing down.

And the booms did not seem as close together as they had been.

No! Not now they don't, by God! Not now!

Dawlish grabbed Egdean's arm and pointed to the logs.

"Look! They're pulling apart!"

It's no optical illusion. The distance separating them was still increasing. The tide's mild ebb was carrying away the downstream boom. He looked astern, saw that there too the chained logs were arcing away.

"Half Speed Astern!" Dawlish pulled telegraph handle. "They've hit their own boom. They've smashed it! We're through!"

A gap, a large and ever-widening gap, had formed astern and it was broadening every second as the sections of the broken downstream boom curled away from each other. *Alpha* shuddered to a halt, water foaming past her sides, then thrust astern, leaving the searchlight beams still edging towards the bank and losing her in the darkness. Another salvo lashed the water ahead of her now-retreating bows.

Now *Alpha* churned astern into the open water below the remaining, upstream, boom and her bows were swinging over to point diagonally across the channel and towards the yacht. The searchlights paused, confused, then swept back to seek their lost prey.

"Full Speed Ahead!" Dawlish ground the telegraph handle forward. "Run across the yacht's bows, Egdean! Then downstream in her lee, and along the colliers' too."

The beams were creeping back but had not yet found *Alpha* as she raced towards the yacht.

Then, suddenly, the beams were gone, blocked, as were the *Nevski's* and *Orlov's* weapons also, by the colliers and yacht. Freed of the blinding beams, the torpedo craft drove through the semi-darkness and ran under the bowsprit jutting from the yacht's bow. A half-dozen pistol shots cracked from her deck as Egdean threw *Alpha's* helm over and streaked along the white flank. None found a mark and soon the torpedo boat was past, driving on to run into the shelter offered by the collier ahead.

"Maxwell! O'Malley!" Dawlish shouted to the sponson gunners. "Hold fire until I give the word. On my word only, mark you! Then the searchlights!"

Past the first collier now.

The moored vessels were still hiding *Nevski* and *Orlov* from sight. But observers on those ironclads must have seen *Alpha* disappear at speed behind the yacht and guess that she was racing towards them. Now, in succession, the searchlights were swinging over to illuminate a huge ellipse just astern of the last of the colliers. If *Alpha* was to reach the *Nevski* on this course, she must charge though that great bright pool on which all the smaller-calibre Russian weapons must already be aiming.

Unless . . .

One chance, a gamble that could buy a minute only. But that might be enough.

I'll take it.

Dawlish reached for the torpedo-firing levers. A toggle safety catch held them down to guard against accidental discharge. He forced the catch up against its spring and exposed the twin handles. They now lay extended towards him and could be raised into the vertical 'Ready' position without activating the discharge mechanism. Pushing them forward through another thirty degrees would open the valves in the compressed air lines. That short push would conduct pressure to the rear of the tubes and hurl the torpedoes into the water ahead.

Now that the moment of destiny was upon him, he felt calm.

Twenty feet of water separated *Alpha* from the side of the second collier as she ran alongside. Confused shouting sounded overhead and a few ineffectual small-arms shots rattled from the deck.

"Egdean! Hard over to port when we reach the stern. Then hard over to starboard to bring us along the next one's side!"

Alpha was past the collier's counter as Egdean threw the helm over and she skidded into the tight turn. Straightening, she ran between the two colliers and on for forty yards with open water – dark water – ahead. Then into the turn to starboard, running parallel to the last of the colliers.

She was on the inside of the channel's curve now and the *Orlov* was visible just off her starboard bow and the *Nevski* beyond.

And their searchlights had not shifted yet, were still illuminating the area between the last collier's stern and the far bank, their gunners tensed to blast the attacker when it sped into it.

A minute passed, a long, precious minute of darkness. Now *Alpha* was drawing away from the collier side and heading diagonally across the channel, prepared to sweep around to starboard to head for the *Nevski's* flank. Her speed could not be less than sixteen knots, despite the loss of draught occasioned by the lost funnel. She was still undetected and –

It could not last.

The searchlight in the *Orlov's* foretop was swinging over, sweeping but not yet finding.

"Starboard Gatling! Go for the light!"

Maxwell and Webb swung their weapon over. It hammered into life, six rounds, pause, six more, pause, five or six again, without effect. And then it jammed. The crew in the port sponson could not bring their Gatling to bear. Until the starboard jam was cleared, the searchlights could not be blinded. The *Nevski's* beams had swung across also and were sweeping like the *Orlov's*.

Tongues of flame flashed from the ironclads' hull ports. Deprived of an illuminated target, the Russians were firing anyway. Falling shells were throwing up white cascades at any point where an over-imaginative gunner mistook shadows on the water for the darting *Alpha*. Then one icy beam separated itself from the others and slewed towards her. It held her for a brief, dazzling, moment before Egdean's manoeuvring shook her free, driving her into protective darkness before a close salvo mangled the waters astern.

The helm was over, carrying the torpedo boat into a long curving turn to starboard that would bring her bow-on towards the *Nevski's* side. A shout of triumph told that Webb's pincers had extracted the jammed round and a moment later the starboard Gatling was chattering again. Accuracy was impossible as the torpedo boat shook and quivered like a crazed animal beneath the gun crew's feet but they still attempting to reach the searchlight in *Orlov's* foretop. Its beam caught again, and held for long seconds before Egdean's weavings shook the battered craft free. She pounded on and her broad turn had brought the *Nevski* just off her starboard bow, opening a line of fire for the port Gatling also. Now it too stammered into action, seeking the searchlight in the larger warship's foretop.

Alpha was in darkness again with only the pale white of her foaming bow wave to betray her. Racing plumes of spray marked shells hitting the water's surface and yet, by some miracle, still not close. *Orlov's* beam was searching astern, but *Nevski's* two searchlights were roaming and probing ahead.

The *Nevski* loomed ahead, black, massive. Dawlish braced himself against the bridge-screen, planted his feet apart and grasped both firing levers. Egdean had positioned *Alpha* so that the ironclad's twin funnels, lined up to looked like one, were dead ahead. Another half-minute's grace might yet yield success.

But cool heads in the Russian tops had realised that their beams had no hope of finding and holding the speeding *Alpha.* Instead, one beam, then another, shifted to flood the water close to the *Nevski's* flank with light. Attack must mean running through it. Dawlish screwed up his eyes against the brilliance of the beams and held his grasp tight on the firing levers.

Now ploughing into the illuminated ellipse. The great ironclad was straight ahead.

"Hold her steady, Egdean."

A half-cable's length, a hundred yards . . .

The ironclads' three and five-pounders were now blazing at almost point-blank range and the waters to port and starboard boiled with their shells. The port Gatling had jammed but Maxwell, in the starboard sponson, was still trying to blind a searchlight. Dawlish felt the deck shudder beneath him and a rush of sound and searing air blasted past him from somewhere aft. He knew that a shell had found a berth on some point on his craft but he did not glance back. The speed seemed undiminished. He grasped the levers tighter.

Eighty yards . . .

He heard the sharp rattle of the Nordenvelts in the Russians' fighting tops between the slower barks of the guns in the hull ports but his eyes were riveted on the precipice-like target that was growing ever larger. He heard Egdean shouting something about watching the port beam, but he ignored it, even though from the corner of his eye he sensed O'Malley swinging his jammed Gatling to port while the loader stilled struggled to free it. His knuckles whitened on the launching levers.

Sixty yards . . .

The *Nevski* filled his whole vision now, a gigantic, sloping wall, tongues of flame flickering from its ports and half-obscured by drifting smoke.

Fifty yards . . .

Discharge was a half-second away when the third and last of the Russian steam pinnaces came bursting into the light from port, having rounded the *Nevski's* stern from some mooring on the opposite side.

It smashed into the *Alpha* a few feet ahead her stern, its bows lifting by a full foot as they tore into the splintering mahogany, spinning the torpedo boat on her axis at the moment that Dawlish was pushing the firing levers forward against the last resistance. The pinnace's impact knocked him to the deck. He twisted, saw the *Nevski* spin out of his view and heard the gasping sound of the two torpedoes being expelled on a harmless course parallel to their intended target.

Alpha seemed to remain locked to the picket boat for an aeon. Both craft spun in a deadly embrace, so close to the *Nevski's* side that the gunners at her ports were unable to depress their weapons enough to bear. O'Malley's Gatling was in action again, its spinning barrels cutting down the three-pounder crew in the pinnace's bows and giving Egdean sufficient respite to shake the *Alpha* free by frantic manoeuvring. The starboard Gatling could not bear on the pinnace but was spraying fire towards the *Nevski's* hull ports.

Dazed and sick with anger, frustration and outright terror, Dawlish staggered to his feet. He dragged out his revolver, loosed off shots towards figures on the pinnace. The torpedo boat pulled away, limping.

Escape was all that mattered now.

"Head for the lower boom!"

"It's going to be slow, sir." Egdean voice was hushed. "This poor old boat is finished."

The last remaining Gatling rounds served to keep the pinnace at a distance as the *Alpha* crawled under the shelter of the *Nevski's* stern. Her speed built up slowly but it seemed impossible to attain more than a third of her earlier maximum. Even now, momentarily protected by the ironclad's bulk from its fire and searchlights, the injured boat must still endure a rain of small-arms fire from the decks above. The port sponson's weapon engaged the pinnace until its rotating stack of barrels fell silent with its last round.

Maxwell and Webb had raised their Gatling to maximum elevation, and were probing for the *Nevski's* mizzen fighting-top as the torpedo boat lurched downstream, out from beneath her stern. And that elevation was still too low and its stuttering bursts of found no target. *Alpha's* course had now exposed her port flank and a Nordenvelt in the top raked her port sponson. O'Malley collapsed across his weapon and lay still and Smithson, his loader, tumbled overboard, blood bursting for his chest.

Alpha was in open water now and crawling towards the downstream booms. The ending of the runs of her two misdirected torpedoes provided a diversion. They had passed across the channel and impacted among the mangrove on the western bank. Columns of water, mud and foliage climbed skyward and the ironclads' searchlights slewed over to probe the area of the explosions. Only this distraction allowed the crippled *Alpha* to reach to within a hundred yards of the downstream booms before the lights came sweeping back to find her. She was down by the stern now, and the after decking was almost awash, but the speed had somehow built up to perhaps five knots. Dawlish ordered Egdean to take her for the western, starboard, shore to find the gap at the boom's end. The possibility of navigating with success into the passage between the floating rows of logs was slight, but it was the only hope.

A searchlight beam swept past, illuminated *Alpha* for an instant and then outran her, lost her again in darkness. Then it paused, moved back. Even as it hesitated, Egdean threw the helm over. The sluggish craft had just begun to turn when the beam caught her again.

The salvo that followed was accurate, deadly accurate. All the shells but one straddled *Alpha*, but that one round struck home in the already mangled stern and the orange flash of its detonation wrecked the steering quadrant. The wheel spun uselessly in Egdean's hands and the now-directionless craft crashed into the boom. Her lifted bows slid over it and hung there as she came to a halt. The impact flung Dawlish and Egdean from their feet. They were struggling to rise as a Nordenvelt opened from *Nevski*, a four-barrel ripple. Egdean dragged Dawlish back down.

Splinters flew from the deck and sides as the volley smashed into them. A pause, then another ripple. A round ricocheted off the bridge-screen and a yell, cut off, told that someone, Maxwell or Webb, had been struck down in the starboard sponson. Small white fountains rose and collapsed to mark the fall of three or five-pound shells. At any moment one or more would hit the stranded boat. It was imperative to leave her, drop into the water, drift downstream.

"Egdean! Get Hickley and Barrow on deck. I'll see to –"

The shell punching into the casing above the engine room cut him off. In the instant before it exploded, he saw shattered fragments of wood flying from the impact. Dawlish threw himself down beside Egdean, arm across his face, heard the shell's detonation and then, worse, far worse, the boiler breaching and clouds of scalding steam erupting from it. He glanced up, saw the cloud billowing skywards. Little remained of *Alpha* aft of the wrecked casing. He hoped that Hickley and Barrow had died instantly.

No more firing from the Russian ships.

Silence now.

Silence and fear and bitter awareness of failure, of lives sacrificed for nothing.

The chugging of the approaching pinnace broke that silence. Its searchlight held *Alpha* in its beam, probed into the wreckage, searched for signs of life. Dawlish spun his revolver cylinder, checking for live rounds. There was one left. He realised, with racing heart, that one last way of escape was left to him. He had often visualised such a moment and weighed its merits with brother-officers in relaxed after-dinner discussions. The choice had always seemed an easy one. Now it was unthinkable. Life, even at this extremity, was too sweet.

The pinnace drew closer still and yet Dawlish dared not raise his head to watch. The searchlight was now bathing the entire foreship in intense light, but the bridge-screen's shadow still hid himself and Egdean.

"I've one round left," Dawlish whispered. "I'm saving it. I'll make a break as soon as that bloody light shifts. I'll drop over the side and let the tide carry me downstream."

"I'll be with you, sir."

They crouched ready, poised to break from cover, but the transfixing beam did not shift. The illumination grew yet stronger Any movement from shelter would be akin to suicide. They heard the nearing throb of the pinnace's engine and a voice calling what must be commands in Russian. Seconds later the craft bumped alongside and a half-dozen armed seamen stormed on board. Their bearing and shouts left no doubt that they were demanding submission. Dawlish pushed his revolver and its single round into the space at the base of the telegraph's pedestal.

Escape was impossible. No option but surrender.

"Get up Egdean. Slowly. Put your hands up."

They heaved themselves to their feet and stood exposed in the searchlight beam, arms lifted above their heads. A voice yelled at them and a figure gestured to them to come down. They descended with caution, conscious that any sudden moment could be their last. Two Russian seamen were looking into the crater where the shell and boiler had exploded. They were shaking their heads. No sign of life there.

Dawlish glanced into the starboard sponson, saw Maxwell crumpled lifeless there, half of his head blown away. Webb lay on his back beside him, moaning, blood oozing through the fingers clutched to his chest.

Three seamen levelled bayonets at Egdean and at Dawlish and motioned them to move. He held his ground. A young officer had jumped across.

"Parlez-vous français?" Dawlish shouted to him. He had read somewhere that most educated Russians did, even conversed in it among themselves.

The officer nodded.

Dawlish pointed to Webb. "Cet homme est blessé. Gravement blessé. Je ne descendrai pas de ce bateau sans lui."

"Il va se faire soigner. Croyez-moi, monsieur." No warmth, but no personal animosity either in the Russian's voice, a professional addressing a respected enemy. He turned and shouted back to the pinnace. Moments later a seaman returned with a blanket.

Webb was moaning as four seamen carried him, slung in the blanket, across to the pinnace. Dawlish reached out to him as they passed, grasped his limp hand, saw that the wounded man was beyond recognising him.

"Je suis seul responsible," he said to the Russian officer. If there was to be retribution, it should fall on himself alone. He pointed to Egdean. "Cet homme ne faisait que suivre les ordres."

"Vous pouvez expliquer que sur le *Nevski*." The officer jerked his head to tell him to step across.

Now time to stumble with Egdean over the splintered deck where his crew had served him so well and so fruitlessly. They stepped across. Three Russian bodies lay around the three-pounder in the pinnace's bow. Dawlish was not surprised when one of the seamen cuffed him when he was thrust against the low superstructure and held there, at bayonet point, with Egdean.

The pinnace chugged in reverse for twenty yards before turning away. Dawlish had a last glimpse of *Alpha*. She was a shattered wreck, all but unrecognisable as the once-trim beauty that had raced with such elan across Killary's waters. Only the boom beneath her forefoot supported her now but she was slithering from it, her stern already submerged. The bow was rising clear and she settled, shuddered and slid from sight. She took with her Dawlish's last hope, his revolver and his last remaining round.

The unharmed *Nevski* lay ahead, as potent as before to wreak havoc with her consort on the world's oceans.

So much loss for nothing.

All my responsibility.

Chapter 20

The pinnace nudged against the curving precipice of the *Nevski's* side. A ladder led to the open entry port above. The Russian officer gestured to it.

"Après vous, Messieurs les Anglais." He smiled, a man proud that he knew of the mad courtesy at Fontenoy.

Dawlish did not stir, did not respond.

"Pas un Anglais alors?"

No answer possible. Admitting that he was an Englishman would not save him. Topcliffe had been clear that prisoners would be disowned and he had accepted that. Now that the reality was upon him, he felt baffled and helpless.

The Russian shrugged and spoke to his men. The nearest caught Dawlish by the shoulder and pushed him against the ladder. He began to climb the tumblehome. The ascent seemed endless.

Suspended hurricane lamps cast a pool of yellow light at the entry port. At its outer fringes he could discern a half-circle of armed seamen or marines in white uniforms, their bayoneted rifles levelled at him. The smell of gunsmoke hung heavy in the air. He hoisted himself to the deck and paused, uncertain whether to advance further.

"Step forward please, sir." The words English, so too the intonation.

He obeyed, but a sound from behind caused him to glance back. Two marines were slipping in from the cover of the bulwarks to left and right, their bayonets directed at his spine. They halted, blocking his retreat. A figure came towards him from the soft darkness ahead, right hand extended in greeting.

Dawlish half-expected to be confronted by some heavily-bearded and elderly officer. Instead, he was facing a tall, slim, clean-shaven man of his own age. He wore no uniform – indeed the white open-necked shirt above equally immaculate linen trousers looked like silk rather than cotton. The curling hair above his chiselled features was golden, the expression pleasant and welcoming. Despite the dead, humid warmth, his brow carried just the faintest film of perspiration. Dawlish caught a distinct whiff of eau-de-cologne.

It could do no harm to shake his hand.

"Prince Vladimir Mikhailovich Krestovski, my dear sir." His English had only the slightest betrayal of a foreign accent. His handshake was firm but from the reluctance of Dawlish's grip he seemed to sense his unease. "Allow me to be the first congratulate you and your gallant crew on such a courageous attack, sir. The spirit of Balaclava is indeed not dead."

Dawlish kept his face impassive, hoped that he showed no flicker of recognition of the heroic failure in the Crimea. Better to stay silent, to let this man talk and get his measure.

"And your name, sir?"

No answer.

"I can understand your reluctance," Krestovski said. "I deem it an honour nonetheless to welcome a gentleman of such obvious courage on board one of His Imperial Majesty's ships." He smiled. "We might have wished to meet in a more pleasant circumstances but, that aside, I'm proud to offer you whatever hospitality is at my disposal in this God-forsaken spot."

He might have been some rich young amateur yachtsman on a summer cruise. But there was also an air of command about him, of lordly assurance and authority that underlay that benign impression. And because of it, Dawlish knew he could not trust him. This man was dangerous.

Yet mention of hospitality had raised hope. The role of chivalrous foe might include humanity, however feigned.

Dawlish pointed behind him. "There's is a wounded man down there whose life isn't worth ten minutes' purchase if he doesn't receive medical attention. Dragging him up that ladder will kill him."

"My dear fellow!" Krestovski's accent was almost, but not quite, that of a cultivated English gentleman. "How very thoughtless of me! My deepest apologies! I should have considered your wounded before. The poor wretch shall have immediate succour."

He turned and called out in Russian, exhibiting an almost perfect profile as he did. Feet scurried beyond the circle of light. The haste seemed to please him.

"The poor fellow will have expert attention," he said to Dawlish. "Your mind can be at rest, sir. And now allow me to introduce you to your adversaries."

He turned and beckoned to two officers behind him. In his gesture Dawlish detected not so much easy contempt as an unconscious assumption of superiority. Both men were bearded and middle-aged. They were sweating profusely and almost bursting from white uniforms stiff with gold braid. Krestovski introduced them.

"Admiral Pyotr Fedorovich Rudnev, Commander of His Imperial Majesty's Oceanic Raiding Squadron."

The older of the two officers bowed stiffly. His grey forked beard extended almost to his waist. His eyes were lifted towards Dawlish's, then dropped again. There might have been a hint of sullen desperation in their lifeless depths.

No handshake, but no suggestion of hostility either. This admiral had also lost men this night, an armed pinnace too, and the *Nevski* had escaped destruction by a fluke. But he was a professional like himself, Dawlish recognised. A man who knew the hazards of naval warfare and accepted them without personal animus.

Krestovski's tone had something like tolerant mockery in it as the second officer, unhealthy-looking and cadaverous, bowed in turn. "And this is Captain Andrei Nikolaiovich Kokoktsov, commanding His Imperial Majesty's ironclad *Alexander Nevski*. A most gallant officer indeed."

The prince turned to Dawlish. "In the present circumstances, I've no doubt that you're reluctant to introduce yourself? No, don't even try to apologise. I can understand. But I must address you somehow. Perhaps Smith or Jones or Robinson?" He spoke as if it were a joke.

Dawlish did not respond. His mind felt numb, unsure of what, or what not, to say. Despair threatened. He could not imagine how this grotesque pantomime might end, how he could make the best of it. But he had he had pledged his honour and he would not yield.

"For the time being, sir, perhaps you would be happy to be known as... as... let us say Smith?" Krestovski paused, amused by his own words. "Mr. Smith, of no fixed abode, of no steady employment and of no known nationality. I think that will suffice. Don't you?"

Better to humour this man who was pleased with his own diplomatic niceties of undeclared warfare.

"Mr. Smith appreciates your delicacy, sir." Dawlish bowed.

Krestovski's tone was curt when he spoke in Russian to the admiral and captain. They disappeared aft. They were educated men, must speak French, Dawlish thought, but knowledge of English would be less probable. That must be why the prince had chosen to address him in it. He glanced behind him and saw that, despite the urbanity of the exchange, the two marines' bayonet points were still inches from his back. Unconcerned, Krestovski reached into his trouser pocket and withdrew an exquisite gold humidor, sized to carry two or three cigars.

He opened it and reached it to Dawlish. The lamp overhead caught the flash of an emerald on one finger.

"Best Havanas, Mr. Smith," he smiled. "A good cigar may prove welcome while we wait for your men to come on board. Would you be so good as to look over there? They're rigging a sling so that the wounded unfortunate can be hoisted aboard in all comfort."

Dawlish accepted a cigar and stooped for the light that flared between Krestovski's cupped hands. The first taste of the smoke was soothing and he drew deeply. The prince applied another lucifer to the Havana clenched between his own flawless teeth.

"I doubt if I should have survived in this cheerless place without the solace of tobacco," he said. "If nothing else, the mosquitoes seem to have a marked aversion to a decent cigar."

Egdean's head appeared at the entry port, relief on his face when he saw Dawlish. He mounted the last rungs. Two seamen converged on him and penned him against the bulwark with their bayonets.

"Have they hurt you, sir?" he called to Dawlish.

"No, Jerry!" Dawlish used his first name, hoped that Egdean would get the hint. No surnames. "Stay quiet! Don't provoke them!"

"Wise words, Mr. Smith," Krestovski said. "That fellow looks quite truculent. A bad loser, no letting bygones be bygones there. He'll have to go to the cell, I'm afraid. He'll be properly treated. You needn't concern yourself on that score."

Dawlish's mind was racing now. He could not to let despair overwhelm him. The reception so far had been better than he could ever have hoped. The prince – and how should he address him to maintain the air of chivalry? Your Highness? Your Excellency? – had chosen to treat him as a gallant enemy, for now at least. There must be same way of turning that to advantage.

He drew again on his cigar and resolved to match courtesy with courtesy.

"Your humanity does you credit, Your Excellency," he said. "Were the roles reversed then I hope that I might display similar nobility of spirit."

Krestovski waved the compliment aside. Webb was being hoisted aboard now, swinging from a line slung on a yard. The pallet he lay on hovered over the bulwark for a moment, was then drawn in and lowered to the deck.

Webb was dying, his head lolling, blood dribbling from his mouth with each laboured, wheezing breath. Disregarding the bayonets at his back, Dawlish, pity-filled, moved to him. Webb's eyes flickered open, gave no sign of recognition, closed again.

Dawlish looked towards Krestovski's splendid profile and saw that he was viewing the injured man with narrowed eyes and obvious interest. Not with the sympathy which his earlier words had implied. Webb was an object and his value was being assessed.

In that instant, Dawlish knew that he would have to establish his position if the prince was not to exploit the situation. Now, immediately. When he spoke, his words were not loud enough to block from his ears the sound of futile suffering which he himself had brought about.

"You should know, Your Excellency, that my crew of knew nothing of these ships' existence until twelve hours ago," he said. "I did. They didn't."

"You expect me to believe that, Mr. Smith?"

"You have my word on it, Your Excellency."

"The word of a pirate, Mr. Smith?"

"The word of a gentleman. I tell you that the responsibility for tonight's action is mine, not my crews'. And as a gentleman I'm honour-bound to tell you nothing more."

He looked Krestovski straight in the eye.

"My men and I are at your mercy, sir. I ask it only for my men."

Krestovski laid an arm on his shoulder. The gesture was almost brotherly. His voice was gentle. "That's understood, my dear fellow! The delicacy of your sentiments does you credit as a gentleman." He paused. "And as an officer."

He raised one eyebrow and smiled, pleased at scoring this last point. Dawlish did not react and stooped towards the dying man. He could speak only hollow words of encouragement, uncertain if Webb could even hear him. Then he stood back and seamen lifted the pallet and carried it away.

I did it to him. I failed him, him and all the others. I failed myself.

Krestovski shook his head. "A sad end for a brave man, I fear. Our good Father Sergei will attend him to the last. Not of the same persuasion, I suspect, but it might give the poor wretch some comfort at the end."

"If I might ask a favour, sir," Dawlish said "That man there," he pointed towards Egdean, "he's of a religious turn. He would have some words to help the man."

"It shall be done, sir!" Krestovski's hand was exerting a reassuring pressure on Dawlish's shoulder, "That man shall comfort him. But now," he began to propel him aft, "I'm sure a glass of brandy would not go amiss before you retire. A cabin's being readied for your occupation. A fever vacated it not four days since, but you'll sleep none the worse for that."

The vessel's vast scale impressed, intimidated, as they moved aft along the deck. Towering masts, rising solidly towards the fighting tops that carried those terrible arc-lights and Nordenvelts. The enormous flat-sided twin funnels. The battery of rapid-fire five-pounders at ports in the high bulwarks, the smell of burned powder hanging heavily around them. Then the curved iron wall of the midships barbette and the ship-killer that it sheltered. Beyond it, abaft the mizzenmast, the fourth barbette stood like a metallic fortress. The wicked muzzle of its forty-six ton breech-loader seemed to mock Dawlish's failure as he passed.

The wardroom was close and stuffy despite the open skylight. The furnishings were luxurious and in a corner an oil-lamp flickered before an icon. A half-dozen paraffin globes shed light over a table strewn with books, magazines and two chessboards, their disorder evidence of the surprise of *Alpha's* attack. A steward approached with a tray but Krestovski insisted on taking a bottle and glasses from it and on pouring brandy himself for Dawlish. He then busied himself, in French, with introducing a number of officers who stood by. None attempted to enter the conversation. Dawlish surmised that few, if any, spoke English. Several, including Admiral Rudnev and the *Nevski's* captain, excused themselves and left. There was an air of resentful formality that Dawlish sensed was directed against Krestovski rather than himself. The man's position here seemed ever more equivocal.

"You are perhaps thinking, Mr. Smith, that we Russians don't know how to celebrate a victory." Krestovski drained his glass. "But you must see what a fearsome place this swamp is. Its shadow lies over us. It has been the death of too many good men. Indeed, had we not brought an extra hand for every three members of the crew needed we would have been severely under-manned by now. Mind you, the excellence of the ventilating provisions has assisted somewhat. But of course, Mr. Smith," he winked as if sharing a secret, "you probably know that already. I suspect that you know as much about the design of this ship as we do ourselves."

Conscious that in his exhausted state he could be too-easily tripped up, Dawlish did not answer. But it took an effort not to register surprise when Krestovski continued.

"And speaking of design, Mr. Smith. Doesn't Mr. Samuel White down in his yard in Cowes continue to surpass himself, year after year? Your vessel was a case in point. Who would have thought that playing with toy boats in water tanks would yield such refinement and speed? And that he should have mounted a locomotive boiler so effectively in so light a hull. Splendid! Truly splendid"

Dawlish kept his face impassive.

"I was once a prospective customer myself for one of White's craft," Krestovski said. "For quite pacific recreational purposes, I might add. I'd come down from Oxford, Magdalen College. I had good friends in England and intended to spend a year or two there before going back to Russia. Then my father died and I had to return home. But the contact with White's yard proved useful. I still receive confidential reports from one of the trusted employees there. So that boat of yours, Mr. Smith, I'll warrant it was one of those wonder vessels that White's been building in such secrecy for the British Admiralty. Am I correct, Mr. Smith?"

Dawlish did not answer.

All Topcliffe's elaborate secrecy had been set at naught.

"And the Cowes regattas," Krestovski said "What happy times! Most especially my last. I was a guest then of your most hospitable Prince of Wales. He's quite a splendid fellow though I rather think that his brother Alfred has a little more intellect." He paused and when he spoke again his voice was cold. "And a member, of course, of the same profession as yourself."

Alfred, Duke of Edinburgh, married to a daughter of Czar. The present threat of war must make that relationship difficult. And more. He was a serving officer of the Royal Navy.

"A profession, Your Excellency?" Dawlish attempted nonchalance, knew he failed. "But you summed me up yourself already, did you not? A man of no steady employment and of no known nationality?"

"I'm fatiguing you, Mr. Smith." Krestovski again laid an arm on his shoulder, affability restored. "Your berth is ready. I'll detain you from your rest no longer."

He escorted Dawlish through dark and humid passages to a small cabin, the accommodation of some middle-ranking officer, little different to that on a major ship of the Royal Navy. A cot fore and aft beneath an open scuttle, too small for Dawlish's shoulders to squeeze through, defined the compartment's width. A stand to the right carried a soap dish, a bowl and a ewer of water. Beside it a carafe of water with a drinking glass. A silver-framed photograph of a kind-looking woman and three children, still stood on the small writing desk to the left. She was a widow with orphans now, though she did not know it A single glass-shielded candle burned on a gimballed mounting above it, illuminating a small icon and a shelf of books. White duck trousers and a white shirt were laid on the bunk beside cotton underwear and a neat pile of towels. A new pair of canvas shoes protruded from beneath the cot.

"Just cast off your soiled clothes, Mr. Smith," Krestovski said. "I've had some articles set aside from my own wardrobe for you. We're about the same build."

"I'm again in your debt, Your Excellency."

"There's one last point. A sensitive one, Mr. Smith. Two sentries will be at your door and their orders will be to kill you if you try to break loose. An unpleasant but necessary precaution, which you'll understand and forgive. And now, good night!"

He closed the door behind him and left Dawlish alone.

Chapter 21

Dawlish sponged himself clean, drew on the fresh underwear. Then he lay down on the cot, resolved to block out the present. His situation was desperate, but he knew that his brain was no less exhausted than his body. Rest was essential if he was to confront Krestovski on equal terms. Years of long watches and of rest in acute discomfort had taught him how to will himself into slumber. His sleep was dreamless.

He awoke as he hit the deck of the still-dark cabin. He flailed with his arms and legs, seeking to escape from what he thought must be a nightmare. But now strong hands were grasping his wrists and ankles, forcing them down, holding him immobile. He flailed his head, saw dim light from the passageway at the open door. A dot glowed and faded and glowed against the dark figure silhouetted there and drawing on a cigar.

"Don't move, Mr. Smith." Krestovski's voice, as calm as it had been hours earlier.

He moved towards Dawlish, said something in Russian, and two other hands clamped his head on either side and held it still.

"I bear you no ill will," Krestovski said. "But you must understand raison d'état"

Then he drew on his cigar again – the tip was bright orange now – and touched it to Dawlish's left cheek, just above the beard-line.

His body arched and he tried not to scream. The pain was intense and he smelled the odour of smouldering flesh and stubble. Krestovski removed the cigar, drew on it to make it glow more brightly, then held it against the cheek again.

Agony transformed drowsy confusion into full consciousness. Dawlish was gasping now in a reality more terrible than any nightmare. He had been on his guard against this man since meeting him, had known that he would be questioned further, but he had expected that it would be in an urbane, even chivalrous, battle of wits.

Not this.

Krestovski was crouched at his left, face half-revealed by light from the passage outside and registering neither pleasure nor distaste. He lifted the glowing point but the pain continued unabated.

The ember danced in the gloom, then steadied and glowed brighter as Krestovski drew on it. He bent over Dawlish, held the orange hip six inches above his face.

"You didn't bring just one torpedo boat to attack this ship, did you?" he said. "A patrol craft's returned with several dead and wounded. And with word that another like it has been destroyed with its entire crew. You had another torpedo boat with you, Mr. Smith, hadn't you? One that our patrol craft put paid to."

Dawlish's eyes were locked on the ember, impotent terror coursing through him.

"So how many more torpedo boats are prowling about this swamp, Mr. Smith?" No mockery in Krestovski's voice as he used the nom-de-guerre. He spoke as a gentle but firm man might state his requirements to an imbecile. "I want the number of boats and I want the location of their base of operations. White's yard was contracted to deliver three of those boats to the Admiralty. Yours reached here. We've found the second. So where's the third? And are there even more?"

Dawlish heard his own voice shout, "You blackguard!"

Krestovski ignored him. "You'll also tell me which ships are lying off the Delta. Which specific estuaries are suspected to shelter us? Which most closely observed? That is the start – but just the start – of what I am going to learn from you. Is that clear, Mr. Smith?"

He drew on his cigar again, quickening its tip to a new intensity. Then he applied it to the same point on Dawlish's cheek as before. This time he did not withdraw it.

Dawlish tried to twist, but without avail, his groans strangled and bestial, his arms and legs pinioned by the seamen. His whole being screamed through that single patch of agony on his cheek. Flashes of light, green and red and white, exploded before his eyes as his spine rose off the deck and was thrust back down again.

An eternity passed before Krestovski lifted the ember. Now he rose from his crouching position, straddled Dawlish, then sat on his stomach. He leaned forward until their faces almost touched.

"I bear no personal animosity, Mr. Smith. Please understand that. I just need to convince you that we're playing a serious game." His voice, soft, quiet and almost caressing, penetrated the mists of pain. "You know that you will tell me what I want. Either now, or in a few hours. It makes little difference to me but it will matter a great deal to you and your men. But I'd prefer, if possible, not to use direct methods again. So, see sense, Mr. Smith."

"I'll tell you nothing!" Dawlish was amazed that he somehow found the courage to invite the torment that he knew must come.

"I could be your friend, Mr. Smith," Krestovski said. "I love England and the English. When these present misunderstandings between our nations have passed, I'll return. I'll be welcome there. We might indeed meet socially, might shake hands and forget this business today, accept as men of the world that it was an unavoidable necessity. But for now, Mr. Smith, you leave me no alternative." And he applied the cigar again.

Dawlish wrenched his head from the seaman's grasp, beating it the deck and flailing it from side to side, but it was impossible to escape the glowing tip.

Krestovski sounded almost pitying. "No, my dear Mr. Smith. This won't do at all. Don't try to twist your head. It will only endanger your left eye. That's not my intention. Not yet at least."

He raised the cigar at last. It had been all but smothered in the bubbling patch on the tortured cheek. The pain, though still intense, lessened somewhat. Dawlish heard himself sob with relief, then braced himself for the next application, wondering how long he could endure before he revealed all, and more, that Krestovski wanted. His eyes were riveted in horror at the dying ember that lifted, stabilised, gained intensity and illuminated Krestovski's handsome features as he sucked on it. He exhaled slowly and spoke again in that terrible, reasonable, quiet voice.

"You'll save yourself and your men much needless suffering if you impart the information here and now, Mr. Smith. I've the rest of the day to demonstrate to you what an infinity of pain one small human frame can endure. Distasteful though it might be, I won't shrink from it. Do you understand, Mr. Smith?"

Only a blind, frantic hatred of his tormentor gave Dawlish the courage to defy him, conscious as he did that this might be for the last occasion before his will broke.

"You blackguard!" he managed to gasp, "You scoundrel, you bloody coward."

His words were lost in a new spasm of agony as Krestovski again applied the cigar end, brushing, then lingering. Dawlish's head was locked now and he could not twist away to find some brief instant of relief.

"You must learn better manners, my dear fellow." Krestovski's voice gave no trace of anger, displeasure or urgency. He sounded, if anything, mildly pained by the discourtesy of Dawlish's resistance. "Your language is distinctly unparliamentary. That's the correct English term I believe, though it's not a concept that worries us unduly in our Autocracy."

He withdrew the butt and Dawlish moaned.

"Your immediate physical discomforts are almost at an end, Mr. Smith, but before we finish you need a small reminder that you must never speak to a Russian nobleman – and especially to the personal representative of His Imperial Majesty – in the terms you've just used."

He reached forward one last time and quenched the cigar in the molten pool on Dawlish's cheek. He ignored the gasp of agony that burst from him. Then he raised himself to his feet and spoke down in a voice as calm as ever.

"Put on those clothes over there. My clothes, incidentally, Mr. Smith. And put on those shoes."

Krestovski spoke in Russian to the seamen. They released Dawlish and he struggled to his feet. His hands were shaking as he pulled on the clothes, felt humiliation when he could not find a shirt sleeve at first. He almost fell while putting on the trousers. They had no belt. Shoelaces had also been removed. Nobody helped or spoke.

He had no sooner pulled on the shoes than Krestovski launched the guards on him again. They scooped him up and flung him out into the passageway. He landed on his hands and knees but already they were coming after him. They did not strike him but they dragged him up and threw him forward at any sign of hesitation. He stumbled along the passage before them, as a reluctant beast might on its way to the shambles. He held the trousers by the waistband lest they fall and trip him and humble him yet further.

Up a ladder, through a companionway and into weak daylight filtering through a canvas awning stretched above the deck. Two seamen fell in behind him, bayonets levelled. Krestovski moved ahead.

"Follow me, Mr. Smith."

They went forward. Three Russian officers stood in a knot before them, Admiral Rudnev, Captain Kokoktsov and another officer. Rudnev came broke from them and came towards Krestovski, his face flushed in anger. He began to speak but Krestovski cut him off, one word enough. Rudnev hesitated, began to speak again, thought better of it and stepped aside.

But as Dawlish passed, the admiral said, "Ce n'est pas ma volonté. Ce n'est pas mon choix."

Not his will. Not his choice.

At the midships barbette, beneath the yawning muzzle of its huge cannon, Dawlish saw Egdean. Beside him stood what remained of *Beta's* crew – Day, the gunner Jarvis, and her helmsman Lowe – all herded against the circular wall.

Day, though he looked exhausted, seemed as relatively unscathed as Dawlish himself. His clothing was in rags and though a bearded marine held a bayonet point beneath his right ear he still had an air of defiance about him. Jarvis stood close by him, his face bruised, his left arm hanging loose but with no sign of blood. On a pallet next to them lay Lowe, ashen-pale, hands clasped to his gory head, blood trickling between his fingers. More blood saturated one trouser leg.

Dawlish saw relief on Day's face but, still unwilling to disclose surnames, shouted, "Charles! Where's the remainder of your people?"

Day had understood. "We're all that's left, Nicholas!"

Now he was racking his brain to recall Jarvis's first name. Was it Tom, or Joe or . . .

It came in a flash. "Matt, are you hurt badly?"

"It's my arm, sir," Pain in Jarvis's voice, but resolution in it too. "It's broke, sir. I've had worse. It just needs is a splint on it."

For an instant their loyalty was more painful to Dawlish than the burn on his cheek. He felt his eyes well with tears. "I'll do what I can for you, lads," he called.

He turned to Krestovski. "What about the wounded man who was brought on board with me last night?"

"He died. A merciful end in the circumstances."

"And that man?" Dawlish pointed to Lowe "Will he have treatment?"

"He'll have mercy, Mr. Smith. Depend upon it. He'll have mercy."

"And that man there?" He pointed to Jarvis. "His arm's broken."

"The surgeon will see to it."

"Will they have food and water?"

Krestovski ignored the question. "Walk with me, Mr. Smith," he said.

He took Dawlish by the elbow, turned him away from the captives, began to stroll sternwards with him. The two armed-seamen followed. In silence, they passed the mizzen and the aftmost barbette. Dawlish glimpsed the breech of its massive gun beneath its open-backed splinter-shield. Onwards to the railing at the stern. No ensign drooped from the staff there. The tide was flowing weakly and the *Orlov* and the other vessels now lay bow on towards the *Nevski*.

"An impressive achievement getting them here, isn't it, Mr. Smith?" Krestovski was leaning on the railing. He gestured to Dawlish to do likewise. "You're a professional, you must appreciate it."

Dawlish stood by him, rested on the rail, ignored him. Below him he saw the stern gallery on which a captain or admiral might take his leisure. It stretched on either side around the counter. His cheek was still an agony. He raised his hand, fearing what it would find, withdrew it at once as new pain stabbed.

Krestovski had noticed. "There'll be nothing worse than a small scar," he said. "Women admire them on a man as long as they're not too disfiguring. I'll send the surgeon to see to it. You'll be returning to your cabin soon."

"You know I'll tell you nothing." But fear haunted him that he might yet do so.

"I've heard that too often, Mr. Smith. Everybody says that at first but they tell everything in the end. Not just for themselves, even more so for others." The tone patient, bordering on sympathetic. "I've no desire to inflict unnecessary suffering. Nothing anarchic, nothing mindless, nothing as bad as the Sultan's Bashi Bazooks unleashed on innocents, on entire Christian towns and villages, in Bulgaria."

A memory flashed in Dawlish's mind of a breakfast table in Zanzibar, of the *Daily News* report that he had first tried to discount and that had then horrified him. Savage cruelties, fifteen thousand dead.

"We're both pragmatists, I believe, Mr. Smith, so we can dispense with casuistry. I know what you are. You know that I do. So tell me, why did you come here?"

He paused, waited for the significance of his allusion Bulgaria to sink in.

"You've come as a defender of a barbarous despotism, Mr. Smith. You've come as an ally, an undeclared one, of the monstrous Ottoman tyranny that your nation – and we can dispense with the fiction that it's anywhere other than Britain – shores up to protect her route to India."

Dawlish felt the temptation to vault across the rail. He might just clear the gallery below him. Once in the water he might have a chance. A miniscule chance, but better than the certainty of pain that would at last break him.

But he would leave his men behind. He owed them too much for that.

Krestovski must have sensed his urge, so too his hesitation. He did not raise his voice.

"I have you, and I have four of your men. You've had a taste, and I regret it, of what might be unavoidable if your obstinacy forces it. Larger matters are at stake. Any agony inflicted here today will occur because you represent the Sultan's interests. Indirectly I admit, but you too must recognise the fact."

One appeal possible, one to any officer's most sacred possession. His honour.

Dawlish had encountered Russian officers before in ports, had dined as a guest on their ships and they had on his, had organised regattas with them in friendly competition. They might drink heavily but they were generous, and often urbane, and never less than gentlemen. He had liked them.

"You hold the Czar's commission, do you not?" he said. "You must know that your threats to helpless men shame you?"

"I hold no naval commission." Krestovski shook his head. "But I hold something infinitely more valuable. His Imperial Majesty's confidence. His trust. Do you think that an enterprise as vital to this can be assigned to simple-minded officers who know of nothing of political realities? Could they be relied on in extremis? No, Mr. Smith, a higher authority and intelligence must govern them and put steel in their resolution."

He could not keep the pride from his voice. Confident, arrogant pride.

Better to indulge it and draw more out.

"So you came here in that yacht?" Dawlish said.

"My private yacht. I enjoy my comforts."

"Why are these ships still here then?"

"You're too curious, Mr. Smith." He took Dawlish's elbow again and began to walk him back to the companionway from which they had first emerged.

"May I see my men again?" Dawlish asked.

"Put your mind at ease about them, Mr. Smith. For the time being at least. You'll go back to your cabin now. Your face will be tended to and you'll be fed. And you'll find a pencil and paper there for answering my questions. In detail. You'll have a few hours to think about it."

The guards brought Dawlish back to his cabin. All was neat again, the disorder occasioned by the assault corrected. He saw a stubby pencil – too short to stab with – and a writing pad on the desk. The family photograph that had been there was gone, so too the carafe of water and its glass, the shade on the candle holder, even the ewer and basin. He understood. Nothing remained that could be broken and used to slit a throat or vein. That escape was barred to him.

Soon afterwards the surgeon arrived, a dignified, middle-aged man with a closely cropped beard. He looked shamefaced, would not meet Dawlish's eyes. An orderly had come with him to carry his instruments and bottles.

"Le blessé qui est mort. Quand est-ce arrivé?" Dawlish wanted to know when Webb had died.

He saw that the surgeon understood French but would not answer. He persisted, wanted assurance that Krestovski was honouring his word about *Beta's* wounded helmsman.

"Et le blessé qui a été amené à bord ce matin? Comment est-il maintenant?"

The surgeon looked directly at him for the first time him, lips tight, held his finger across them, gave his head a shake so slight that his orderly could not have noticed. His silent massage conveyed that he did not like the situation and that he was forbidden to speak. He gestured to the cot and Dawlish sat on it. With great gentleness, the surgeon began to swab the burned cheek clean, then applied some stinging antiseptic and finished by rubbing on ointment. He waved Dawlish's thanks away when he left.

Soon afterwards the food came, a steward carrying a silver tray with a white cloth. Black bread, slices of smoked sausage, a banana, water in a carafe. A seaman stood behind the steward, watching him pour three glasses in succession for Dawlish. It had the unmistakable taste of distilled seawater. He was thirsty, hungry too. This might be his last meal ever and he tried to savour it. He gestured to the steward to leave the water and the glass but the man shook his head, said only, "Nyet!" and put them on the tray to take away. Before they left, the seaman opened the door and from outside brought in a bucket with a wooden cover. He put it in a corner, its purpose obvious. One glimpse of two other guards outside and then the door closed again.

Dawlish was alone. The ointment had soothed, but not removed, the pain of his cheek but that was nothing to the despair welling inside him. He knew now that Krestovski's power was absolute here, as much over the admiral and the officers as over his captives. He had already shown his willingness to employ pain and humiliation, use them without emotion, without hesitation, even without rancour. He would do so again if needed.

Raison d'état

The same term that Beaconsfield had used. A reason of state, of national interest. The term that justified any crime.

Despair was rising now. Dawlish saw the paper and pencil on the writing desk. A small wheedling, yet pragmatic voice inside his brain told him that, before this day was out, he might be grateful to scribble all that Krestovski wanted.

But he had given his word, had pledged his honour. He could not yield it easily, all the more since he had failed in everything so far. He took the pencil stub, broke it, threw it out through the small scuttle. Better to remove temptation.

He forced calm on himself, considered his situation as if it involved some other man. Krestovski must be waiting for a message, he reasoned, one brought from the nearest port that had telegraphic contact with Europe. Perhaps Madeira. A small fast vessel, another yacht perhaps, might be waiting in the harbour there to make a dash, carrying with it the order to ravage Britain's trading routes. Until then, the *Nevski* and the *Orlov* and their colliers would swing at anchor here. That malaria might deplete their crews did not matter. That had been allowed for and Russia could afford to be prodigal of lives. When that message would come, Britain would have nothing to counter a threat transformed into reality.

But timing was everything.

The message would not come until Britain hovered on the brink of intervention. That was the time when appearance of the ironclads might stay Britain's hand or, if not, would herald a devastating attack on British commerce. But leaving the Delta too soon, brushing past *Nomad* and *Volage* while a state of peace still existed, would force the Russians to wander on the ocean to deplete their bunkers and eat up their colliers' stocks, without hope of replenishment from captured merchantmen. With speed reduced to conserve diminishing fuel, even the slowest tramp might well outrun them.

Dawlish saw now that being driven to that measure must be haunting Krestovski. *Alpha's* attack had almost succeeded. Had *Beta* not been lost, then the *Nevski* might by now be settled in the mud of the channel's bed, her upper masts and yards standing stark above the water surface like grave markers. It would have been all the more probable still, had the *Gamma* not come to grief at Killary.

Krestovski knew that three boats had been built by White's at Cowes. For him it would be reasonable to assume that all three had reached the Delta. If so, the third craft might have accompanied the two the previous night, last in line, might have retreated when *Beta* was destroyed ahead of her. She might, even now, be lurking somewhere close. And worse, there could be other boats too awaiting their turn . . .

The *Nevski* had come within a hair's breadth of destruction. Her luck might run out in another such attack. To escape that possibility, Krestovski might even now be weighing the option of leaving the Delta.

To wander.

To see the squadron's offensive capability withering day by day.

For Britain, for Dawlish, for his crews, that would be victory of sorts.

But only silence in the face of Krestovski's savagery could buy it.

Chapter 22

They came for him again in what must be early afternoon. No Krestovski this time, no violence either, just a young officer who avoided his gaze when he beckoned him. He went ahead of Dawlish, two guards following as before. Heavy rain was beating on the canvas awning when they emerged on deck.

To the central barbette. Day stood against it, Egdean and Jarvis by him, penned there by half-a-dozen seamen. All were in the same clothes in which they had come aboard. Day's face was bruised now, one eye black, as if from punching. So much for Krestovski's assurances. Jarvis's left arm was now in a sling but otherwise no worse than earlier. Egdean looked untouched.

"I've told them nothing, Nicholas!" Day shouted

"Where's Lowe" The wounded helmsman was not with them.

"We haven't seen him, Nicholas!"

Hope flared. The surgeon who had treated Dawlish's cheek with such compassion would not have withheld it from a worse-injured man. The clean white sling indicated that Jarvis's arm had received proper care.

"Be quiet, Mr. Smith, and sit down over there!"

Dawlish turned, saw that Krestovski had come behind him. He was gesturing to two camp-chairs placed just beyond the barbette, a small low table between them. A man in a cream civilian suit stood behind. Admiral Rudnev and Captain Kokoktsov, two other officers with them, stood far enough beyond to give an impression of wanting no part in this, but forced to be here nonetheless.

"I'm told that the paper left in your cabin is blank," Krestovski said. "Perhaps you'd prefer to tell me face to face instead?"

Dawlish shook his head, then stiffened, his nostrils catching a sharp smell. A coke brazier was glowing at the deck edge. The air above it shimmered and three irons protruded from it.

He fought down the urge to scream, to find release in the solace of insanity rather than accept the suspicion that sprang to his mind. He looked from the brazier to his men and then to the spotless and elegant figure that contrasted so starkly with those husks of suffering. He looked Krestovski in the eyes, searching for some trace of sympathy.

"For God's sake," he heard himself croak, "don't disgrace yourself by abusing these wretches. Haven't they endured enough?"

"They helped kill a dozen of our people. They destroyed a patrol boat." Krestovski said. "There are six Russians in this ship's sick-bay – that's the word you use in your navy, don't you? One is likely to die and two others have lost limbs. And you ask me if your men, common pirates attacking under no national ensign, deserve sympathy?"

He shook his head and laughed. And the laugh did not sound hard, or bitter, or sarcastic, but it had a quality of pure amusement about it, just as an adult might be amused by a child's incomprehension.

"But, of course, more suffering may not be necessary, Mr. Smith."

He took Dawlish's elbow and led him towards the canvas chairs. He motioned to one and Dawlish took it. He saw that face of the shaven-headed civilian standing behind looked Asiatic, not Russian. He settled himself, then felt something nudging through the canvas and against the base of his spine.

"My servant's an Uzbek, Mr. Smith," Krestovski said, "A pitiless race, if a loyal one, and this particular specimen's my man entirely. He should be. I saved him from hanging."

Dawlish glanced back. The Uzbek's eyes, set in a high-cheek boned skull that looked as if it had parchment stretched tight over it, had all the coldness of a viper's.

"His presence should dissuade you from seeking death by a dash over the rail," Krestovski said. "He'll give you no easy bullet in the brain. At the first unexpected move he'll squeeze the trigger and leave you a rational and conscious cripple. I can assure you, as an eyewitness of such treatment, that death will take a minimum of twelve hours. And during them you'd be well capable of full cooperation."

Dawlish nodded, his teeth clenched, hoping not to betray the nausea threatening to overwhelm him. He tried to look away, but always his gaze was drawn back to the pitiful group at the barbette. He forced himself to be calm, to convince himself that there must be some way out.

"I appeal to you, as a rational man –"

Krestovski cut him short but his voice was calm. "Let's not start all that again, Mr. Smith. As a rational man, you know that you leave me no choice. You must know our mission. You must have guessed that a despatch vessel waits in a certain port that has a telegraph link to Europe. It'll carry us news of our armies' arrival at the gates of Constantinople, as they will do. When that message arrives it is I, the Czar's personal representative, who will send these ships into history. Am I to threaten that destiny for the sake of your sense of honour?"

He was leaning over to Dawlish now, lips close to his ear.

"I know your type." His voice was low. "You'll bear a lot yourself before you break. But it's not you I'll make suffer in the body – you understand? And so, I'm asking you again. Will you tell me what I need to know?"

Dawlish shook his head in mute misery, not trusting himself to speak. The seconds that followed were endless.

"Your cheek hurts, does it not?" Krestovski asked at length. "That little episode gave you an insight as to what would come, did if not? And your answer is still 'No'?"

"No." A whisper, barely audible. The most difficult word he had ever uttered.

Krestovski sighed and stood up. He looked down at Dawlish and shrugged his shoulders with the air of a reasonable man whose patience had been tried beyond its limit. He turned and clicked his fingers towards Admiral Rudnev. The admiral, face flushed with anger, spoke to one of his officers and sent him to Krestovski. Brief orders and then the officer went below.

No other sound now but the drumming of the rain, of the torrents spilling off the awning, curtaining off the view of the endless green mangrove beyond. Dawlish's mouth was dry. Blood pounded in his brain and his fingers locked on the arm-rest of the canvas chair lest his trembling be too obvious. He was close to breaking and he knew it.

Two men in white jackets approached from aft and were carrying a stretcher. Dawlish recognised the first as the orderly who had helped the surgeon treat his cheek. No sign of the surgeon himself now but the officer who had been sent on Krestovski's errand was following. His face told that he found his task distasteful, shameful even.

And Dawlish saw what that officer had guessed and dreaded. Lowe lay on the stretcher, no sheet or blanket covering him but in a clean white night-shirt, his head swathed in bandages. His wounded leg must have been dressed also, for no red blotch had soaked the white. Dawlish had been correct in his positive estimation of the surgeon.

Lowe stirred, raised himself on one elbow, seemed uncomprehending, fell back. Krestovski was standing by the brazier. He pointed to the deck at his feet and ordered the bearers to lay down the stretcher.

Lowe was trying to raise himself again. but had not strength enough. For one brief instant, his bewildered gaze settled on Dawlish. He whispered something but it was inaudible. Krestovski beckoned to the officer and demanded something from him. The officer handed him a revolver.

Krestovski cocked it, stood back a little, motioned to the orderlies to stand aside.

Then he fired into Lowe's head.

He handed the pistol back to the officer, gave him some other order, then he walked back to Dawlish.

"I promised that he'd have mercy. He's received it. Nobody else will."

No sound now but the beating rain Then a voice roaring from the barbette wall.

"God will punish you," Egdean shouted. "God will –"

Day had caught him by the shoulder and was urging him into silence.

"You're a bloody murderer, Krestovski." Dawlish felt the Uzbek's revolver pushed yet harder against his lower back.

"And you're a common pirate, Mr. Smith." Krestovski seated himself next to Dawlish again. His voice no less calm and reasonable than before. "You flew no ensign, you wore no uniform, you're protected by no law. You know that I'd be within my rights to hang you and every man of yours from the highest yardarm on this ship?"

"Then hang us then, and be done with it!"

"It won't be that easy, Mr. Smith. But you know now that I'm serious."

Krestovski clicked his fingers at the two orderlies who stood frozen by the stretcher and looking down, appalled, at Lowe. Half his head had been blown away. Blood, bright red against the holystoned white of the cambered planking, was trickling down the slope towards the scupper. Krestovski had the orderlies' attention and he called to them. They looked back, bewildered, made to move, then stood back again. One was shaking his head and the other turned to the officer with them, as if asking for confirmation. The officer, as shocked as they were, nodded.

They lifted the stretcher and tipped Lowe's body over the rail.

Admiral Rudnev had watched from a distance. Now he came forward, distaste clouding his features. He spoke to Krestovski in a low voice. The words were unintelligible to Dawlish but their intent was obvious. Krestovski was shaking his head but the admiral persisted, disgust as well as anger in his tone. At last, he turned away and stalked back to join his officers.

"You have an advocate, Mr. Smith," Krestovski said. "I'll humour him. I'll give you two hours more to reconsider. I'll have a new pencil sent to your cabin. Think about it, think hard. Our soft-hearted Admiral Rudnev needs the information just as much as I do. He won't intercede a second time."

And Dawlish was returned to his cabin, the Uzbek still holding the pistol against his spine until he handed him over to two guards at the door.

It closed.

And another stub of pencil lay on the clean pad of paper.

Temptation.

*

It was longer than two hours before they came again, long enough for mental agony, long too for enduring the pain of his burned cheek that reminded him that worse might yet come.

Dear God, let that be only for myself and not for Day or Jarvis or Egdean. I'll break, my screaming flesh will conquer my spirit. But let that surrender not be immediate. Give me strength to bear the agony until the involuntary moment comes.

The rain had ceased and the air was still and hot and humid. The brazier still stood by the rail, restoked and glowing, three irons pushed into it, cherry-red as far as their wooden handles. Krestovski was already seated on his canvas chair, gesturing to Dawlish to take its twin. No sign as yet of the other prisoners.

"I understand there's nothing on your writing pad, Mr. Smith"

"Nothing." Dawlish had thrown the second pencil also through the scuttle.

A white-jacketed steward was placing a silver tray on the table separating the chairs.

"Tea, Mr. Smith? From Georgia. Better, I assure you, than Darjeeling."

Dawlish shook his head. The Uzbek's weapon was in place against his spine again.

"You're sure? You're really sure?" Krestovski sipped his tea delicately through a lump of sugar gripped between his teeth. "You think this business cruel?"

"Unspeakable."

"No worse than the Turk you defend, Mr. Smith." There was smugness in his tone, a hint of confidence that the end might be near.

Guards brought Day and Jarvis and Egdean on deck, pushed them again against the barbette, levelled bayonets towards them. Shoulders slumped, faces drawn, all three looked close to collapse. Dawlish knew no words to call to them that would not sound hollow.

"I think we'll start with that fellow with the injured arm," Krestovski said.

"Take me instead." Dawlish had rehearsed the statement again and again in the cabin. Trembling as he did now, he was yet relieved that he did not hesitate.

"Too easy, Mr. Smith."

Until that moment Dawlish's mind had held back from accepting the full reality. He had wanted, against all evidence, to believe Krestovski rational. Ruthless and amoral perhaps yet governed by a logic based on raison d'état alone. But he could shy away from reality no longer. This man was not mad. He was something worse. He was malignant, had willingly crossed beyond the boundary of human worth and saw himself now, as Caligula or Nero had in their times, a god glorying in absolute power within his own domain.

Seamen moved now to Krestovski's orders, pushing between the guards surrounding the prisoners. Day and Egdean were trying to shield Jarvis but they were thrust aside. Blood stained Egdean's shirt from a blow across his mouth and Day doubled from a rifle butt punching his midriff. Both men went down and when they rose it was with bayonet tips touching their throats.

Two seamen had caught Jarvis, were dragging him with them towards the rail. He was trying to struggle, but the pain of his broken arm had sapped his strength. His face was waxen-pale, his eyes locked open in terror and despair.

Krestovski rose, walked to where the seamen who held Jarvis against the rail. He bent down on one knee, rolled up Jarvis's tattered trouser leg to expose the calf. Then he wrapped a handkerchief around his hand, went to the brazier and pulled out an iron. The tip was almost white. He turned towards Dawlish, one eyebrow raised in question, saw no response.

He can't do this. He won't, he can't!

"Whatever you want! Whatever you want, I'll tell you!" Jarvis's voice was a scream. "For God's sake! I'll tell you anything I can!"

Krestovski had come closer, was looking down at Jarvis's bare calf, relaxed, almost pensive, as if studying an abstract problem. Jarvis was babbling now, his words incomprehensible.

He'll do it. He won't hold back.

A long scream, despair incarnate. The iron floated an inch from the bare skin, was hovering there. Even from where he sat, the Uzbek's muzzle rammed yet harder now against him, Dawlish caught the stench of the hairs frizzling from the heat. He looked away, had not the courage to watch, saw that even the guards around the barbette were glancing uneasily over their shoulders towards the Krestovski and his victim.

The iron was yet closer now, the skin yet untouched, but scorching. Jarvis's scream was continuous now, an animal howl beyond pleading, beyond despair.

Then Day broke.

Dawlish had not expected it. He had never known Day before meeting him on *Nomad.* His appraisal of him had been formed in the weeks since – a more than competent officer, a little unimaginative perhaps, but steady and methodical and likely to show dogged courage in adversity.

But now a commotion was erupting at the barbette. Day was shouting and trying to push through the guards there. With one hand he was trying to deflect the bayonets that blocked his progress and had raised the other to hide his face, ashamed of his weakness.

"I'll tell you all," he yelled. "I'm an officer! I'll tell you all you want, and every last detail too!"

Krestovski turned from Jarvis, thrust the iron back in the brazier, then signalled to the guards. They stood aside, let Day through, closed again to pin Egdean against the barbette again. Two seamen followed Day with levelled bayonets. Krestovski advanced to meet him, smiling, hand outstretched in welcome.

"My dear fellow –"

Day's kick into his groin silenced him. He doubled, gasping in pain.

The bayonet lunge of the quicker guard caught Day on the side below his right arm, tearing through a fold of flesh and opening a scarlet gash. The wound was not incapacitating, for he was agile enough to avoid the thrust of the second bayonet. Krestovski was reeling in his path, blocking him, but Day shoulder-charged him and hurled him sprawling on the deck.

Now a diversion erupted at the barbette. The attack on Krestovski had distracted the guards and had turned heads. Egdean seized his moment, dashed the bayonet that threatened him aside. He snatched the guard's rifle by its muzzle, was spinning him around, locking the man's neck in the crook of his left elbow, holding the weapon's point against his neck. It happened fast, had won seconds that froze the other guards into shocked immobility.

"Go on, sir! Go on!" Egdean bellowed.

Day was racing towards Jarvis and the two men holding him against the rail. One of them released him and moved to block Day. They collided and Day smashed his fist into the man's face and knocked him down. He stooped, grabbed the brazier by its thin tripod legs, spilling embers as he lifted it. Then he heaved it towards the seamen close on his heels. Orange coals showered against them and one cried in pain and the others' charge faltered. Jarvis was struggling, twisting to free himself from the grip of the single seaman still holding him. Effectively one-armed, he was not succeeding but he had the man off balance and diverting his attention from Day who was sweeping up one of the still glowing irons from the deck. The guard grappling with Jarvis saw too late that Day was driving at his shoulder with the with the iron. He howled as it struck, released Jarvis, staggered back.

For one brief instant Dawlish saw Day turn towards him, eyes full of regret and despair. And, worst of all, reproach.

Day was grabbing Jarvis now, lifting him, throwing him across the rail. Then he vaulted behind him. A loud splash told that they had hit the water below. Dawlish half-rose to his feet, only to freeze as the revolver was rammed still harder against his spine. He dropped back into his chair.

Krestovski had regained his feet and was fighting to catch his breath and gasp an order. For the first time Dawlish saw him in a rage. He lurched towards him, face contorted, teeth grinding. He grabbed Dawlish by the shoulder and dragged him towards the entry port where he had been brought on board the previous night. The Uzbek followed like an evil shadow, never relaxing the revolver's pressure.

"I'll show you the consequences of escape," Krestovski gasped. "They won't get a hundred yards before we have them and they'll pay! They'll pay."

No sign of Jarvis. Encumbered by his broken arm, he must have already gone under to the merciful death that Day had bought for him. Dawlish's heart leaped as he saw that Day was swimming towards the mangrove, had already covered almost a third of the distance. A vee of ripples streamed back from his bobbing head. Strongly as he was stroking however, he could not hope to outdistance the two cutters that had been lying alongside the *Nevski* and which were now converging on him with steady, measured oar-beat.

Dawlish ignored the jabbing pistol and yelled out: "Come on, Charles! Good fellow! Don't let them take you! Come on!"

Krestovski was beside him, quivering with anger. He had thrust one fist into his mouth and was gnawing it as he watched the boats bear down on the swimmer.

The first cutter sliced in front of Day. The rowers backed water to check the forward momentum. Day ducked under and was lost to view. He was gone for seconds before bobbing to the surface again, yards beyond the cutter's other side and still heading for the mangrove. The boat crew responded to shouted orders from the sternsheets and pulled around to follow him.

Day might well have gained the bank, for all the good it could have done him, had the second cutter not lurched ahead of him. His path was blocked and in moments the two boats hemmed him in. They lay parallel to each other with his head equidistant between. Any movement of his was countered by a similar movement by the cutters. Boat hooks reached out to snag his clothing. He seemed exhausted now and in no state to repeat his tactic of escaping under one of the boats.

Sick with impotence to assist, Dawlish watched as Day, treading water, rotated slowly until his despairing face turned towards the *Nevski*. He seemed to hang there forever, oblivious of the grasping boat hooks. Then, as if with infinite sorrow, he raised his arms to the vertical and went under. He slid out of sight before coming up twice again, choking. Somehow, he still avoided the hooks and raised his arms once more and sank. He did not reappear a third time.

Fury in Krestovski's voice when he spoke to Dawlish. "We're not finished, Mr Smith. There's still that peasant ox to deal with."

He gestured towards the barbette. Egdean still had his terrified hostage's locked in his elbow and the bayonet point was just beneath it, ouching his neck.

"Tell that man to yield, Mr. Smith."

Dawlish shook his head. Egdean deserved the dignity of choice.

Krestovski spoke to the Uzbek. The man grabbed Dawlish by the shoulder, dragged him to his feet, spun him around so Egdean could see the pistol rammed against his lower back.

"I'm counting to five." Krestovski had walked to the barbette, was calling to Egdean. "You've that much time. After that I'll have my man cripple your commander."

Egdean dropped the bayonet, released his hostage and held up his arms.

No blows.

And only he and Dawlish remained to return to their separate incarcerations.

Chapter 23

The cabin was as orderly as when Dawlish had first entered it. A bowl and ewer of water stood on the night stand again, a carafe and glass next to them. A guard gestured to him that he might drink and wash his face and hands. He watched him as he did and took the breakable items away with him when he left. Dawlish sat on the cot, oppressed by the thought that this must be the prelude to some new bout of ingenious cruelty. The door opened again, the Russian surgeon, alone this time. He was as silent as before despite Dawlish probing him in French, and he would not look him in the eye, though he attended with delicate competence to the burned cheek. The pain, scarcely felt during the horror of the previous hours, was back.

Dawlish lay down, the cotton pad that the surgeon had left him held to the throbbing burn. It was nothing, he knew, compared with what Krestovski would wreak on Egdean. He would plead again to take his place – the idea unmanned him, but he must force himself to it – but he knew that Krestovski would reject it. He would yield at last, no doubt of it, for the faithful seaman's sake, but each hour's delay until that moment would increase the Russians' fears that other torpedo craft might be waiting to attack. That fear might drive them from this anchorage, out too soon into the open sea. At last drowsiness conquered pain and despair and he lapsed into uncomfortable sleep.

It ended with an awakening more gentle than the first this day. The cabin was dark and a young officer was shaking his shoulder while a seaman stood behind him with a lantern.

"Son excellence le prince, vous invite à dîner avec vous, monsieur." No sarcasm in the tone but an impression of words repeated, by order, verbatim. And with distaste, maybe pity.

An invitation to dine. A euphemism? Some new game of cruelty?

Dawlish stood, pulled on his laceless shoes. His knees were weak but he moved to the door without urging. Through the ages, many men, and women too, their spirits quaking within, had gone with outward composure to hideous death on the scaffold. He would try to do so with similar dignity.

Until . . . Until the flesh could endure no more.

They turned left at the door and not right as before. They were heading aft down the passage, the young officer leading, two guards close behind Dawlish. They passed other cabins. A panelled wooden door ahead, then a knock. A steward answered, bowed. The officer gestured to Dawlish to enter and but did not follow. The door closed.

He found himself in the semi-circular saloon directly below the quarterdeck that occupied the entire stern of the vessel. It must be Admiral Rudnev's but there was no sign of him. Krestovski, in clean clothing and wafting eau-de-cologne, was advancing, smiling, again with hand outstretched.

"A truce, Mr. Smith," he said, "We'll be back to business soon enough – and unpleasant business too for you, I fear, and there's no help for that – but we can forget it for an hour, can we not?"

Dawlish almost recoiled as he forced himself to take the proffered hand and let Krestovski pass an arm over his shoulder like an old friend. Somehow, he must play for time with this pervert.

"A civilised solution, Your Excellency." He had not addressed him so all day but now he tried now to inject some courtesy into his tone.

"Like Saladin and the Lionheart then!" Krestovski was once more the prince whom Dawlish had first met, urbane and chivalrous. He guided him across the saloon.

To port and starboard, open doorways gave access to the wrought-iron gallery that ran around the stern. A row of large square casements disposed along the curving transom gave an unobstructed view out across the dark waters without. The transverse bulkhead formed the other wall. It was panelled with inlaid woods to depict a battle on a frozen lake, shaggily-clad warriors axing down mail-clad knights and hamstringing their mounts even as they crashed through the yielding ice. An open door on the far side must lead to the admiral's cabin. Despite the open casements, and the skylight above, the saloon was oppressively hot, with just the slightest cross-current of air to alleviate the humidity and make the oil lamp flicker before an icon at one side. A dining table had been set for three.

A stifled sound caused Dawlish to turn. To the left of the door that he had entered through he saw Egdean, his hands and feet bound to the arms and legs of a heavy wooden chair. He was gagged but trying to speak. Krestovski's impassive Uzbek sat on a stool next to him, knife in hand.

"You might tell your peasant to be quiet," Krestovski said to Dawlish. "He'll be the guarantor of your gentlemanly behaviour at dinner. Your backbone will be out of immediate danger but at the first hostile movement my servant will blind him."

Dawlish saw fear in Egdean's eyes. He raised a finger to his lips and shook his head, hoped that Egdean understood his meaning.

Be patient. I'll do what I can for you.

Admiral Rudnev entered, extended no hand. His face was flushed and sweating and he smelled of alcohol. He slurred something when Dawlish wished him Bonsoir, then lumbered past and sunk into a chair of the head of the table.

"It might be more congenial if we speak in English," Krestovski jerked his head toward the admiral. "He's half-drunk already and he won't be a good conversationalist tonight. I prefer English it to French anyway and there's no need to maintain the charade that you're anything but a British naval officer."

Once more the personification of urbane good-fellowship, he invited Dawlish to sit at the table and took his place opposite him. Behind him, Czar Alexander II was frowning from a portrait in oils.

The meal was better than could have been expected in the heart of the swamp. Dawlish commented on it.

"My own chef," Krestovski said. "French. I sent for him to come over from my yacht."

A lightning flash outside, and a thunderclap seconds later, announced the beginning of the night's downpour. Through the open doors Dawlish saw grey walls of rain.

The steward came and went like a silent wraith with course after course. Dawlish and Rudnev toyed with the food and neither ate but Krestovski relished what was put before him. When the steward moved to fill Dawlish's glass, he ordered him to place the wine bottles on the table, then waved him away before filling the glass himself. Rudnev looked embarrassed and morose. He lapsed into silence after a confused attempt to apologise in French to Dawlish. Krestovski cut him short in Russian with a remark that sounded slighting. Thereafter the admiral contented himself with draining glass after glass of colourless liquid from the bottle before him. Krestovski ignored him, was reminiscing fondly about his time in Oxford and his circle of English friends.

But one acquaintance he valued above all.

"Prince Alfred. A naval officer, like yourself. Perhaps you know him, Mr. Smith?"

"The Duke of Edinburgh?" Dawlish said. "I don't move in such circles." The Queen's second son had a good reputation as a competent officer, based as much on his merits as on his birth.

"An admired man in Russia, Mr. Smith And popular! We even have a warship named for him, the *Gerzog Edinburgski,* a sister of the *Orlov*. An irony in these present circumstances, is it not?"

Dawlish was listening with only half an ear and was studying the saloon. The slightest movement of heavy air was passing through the two doors thrown open to the stern walk.

"You know the duke then?" Dawlish feigned interest. He had to raise his voice since the skylight above was open but the torrents of rain were beating loudly on the canvas awning above the deck.

"Know Prince Alfred! I've had the honour to be on the most intimate terms with him ever since he first visited Petersburg to solicit the hand of His Imperial Majesty's lovely daughter, Maria." Krestovski drained his glass, then refilled it. There was no trace of irony in his voice.

There seemed to be no sentry on the stern gallery though there might well be one or more on the quarterdeck overhead, and in the passage leading to the saloon. And for the first time Dawlish was free of the threat to his spine.

Eight paces would bring me to a door . . .

"You introduced Prince Alfred to the delights of St. Petersburg?" Dawlish said. "That must have been a pleasure."

"In more ways than one, Mr. Smith! We had several memorable nights with the gypsies on the islands!" Krestovski laughed, filled his glass again, emptied it and filled once more. "I can assure you that the wedding might have been off had His Imperial Majesty come to know some things about those nights!"

There was still Egdean to be considered but if only. . .

"I suspect discretion was in order, Your Excellency?"

"Discretion that was well merited! Because Affie was even more concerned about his own dear mamma getting wind of his recreations than His Imperial Majesty might. And I don't blame him, Mr. Smith! That lady's daunting!"

The steward who's been moving in silence from and to the small pantry partitioned off from the saloon is slightly built and would offer little opposition…

"You've met Her Majesty then?"

"I've been her guest at Balmoral. Twice."

Krestovski shook with mirth when he recalled Affie's practical joke at the expense of a German princeling when they were stalking stags. The wretched man had been made look like a fool. And that triumph had been exceeded only by the crassness of his elder brother's efforts during Cowes Week the following year.

He drained his glass. And filled it again.

Only the motionless Uzbek threatening Egdean's eyes stood between Dawlish and a dash for freedom. The small, wheedling, cowardly voice was back in his brain and whispering temptation. Once in the water he would have a chance, however remote, of reaching Camp Beaconsfield. Egdean would suffer, but larger issues were at stake. And then he recoiled from the thought, appalled by how soon he had come to accept pain as a currency with which to barter.

And yet . . .

"You must know that I've no greater affection for any foreign country than for England." Krestovski's voice was slurring, its tone was almost maudlin. "I completed my education there. I had friends there from every class, every class, Mr. Smith, highest to lowest."

"Even in White's boatyard?"

Krestovski paused, frowned, realised the irony and then laughed. "Even at Sammy White's, Mr. Smith! But look, sir, I don't want to discuss shop over dinner. Talking shop, that's a splendid English way of putting it, isn't it? And nobody would be more overjoyed than me if we could settle this current unpleasantness amicably. To His Imperial Majesty's satisfaction of course."

"As, Your Excellency said. No shop."

The meal ended. Krestovski dismissed the steward and reached for another wine bottle. He shook his head in mock exasperation at Dawlish's refusal.

"The Prince of Wales, Mr. Smith, now there's a good judge of wine! I remember a dinner at Marlborough House when . . ."

Dawlish scarcely heard him. Each time he took a surreptitious glance he saw that the Uzbek was staring back at him, his face as immobile as an automaton's, his eyes unblinking and watching his every move. Egdean's head was bowed. Probably praying.

Krestovski's glass was empty again and was pouring from a new bottle, vodka this time, not wine. His hand was unsteady. His English was faultless in his latest tale of regal, if boorish, good-fellowship still but he was now slurring more. He must be close to the limits of his tolerance for drink.

Dawlish looked down at the dessert knife on his plate, the only item of cutlery that had not been removed. It was short, blunt and round-nosed. He looked up and measured the distance to the Uzbek. Five paces – and the man's reptilian eyes were still fixed on him. He looked away, his mind racing over a host of possibilities, all hopeless.

A sob broke his concentration, a moan of anguish from the admiral. The bearded figure, so quiet until now, raised his glance. His eyes brimmed with tears and his expression showed equal parts of deep internal agony and drunken self-pity. With another groan he fell himself forward on the table with his face buried in his hands. His huge frame shook with sobbing that interrupted a stream of incomprehensible Russian. Krestovski was no less surprised than Dawlish but as he began to follow the admiral's confused drift he began to laugh.

"The old fool has broken before you have, Mr. Smith." Krestovski's voice was bitter with contempt. "That's the sort of cringing peasant we have for admirals in our Imperial Navy! Some spilled blood and singed flesh and he whimpers like a child. His honour won't permit him to stand by and see a repeat performance of today." He threw back his head, and drained the half-filled glass in a single gulp. "Rudnev's honour, by God! His great-grandfather was a valet, ennobled for procuring whores for Potemkin. And he talks of honour!"

The admiral must have guessed something of the words' meaning and he looked up with hatred in his eyes. Krestovski saw it too, seemed pleased. He spoke in Russian, his voice heavy with sarcasm, and slow enough that even the drunkest of men could understand the import. It must be the same gibe about ancestry as before, for Dawlish recognised the word 'Potemkin'.

Rudnev lurched to his feet. Tears coursed down his cheeks He stammered a speech that drew some new slight from Krestovski. The wretched man turned from him and staggered towards the corner where the lamp burned before the icon. He threw out an arm, pointing to it and, fixing his gaze on Krestovski, began a tirade that seemed half-sermon, half-denunciation.

Krestovski snapped.

There was no trace now of the English gentleman, of Prince Alfred's bosom friend, as he started to his feet, his face contorted with rage. He was almost foaming, but still speaking English. "Coward!" he spat. "You dare to call yourself an Imperial officer?" And then he shouted in Russian, again some reference to Potemkin.

Dawlish's heart was thumping but he stayed immobile, fearful that any premature movement might distract Krestovski. From the corner of his eye, he sensed the Uzbek moving, not stirring from his stool but leaning forward, intent on the drama being played out by his superiors and minimally relaxing his attention to Egdean.

Fury had replaced the Rudnev's disgust. One arm gestured towards the icon and the other extended towards Krestovski in an attitude of denunciation. He was shouting now.

It was too much for Krestovski. He picked up a glass from the table and hurled it at his accuser. It missed and shattered on the bulkhead beyond. Rudnev rushed forward, surprisingly agile for a heavy man so far-gone in drink. A great hand grasped Krestovski's throat and dragged him forward. A second hand joined the first, the fingers interlocking behind the neck, the thumbs biting deep. A gurgle issued from Krestovski's parted lips. His eyes began to bulge and his hands clawed at the admiral's huge paws.

Dawlish waited for a second after the Uzbek moved forward to aid his master. Only when the man was two paces beyond Egdean did he reach for the blunt dessert knife and hurtle at him. The wiry Asian had been well trained, for he had half-turned so as to cover Dawlish as he edged around the table, but he was unsure how to intervene in the quarrel between his betters. His hesitance gave Dawlish his chance.

The Uzbek's knife, long, wicked and sharp, was grasped in his right hand but Dawlish was fast with the speed of desperation and he was kicking up between his adversary's legs before he could lunge at him. The man doubled with pain and his knife blade flailed past Dawlish, who was even then dodging behind him and grabbing for his close-cropped skull. His left hand slipped on the stubble of black hair before his searching fingers hooked into the eye-sockets. The Uzbek's mouth was opening to scream as Dawlish smashed his head backwards, noticing as he did the rearwards-swinging knife that the pain-crazed man dug at him. He twisted to the left and felt the blade go slicing past his thigh, ripping the trouser fabric but drawing no blood. Before the Uzbek's arm could come forward for another blow, Dawlish brought up the round-nosed knife and drove it into his throat below the right ear. A spasm convulsed the Uzbek's body. He tottered forward, burbling, letting his own weapon drop as he groped to pull the protruding knife from his throat. He hit the edge of the table and collapsed on top of it.

The two drunken combatants at the other end of the table were too intent on their struggle to see Dawlish's action. Krestovski's face was purple, his eyes bulging, his tongue protruding. Dawlish felt savage joy as he heard the agonised spluttering of his tormentor. He glanced about for a weapon, saw an unopened bottle on the table. He grabbed it and sprang towards the struggling pair. Rudnev was oblivious of his approach and intent only on finishing the prince.

The heavy bottle ended its arc on Krestovski's head. His body stiffened for an instant, then slipped down, pulling Rudnev with it. Dawlish felt a stab of guilt as he raised the bottle again, remembering the admiral's sympathy, but there was no time for sentiment now. Rudnev had raised his half-comprehending face and was opening his mouth to speak as the bottle flailed down for a second time. It smashed his nose and sent him sprawling backwards on the deck.

Dawlish stepped across Krestovski's inert body and kicked the bleeding admiral twice in the midriff as he tried to struggle to his feet. The man's strength must have been superhuman for he was almost up when the bottle's next blow caught him squarely on the top of his head. This time he toppled into a silent and motionless heap.

Blood pounded in Dawlish's head as he leaned, panting, against the table's edge, reviewing his options. The open doors were beckoning, but only minutes, perhaps seconds, were available before some steward or sentry would come blundering in and raise the alarm. The Uzbek had rolled off the table and lay twitching on the deck. A gargling sound issued from his throat and his feeble hands were fluttering around the terrible weapon jutting from his neck. His knife, which had so nearly slashed Dawlish's leg open, lay close. The sight stirred him into action. He picked it up and in seconds had Egdean free from the bonds lashing him to the chair. As he sawed at the manila rope he poured out his immediate plans in an urgent whisper.

"If we drop off the gallery, we've a good chance of making it into the swamp."

He removed Egdean's gag. The seaman's brain was working as quickly as Dawlish's. "The tide must be well turned by now, sir. It'll be flowing strongly. It'll carry us back into the swamp if we drift with it."

"So much the better. Now you're free! Come on!"

Dawlish pushed the Uzbek's knife into his waistband. They crossed to the port door and looked out on the iron lattice-work gallery. The rain was still cascading and only dim pinpricks of light identified the *Orlov* and the other vessels. No alarm raised on the *Nevski* yet. Sounds of drunkenness in the saloon or wardroom might not be unusual and common seamen guards would hesitate to come between their officers.

Egdean rubbed his wrists and ankles, stimulating the circulation at the red weals where the ropes had bitten into his flesh.

"A moment please, sir," he said. "I can hardly feel anything."

More lightning, more thunder, a long half-minute of it, and the downpour strengthening. Dawlish glanced around the saloon. The only movement came from the dying Uzbek. The lamp still guttered before the icon, its reflected flame glinting on the row of wine and vodka bottles on the table.

And in that instant Dawlish had a sudden fleeting vision that offered the chance of vengeance. The merest chance, but of vengeance absolute. He pulled at Egdean's sleeve.

"Take one of the unopened vodka bottles," he said. "Put it inside your shirt. I'll find matches. Quickly now!"

He bent over Krestovski – laborious breathing indicated that he still lived – and felt his pockets. The shape of the golden humidor was unmistakable and with it was a box of lucifers. He extracted them. The humidor should be airtight, for the top pulled free with a slight sucking sound. He spilled out the cigars, opened the matchbox and pushed its contents into the gold cylinder. Then he put it in his trouser pocket.

"You have the bottle, Egdean?"

He nodded. It made a bulge in his shirt. Dawlish laid an arm on his shoulder.

"We're not finished here, Egdean." He knew that what he was about to ask was in all probability beyond his own and the seaman's weakened capacities. "We're going to drop into the water as silently as we can. Then we'll swim forward until we're under the forward sponson. I'm going to find a way up into the barbette."

"Aye, aye, sir." Egdean's expression showed that the idea frightened him, but long years of service made the idea of refusal impossible.

They stepped on to the gallery. The iron grating creaked beneath them. The water beating on the awning all but drowned out some brief exchange in Russian from somewhere forward. It sounded unconcerned, perhaps bored sentries' observations about the storm's fury. The alarm had still not been raised.

Dawlish swung himself over the rail and then, hanging by his hands, lowered himself until his feet were dangling over the water, some ten feet below. He waited until Egdean did the same, then nodded to him.

They dropped together.

Chapter 24

The splash was like an explosion in Dawlish's ears. He seemed to descend forever through the dark water before his downward velocity was checked and he could kick himself surfacewards. His head emerged well astern of the *Nevski* – the tide was indeed flowing strongly.

And still no alarm from the ship.

He relaxed for a moment and let the warm, muddy waters carry him into the darkness while his eyes adjusted. Over to the left he discerned the black lump of Egdean's head ploughing against the rain-pocked current towards the ship. He struck out after him. The water tore at him and it took almost his last reserves of energy to prevail against the stream. At last he gained the stern and swam for several yards along the port side. His clutching fingernails held on to an overlap of one plate on another. Slimy as it was, it afforded some purchase. Several yards ahead he could make out Egdean using similarly precarious handholds to drag himself forward along the ironclad's flank.

Dawlish paused to regain his breath, then continued his agonised progress. It was marginally easier to pull himself along by the plate-edges and rivets than to swim against the tide. They were just minimal holds, many too coated with slime to offer any substantial grip. He lost his position several times and drifted a few yards sternwards before anchoring himself again. He paused again to catch his breath. Light and voices issued above him from the row of the secondary battery gunports. The sounds were of as men off watch, yarning, perhaps playing cards, at mess tables between the guns. His head pounded by the rain, he went on, yard by painful yard.

Aeons passed before he could make out the overhang of the sponson carrying the port forward barbette. A half-minute's further progress brought him alongside Egdean who hung, panting, to the lowermost rung of the ladder set into the ironclad's side just forward of the barbette. They looked up. The rungs were lost to view beyond the curve of the tumblehome and they could only hope that they continued to the deck.

Two minutes passed in silence as they rested. Both knew that they were close to the limits of their strength. There was still no indication that the carnage in the admiral's saloon had been detected but their unspoken fear was that a sentry might be posted directly above them here.

The dull exhaustion in his own voice shocked Dawlish when he at last whispered, "Take the knife, Egdean. You go first. I'll be after you. If there's a guard then kill him while I slip into the barbette. If there's none, then go into the barbette yourself. Now give me the bottle. And good luck!"

The transfer was quick and Dawlish nestled the bottle inside his shirt. Egdean heaved himself from the water and began pulling himself up the ladder. Dawlish followed.

The rungs clung to the tumblehome all the way to the very top of the bulwark and had reached a point where the barbette's curve cast a deep shadow. Egdean raised his head above the edge. The deck before him was bathed in yellow light from hurricane lamps suspended beneath the awning. An armed sentry stood not ten yards away, towards the bows. His back was turned. Egdean lowered his head and gestured to Dawlish to follow. Then he raised himself cautiously until he was standing on the bulwark-top.

The sentry turned and moved a few paces aft. Egdean froze, unnoticed in the shadow. The bored sentry turned again, heading forward. The bulwark-top was a flange a scant eight inches wide and it took a fine sense of balance to edge along it to the barbette wall that rose three feet above it. The monster gun was trained forward and the open back of its splinter shield gave access to the barbette's interior. Egdean rested one hand on the wall's top and rolled over. He dropped into the sheltering darkness of the barbette itself, where the bulk of the gun mounting all but filled the enclosed space.

Dawlish, still on the ladder, peered over the bulwark, then ducked. The sentry was coming back. It would have been impossible to gauge his position by sound, even had the cascade not been drubbing on the awning. A minute passed. Then a muffled speech in Russian, a petty officer making his rounds perhaps, exchanging brief words. Dawlish waited a half-minute, then raised his head above the bulwark. The sentry had gone forward again, back turned. There was nobody else in sight.

No time now to hesitate.

He gained the interior of the barbette with as little difficulty as Egdean had, even though the fifteen seconds needed for it were terrifying. The bottle inside his shirt clinked on the on the top of the armoured barbette as he rolled across it. The sound seemed deafening to him but it raised no alarm.

Huddled in the narrow space between the monster gun and the curved wall, Dawlish whispered, "There must be a trap-door that reaches towards the magazine. They've probably got to return the gun to this bearing to reload it, so it must be by the breech."

More lighting now, irregular but continuous, the thunder's delay indicating that it was far distant. They wriggled along the edge of the mounting until the breech loomed above them. There were a number of hydraulic cylinders for raising the shell and charge in a cradle, and for ramming it home, but it was the davit assembly there that confirmed Dawlish's guess to be correct. Below it were the outlines of a hatch about four-feet square. A ring on one side showed where to lift it. This was the access to the magazine deep in the bowels of the ship from which the davit would hoist shells and charges. The fear that this closure might be bolted from beneath remained unspoken while Egdean positioned himself to lift it.

"Wait Egdean." It was impossible to know what noise it might make when raised. Better to wait until. . .

Until the lightning rippled again. One second, two, three. . .

And then the thunder, loud enough, even over the rain's pounding, to drown any creak.

"Now lift it, Egdean!"

It held for a moment and then yawned open. A square shaft extended into darkness, with ladder rungs set in one wall.

Dawlish removed the bottle from his shirt, handed it to Egdean and motioned to him to remain. Then he swung himself into the shaft. He ignored the feeling of claustrophobia that threatened to engulf him as he descended into the blackness, an ever-receding square of dim-light above.

He counted rungs . . . twenty-five, twenty-six . . . thirty-one, thirty-two, thirty-three. . .

About ten inches separated each so he reckoned that he must be below the waterline by now. He lowered his left foot again but this time it encountered not a rung but a solid surface. It turned out to be another trap-door. He stood on the lowermost rung, steadying himself with his left hand while his right moved over the trap-door's surface, searching for a lifting point. His fingers made contact with a ring almost directly beneath his feet and he pulled. The closure was heavy – it must have been solid plate, an inch or more thick – and it took an agonising effort to raise it into a vertical position. The lifting ring clicked into a retaining clip set in the bulkhead behind to hold it open.

Dawlish's foot felt the first rung below the trapdoor and he lowered himself. Twelve more rungs took him to the bottom of the compartment. The smell of powder left him in no doubt that he had penetrated the magazine. He groped forward in the darkness, arms outstretched. His fingers contacted something smooth, cylindrical and metallic, over a foot in diameter. He moved to the left and encountered more of the same. These shells were not what he sought and he felt his way to the other end of the chamber. His hands detected the unmistakable touch of silk, which would vaporise and leave no residue in the barrel, telling him that he had located the bags containing the powder charges. Through the fabric he could feel the florin-sized hexagonal discs of brown cocoa-powder that he had read that the French Navy had recently adopted. The *Nevski* had been supplied with the best propellant charges available.

He felt for the top of the nearest pile and dragged the uppermost bag towards him. It weighed about a stone. The size was ideal – ideal for lodging in the rungs of the access shaft to provide a flash path from the barbette interior to the magazine. All he needed now was time. His spirits were lifting above the dumb, dogged endurance that had carried him this far.

There was enough slackness in the charge bag that he lifted to his shoulder for it to mould itself to it and he could keep it in position by inclining his head against it. He began to climb the ladder. Egdean relieved him of the bag at the top.

"Push it under the breech," he hissed.

He left Egdean to it and climbed back down to the magazine – the descent seemed shorter this time – and selected another bag. He climbed again, panting from the effort, until he was almost at the top. This bag he wedged just below the upper trap-door.

Down again. He collected two more charge bags, jamming one about half-way between the barbette and the lower trap-door and the other at the trap-door itself. He descended into the magazine for the last time and piled a dozen bags at the bottom of the ladder. Any flash penetrating down the shaft would impinge directly on them. His hands were shaking with excitement and he had forgotten his exhaustion as he lifted the last bag to his shoulder and began to climb.

Egdean was helping him through the topmost trap-door when the alarm was raised aft. A single shout, running footsteps and then much more yelling.

The slaughter in the Admiral's saloon had been discovered.

Orders were being called and feet stampeded past the other side of the iron wall. Dawlish resisted the urge to hurry, telling himself that the forward barbettes would be the last places searched.

"Slit this sack open," he whispered to Egdean, pushing the bag at him. "Empty it in a heap by the trap-door."

Egdean's knife slashed through the silk and he emptied the powder in a mound by the open mouth of the access shaft. Dawlish's heart was thumping and his hands were shaking as he pulled Krestovski's humidor from his pocket. He pulled it open. The top came free with a reassuring sucking sound – it had stayed watertight. He emptied the matches into his palm. This was the moment of decision.

"Drop overboard, Egdean. I'll be right after you. Strike away from the ship and drift with the current. Go now!"

Egdean nodded, crawled around the gun-mounting until he was at the outer edge of the barbette. Then he raised himself and vaulted over. Even before he splashed into the water Dawlish had smashed the neck of the vodka bottle against the iron wall behind the powder heap. He poured the clear liquid into a pool on the metal deck beside it.

He selected a match, struck it against the iron but it would not light, neither would the next, nor the next again. He was desperate now and he took the whole bundle in his hand and scraped them along the rough side of the gun mounting. There was a spark, then a flash of flame as twenty-five or thirty match-heads took fire from each other. For an instant he saw their light reflected in the pool of vodka before he dropped the burning mass into it. A blue flame licked back at him and hovered over part of the surface of the liquid. In seconds it must reach the powder.

He had never known terror like this. He flung himself towards the barbette wall and clawed on top. He rolled over and fell into the blackness as a voice yelled out and a rifle blasted somewhere behind him.

The impact with the water winded him, for he had fallen unhandily, and he went under. He was choking when he reached the surface again but he struck out at once. The tide was flowing very strongly now and he was drawn parallel to the *Nevski's* side. The knowledge that hell was brewing behind him lent extra power to his strokes. He was almost past the stern when Egdean's voice reached him from the darkness.

"I'm close to your left, sir," he yelled, all attempts at concealment abandoned. Dawlish realised that Egdean had remained hanging on some protrusion by the stern, waiting for him lest he needed assistance.

"Keep going," Dawlish gasped. "Swim for your life!"

A searchlight flashed into life on the mizzen mast and stabbed into the darkness to his right. The first ignition roared behind him and an orange glow lit up the creek, the mangrove and the sky itself. Involuntarily, he found himself rolling on his back, overcome by the urge to see the outcome of his work.

A flame-flecked column of smoke was billowing up from the overhanging port barbette. The masts and yards stood etched in black against the red. Then, in succession, four more explosions, so close together as to be almost one, sent fresh plumes of flame belching skywards from the great iron cylinder, all but engulfing the vessel's top-hamper. A wave of heat blasted across the water, driving rain with it horizontally, searing his eyes, close as he was to the surface. Pieces of debris arced off into the darkness from the inferno's glowing heart. He saw the massive barrel of the forty-six ton gun rearing upwards, as if attempting to escape from its mounting. in its agony It remained in its position until the next explosion, the largest yet, which signalled that the successive detonations in the access shaft had set off the main magazine, not just the charges but the shells as well.

An orange ball of flame blasted horizontally through the plates of the ironclad's side, beneath the sponson. The entire weapon, and the huge barbette that had sheltered it, bereft now of support, toppled outwards and crashed with a shower of spray into the water beneath. A jagged hole had been torn in the *Nevski's* flank and deck and within it a furnace raged. Against the fiery column that still clawed skywards, the foremast was toppling into the glowing pit. As it collapsed into this dreadful abyss another explosion, as terrible as the last, engulfed the whole forward section of the ship. The other forward sponson's magazine had also exploded, ripping the entire structure, the gun-mounting and its protective breastwork, as a single body from the hull and casting it into the darkness beyond. A sheet of fire rushed aft over the deck, enveloping the twin funnels and the already staggering mainmast.

The *Nevski* was in her death throes. The section of the hull abaft the now-missing sponson positions parted from the bows and the blazing pit of fire opened out to become two separate walls of flame. The stern section rotated so that it began to drift beam-on with the flooding tide. For a brief moment Dawlish feared that it might bear down on himself and Egdean but then it began to roll over. Beyond it the bows were already disappearing in a cloud of steam.

The after section rolled over further, exposing its whole blazing deck. A series of smaller explosions rippled across its flame-washed surface as the ammunition for the lighter weapons detonated. The tortured hull rotated more and frantic human figures were scuttling through the fire. The funnels were tearing free to follow the falling mainmast. Further and further the hull rolled. The midships forty-six tonner cannon tore itself loose, wrenching from the barbette and ripping a new access for the flames to the entrails beneath.

Its disappearance triggered the last and mightiest detonation of all as the midships and after magazines erupted simultaneously. The fireball that blasted from them dwarfed all earlier explosions and the searing wave of heat that blasted over the anchorage forced Dawlish to duck his head below the water.

When he looked up again, shaking droplets from his eyes, the last traces of the *Nevski* had disappeared. Only the column of smoke rising skywards remained to show that she had ever existed.

Chapter 25

The *Orlov* was coming alive as the tide carried them past at a separation of fifty yards. Lights danced on her deck, and shouted commands urged men to their stations. The first boats were already pulling away to search for survivors. Nobody noticed the two heads, dark against the dark water. They drifted onwards then, past the colliers – a boat was drawing away from the second – and past the yacht.

Dawlish came to rest with a bump against the remains of the floating boom, the undamaged upstream half. He had been swimming on his back and he clutched at the log. Exhausted, he knew that it would need an effort of will to get under and, then release it to drift on into the swamp, like flotsam, with the tide. He looked back. The rain was dying. The first boats had reached the site of the *Nevski's* loss from the other Russian vessels and the *Orlov's* searchlights were sweeping across the debris-strewn waters. The entire anchorage reflected flames from still-burning flotsam and smoke drifted and billowed overhead.

"Sir!"

Egdean had also reached the boom a few yards to Dawlish's left, and was pulling himself along it towards him. With much difficulty, he was dragging a half-submerged log that had been held against the barrier by the current.

"Here's something to hang on to, sir," he said. "If we can push it across we can hang on to it as we drift upstream."

Dawlish shook himself from the half-dazed reverie into which he had sunk. He found it impossible to wipe the *Nevski's* fiery end from his mind, yet he felt no joy at his victory. Twenty-one men, including Tobin, had set out from Camp Beaconsfield. Now just Egdean and himself remained. And for how long?

It took long minutes to shift the log over the boom, for their fatigue had all but robbed them of their strength. In the end it was only by Egdean getting underneath and heaving it upwards, while Dawlish guided it across the slippery boom, that the log finally slid across. They ducked under the barrier and reached for the it. It all but submerged under their combined weights. They clung to it, stupefied with exhaustion, deaf to the clamour of activity downstream.

And the flooding tide, slower now, carried the sodden log and its two bedraggled parasites deeper into the swamp.

*

Dawlish struggled into consciousness. He was shivering and very cold. His limbs were stiff and aching. Pain raged in his burned cheek. He touched it, found it wet with pus. He was lying on a patch of mud, half-sunk in it, ill sheltered from the steady downpour by the mangrove above and around him. Egdean was crouching with his back towards him and peering out through the foliage at the creek beyond. He turned as he heard Dawlish's movements. He looked like a mud-smeared scarecrow. Dawlish knew that he himself could look no better. He tried to restrain his chattering teeth but failed.

"I hope you're rested, sir," Egdean said. "When I got you here last night, I was afraid you'd never see the light of day again."

"You brought me here?" It was an effort to get the words out.

"Some sort of fainting fit overtook you on that log. It was the Lord himself who gave me the strength to keep your face out of the water."

Dawlish had no recollection of anything since crossing the boom. But, aching and wretched as he was, he felt that he was less exhausted than before. It was not surprising – judging from the elevation of the sun's glow beyond the leaden clouds he must have slept for several hours.

"You saved my life again, Egdean," he said. "You have my word that I'll see you rewarded for it if we ever see England again."

"Do you think we'll make it, sir?"

"It's either that or die in this filthy morass. Have you any idea of the time of day?"

"About midday, sir. 'twas just getting light when I woke myself. 'tis been four or five hours since an' it's rained for most of them."

Dawlish felt both hunger and thirst. There was rainwater aplenty to drink but there was no immediate prospect of food. He moved over beside Egdean and looked out over the creek through the foliage. It was narrow here, not more than twenty yards, and they had obviously been carried far from the Russian anchorage by the tide before Egdean had decided to risk coming ashore. An assembly of sticks, not unlike a half-submerged wattle fence, rose from the muddy water in mid-stream. It was a fish trap, similar to so many others they had passed on the journey from Camp Beaconsfield. It was one of a half-dozen in a line parallel to the bank

"Any sign of life?" Dawlish asked. "We need a canoe."

"A few blacks came here this morning, sir," Egdean said. "They emptied the trap. There was a couple of canoes with two boys and a man in one and two women in t'other. I reckon they'll be back towards nightfall to check if they've caught anything. We might be able to surprise them then."

"You've still got the knife?"

Egdean held it up. It seemed a puny weapon with which to win their way to deliverance but it was all they possessed apart from their mud-caked rags.

"It don't seem right, sir, to use it on some poor heathen as never did us no harm."

The remark was insubordinate, but Dawlish let it pass. He hoped that they would not need to use the knife but, if there was no option, it might be unavoidable.

Raison d'état.

An awkward silence. Egdean broke it.

"It was tough on the lads we left behind, sir," he said "An' not for them alone neither. There'll be many an orphan and a widow-woman who'll know the inside of a workhouse before the year is out."

He paused, hesitant to continue, then asked: "Was it necessary, sir?'

Dawlish did not answer. He guessed that the question would trouble him for years.

"We can mourn our people later," he said at last. "The best tribute we can give them is to get back to Camp Beaconsfield. If we can get word to *Nomad* there's a chance she can trail the Russians if they leave. The *Orlov's* the threat now."

They lapsed into silence again. Dawlish eased his thirst by wringing out his sodden shirt into his mouth – the unceasing rain at least offered fresh water. Hunger gnawed but he knew that he could keep going another day, maybe two, without food. He kept watch through the afternoon, ignoring the torment of his wounded face, and cleansing it with rainwater as best he could while Egdean dozed in discomfort on the mud. There were no sounds other than the persistent swishing of the rain and the cries of distant monkeys. Once he watched in horror as a crocodile slipped by, its eyes alone breaking the surface. He shuddered at the sight, knowing that at some stage he would have to enter the water again.

The afternoon passed. Attempts to trap any of the small crabs that peered from holes in the mud, and scuttled from one to the other, proved futile. He occupied himself by scratching on the mud with a twig as much of the Delta's geography as he could remember, trying to sketch the maze of creeks through which Tobin had guided *Alpha* and *Beta* from Camp Beaconsfield. It was an almost impossible task. Judging from the narrowness of the creek in which they now sheltered, he estimated that they were two or three miles north of the *Nevski's* grave, and somewhat to the north-west of Elepa. The best chance for escape lay in striking due east, leaving Elepa to the south, and to continue in that direction for eight or ten miles before attempting to follow the tangle of waterways south-easterly to either Camp Beaconsfield or Bonny. Arthur West had managed it somehow, dying though he was, so it must be possible.

All it needed was determination.

And a canoe.

*

The sun was long down and the was tide beginning to flood again, sluggishly at first, when Dawlish woke Egdean and outlined his ideas on how to cope with any passing canoe. None had appeared all day and the unspoken fear between them was that this might be a poor fishing area, seldom visited. Cold, sodden and hungry as they were, the prospect of another night on this pestilential mudbank was depressing. Two hours passed, made wretched by mosquitoes.

Dawlish sensed that Egdean wanted to say something, yet was holding back.

"We're going to make it back, Egdean," he said with as much conviction as he could muster.

"It ain't that that worries me, sir." The words were hesitant, had a tone of deep sadness. "It's why 'twas me as was chosen, sir."

"Chosen?"

"By the Lord, sir. For there were better men than me on our boats and maybe even on that Russian ship too."

He hesitated, fearful that he had gone too far, and then, sensing Dawlish's sympathy, went on in a rush.

"Ned Webb, sir – he was a good man. Six little children he had too. And Jacob Browning, sir – a sound Methody Christian, an' a teetotaller to boot. An' Bill Barrow, sir, and Mr. Hinckley. Even Jack O'Malley, though he were a Roman, and that Tobin, though he were a pagan. All good men, sir, with nothing to be ashamed of. But 'twas me who was spared"

Tears were glistening in the corners of his bloodshot grey eyes and there was a catch in his voice.

"But the Lord had a purpose for you, Egdean." Dawlish hated himself for drawing on the authority of a Deity of whose existence he was never sure, yet was ready to say anything that would sustain Egdean's spirit for now.

"But I'm not worthy, sir. I carry a burden, sir, like the pilgrim Christian in that book, but I can't lay it down like he did. It was the others deserved to live, sir, not me and – "

He stopped, stiffened and pointed downstream.

The sounds of voices and paddles were unmistakable but Dawlish could see nothing. He pushed forward to see better through the mangrove screen. A hundred yards distant, at the bend of the creek, a pinprick of glowing red. It was creeping towards them, a single dugout with an earthen pot of fire amidships to give light. His cold numbness left him as his excitement rose.

He reached across, touched the seaman on the arm.

"I need you, Egdean. Don't fail me now, not after so much. The Lord chose you for a reason, and he's still with us."

The light came closer with excruciating slowness. It stopped for minutes on end, apparently busy with another fish trap, then resumed its progress. Dawlish eyed the distance to the trap opposite him – ten or twelve yards. Swimming with caution, it would require less than a half-minute to reach it. He whispered his last instructions to Egdean. Their eyes were now riveted on the canoe.

"We'll drag them out, Egdean. You have the knife?"

"In my shirt, sir."

"Don't use it unless you have to." He had nothing against the occupants. It was close enough for them to reach the shore. There had been killing enough already.

Long minutes passed before the canoe drew level. They could see the outlines of two people but the overcast sky made it impossible to make out any details despite the light flickering from the pot. The figure in the stern guided the dugout against the fish trap with skilful strokes while the occupant of the bows was crouched over, intent on tying up. Now was the time to act.

Dawlish shuddered at the memory of the crocodile he had seen in the afternoon but it was too late to hesitate. Egdean had already slipped noiselessly into the water and he followed. The soft mud clutched at his feet but he pulled himself free and began to swim, keeping abreast of Egdean.

The canoe's occupants were oblivious of their approach. Egdean was heading for the stern – the figure there, armed with a sharp-bladed, leaf-shaped paddle represented the greater hazard and would have to be dealt with first. The occupant at the bows was bent over the trap, drawing something from its depths on a rope. Only the sound of this effort broke the silence.

They were now so close that the curving side of the dugout was overhanging their heads, and they were still undetected. Hissing "Now!" to Egdean, Dawlish reached up, grabbed the gunwale with both hands and heaved himself upwards, as if to hoist himself on board. The canoe rocked violently, threatening to roll on top of him. He pushed himself half-out of the water, kicking upwards so that he could rest his entire weight on the edge. The man at the stern shrieked with surprise, lost his balance as Egdean grabbed him, then dropped his paddle and fell overboard with a loud splash. Another voice, more high-pitched, screamed from the bows. There was a threshing in the water and then the flow carried the paddler away with it, still gasping and struggling.

Egdean shouted: "He's gone, sir!"

The figure in the bows was edging back now, crouched down and holding the gunwale for support. Dawlish, in the water, hanging on beyond the glowing pot, was still rocking the little craft. With the advantage of surprise lost, he realised that it would be difficult to overbalance and dislodge this second adversary.

"Be careful, sir! Stay out of his reach!" Egdean's voice called out from the darkness. "I'll deal with him!"

Egdean reached for the overhanging stern and began to pull himself on board. Dawlish released his hold on the gunwale and kicked back in the water, hoping to circle behind the crouching form and provide distraction while Egdean approached from its front. Then he froze, for the glow of the fire-pot had lit up the figure's features for the first time.

This was no native of the swamp.

The pallid face, desperate and terrified, was that of the bedraggled white woman he had seen a few nights before in Ephraim Loveday's war-canoe. Clad now in a loose wrapper of nondescript grey, her tangled hair lank around her drawn face, she watched, horror-stricken, as Egdean levered himself over the stern. She reached down with shaking hands and picked up the pot. Her intention of dashing its embers in Egdean's face was obvious.

Dawlish, treading water, was too far away still to restrain her physically but he shouted with all the authority he could muster.

"Put it down, woman! I'm a British Officer! We're your friends!"

The woman started and glanced around, her face fully illuminated by the pot's red flicker. An expression of something like hope flashed for a moment across her features, only to disappear at once and be replaced again by a look of sheer terror.

"You bleeders!" She shrieked into the darkness, her voice a mix of fear, anger and hatred. "Mock me again, would yer?"

The accent was Cockney. Desperate as the situation might be, Dawlish felt a rush of hope.

"Calm yourself, woman!" he shouted. "We're Englishmen!"

Egdean had dragged himself on to the rocking stern and he crouched there with his left arm thrown across his face to shield it from a possible shower of hot cinders. The woman was not more than eight feet from him. She raised the pot over her head, throwing her face into shadow again.

"Not another step, you bastard, or I'll roast you," she screamed. "You don't fool me with yer mimicry! Get back or I'll let you have it!"

For all her defiance, Dawlish detected a note of uncertainty.

"We're your fellow-countrymen, ma'am! For God's sake don't throw that pot!" He saw her pause, uncertain. "We're going to show you what we are. Egdean! Let her see your face!"

Egdean lowered his left arm. The woman did not cast the fire-pot as she had threatened but instead inclined it so that the amber glow lit up both her own features and Egdean's. She seemed transfixed by the sight of the ruddy and unmistakably European countenance before her. And then a sob convulsed her.

"I thought I'd never see an Englishman again," she said. "Them bleedin' Russians was as bad as Ephraim's lot. No! Worse they was!"

Dawlish swam to the side of the dugout and hoisted himself in. All the woman's fight was gone. She was weeping without restraint as Egdean gathered her to him, comforting her like a child, his face full of compassion.

Chapter 26

They had pulled in to the bank. Dawlish was impatient to move immediately but the woman clung to them and poured out a long, sob-interrupted stream that was difficult to interrupt. He decided that it was worth hearing her out to calm her down. She appeared at home in the swamp. With luck, she might well prove a useful guide back to Bonny, if not to Camp Beaconsfield. The disappearance of the other paddler did not seem to concern her. When she at last quietened, he began to question her.

"What's your name, ma'am?"

"Polly Cringle, sir."

"What ae you doing here, Polly?"

"It's a long story, sir." She looked from Dawlish to Egdean and back again, eyes pleading. "Can you save me, sir?"

"We'll do our best, Polly, we'll do our best. But who are you?"

"I ain't no lady, sir, if that's what you mean. Born in the Bethnal Green workhouse, I was, not that it's nothing against me. My ma scarpered a week after. Not that I blame her. I'd have done the same myself if I'd had her trouble." She said it without bitterness.

An East End orphanage had raised her and she remained a charge there until a situation was found for her as scullery maid in a Wapping tavern. She was about thirteen then.

"Maybe one of you two gents knows it?" She brightened a little. "The Rose and Crown. Very popular with seafaring men, it was. Five years I spent there and 'tweren't bad at all. Put me behind the bar, they did, cos the customers thought I looked right saucy. The landlord, he was a bit partial to me, if you receive my meaning, an' generous with it, but his wife, the bitch, she kicks me out after she finds us in the cellar together one morning. Just havin' a bit of fun, we was, all harmless like. So I packs my traps and I'm off down the road to the Star of the East. Put behind the bar there, I was. A nice dress, good money too. And 'twas there I met Tom Devlin."

Tom's memory brought on a new spasm of weeping. When she became coherent again it emerged that he had been a self-styled palm-oil trader, encountered while he was on a drunken spree while on leave in London. He had survived three years in the Delta but in two weeks had squandered his accumulated earnings and was heading back to West Africa for another three to four years. Polly had been impressed by his open-handedness and had allowed herself to be talked into returning with him.

"He seemed like a real gent at the time." She was sniffling now. "We did have a good time while he had money, I'll give him that. Don't get me wrong – he were a decent cove, but he weren't no trader hisself, just a clerk for Goodbody and Nagle. He said I'd be a lady in Africa, with black servants to do my bidding. An' I believed him, God help me! Poor Tom had little more than a shack at Goodbody's depot at Forcados, an' a right dirty hole that is, I can tell you"

She had rotted there with Tom for eighteen hopeless months until a combination of blackwater fever and delirium tremens had swept him away. He bequeathed her on his deathbed to his bosom companion, Alf Gilmore.

"Look after her, Alf, she's one in a million, them was his very words, sir, and he was gone within an hour of utterin' them. But Alf, he was a pig, sir, and he'd already half a dozen black biddies to warm his bed, so he was in no need of an Englishwoman who had his measure. An' that I had, sir, that I had!"

Alf's inheritance coincided with news of Ephraim Loveday's ambition to add a white wife to his harem. So much Polly had deduced later. She had woken from a drunken stupor to find herself trussed in the bottom of a canoe, en route to Ephraim's capital at Elepa. Alf's reward had been paid in palm-oil.

More she would not tell immediately, so deeply had the horror of what followed scarred her. She spat out Ephraim's name with loathing.

"What that animal made me do – but no sir! You're a gentleman and don't need to know it. He were a real pig!"

She was sobbing again. Egdean held her to him and cushioned her head against his shoulder. And then anger overcame sorrow.

"He even made me catch his bloody fish and cook it with my own hands, the pig!" Polly was shaking with rage now. "And that bastard Festus – him that this gentleman did for just now, and good riddance too – Festus was set to watch me like a dog. Watched me day and night, he did, an' reported every move to Ephraim. 'twas Festus who pegged out the senior wife to drown at high tide to make room for me. Screaming and gurgling and spluttering something awful she was, though it didn't help her none."

Egdean's presence seemed to reassure her and she cheered up somewhat.

"Did you gents have anything to do with the big Russian ship that blowed up last night?" she asked. "Terrible slaughter it was, Ephraim said. He went there to see it today. Gave him a nasty turn it did, especially seein' they was such good friends of his before."

There was no gain to be had from concealment.

"We did it, Polly," Dawlish said. "With good reason too. Those people are enemies of the Queen."

"The Queen wanted it done, did she, sir?" Polly's voice was hushed with reverence.

"She did indeed, Polly, and she can't wait to get news of it. But now we're stuck here. We need to get to Bonny as soon as possible so she'll know. Could you guide us there?"

She shook her head sadly. "I know the creeks round here," she said, "and on the far side of Elepa too, but beyond that I'd be lost."

"Look, Polly, this isn't the first time we've seen you. A week ago we saw you with Ephraim in his war-canoe. He was coming back from burning a village."

"He burned it all right," Polly said, "and half the people in it, babbies and old people too. I told you he was a pig."

"Could you find your way to that village, Polly?" Dawlish said. "If you can get us that far I'm sure we'd manage from then on. We'll take you with us. I guarantee that if we make it to Bonny, I'll have you back in London within a month. Back in the Star of the East or anywhere else you want, and money too to get you started."

"It won't be easy sir, but I'll do my best." Polly said, and there was a note of determination in her voice. "We'd need to start now."

There were two paddles in the canoe. Dawlish and Egdean began to stroke. On Polly's instructions they dropped downstream while she, using Egdean's knife, gutted the fish she had just caught and roasted them over the charcoal in the pot. They passed seawards down the creek for a mile before Polly directed them into an intersecting waterway to port. It was very narrow and overarched with mangrove. They pulled into the shadows to devour the half-cooked fish. It was charred on the surface and almost raw within but nothing had ever tasted better to Dawlish.

The sky cleared partly in the course of the night. The moon lit up their progress through the creeks and reference to the stars confirmed that their general course was easterly. Polly advised giving Elepa an even wider berth than Dawlish had anticipated since she was concerned by the intensity of the fishing activity in the area by night.

"Won't you be missed, Polly?" Egdean asked. "Will they come searching for you?"

Bitterness in her laugh. "Not tonight," she said. "Ephraim's got a new wife today, from Degema. He'll be busy enough with her. He was reckonin' on Festus watching over me and he'll never miss us before morning."

"You're sure we'll be clear of Elepa by then?"

"Well clear, sir. There's a hut this side of there. It's like a church to them, a shrine. We could rest there. Ephraim brought me there once. Nobody comes there normally, dead scared of it, they is. Say it's haunted by spirits they does, the heathen pagans, but I don't believe none of it."

The night was one long, monotonous session of paddling, marked only by the turns in the creeks and channels. Polly's navigation was impressive but not infallible. Three times they found themselves in a creek that narrowed to a trickle, forcing retreat, then pressing on, always eastwards, despite their meanderings.

They met no other canoes. Aching in every muscle and bone, plagued by itching bites, both men were glad to let Polly relieve them at intervals. She was not only fresher, but more skilled with the paddle, and the dugout seemed to leap forward when she replaced one of them. The burn on Dawlish's face was a running sore now, a magnet for insects. The weals from the cords that had bound Egdean's wrists and ankles to the chair in the *Nevski's* saloon were broken in places and oozing blood. Each forced from his mind the concern that several more days of such paddling lay ahead and they concentrated on nothing but the next stroke.

Only once did the generally eastwards trend of their journey force them to cross one of the wide channels running north to south. They were lucky, for there was no sign of human activity in the vicinity. They crossed rapidly nonetheless, crouching low in the canoe, conscious that they stood out dark against the shimmering, moonlit waters.

Finding the shrine proved more difficult than Polly had expected and they made two more wrong turnings, wasting time in retreats. The sky was brightening in the east when they entered the narrow waterway, at the head of which they found the hut. It stood on a sand hummock that rose above the mud, surrounded by palms and thick undergrowth inside the outlying fringe of mangrove. Here a foetid odour of decomposition overlay the swamp's own heavy miasma.

Dawlish examined the place while the others dragged the canoe from the water and secreted it in the foliage. It was a tumbledown, mud-walled, palm-thatch structure and it was beyond his comprehension that such a dismal and insignificant place could be filled with so much dread. The lop-sided hovel sheltered a few crude carvings, a white-daubed clay figure and several earthenware pots. Three mould-covered skulls lay in a corner, half-buried in rotting leaves. Apprehensive of what he might find, Dawlish lifted the lid of one of the pots. He found, to his delight, that it was half full of over-ripe bananas. Another pot contained a pawpaw and the remainder, foul-smelling cassava. The deity must have received its offerings in the very recent past. That must make a repeat visit unlikely in the near future. Polly advised against the cassava – it could be poisonous if not steeped long enough in water before consumption – but they divided the fruit in equal shares and wolfed it down.

The shrine, miserable as it might be, offered shelter against the rain that began again in mid-morning. They stood watch in succession, staring out into the little creek while the others slept. In the afternoon Dawlish took his turn, trying in vain to ignore the ache of his suppurating cheek and his growing hunger. He had maintained an air of confidence while with the others but now, alone, he admitted to himself that reaching safety was probably all but impossible. Death in the swamp would be slow and squalid. Regrets crowded in on him. Not just for the loss of his crews – and that was most painful of all – but for the years that would be denied him, of striving and achievement, of a woman's love perhaps, and maybe of children too, of honourable old age.

My name is writ in water.

A grey curtain of rain reduced visibility to tens of yards. He forced himself to ignore the insidious temptation of despair and occupied himself by watching the jerking movements of the mud-skippers that flitted between the exposed mangrove roots.

He heard stirring behind him. It was Polly. In daylight she looked even more wan and pathetic than she had done in the fire-pot's glow. She was feeding it with twigs now, her body thin and pinched, her face wasted and pallid. Scars of insect bites that had once turned sceptic blotched her neck and arms. She missed several teeth and her hair was like filthy straw. She saw that he had noticed her and, when he smiled, she came over.

"I don't want to trouble you, sir," she said, "but I couldn't sleep no longer." She lapsed into silence, more shy and deferential than on the previous evening, more conscious of the social chasm that divided them despite their shared wretchedness.

"How old are you, Polly?" Dawlish felt a surge of compassion.

"I think I'm twenty-three, sir, but I'm not sure." She looked nearer to fifty than to half that and yet, despite her decrepitude, there was a noticeable determination about her.

"You want to see London again, Polly?"

She nodded. "It's a paradise compared to this, sir. I'd crawl there on me hands and knees. But I'm sure I don't know why a gent like you would ever leave it willingly."

"Ambition, Polly, ambition."

"Ambition, sir?"

He saw that she was puzzled and could not understand the concept but he outlined what had brought himself and Egdean here. She laughed when he told her how the *Nevski's* destruction had been encompassed.

"Don't lose no sleep over them Russians you blowed up sir," she told him. "They'd all of 'em been dead anyway in another six weeks. Dyin' like flies, they was already, from fevers and fluxes. Never a day without one of them being planted in the cemetery they made near Elepa. Sometimes two or three together. Right doleful it was too, with an old cove with a beard moaning and singing over them."

"I saw somewhat of it myself, Polly. A funeral. When I came to spy out the lie of the land."

"Couldn't stand the heat, they couldn't, sir, seein' as how they comes from such a cold place theirselves. One of them hanged himself too – I seen it myself – one of the blokes as came to Elepa to buy fruit. Ephraim, rot him, would never let me out of the hut when there was white men about. Didn't trust me with me own kind, he didn't, but I saw it through the thatch. Couldn't take it no more, poor chap, so he hanged himself from a tree. They didn't bury him with in the others but out in the mud, near where Ephraim's wife was pegged."

She spoke in a conversational, even gossipy, tone. She seemed to have passed the stage of disgust and found the incidents she related interesting only in a neutral way.

"Then there was two Russians as tried to escape. They stole a canoe but didn't get far. They was flogged on the big ship, beaten with a sort of cat. Ephraim was invited to watch, an' he liked it, he did. Died under the lash, they did, poor souls, and Ephraim could talk of nothin' else for days. Giving him ideas, them bleedin' Russians was, an' God knows he was bad enough to start with."

A note of fear had crept into her voice and she shuddered. She grasped Dawlish by the wrist and looked straight into his eyes.

"If they should catch us, sir," her voice was very quiet, "or even if you think we're cornered, don't let them take me alive, sir."

"They won't corner us, Polly. They've other concerns now."

She would not be comforted. "It would be a mercy if you was to slit my throat, an' that other gentleman's, an' your own too, sir. But me first, I'm beggin' you. That Ephraim, he's a demon." She lapsed into silence, overcome by some private memory. Dawlish did not press her further. Then she said: "You'll promise me, sir? Won't you?"

"I promise, Polly."

He reached out and shook her hand. It was small, but hard and scaly. Then silence again, each sunk in a gloom made deeper by the miserable scene before them.

His own thoughts drifted back to the *Nevski*. To the shock of Krestovski's transformation from chivalrous foe to devil incarnate. To the bestial treatment of his victims. To the final inferno that had engulfed ironclad. He forced himself to cold evaluation. Terrible as the price had been, the main threat to the Royal Navy was eliminated, the only threat that its proud group of first-rate ships could not challenge with confidence. In that, he had succeeded against the odds.

But the thought of the *Orlov* reproved him.

Sleeker but less powerful than her consort, but a fast and lethal raider nonetheless. She alone was capable of fighting her way past the *Nomad* and *Volage* if she had to and any other British ships lying off the Delta too. Unless she proved unlucky, she would reach the open sea to wreak appalling havoc on Britain's shipping lanes before she could be brought to bay.

In the remote recesses of his mind the memory stirred of himself, a boy of nine or ten, reading on his bed beneath the sampler that proclaimed that God is Love while a branch of the elm outside brushed the window in the breeze. The book, 'Deeds of Famous Admirals', a gift from his Uncle Ralph, had shaped his life. One dictum he had never forgotten, a saying of Nelson's, stern and unremitting.

"Now, had we taken ten sail, and allowed the eleventh to have escaped when it had been possible to have got at her, I would never have called it well done."

The *Orlov* was like that eleventh sail.

It could not be called well done.

And for all that the *Nevski* was gone, Dawlish knew in his heart that he had still failed.

Chapter 27

It was just before sundown and they were cooking the remains of Polly's catch. Egdean was on guard. He stiffened suddenly and gestured for silence.

"Here, sir!" Polly handed Dawlish the knife with which she had been cutting the fish and covered the fire pot, cutting off its smoke. The sound of an approaching paddle was unmistakable.

Egdean flattened himself against the wall at one side of the hut's entrance while Dawlish crouched at the other. He peeped out. A single dugout, a small one, eight feet or so long, was threading its way up the creek. An old man was huddled in the stern, deftly manoeuvring it. His withered body was smeared with ashes, which gave him a white and leprous appearance. He was alone.

Dawlish pulled Polly to her knees beside him and signalled to her to peer out. Her face lit up in recognition.

"It's Iziki," she whispered "The wizard. Ephraim's uncle. He ain't a bad bloke. He was the only one of 'em to treat me decent."

Iziki drove his canoe against the bank and stepped out stiffly, sinking to his shins in the mud. He dragged the craft out of the water and on to the dry patch of ground with slow and rheumatic movements. He appeared to have no suspicion of anybody else being close. Having beached his dugout, he reached into the bottom and pulled out a sack. Then he came hobbling towards the hut.

Dawlish and Egdean were poised on either side of the doorway. Iziki entered, blinking his eyes against the gloom within. He paused on the threshold, still oblivious of their presence, but his nose was sniffing and twitching as he detected the smell of the cooking fish for the first time. Terror flashed across his face but before he could cry out Egdean had stepped forward and grabbed him. One arm encircled his body, trapping his arms, while the other locked on his throat. Dawlish sprang in front of the terrified captive and held the knife's point against his breast. Iziki's eyes bulged and his horror was compounded when Polly stepped from the shadows.

"Don't kill him, sir," she said. "We can just truss him up and leave him here. Nobody'll come looking for him for a day or so."

"Ask him if there's a search on for you, or for us." Dawlish raised the knife to Iziki's cheek to emphasise the value of co-operation. He nodded to Egdean to release his headlock.

Polly unleashed a stream of incomprehensible pidgin at the quaking wizard. His answer came in a babbling rush. Polly shook her head and turned to Dawlish.

"It ain't no good, sir," she said. "He's too frightened. He's just about able to think of beggin' for mercy."

She spoke again in the involved West Coast pidgin that seemed to have more in common with the local languages than with English. Iziki answered hesitantly, his fear-haunted eyes locked on the knife. A lengthy question and answer session followed before Polly translated again.

"He says the Russians is gettin' ready to leave sir."

They must fear the presence of a third torpedo boat, must want to take no chances.

"They don't reckon that it's safe no more in the creek," Polly said. "There's a gang of 'em in Elepa now and they're holding Ephraim and most of his headmen hostage until enough fresh fruit supplies is gathered for them. It'll take time. Ephraim's people will have to trade for it. It comes from the land above the swamp."

"How soon then before the Russians can leave, Polly?"

"He don't know but he says that the creek is like a slaughterhouse. Half of Elepa is in their canoes fishin' out corpses for the Russians. Terrible tore up and burned most of them is. They're planting them in pits twenty at a time and Iziki reckons it'll bring bad luck on Elepa. He thinks Ephraim will have to move the village somewhere else after this."

"But is anybody searching for you, or for us?"

"He don't think so, sir. They're too busy trying to clear up the mess that you and Mr. Egdean made. And nobody missed Festus or poor Polly."

She resumed her questioning of Iziki. He stammered his replies, obviously anxious to please, his bloodshot eyes never leaving the knife. Polly translated again.

"He thinks the Mami Wata destroyed the ship."

"Who?"

"She's a spirit. She lives in the swamp, they say. They're terrified of her. An' she don't like Ephraim making friends with strangers, the Mami Wata don't, Iziki says. Ephraim's terrified of the curse he's brought on hisself an' he sent Iziki to get the bleedin' Mami Wata on his side."

Iziki might not have understood a word but he was nodding his head in furious agreement and attempting a fawning smile.

"Brought a few offerings for the Mami Wata, he did. They're in that bag."

Still holding his knife poised, Dawlish dropped to one knee and reached for the sack that Iziki had let fall. He shook the neck open and threw its contents on to the floor but recoiled immediately. Three heads – African heads, blood smeared and fresh – rolled across the floor. He looked away, his stomach heaving. Iziki was grinning and nodding, anxious to please. Dawlish deliberately lowered his knife, repressing the desire to drive it into the stomach of the ash-smeared wretch. He knew that he was on the point of losing his self-control.

Polly alone was unmoved. She kneeled down, scrutinised each head with obvious interest. Her voice, when she spoke, had a dreadful air of exultation about it.

"They're three of Ephraim's wives, the bitches. I'll shed no tears for any of 'em. Gave me hell they did, the poxy whores."

"It's a sacrifice, a heathen sacrifice." Indignation as well as horror in Egdean's voice.

Polly spat at the nearest head. "Ephraim didn't offer the Mami Wata nothin' he wasn't tired of already," she said. "He'll have another three within the week."

Dawlish felt an urge to look at the loathsome objects at his feet but he forced himself not to do so. Nausea was rising in him but he managed to choke it back.

"If there's rope in his canoe, Polly, fetch it." he said between gritted teeth. "He won't die, because you asked me. But hurry. My patience won't last."

The wizard had sensed Dawlish's anger and had dropped his ingratiating manner. He was now blubbering in abject terror and entreaty. Egdean's grip tightened on his throat, half-choking him. Dawlish turned away in disgust.

When Polly returned with a length of sodden rope, they used it to tie Iziki hand and foot. A filthy and blood-soaked rag torn from the sack served as a gag. Egdean threw him down in the centre of the hut, his face just inches from the fear-contorted features of one of the heads he had carried from Elepa.

Dawlish looked with revulsion at the squirming wretch, then rushed from the hut and vomited.

*

Their travel through the swamp that night was all the faster for their desire to leave the shrine's squalid horror far behind. They had paused only to take Iziki's reserves of food and to hide his dugout in the mangrove before winding their way back down the creek and striking out south-easterly. The knowledge that the *Nevski's* fiery end had imposed chaos on Elepa increased their hopes of evasion and Dawlish's spirits had risen. Two nights' paddling, he estimated, might get them to safety. Bruised, hungry and exhausted though they were, that goal might just be attainable. The aching limbs, the blistered hands, the raging insect bites – so numerous now that they had fused into a single blazing rash – and the slow agony on Dawlish's cheek, all seemed slightly more endurable as the hope of survival increased.

They paddled steadily through the night, doused again by a heavy downpour, hindered at first, then aided, by the tide. Now they were hugging the bank as they dropped down some broad waterway, now turning into a twisted and narrow creek all but roofed by the overhanging mangrove, now crouching low and scurrying across the broader stretches of open water in their path. Haste did not help however. The leaden sky above blotted the stars from sight and only a short break in the cloud revealed that they had taken turns that had headed them westwards again. How far to the west, it was impossible to judge.

"We're lost, sir." Polly had begun to weep. "I'm sorry, sir. We're lost."

"No, Polly. We're not lost. Just a little astray." Dawlish spoke gently even though fear was growing within him. She was still their only hope, must not be let despair. "We'll go back to the last fork. You'll find our way from there. I know you will. You've done so well so far."

Back then. More twists, more forks, rain cascading again to deluge strength, visibility yards only, sense of direction increasingly uncertain, a retreat from a dead-end creek, a grounding on soft mud that necessitating Egdean going overboard to drag the canoe free. Nothing to be done but hope and endure the hours of aching fatigue with dumb resignation.

*

Almost dawn.

Egdean and Polly were paddling and Dawlish was taking his turn in the bows as lookout when the sight of a dark outline jutting from the shadows of the bank ahead froze his blood. His hissed warning brought the dugout to a halt. It nudged against the overhung vegetation while he strained his eyes to separate the dark and threatening shape from the yet darker mass behind it. The rain had stopped now but because of the shreds of cloud passing across the face of the moon there was little light.

He signalled to Egdean to propel the canoe slowly forward and they halted again after twenty yards. Now he could discern the sharp, man-made outlines of a craft larger than any dugout. No lights showed from it. A chilling recollection of the picket boat skulking in wait – it seemed so long ago – caused his body to tense in anticipation of a hail of fire bursting from the dark bulk.

And yet . . .

There was something familiar about those lines, broken and deformed perhaps, but still familiar.

He gestured to Egdean to stroke forward, his excitement rising. The shape was definitely longer, sleeker and less bulky than any Russian pinnace. They moved still closer and the outline of the *Beta*, battered and half-sunk though she was, became unmistakable.

There was no sign of life. The bows lay embedded in the mud and mangrove of the bank and the hull listed heavily to port. The entire centre section had been torn open by the boiler explosion. The stern was submerged. It was difficult to recognise in this maimed and twisted wreck the pride of White's boatyard that had sped so bravely into action only a few nights before.

A dozen paddle strokes took them alongside. Dawlish clambered aboard, hoping to find some discarded weapon to supplement the Uzbek's knife that constituted their sole armament. It was all too evident that the decks had been hellishly raked by Nordenvelt fire before the Russians had boarded. He could only marvel that any of her complement had survived to be taken captive. Dark patches on the remaining deck must be dried blood but there was no sign of bodies. They must have been dumped overboard and his mind drew back from imagining how the swamp had treated them since. There was no sign of anything useful either. Somebody had taken a sledgehammer or similar implement to the breeches of the Gatlings.

Dawlish moved forward and pulled himself up on to the bridge structure. It was canted crazily to port – the buckling of the deck by the boiler explosion had almost thrown it overboard. He looked aft in sadness, remembering his own desolation as he had crouched on the bridge of the *Alpha*, waiting for the Russian picket boat, accepting that surrender was inevitable. Day's agony of mind could not have been any less in the moments before capture.

His hand rested idly on the catch over the torpedo-firing levers. There seemed a dreadful irony in the idea of this little vessel being transported so far, at such a price, only to be abandoned useless in this swamp with these levers still unpulled.

And at this thought he started with excitement.

Could the torpedoes still be intact? Had they escaped the Russians' attentions in the confusion? The fact that the bow was lodged, undamaged, in the bank, indicated that they had not exploded.

If only –

But no! The thought was too fantastic.

He was flushed with excitement as he swung himself down from the bridge and crouched beneath. The starboard Gatling mount had collapsed and blocked access to the rear of the launching tube on that side. To port however, the tube seemed undamaged and access unhampered. He grasped the brass wheel that operated the locking lugs on the tube's rear closure. It turned easily. He spun it and the circular door swung open to reveal the torpedo's propeller and rudder assemblies. They seemed undamaged. He moved over to inspect the contents of the steel toolbox on the bulkhead between the two tubes. It had been overlooked in the general pillage and the spanners, screwdrivers and other implements needed for disassembly and readjustment of the torpedoes were still inside.

It was as if fate was making it impossible for him to follow any course of action other than that which was forming in his mind. From a hundred confused ideas and possibilities, the nebulous embryo of a plan was taking shape. He must calm himself and think the prospect through.

The sky was brightening in the east. It would be full daylight in a quarter-hour. He sat on the remnant of the bridge, his head grasped in his hands, sweat running through his fingers. He must assume for a moment that the torpedo was intact. That presupposed positive answers to a string of 'ifs'.

If the air reservoir was unpierced.

If the pressure had not leaked through defective seals.

If the depth-control 'Secret' and its associated linkages and control rods were serviceable.

If the pneumatic-drive motor was unharmed.

If the firing pistol was still operative.

All 'ifs' that could only be checked with time and patience.

But if the torpedo was indeed intact, then he still had one last chance of smashing the remaining Russian man o' war. Nelson's 'eleventh sail' had indeed escaped but it might yet be at his mercy if he could somehow transport these fifteen feet of death to it. He glanced aft at the torn deck where the boiler had erupted. Had the vessel's disabling taken some other form, there might have been some faint hope of delivering the missile in the manner intended.

He looked down at the canoe alongside. His two companions, obviously keen to press on as far as possible towards safety before full sunrise, glanced up, faces slack with exhaustion.

They were his hope.

He refused to listen to the small reasonable voice within that told him that it was an impossibility. But with determination, and luck, it might just be done. He had passed this way with Tobin on the reconnaissance mission some time before midnight. Sufficient hours of darkness had remained for them to reach the Russian anchorage by dawn. He strove to remember the details of the night of the torpedo boat attack. Surely no longer than thirty minutes had elapsed between the furious battle in this creek, so fatal for the *Beta*, and his own arrival at the Russian boom? Half an hour's steaming for the *Alpha*, a full night's paddling for two men and a woman, all exhausted. Closer perhaps to two nights with the torpedo towed astern.

It might be possible, but only just.

His mind swung back to the information provided by Iziki. The Russians were apparently occupied with recovery and burial of their dead, but fear was also driving them to prepare for departure. The vicinity of the anchorage would be busy by night and by day. Their boats would be to-ing and fro-ing with the corpses. Canoes from Elepa would be ferrying the fruit that would be so important for the long scurvy-threatened months at sea that lay ahead of the *Orlov*. The lookouts would be even more alert in the aftermath of the *Nevski's* destruction. In his mind's eye Dawlish could visualise the searchlights sweeping the channel by night while the nervous gunners blasted at any suspicious piece of driftwood with their Nordenvelts.

There could be only one reasonable conclusion.

Attacking the *Orlov* at the anchorage could offer no hope of success.

But there was one alternative – to lie in ambush between the anchorage and the sea, waiting at a point which the *Orlov* must pass. There was a chance, a very small one, that the remaining torpedo could be made to reach her as she escaped seawards.

Dawlish sat for several minutes, weighing the odds for a successful attack. When he compounded the chances of transporting the torpedo to the channel in time to catch the escaping *Orlov* with the chances of scoring a hit, he had to admit that the overall probability of success was close to zero.

Camp Beaconsfield was forty-eight hours away, less perhaps. If he were to press on now, leaving the *Beta*, never mentioning his discovery of the potentially serviceable torpedo, then no reproach could ever be levelled against him. Given the opposition and the odds, he had done as much, and more, than could ever have been expected of him. The *Nevski* had been ripped apart, eliminated. Not even Topcliffe could ask for more. The *Orlov*, powerful as she was, could eventually be run down and sunk. The threat that she represented to the Royal Navy was serious but by no means insuperable. Deliverance for Egdean, Polly and himself was in his grasp. Reason told him he should forget the torpedo and press on towards Camp Beaconsfield.

And then, without warning, agony knifed through his bowels It was for the third time since leaving the hut. The over-ripe fruit had done its work and he, like the others, was racked with diarrhoea that was as painful as it was degrading. He moved to the side of the vessel, out of sight of Egdean and Polly, and hung there, gasping with pain. The spasm passed, but there were traces of blood, and that worried him. When he drew his trousers about him again, he felt weaker than before. The others could not be much better.

He sat again by the tube, shivering, sweat coursing from him, head aching. His misery absorbed him and the logic of heading at once for refuge seemed ever stronger. And then, suddenly, the memory of Lowe despatched like a dog and thrown overboard from the *Nevski*, thrust itself to the forefront of his mind. And Jarvis's screams as the glowing iron hovered just above his flesh and hairs frizzled from the heat. Day's break for freedom. Egdean's sight at risk. And yes, his own burned cheek. But bitterest of all, Krestovski's delight.

Cold anger shuddered through him. The bottle smashing into Krestovski's head, the waves of flame washing across the *Nevski's* deck and the great black hull rolling over in its death agony seemed but meagre payment for the sufferings endured. His men deserved a yet fuller settling of the account.

He looked down at his hands and saw that the fists had closed involuntarily, the fingernails biting deep into the palms. There was no choice but to drain the cup to the dregs. Until now he had been driven by vague concepts of duty and ambition. He had first committed himself because of Topcliffe's shabby offer of patronage and everything since had followed inevitably from that.

He would use his last torpedo.

But not on behalf of their Lordships at the Admiralty, nor of Topcliffe, nor of Beaconsfield. No, not even for that remote widow in Windsor whom they were all so eager to serve. No! Not for the preservation of the road to India, nor for Turkey's continued control of the Straits nor for its freedom to massacre Bulgarian Christians.

No, by God! That last torpedo would settle his personal debt.

He reached down and touched a propeller blade.

The screw rotated smoothly, with just the slightest resistance, as it should.

It was promising.

Chapter 28

Dawlish's heart went out to Polly and as Egdean when he saw them, half-dozing, in the canoe. Poor wretches, they must be confident that they would soon be underway towards safety. There was no way to sweeten his message.

He roused them, outlined his plan calmly but bluntly, did not hesitate to minimise the hazards. While he was speaking, he saw disappointment fill their faces. For one long, unworthy, moment he realised that there was nothing to stop Egdean using the knife he carried to finish him here and then journey on with Polly. The moment passed as the seaman nodded. Dawlish felt ashamed.

"I can order you, Egdean," he said, "but we're beyond that now. You and Polly are as important to this as I am. If you believe you can't manage it, then I'll take you at your word and that's the end of it."

He turned to Polly. The bedraggled girl had begun to weep. After months of degradation and despair, deliverance had seemed unexpectedly at hand. Now, with salvation still possible, she was being drawn into an undertaking that would carry her back towards the hell she had just left.

"I can't order you, Polly," his voice was quiet, "but I can't find the way without you."

She dashed her tears aside. "You was good to me, sir," she said. "I'll guide you."

"You didn't leave me at Pemba, sir," Egdean said, "and I ain't about to leave you here."

And so they worked with grim intensity, Egdean flinging himself into the task with almost greater determination than Dawlish, and Polly assisting with a vigour that was surprising from a frame so gaunt and wasted.

They took the mooring cable from the *Beta's* bows and slung it from the bridge platform, then used it to take the weight of the torpedo as they inched it, with boundless caution, from the tube. Dawlish stood by the rear opening with a crowbar improvised from part of the wrecked Gatling mount, guiding the long cylinder into a resting place on the crumpled deck beside the ruptured boiler casing. Egdean and Polly heaved on the cable, taking the greater part of the weapon's weight as it slid further out. It was hard, brutal work that strained their muscles to the limit, made nerve-racking by the knowledge that one slip would smash the vital rudders down on the deck, damaging them beyond repair. Sweating and groaning from the effort, they somehow managed to complete the extraction and lay the torpedo down safely.

Time now to rest, however briefly. Polly dropped into uncomfortable sleep beneath the bridge and both men sat on the deck, their backs against the torpedo. Insect bites had by now swollen their faces and arms and itch added discomfort to fatigue, aches and burns. Dawlish noticed that the weals on Egdean's wrists and ankles were now as foul with pus as his own cheek, but the seaman had never complained of it.

The air was warm and heavy with the promise of thunder. The silence was broken only by the distant scream of monkeys. It grew until a troop could be seen scampering through the foliage fifty yards down the creek. The sight was somehow pleasing.

"They know well enough how to live here," Dawlish said. "If only they could –"

But one had tumbled with a splash into the muddy waters beneath an overhanging branch. He surfaced and struck for the bank, the tip of his tail protruding, while his fellows urged him on with furious chatter.

"He's a brave little chap, sir," Egdean said, and then, "Dear God!"

Something was lashing up from beneath and the monkey was screaming like a child in torment. There was a brief glimpse of a long, brown snout and snapping jaws and then only a circle of ripples and the frenzied chatter of the fleeing troop.

"Crocodiles frighten me, sir," Egdean said.

It was the nearest he had ever come to admitting weakness. They lapsed into a long silence, as if the small tragedy had been an omen. It was Dawlish who spoke at last.

"I never thanked you for answering my telegram so promptly." Death's presence seemed so close now that the chasm that separated an officer from an enlisted man had shrunk to nothing. "I'm sorry that I tore you from your family."

"You'd said I could call on you as a reference, sir, if there was any problem." Egdean paused, and when he resumed there was a catch in his voice. "I valued that, sir. I wouldn't have dared go back without it."

He told of his return, of the child meeting him in the lane and guessing who he was.

"And so, sir, I saw my brother again, an' had there been more time I'd have seen my sister too."

"How long since you had last seen them, Egdean?"

"Since I enlisted, sir." There was a quaver in his voice and tears were trickling from his eyes.

Dawlish looked quickly away but a single glance had told him of an agony deeper than loneliness, sharper than fear of the death that the coming time might bring. Egdean, faithful, reliable and fearless, the rock on which the last desperate ambush would depend, was near to breaking.

"The trouble you mentioned in Zanzibar –" Dawlish hesitated, uncertain whether to continue as the seaman suppressed a sob. "The trouble that kept you away from England, Egdean –"

"I'm a defiled creature, sir. An' not worthy to have lived when better men died." The words came in a rush and he was weeping now.

Dawlish fought down rising panic. No appearance of a Russian picket boat could be more threatening to this last mission. Without Egdean, nothing could be achieved.

"But it's past now, and it's long forgotten, isn't it, Egdean?" He forced calmness and compassion into his voice.

"My brother told me, sir. He'd heard for certain that the man is dead."

"What man?"

The story, pent up for years, came tumbling out. It was a common enough one, and Dawlish had heard variants before. And always the teller had thought himself unique and had carried the shame with him like a hidden ulcer until the act of confession had purged him of it for ever.

"It was bad, sir. Very bad." Egdean shuddered. "The Lord destroyed a city for that same sin. It's in Genesis, sir."

A youth recruited by his older brother, an assistant gamekeeper then, to act as a beater on a shoot. A guest of the master's, a wealthy middle-aged bachelor sportsman, impressed, he said, by the lad's strength and intelligence. The offer of a position as a deckhand on his yacht. A month on board – a cruise to the Channel Islands and back to Ryde – and the revelation of the sea as a challenge to be mastered and enjoyed. The God-fearing youth's growing confusion and unease at raucous laughter and stifled noises in closed cabins as the owner's hospitality was shared equally with titled gentlemen and illiterate boat-boys. His disgust at certain allusions.

Egdean stopped. His voice trailed away.

"You must continue now," Dawlish said quietly. "Tell it. Once only and for the last time ever."

A pause, and then the inevitable climax. A quiet evening and the summons to the saloon. The offer of drink, foolishly accepted, half-drunkenness and then suddenly hands being laid upon him and clothes being stripped away. The sycophantic laughter of the two ragamuffins who held him writhing across a chest as the yacht's owner thrust at him like a rutting stag. Tears, pain, shame and the offer of money afterwards.

Egdean lapsed into silence, panting with anger.

There was more. Dawlish could feel it.

"But that wasn't the end of it, Egdean? I wouldn't respect you for the man you are if it were."

A pause. "I waited until he was asleep, sir." The words were an effort and they had an edge of fury. "I was a coward maybe, but I was just a lad. I meant to kill him – and God forgive me, but I'd do it again if I could. But he woke up."

"You killed him?"

He shook his head. "He grabbed at me and I stabbed him and he fell down bleeding and quiet and I thought he was dead. I dropped overboard and swam ashore."

"And you enlisted. You called yourself Egdean."

"It's just a name that came into my head. A place nearby my home."

"And you heard afterwards that he was alive? That the police were looking for you?"

Egdean nodded.

"It's finished, finished forever," Dawlish said. "You've nothing to fear now, and you've never had anything to be ashamed of." He drew him to his feet. "Give me your hand," he said, "and I'll warrant that I'm neither the first nor only officer to respect Jeremiah Egdean."

"You mean it, sir?"

The swamp was vast and hostile around them. With terrible clarity, Dawlish recognised that even this might seem precious when his last moments came. And that might be very soon. So now this was a time for honesty.

"We're going to face death together, Jerry." Dawlish had only once before used the seaman's first name. "At this moment I'd choose no other man to have by me."

In the firmness of the handshake, he knew the old Egdean, solid and indomitable, would be with him to the end, whatever it might be.

Behind them was the noise of Polly stirring in her sleep. It would soon be time to get to work again.

*

The high stakes involved justified taking chances and they must work on through the daylight hours.

Dawlish began his checking of the torpedo's mechanisms. He sent Egdean and Polly westwards along the creek in the dugout. Danger would be most likely come from that direction. They were to keep watch from the nearest intersecting waterway and warn him of the approach of danger by a single long whistle from Egdean's powerful lungs. In the worst event, they were to leave him to his fate and continue eastwards to safety once the coast was clear.

He exposed the air reservoir and found it undamaged. The small integral gauge indicated almost full pressure. The leaks through the India-rubber seals had been almost negligible since the last charging. He removed the cover that gave access to the 'Whitehead Secret'. The diaphragm and the linkages it operated were in as good a state as when he had last inspected them at Camp Beaconsfield. The previous depth setting had been fifteen feet and he changed this to eight. Given the unconventional way he intended to launch the weapon it was better to minimise the extent to which the Secret must work to establish the running depth. The horizontal rudders waggled up and down in response to his finger's pressure on the diaphragm. There was no hint of slackness in the linkages. He opened the valve operated by the starting lever in a pocket on the side and the motor hummed into life and sent the screws spinning. Satisfied that the mechanism was operating as it should, he closed it off at once, unwilling to waste any of the precious air. He deliberated over stripping the firing pistol but decided against. It was unlikely to have become inoperative since last inspected and the less he tampered with it the better. He limited himself to checking that the arming fan would spin loose as the torpedo moved through the water, so freeing the pistol's detonator plunger to explode the weapon when it struck the target.

It took two hours of intense concentration to complete the inspection and the sun was high when he at last decided that it was fit for use. He climbed to the bridge and gave a long whistle and, after a pause, another. The canoe emerged from the mangrove tangle by the creek's bend and stroked towards him.

It proved as difficult to manhandle the torpedo from its resting-place, down the sloping ramp of the buckled deck and across the jagged wreckage, as it had been to extract it from the tube. Time and again the long cylinder jammed and only brute force, exerted through the rope and crowbar, succeeded in dislodging it. Dawlish did not relax until it slid at last into the water, liberated from the fear that a knock on the delicate propellers or azimuth and depth-regulating rudders would bring his hopes to naught. Floating awash in the muddy water, cradled in its own element, the torpedo looked like some evil metallic pike, hungry and patient.

He had intended to tow the torpedo astern of the dugout but a short trial showed that, if pulled this way, its length and inertia made steering impossible. If narrow and twisting creeks were to be negotiated, then there was no option it but to lash the weapon alongside. Though the curve of the canoe's hull overhung it, there was still a considerable strain on the paddlers on that side, who were forced to lean out further to make an effective stroke. The problem was all the greater since the asymmetrical drag imposed a constant tendency for the craft to swing to starboard, the side on which the torpedo was secured. Thankful now that they had a third paddle, that from Iziki's dugout, they commenced their slow and laborious progress with two paddlers to starboard, one to port.

And all three of them were tired, very tired.

Chapter 29

Despite the added danger of detection that movement by daylight could bring, Dawlish was determined to push on as far as possible from the *Beta's* wreck before hiding. Their course was south-westerly now. The goal was to strike the channel which the Russians must descend seawards at a point several miles south of their anchorage. Dawlish did not voice his fear that, in their haste to depart, the enemy might even now be slipping out, rendering futile this clumsy race across the swamp. Progress through the narrow and serpentine creeks was slow and painful due to the need to counteract the swing to starboard. Beyond the grey clouds the sun was high and its heat had turned the swamp to a gigantic steam bath in which the air seemed to offer solid resistance to motion.

Sweat saturated the paddlers and the blisters on their hands were now broken and raw. Each was sunk into a near-stupor from which all reality had faded other than the need to somehow lift the paddle and sweep it forward for always one more muscle-numbing stroke. The chattering of unseen monkeys sometimes mocked their snail-like progress but, except for the odd crocodile lazing on a mudbank, a solitary black and white fish-eagle vigilant on a branch high overhead, or the quick metallic flash of a kingfisher, there was no sign of life.

They paddled for almost four hours and Dawlish estimated that their tortuous progress had taken them no more than three or four miles in a direct line south-westwards. Then they pulled up a side creek. They could find no hummock of ground above water level and so were forced to remain in the canoe, embarrassing as it was, for diarrhoea still tore their bowels, even when logic argued there was little left to void. The remains of the fish that Polly had caught the night they had met her, and of Iziki's food, were all they had to eat. The prospect of being able to steal from fish traps and of stripping shellfish from mangrove roots at low tide was now all that stood between them and starvation. Only of fresh water was there an abundance, for it was raining again.

Dawlish took the first watch, perching on the stern to let the others stretch out with scant comfort in the bottom. Despite the cramped position and the presence of an inch of water they were soon asleep, two filth-encrusted human wrecks, insect-bitten and half-starved, who must somehow assist him in the destruction of a powerful warship. For all its armed might, Britain's significant naval power boiled down at this moment to a single exhausted lieutenant, a weakened seaman and a worn-out Cockney barmaid. Now only the torpedo wallowing alongside went some way to redressing the balance.

He sat staring out into the rain's grey mist, thankful for the tepid water that flowed over him and somewhat eased the nagging of his bites. Heavy as the downpour was, it did not seem to disturb the rest of the two unfortunates before him. He envied them their oblivion. Fatigue ached in his every bone and muscle, smothering with its dull misery the sharper pains in his shoulders and on his cheek. His itch was a torment beyond belief, sometimes a dull fire across his whole body, at others a blaze that erupted unexpectedly at a single spot and made the urge to scratch and tear at the skin irresistible. The hollow ache of half-satisfied hunger was passing now, replaced by a general debility. What little nutrition had been afforded by the meagre food of recent days had been nullified by his stomach problems and did little to fuel the efforts demanded.

Another twenty-four hours like this might well finish him, he knew, leaving him incapable of anything but drifting coastwards with the ebbing tides. Egdean would be good for a similar period, perhaps even a little longer, and Polly also, driven by her desperation, but for all of them the limits were defined. Within that remaining twenty-four hour period they must reach a position from which the torpedo could be launched into the *Orlov's* flank.

His brooding was interrupted by Polly rising.

"It's hard to sleep at a time like this, sir," she said, "though God knows we need it. If you'd like to lie down, I'll gladly watch for you."

Her voice was lifeless. She must be very close to the end of her tether. Dawlish was moved to a pity all the stronger for knowing that he could do so little to alleviate her misery.

"It won't be much longer now, Polly." He recognised the hollowness of the words, and so too must she, even as he spoke. "Once this torpedo's done its work we'll be dropping down to the sea with the tide. A few days should see you an honoured guest on a ship of the Royal Navy."

"Me? An honoured guest, sir?"

"I shouldn't be surprised if the Queen herself didn't invite you to Windsor to thank you."

Polly laughed without mirth and shook her head. "I could sink ten of them Russian ships for her, sir," she said, "and there still wouldn't be a lady nowhere who'd as much as want to spit at me. The Widow o'

Windsor don't need to see the likes o' me. I'll be content enough if I'm back drawing ale at the Star of the East while you're dinin' with your gentlemen friends."

He found it hard to answer. Polly had recognised that the companionship forced by their shared plight could not bridge the social gulf that would yawn were they to reach the safety of the outside world. But still he wanted to comfort her and yet respect her honesty. The tears were welling up in her exhausted eyes as she looked out over the dismal channel. Then, with an impatient gesture, she swept her hand across her face and nodded at Egdean's recumbent figure.

"Does you know Mr. Egdean for long, sir?" A tremble in her voice.

"For more than three years." Dawlish was glad to change the subject. "We served together on the other side of Africa. He saved my life." He paused, thinking again how easily the 'we' now came, distinctions between lower and quarter decks now so irrelevant. "I doubt if a finer or braver man serves in the Navy in any rank, or in any post." He meant it.

Polly nodded and the bitterness seemed to fade from her as she glanced at Egdean's bedraggled hulk. "He ain't no gentleman, sir, not a real gent, that is, an' he don't hold with no drink – he told me so himself – but he treats me like a real lady, he does. I don't wish for much for myself but I hope he don't get hurt."

He realised that there was some crumb he could offer, some recompense he might claim from Topcliffe.

If we survive.

"It's up to Mr. Egdean of course, Polly," he said, "but if he should wish to leave the service before the end of his term, I'm quite sure I can arrange it when we return. Many an old sailor's glad of an appointment to the Coastguard. It usually brings a comfortable cottage with it."

"His own place, sir?"

"His own, Polly." He paused, saw something like longing in her eyes. "And I don't doubt that he'd appreciate having a lady to housekeep for him. It would be up to him of course but I'm confident that I could secure such an appointment."

"I don't think he'd hesitate, sir," Polly was smiling wanly. "He was speaking about it himself. An' he said that he wanted to look after me."

"No more Star of the East then, Polly?"

"He said we wouldn't talk of that time no more. Not never."

Dawlish wondered what promises had passed between the ill-assorted couple while he had worked on the torpedo. He felt thankful that some glimmer of hope had entered into Polly's thankless existence. And into Egdean's too for that matter. It might well be the spark that would carry them through the final stage.

He was tired, too tired to think further about it. He left Polly on watch, with orders to rouse Egdean when she thought two hours had passed, and then lapsed into a comfortless and mosquito-tormented sleep on the dugout's sodden bottom.

*

Egdean woke him as darkness fell. He was cold and shivering as he fought his way back to consciousness. Sleep had taken the edge off his fatigue but had done nothing to ease his other aches. While he had slept, Polly, with immeasurable patience, had caught almost a dozen of the small crabs that infested the mud of the bank. She had roasted them over the remaining embers in the fire-pot. Less than a single mouthful could be scooped from each shell but it was enough to stay their cravings for nourishment for precious moments. Dawlish assured her that this supper would be repaid with one of oysters and champagne in London, but the mention of a world other than this doleful universe of dripping mangrove and muddy creeks served only to emphasise their misery.

The clouds had cleared. A bright moon lit their way as they dropped down the creek.

And so began the last leg.

Ahead, they hoped, and feared, lay their rendezvous with the *Orlov.*

*

This night was the worst yet, for the mental as well as the physical effects of extreme fatigue were now manifesting themselves. Dawlish stared ahead into the half-darkness, striving to keep awake by reciting half-remembered fragments of Gray's Elegy and of verses by Keats, by listing the shires of England and the plays of Shakespeare. Polly fell forward once, babbling in sleep, wakening when her face hit the side of the dugout. Only Egdean, stroking resolutely at the stern, was fully awake.

Early in the night, they encountered a party of fishermen, luckily visible from a distance because of the usual glowing fire containers. They pulled in beneath the bank's foliage and crouched there with thumping hearts until three unobservant canoes passed without detecting them.

The meeting made them more cautious. They were coming into a more frequented area and they clung to the shadows during their subsequent progress. This caution betrayed them however for, in their eagerness to follow darker and narrower creeks, where the risk of an encounter would be lower, they found themselves in a twisting channel that died out in a trickle beneath a canopy of mangrove. They could only than paddle back, stern first, thus putting the rear of the torpedo at risk. They were used by now to paddling so as to compensate for the drag to starboard but were so unhandy at the reversing operation that the dugout stuck against one bank, catching the stern section of the torpedo in a submerged mass of mangrove roots.

Dawlish's heart pounded as he groped beneath the surface. A tangle of rubbery sinews was gripping the fragile propulsion and steering elements. He shuddered at the thought that a crocodile or snake might be slithering through the muddy waters near him but there was no alternative to taking the knife and sawing through each tendon in turn. He persevered, heart thumping, for the viscous mud held the roots tight and made work by touch-only difficult. It seemed like hours before the torpedo broke loose and they could resume their painful way back down the cul-de-sac.

They regained the broad channel that they had left so unwisely. The tide was ebbing, helping them somewhat. The dugout drifted with it, Egdean alone plying his paddle, and then only as a rudder to hold them in the shadows. The thinning clouds had revealed the stars above, making navigation more straightforward.

The waterway swung around to almost due south. It widened, then split. They followed the right-hand fork, still headed south-westwards. It narrowed and the current increased.

Another branch. Polly motioned to starboard. It was full ebb now and the waters were running ever faster, exposing three and four-foot banks of black mud at the creek sides. They travelled still further to the west, then south, then another fork, southwest by south. Dawlish tried to summon to his mind's eye as much of the complex geography of this section of the Delta as he could remember from Tattersall's map but it helped little.

Polly leaned forward and whispered, as if reading his mind, "There's one more big channel, sir. A quarter-mile across if it ain't more. After that there's just one narrow bit o' swamp and then we'll be in the Russians' channel."

The crossing of that one remaining broad watercourse was a nightmare. It was every yard, and more, of Polly's estimation. Its surface was mirror-like and unrippled in the moonlight. Regardless of visibility, they had to go straight across. The ebb was slackening however, making the transit more direct than it would have been an hour earlier. For fifteen or twenty minutes on end the dark ribbon that was the opposite bank seemed to draw no closer. The beat of their paddles sounded loud enough in their own ears to draw the attention of the entire swamp yet, in the end, they gained the farther shore unobserved.

The final section of swamp was, as Polly predicted, no more than a finger, a half-mile strip of mangrove-shrouded mud lying between the two great waterways and itself criss-crossed by narrow and convoluted creeks. One such creek carried them across. They emerged on to another broad channel. It was over a half-mile wide.

"Here it is, sir," Polly sounded weary and pointed northwards. "Them Russian ships is up there. If they ain't gone already, that is."

Dawlish's heart sank at the sight of the vast expanse of water. The torpedo's maximum effective range was little over six hundred yards, and that depended on launching from a tube. With the canoe, it would be essential to get closer, much closer. Even had he been prepared to head north, where intensive Russian patrolling could be expected, he would find no appreciable narrowing of the channel. Southwards, seawards, it would funnel out to still greater breath. His hopes of mounting his attack from the cover of the mangrove faded. The escaping ironclad would be keeping to midstream. The attack would be as much a forlorn hope as would be an assault through a breached fortress wall.

It must by now be four-thirty or five o'clock. Dawn would be breaking soon. The tide was turning and it seemed unlikely that the Russians, if they intended to make their dash in the next twelve hours, would depart from their anchorage before high water. There was time for rest. They pulled in under the overhanging foliage. Dawlish took the first watch while the others stretched out in the cramped bottom. Soon afterwards it was full daylight.

Shivers racked him but he had no means of doing anything about it. He noticed that he had lost his craving for food. He wondered if this would be the day of his death. Fatigue had done much to rob the idea of its terror. He tried to summon up memories of how he had faced death on other occasions.

Crouching in a foul ditch, waiting for the signal that would send him and a thousand others plodding across the mud flats towards the Taku Forts.

Howitzer fire throwing up great fountains around the grounded *Odin* in '64 and coming closer with every salvo.

Manning the pumps on the wave-lashed *Sprightly* in a North-Pacific gale in '66 while her engine laboured on the edge of failure.

Caught in an ambush in the gloom of the Ashanti thicket.

Dragging Egdean through the millet on Pemba as the Arab slavers outflanked them.

All desperate.

And yet this was different.

On each of those occasions he had been fit and healthy, not debilitated by privation and hunger, and the urge to live had been strong. But Death now seemed like a welcome friend who offered rest and oblivion and he must fight the temptation to yield to its treacherous blandishments.

The memory of his home was strong now, and of those dinners with his father when they had bored and exasperated each other, and had somehow loved each other through it all. He longed to listen again, even if just for one more time, to the old man's stories of petty legal triumphs. He though too of how his father would react to news of his death, dressed up in a lie of Topcliffe's. He wished he could ease the sadness that would be so terrible, the grief of the loss of a second son. But even that pain would dull at last.

And yet all these thoughts, all these regrets, faded into nothing in the face of his longing for rest.

Chapter 30

Dawlish struggled into wakefulness. Egdean was shaking him. His voice was quiet and awe-struck.

"They're coming," he said. "They're just coming into sight."

Still blinking against the light, Dawlish rose to a kneeling position. It must be late morning, even though it felt only like minutes since Egdean had relieved him.

"There, sir."

The seaman was pointing northwards. Rising high above the foliage of the swamp, the masts and yards of the Russian vessels were unmistakable. No sails were set and the hulls were still obscured by a slight bend in the channel but five separate plumes of black smoke drifted skywards – the *Orlov*, the three colliers and the yacht.

Dawlish glanced to the water by the canoe's side. It was lapping high against the bank and there was no sign of flow. Soon the ebb would be speeding the flotilla yet faster on its way. It was full daylight and the Russian commander's sensible decision not to risk the passage of the swamp and bar by night had robbed Dawlish of his only cover, that of darkness.

There was an almost hypnotic quality about the ships' stately advance, so slow as to be almost imperceptible. At last, the first vessel emerged into full view, the tubby hull identifying one of the colliers. Dawlish estimated the distance as a mile and a half. Astern of her, the next ship became visible, the *Orlov's* long and rakish lines unmistakable. Though still far off, the central battery's open ports could be picked out – the ironclad was cleared for action and ready to blast her way past any blockading British warships that might be waiting outside the Delta. Her main armament would be more than a match for *Nomad* or *Volage* and her six-inch armour would be impervious to their guns. They could only trail at a safe distance, not confront. The two other colliers followed in the *Orlov's* wake. And, last of all, the white steam yacht.

None of them spoke, not Dawlish nor Egdean nor Polly, each transfixed by the sight of the flotilla bearing towards them. The ships grew taller every moment and made the idea of opposing them with a dugout yet more preposterous.

Dawlish broke the silence.

"We're going to paddle towards midstream." His voice was hushed in involuntary awe. "We've to behave as if we were fisherfolk. Polly, you'll have to stand up and wave at them when I tell you. And you, Egdean, you and I, we'll keep paddling the dugout into position."

They both nodded, neither breaking their stares away from the approaching ships.

"I want to get within three hundred yards of the *Orlov*. Less if we can." Dawlish found the words hopelessly optimistic even as he spoke them. "We'll swing our bows around to face a point about a hundred yards ahead of her. Do you follow, Jerry? I'll slip overboard, cut the torpedo loose and activate it. Remember that you'll be responsible for aiming up to the last moment. You understand?"

Egdean nodded. His face was a mask, drained of all emotion.

"You need to pull me from the water as quick as you can after that or the explosion will do for me. Then we'll paddle hell for leather for the shore."

Egdean was removing his shirt. "Begging your pardon, sir," he said "I think you'd better be doing the same yourself. If we smear a bit of mud on ourselves, we'd look a bit more like blacks."

They reached down, drew handfuls of mud from around the mangrove roots and plastered it on their faces, arms and torsos. Polly's eyes stood out wild with fear as she covered herself in the foul-smelling ooze and she seemed incapable of tearing them from the ever-closer vessels.

Now time to strike out.

Dawlish, sick with apprehension, could find no words of encouragement for his companions. He reached out and touched their hands, first Polly's, then Egdean's. In neither face could he recognise anything but desperation. He moved to the bows, crouched down and picked up his paddle. Polly squatted by her accustomed place amidships and Egdean, at the stern, urged the craft out from the cover of the bank with a powerful stroke. Dawlish kept his head down and concentrated on paddling, avoiding looking up at the increasing bulk of the first vessel in line, now little more than a mile away. Blood was roaring in his head and he was badly frightened. He willed his hands not to shake and, as he did, realised that his fatigue had left him.

The ebb had now set in but was yet so slight as to offer no appreciable difficulty for maintaining a direct course across the channel. They were already two hundred yards from the shoreline and heading diagonally upstream towards the centre of the channel before Dawlish glanced up. The first lumbering collier was no more than a thousand yards upstream. He could discern lookouts on her yards and tops. Black smoke billowed skywards from abaft the foremast, losing itself in the light and spasmodic breeze. Dawlish stroked harder still, the splash of his paddle keeping rhythm with Egdean's insistent beat. The *Orlov* was now blotted from view by the dark mass of the leading ship, only the drifting pall of her smoke betraying her presence next in line.

The range was closing, with the dugout clawing its way towards midstream while the quickening ebb bore the Russians on with it. Dawlish looked down to check that the knife was secure in his waistband. It would be needed soon. Again he dug his paddle deep.

Now less than six hundred yards separated the leading collier from the dugout. The *Orlov* came into sight astern. Her battery's menacing snouts extended through open ports. Dawlish stiffened. Now was the time to play to the full the roles of swamp fishermen. He turned and called to Polly.

"Get up and wave! Hold up the pot. Just as if you were offering them fish."

Polly struggled to her feet, bracing one foot against the gunwale to keep herself steady. She held the now-cold fire-pot on her shoulder and waved with her other arm. No immediate response from the collier. The canoe was already closer to the Russian ship than Dawlish could have hoped. It was now beam on and sweeping past without concern. At its bulwarks a few faces were turned towards the dugout and somebody waved back.

Now the moment of decision.

The *Orlov* followed in the collier's wake, still two hundred yards away and ploughing down the centre of the channel. The canoe's axis, if extended, would intersect the ironclad's course at a point two hundred yards ahead of her. Time to hold this heading and let the *Orlov* come on. In moments would come the ideal – the only – instant for launching the attack.

Dawlish turned aft. "I'm going over, Egdean!" he yelled. "Keep her dead steady on this heading! We'll get her amidships!"

He pulled the knife free and clambered aft past Polly. She was still gesticulating, was like a madwoman now. He leaned down and hacked through the first rope, that aft, that bound the torpedo alongside. He glanced towards the *Orlov*. Her course was unchanged but now, to his horror, he saw figures along her bulwarks pointing towards the canoe. The metallic tones of an alarm bell came ringing across the water.

The chattering of the Nordenvelt in the *Orlov's* foretop reached his ears as the water ten yards to port of the canoe was lashed to froth. He did not hesitate, nor go further forward to sever the second rope, but vaulted over the gunwale and splashed down just outboard of the torpedo.

The Nordenvelt's hammering stilled for a moment, but he scarcely heard it, intent as he was on shaking the water from his eyes and groping along the metal cylinder, seeking for the firing lever's recess. The gun exploded into life again and was joined by a second. A churning patch of water moved without mercy towards the dugout. The *Orlov's* immense black hull was filling his vision but he tore his eyes away and concentrated on finding the all-important lever. His fingers slipped on the now-slimy metal surface, then locked into the pocket. He pushed his hand inside and closed it over the activating lever within.

He pulled.

The weapon's screws began to churn, urging it forward against the bond that still secured it to the canoe – and then he heard Polly's scream. He glanced up, horrified. Chunks of wood were flying off the gunwale and Polly was collapsing backwards, turning slightly as she fell, her jerking body a single gaping wound, scarlet, torn.

Around him the water boiled. The torpedo was straining forward, dragging the canoe with it. It was pulling Dawlish also – his fingers were still locked on the lever. He reached for the remaining rope and sawed through it with the knife.

The torpedo surged away, flinging him aside as its whirring screws shaved past. His head went under and he choked. He fought his way to the surface and realised that the Nordenvelts had fallen silent. One thought dominated him now, to hoist himself from the water before the torpedo struck home. He shouted for Egdean, but got no response. He reached for the splintered gunwale and heaved himself upwards. The dugout rolled over towards him. As he fought to get one leg over the side, he saw Egdean collapsed, groaning, in the stern, his shoulder a mass of blood. The dugout rolled further as it took Dawlish's weight, almost tipping the Egdean overboard. He managed to topple over into the craft but he dared not look out from it.

The canoe shuddered as the Nordenvelts chattered into life again, sweeping past the shattered bows, but missing this time. Dawlish cowered, with Polly's lifeless and bloody form only inches from his face.

He knew that he had just seconds to live. A third weapon joined in but had not yet found the range. He was shaking and he did not want to die.

How much longer . . .

Curiosity was stronger than fear. He raised his head, could spot the torpedo's trail of bubbles heading with ponderous slowness towards the axis of the *Orlov's* advance. The torpedo would hit close to the bow.

But no!

It was curving over to port ever so little. The launch had not been perfect and straight-running setting of the rudder might have been disturbed by a fraction of an inch when manhandling the weapon from *Beta's* tube . . .

And it missed.

It must have crossed the *Orlov's* path scant yards before her bow wave, running on harmlessly towards the distant bank. The Nordenvelts fell silent as the vessel slipped past, close enough to see the expressions of surprise on the faces of officers looking down from the bridge wing. Dawlish dived for cover again, heartsick with failure. At this moment death seemed preferable to the despair raging within him.

And then an explosion louder than any thunderclap.

Hope soaring, Dawlish rose to his knees and saw that a white column of water that was rising, slow and majestic, not on the *Orlov's* side but at the collier now a cable and a half ahead of her. For one moment he thought that his torpedo must have strayed so far off course. But then another explosion, one that must be beneath the collier. The entire hull was lifting on a mound of water that rose past its flanks to hide the bridge and funnel behind a frothing curtain. Even as the white cascade reached its apogee and began collapsing back, it was obvious that the vessel's back was broken. The bow section, now parted from the stern, was rolling over to starboard, the foremast describing an enormous arc as it pitched over, its snapped shrouds whipping. The falling column engulfed the doomed ship in a cauldron of spray and when it cleared only the sinking stern portion was visible. The mizzenmast still stood but the main lay toppled over the side in a tangle of cordage.

Dawlish stared in amazement. His torpedo could not have done this and an explosion a moment later at the opposite bank confirmed that it had run on that far.

The *Orlov* was ploughing on, helm over to avoid collision with the dying collier ahead, straightening to pass along its port flank. She was level with it when the sea rose again, this time at a point some fifty feet abaft her bows. Higher and higher it climbed, a feathery plume that rose until it blocked from sight the foremast behind it. The whole great ship seemed to shudder and stand still in the water. A black object, its limbs flailing, separated itself from the mainmast's fighting top and dropped downwards. The mast itself whipped like a sapling in a gale.

The wave that rolled back from the *Orlov* flung Dawlish into the bottom of the dugout and half-swamped the tiny craft. He struggled to his knees again and saw the spray from the now-disintegrating water column showering down over the stricken warship. He crawled towards the stern, dragged Egdean into the bottom and grabbed the blood-smeared paddle that the seaman had so recently dropped. He plunged it into the water and began to turn the waterlogged dugout towards the shore. His strength was that of desperation. Almost berserk now, he drove the craft forward with long strokes. The ebb was strong now and it carried him with it.

He risked a glance over his shoulder and saw that the *Orlov* was down at the bows. Her forecastle was almost awash and the foremast had toppled forward to lie in a tangled mass above the bowsprit. She was beyond saving, her stern rising to expose her rudder, her still-rotating screw, her copper sheathing. Some men were leaping from the bulwarks and others were attempting to launch boats amidships. The sounds of shouting – and of revolver shots, perhaps to quell panic – carried across the water. There was no sign of fire but black smoke still belched from the funnel. The collier next in line, the second, had swung over so as to pass to starboard of the *Orlov* and of what remained of the first. The third collier, the last, seemed to be approaching the ironclad to render assistance.

The white-hulled yacht was still coming on, speed building as she did, as if disdainful of the *Orlov's* distress, and adjusting her course to run close past. She ploughed through the bodies struggling in the water, drove on without pause towards the open sea.

Dawlish rested on his paddle and then, still bewildered by the explosions, felt fierce delight course through him.

Paid back!

Then he looked down. Polly's ripped body lay before him like a side of beef in a butcher's shop and her open-locked eyes conveyed disbelief rather than pain. She had deserved better. At his feet Egdean was moaning and slipping into unconsciousness.

Tears sprang to his eyes and he began to weep. Sobs racked him. For Polly, for Egdean, for his crews. And for himself.

The *Orlov's* bows had sunk much lower. The stern was rising clear, exposing the keel beneath the stilled propeller. The third collier had drawn alongside and men were leaping across. Downstream, two cables ahead of the *Orlov*, the second collier, that which had passed her before, was now coming about to assist. She was beam on to the current and responding poorly to the helm. Still sobbing, Dawlish turned his back on the scene and began to propel the dugout towards the shore again. He had no clear idea of what he was going to do there, other than rest.

The muffled roar of another explosion spun him round. He looked to the *Orlov*, expecting to see her rent by a secondary detonation but, to his surprise, her situation was just marginally worse than it had been a moment before. But glancing downstream he saw a huge pillar of water rising to port, and beyond, the turning collier. She slipped past the now-collapsing column of white spray. Though rocking, she seemed unharmed. She held the turn, all intent of assisting the *Orlov* abandoned, until her bows pointed towards the sea again and she headed downstream.

Dawlish's attention was drawn from this mysterious explosion to the last moments of the *Orlov's* agony. The collier that had come alongside to assist was drawing away as the dying vessel's stern rose yet higher. The bowsprit and fallen foremast were submerged by now and the hull rose at an angle of thirty degrees above the water's surface. Figures clambered over the bulwarks and cast themselves into the widening gulf between the *Orlov* and her retreating rescuer. Others were swarming up the standing rigging of the main and mizzenmasts in a frantic attempt to escape the rising waters.

Higher and higher the stern rose. The funnel tore itself free and crashed into the water. Black smoke vomited from the gap left in the deck and this seemed to be the signal for the final slide of that beautiful slim hull. The rising waters choked off the smoke and replaced it with a sudden billow of steam. The *Orlov* settled deeper, submerging the central battery. The main mast began to topple forward and the ship began to roll over. For an instant the stern, with its rudder, screw and still-flapping ensign, seemed to stand motionless before she disappeared. The waters, dotted with the heads of swimmers, boiled and raged as huge bubbles erupted from the sunken hull.

The *Orlov* was gone.

Dawlish looked away from the seething pool left by the ironclad to watch the last seconds of the devastated collier. Its end was less dramatic. Only the stern section remained and it sank on an even keel, so that the lapping waters rose around the upright mizzen, up which a few desperate wretches were still climbing. The remaining collier was passing on to join her sister heading downstream. And the yacht was a distant white dot now, still running seawards.

Dizzy and light-headed, Dawlish was paddling again. His strength was gone now and his strokes were weak as he headed towards the eastern bank, his tired brain probing the mystery of the explosions that had doomed the *Orlov* and the collier. They were none of his doing.

The question seemed too large, too overwhelming to comprehend. He was still baffled by it when a bright light seemed to explode in his head. He collapsed forward with his face resting on Egdean's chest.

The dugout drifted seawards with the ebbing tide while, astern, the shouting of the Russians struggling and drowning in the debris-strewn water grew ever fainter.

Chapter 31

The bump of the cutter drawing alongside the half-swamped dugout stirred Dawlish from his stupor. He clawed into consciousness to discern the flash of a white sail and hear the sound of voices but the effort was too much for him and the abyss of oblivion too tempting. His eyes closed again as the canoe rocked beneath the heavy figure that came thudding down next to him. A huge hand closed on his hair and dragged his face upwards. He struggled weakly, fully awake now, but the will to resist was all but dead in him. Had it not been for the accent and the words he might have lapsed again into his semi-coma despite the rough handling.

The Liverpool tones were unmistakable.

"It ain't a black, Harry! It's one o' them bloody Roosians!"

Then a half-choked gasp of horror.

"Jesus! Harry! There's another one here too, an' woman also. A white woman an' she's fair tore up!"

Dawlish felt himself dropped back on the bottom. Despite the sun's brilliance and the pain blazing in his head, he could make out a second figure swinging down into the canoe. Beyond he could discern a row of faces looking over the gunwale of a cutter. Somebody was leaning over him now and shaking his head. Only then did he remember Egdean, and Polly, and the last terrible hail of fire.

The Liverpool voice called out again. "The poor bitch! Dead as mutton she is!"

"Fancy bringing a woman to a place like this." Another voice, West Country. "Some bleedin' Roosian officer's whore, I'll be bound."

"What'll we do with her, Harry?"

"Tip her over and be done with her, Fred. She won't be missed."

The canoe heeled over. Then a splash and it righted itself again.

Dawlish found himself sobbing as he tried to raise himself from the water sloshing in the dugout bottom. Not just for Polly but for relief that he was with British seamen. He had almost risen on his knees when two powerful hands grabbed him from behind and pinioned his arms. He saw Egdean stirring, moaning in half-consciousness, his shoulder bloody.

"There's life enough in these other two bastards." Fred was shouting close to Dawlish's ear. "What should I do with 'em, Harry?"

"Lieutenant Melville said nothing about no prisoners." Harry's Devon tone was dismissive. "Seein' there's so many of the buggers in the water already two more won't make no difference. Just knock 'em on the head, Fred, and drop 'em over."

Dawlish's grip on reality was just enough for him to grasp the import of Harry's advice. He summoned his last reserves of strength and bellowed in a voice trained since boyhood to shout commands in an Atlantic gale.

"You bloody idiot! Don't you recognise a British officer?" he yelled. "I'm Lieutenant Nicholas Dawlish, Royal Navy! Let me go!"

His captor recoiled as if he were a hot coal. One of the seamen in the dugout grabbed him as he fell forward. A look of recognition spread over his features.

"I know you, sir!" he shouted. "D'ye remember me, sir? Joe Rawlins, foretopman in the old *Sprightly* in '66."

Dawlish would not have recognised his own father, for he was falling once more into the dark pit of insensibility. It did not matter now.

He had returned to the Royal Navy.

*

When he awoke nine hours later, Dawlish knew neither where he was nor how he had arrived there. His sleep had been deep and total but it ended with a nightmare that jolted hm into consciousness, one of interminable rain, mangrove, hammering Nordenvelts and scorched flesh.

And Polly writhing in a leaden hail.

He was still in half-delirious confusion when the door was thrown open and daylight flooded in. He quietened, realising that he was in a damp mud and palm-thatched hut, enveloped by a mosquito net and lying on a rough cot, and that a European, clad in white duck, was bending over him. His visitor's voice was calm. And English.

"Calm yourself, Lieutenant Dawlish. You're among friends."

He looked up into the kindly, bearded, face of a man not much older than himself.

"Lieutenant Phineas Melville at you service, sir. No! Don't try to rise! You must rest."

Dawlish lay back, more confused than ever.

"Thank heaven you've awakened," Melville said. "We'd quite despaired of you."

Dawlish took the hand extended to him, found his grip weak.

"Where am I?" His voice was a low whisper.

"Camp Disraeli," Melville said.

"Where?"

"Camp Disraeli. West of the San Bartolomeo Channel."

"Where?" Dawlish was confused.

"Camp Disraeli." Melville's tone was quiet and patient. "The place Admiral Topcliffe chose as our base of operations."

"Topcliffe? Is he here? Did Tattersall bring him?" Dawlish was trying to sit up. "I must talk to him. Now! At once!"

"Calm yourself," Melville pushed him back on the rolled blanket serving as a pillow. "You can rest until he arrives. We expect him soon. He intends to witness the descent – and we hope the sinking – of the second ironclad."

"What second ironclad?"

"The *Alexander Nevski.* She's still waiting up the channel. We're ready for her."

"She's gone! She's gone, I tell you!" Dawlish babbled. "Tell Topcliffe that!"

Pity on Melville's face, the pity that a decent man would feel for a lunatic.

"The *Nevski* and the *Orlov*, they're gone, both of them!" Dawlish shouted. "And so's Krestovski, he's gone too, and *Beta* and *Alpha* and Polly and Egdean and Day and –"

"There, there," Melville said and he patted Dawlish's shoulder as he drifted off once more into an uneasy sleep.

*

Dawlish was calm when he awoke again. He opened his eyes to see chinks of light showing through the palm-thatch roof above. A whole night must have passed. He sat up.

"Be careful, Lieutenant Dawlish." Melville's voice. "Don't attempt to rise. I'll have some food brought for you."

Melville had been sitting on a stool by the head of the cot. Now he went to the rough doorway and spoke quietly to somebody outside. Then he came back and sat by Dawlish's side.

"We'll get some broth inside you," he said, "and then you'll feel better. Do you feel fit enough to talk now?"

Dawlish nodded. His whole body felt stiff and badly used. He put a hand up to touch the gnawing ache on his left cheek, found a pad covering it and smelled antiseptic. And then he remembered.

"You had a narrow escape, lieutenant," Melville said. "If Rawlins hadn't been in the cutter, I doubt that you'd have lived to tell the tale." He hesitated, as if finding words that could not be easy, then said, "I'm afraid your lady companion was already dead. I was angry when I heard her body had been dropped from the canoe. It shouldn't have happened. We'd have given her a decent Christian burial."

Dawlish groaned. "She died very quickly," he said. "She couldn't have felt anything." Tears started to his eyes. "And Egdean? He's –"

"The chap with you? He's weak, and badly wounded, but the surgeon thinks he'll pull through." Melville motioned to the other side of the hut and Dawlish was aware for the first time of a second cot and a bulky and inert figure stretched on it. To his embarrassment, he found himself weeping and he tried to brush the tears away.

"There now, old fellow," Melville was himself embarrassed, and to cover it he rushed on. "Topcliffe advised me that he'd sent a small reconnaissance party into the swamp from another direction. He wasn't very specific and I didn't press for details. You know how close to his chest he likes to play his cards."

"A reconnaissance party?" Dawlish looked blank.

"The Admiral said it was a special group for scouting the ironclads' location. But he said nothing about it consisting of just one officer and a seaman. And a woman! I call that most irregular. Who was she?"

"A noble woman. She was good and kind and brave." Dawlish didn't want to say more. He had mastered himself now and found an air of unreality in Melville's talk. Then came remembrance of something in their previous, brief, conversation. Something amiss.

"What did you call this place?" he asked.

"Camp Disraeli." Melville said. "After the Prime Minister, you know. It was the Admiral's idea."

"You surely mean Camp Beaconsfield?" Dawlish was more confused than ever.

Melville was smiling, "You're coming round well now. I can see it."

"You said Disraeli? Don't you mean Beaconsfield."

"The same man. Mr. Disraeli was ennobled as Lord Beaconsfield not so long back. But Admiral Topcliffe insisted on calling this camp 'Disraeli' even though I mentioned that to him. I can't imagine why he was so insistent on the point. But he's not a man to press."

"Is Tattersall here?" Dawlish's suspicion was stirring.

"Tattersall?"

"Lieutenant Frank Tattersall."

"Tattersall? There's no officer of that name here," Melville looked surprised, "and indeed I'm the only Lieutenant at Camp Disraeli. I'm in command here, rather than a more senior officer, because of my expertise in submarine mines. I shouldn't boast but, by Jove, we really did prove their capability!"

"Mines? What mines?"

"You must have seen that *Orlov* ironclad going to the bottom, and that collier too that was with her. You were running downriver ahead of them to tip us off, weren't you? But they overtook you. We caught them just in time to save your bacon!"

"Caught them?"

"Sunk them. And when the *Nevski* comes down the channel at last you'll see us finish her too in just the same way!"

"But the *Nevski* is gone already!" Dawlish cried. "It was four or five nights ago, I don't know how many. I blew up her magazines after our torpedo attack failed. And afterwards I salvaged the remaining torpedo and I used it on the *Orlov*!"

Melville was looking at him in amazement.

"I think you had better lie down again, Dawlish. There's a good fellow." He spoke in the soothing tones of one humouring a child or a madman. He gestured towards a seaman entering with a steaming bowl. "Look! Here comes your broth. My word! It does look appetising! You'll like it, won't you? It will do you a power of good and then you can sleep again."

In a single flash of enlightenment Dawlish understood. He pushed away the bed covering and struggled to his feet. He was tottering, but he was flushed with excitement.

"You haven't heard of Tattersall or Camp Beaconsfield!" he shouted. "No! And I'll wager not about the *Alpha* nor the *Beta* neither, though they were the fastest craft in the Navy!"

Melville tried to push him back on the cot, gesturing as he did for assistance from the seaman who had brought the broth. His face registered pity as well as alarm. Dawlish realised that he was being taken as demented.

"And Topcliffe told you nothing of my mission to sink the *Nevski* and the *Orlov* at their moorings?" he cried. "You think I'm deranged, don't you, Melville?"

"Just a little overwrought. A touch of the sun perhaps and –"

"I'm as sane as you are, Melville, if indeed either of us are, for both of us have been the dupes of an infernally clever plan."

Melville stepped back, uncertain whether to order the seaman to restrain him. But Dawlish would not hold back, would be heard.

"You speak of mining, Melville. I believe you. But I myself, and Polly and Egdean too, we launched my last torpedo towards the *Orlov's* side and I'd have sunk her too, by God, if it had run straight. Your mines took her, and that collier also, and they went down with no help from me!"

Melville paled, half-recognising the possibility of truth.

"Of course the channel's mined," he said. "It's been mined for almost three weeks. Topcliffe sent me out in the *Druid* to oversee the mining of the channel. He gave the most minute instructions, right down to the naming of the camp."

"Disraeli. Not Beaconsfield? You're sure of that?"

Melville nodded.

"When did you last see Topcliffe?"

"Not since we left Portsmouth. But I've been getting instructions from him in the last week. He's been out beyond the bar, in *Nomad*. He's heard already about the *Orlov's* sinking and he's arriving any time now to see us destroy the *Nevski* when she comes out."

"Tell me about the mines," Dawlish said.

"Two belts, forty mines each," Melville said it with obvious pride. "The furthest up the channel contains twenty active and twenty contact. Electric cables link the actives to an observation point on shore – I can show it to you. A vessel doesn't even have to touch the mine. If one comes close enough, we throw the electric switch onshore and up she goes! And the passive contact mines, they're hundred and ten-pound charge units. Fitted with Hertz chemical horns, very sensitive indeed. Anything drawing more than fifteen feet will set them off. That must be why that yacht passed through safely. She must draw less."

"But then the first collier must have passed safely through the upstream belt?"

Melville nodded. "She was lucky, damn lucky not set off one of the contact mines in the first belt and I didn't want to waste an active mine on just a collier. I wanted to keep all I have for the ironclad coming on astern of her."

"And she ran out of luck on the second belt?"

"I blew one of the electric mines there. And then she ran against one of the contact mines by herself and set it off."

"So you destroyed the *Orlov*?"

"Yes. She must have been damn near directly over the active mine in the first belt that I set off. It was a hit and miss business judging location because we couldn't risk setting marker buoys lest the enemy see them. But the luck was on my side."

The *Orlov* had been already doomed without the dragging of that torpedo alongside the canoe though the creeks. Without Egdean's resolution. Without Polly's death. It had been all for nothing. The *Orlov's* death had been Melville's triumph.

"What about the other colliers?"

"We touched off another electric close to the second when she drove over the belt. It didn't damage her but she ran on for a half-mile and then loitered. She did good work and picked up as many survivors as she could as they drifted down. Not like the damn cowardly master of that yacht that showed us nothing but a clean pair of heels. And the last collier had taken whoever she could from the *Orlov* and then ran so close to the wreckage of the first that she came through unscathed. I didn't wish to waste any more of the active mines. I need them for the *Nevski*. It can't be long before she comes down. And she's the real prize!"

Dawlish shook his head. "She'll never come down," he said. "She's gone already, don't you see? Did you hear nothing? See no great light in the sky?"

"There's thunder and lightning every night."

"It doesn't matter. She's gone anyway. And you and I have been unknowing partners, Melville. We've even worked from Camp Beaconsfield and Camp Disraeli, different names for the same man. You set the bear-trap and I was sent to chase the Russians into it."

Bitterness ran through him as he realised the full enormity, the bottomless guile, of how he had been used. His voice was angry now.

"It didn't matter whether my torpedo attack succeeded or not." He could feel the terror and excitement again – the battles with the Russian pinnaces in the creeks, *Beta's* destruction, the lost crews. All that passion, all that courage, foredoomed to failure. "It didn't need for me to succeed. It mattered only that the attempt was made to show the enemy that his anchorage was no longer secure and so drive him into your minefield!"

The memory of the wounded but defiant *Alpha* slewing towards the *Nevski* in a blaze of icy light and barking gunfire was as real now as on the night itself. And all of it nothing but a deliberate sacrifice of unwitting heroes.

"They'd have run into the mines sooner or later. But I was sent to make it sooner."

Now he was back on the *Nevski's* deck, with Krestovski mocking and tempting by his side, and the rain drizzling down and the smell of scorched flesh . . .

"And the irony – no, Melville, not the irony, the tragedy rather – is that I succeeded anyway and I did blow the *Nevski* to kingdom come."

In that blazing hecatomb, convulsed by explosions and engulfed by flame, Krestovski had died. That was some bleak satisfaction.

"As for the *Orlov*, she was yours, Melville, and she took the bravest of all my crews with her!" He saw Polly again, she who possessed nothing but hope of a future in a coastguard's cottage, losing even that in blood and agony as the Nordenvelts stammered.

Dawlish stopped, for there was a lump forming in his throat and his eyes were misting over. It was all one picture now, the shattered deck of the *Alpha*, the defiant survivors hedged with bayonets against the barbette, Day's conscious choice of death rather than risk his resolution breaking, Egdean's unfailing strength and Polly's loyalty up to that last moment when the torpedo sped on its futile way.

And worst of all was the recollection of his own first meeting with Topcliffe in that Pall Mall club, the cynical bargain he had been offered and, dreadful now to recall, his own cynical acceptance of it.

I have nobody but myself to blame. Not Topcliffe. Not Beaconsfield.

His own ambition had bought his triumph and his tragedy.

Ashamed of his emotion, he turned away from Melville. "Forgive me, Lieutenant." He brushed his tears away. "It's just that the victory was dearly won, but won it was. You can forget the *Alexander Nevski*. She's still up in the channel all right, but she's at the bottom of it, blasted and disembowelled and harmless forever."

At that moment a seaman appeared at the door, begged pardon and informed Melville that Admiral Topcliffe was just then stepping ashore.

Chapter 32

Nomad's stokers had reason to regret Topcliffe's demand for haste as she ploughed through tepid waters beneath a sultry sky, first west, then north, along West Africa's great bulge. Vomiting smoke, her boiler seams straining, her furnaces consumed coal at a rate only normally achieved during speed tests on the measured mile. She was heading for Madeira, the tiny Portuguese-held island that was a staging point for telegraphic cables linking Europe and the Americas. It was through there that the message from Saint Petersburg to Krestovski to unleash the *Nevski* and the *Orlov* would most probably have come. And it was from there now that Topcliffe would flash notification of their destruction to London.

The great Delta lay two days astern when Dawlish emerged on deck, still weak, still unsteady, clad in borrowed uniform. The prohibition of discussing his mission with any but Topcliffe made his relations with the ship's officers stiff and formal, his position even more difficult than on the voyage out. He sensed from their embarrassed mingling of pity and curiosity that his transformation in a fortnight from rude health to a hollow-cheeked scarecrow would in any case have made him a man apart. The unspoken question as to the fate of his torpedo boats and crews was written on every face. Nobody mentioned Day to him but his unexplained absence hung like a miasma over even the most trivial conversation.

Egdean had come on board, weak, often delirious, but enjoined, in the moments of his lucidity, to secrecy. The whole ship's company knew that he now lay in the sick-bay, the only survivor of the *Alpha* and *Beta* crews whose mission had evoked such curiosity on the voyage out from Britain. Yet Dawlish had few worries on the score of the faithful seaman's ability to keep the secret. He had carried one yet more terrible for himself locked within him for over a decade and a half.

Dawlish's own body recovered quickly. His abiding legacy would be the livid, strawberry-sized scar on his left cheek. He would grow the line of his beard a little higher but that could not disguise it fully nor cancel remembrance of the stench of singing hair.

Already, he realised, he had become a man apart, one around whom rumour and speculation would grow like weeds and barnacles on a hull too long in arduous service, a man to whom certain direct questions might never be posed, a man respected, and feared more than a little, a man who would never again be received with total ease into the company of his fellows. He had passed through an invisible barrier on the *Nevski's* deck and there could be no return.

Now, when he looked at Topcliffe, he saw himself.

In that terrible moment of clarity when Melville's story had forced him to accept the burden of his own decisions, he had decided that there would be no hint of recrimination when he related all to Topcliffe. And somehow, he had managed.

The admiral's features had shown mixed shock and delight, and perhaps even shame, when he entered that shack at Camp Disraeli.

"I should perhaps have expected you to make it, Dawlish," he said, something like compassion in his voice as he took his hand and urged him back to his cot.

And then the old Topcliffe, remote and imperious, was back and dismissing Melville. A single glance towards Egdean's pallid and sleeping form told him that there would be no witness to the confidences that would follow.

"The *Nevski's* gone," Dawlish said.

"And you did it."

A simple statement, never to be forgotten.

Topcliffe had already received independent confirmation from Tattersall that the distant convulsion rending the night sky, and seen from Camp Beaconsfield, had been something other than a violent thunderstorm. Tattersall had sent patrols westwards. They encountered terrified refugees fleeing the pall that had settled on Elepa after the destruction of the great black ship.

Topcliffe listened to Dawlish's account in total silence, only showing surprise, quickly suppressed, at the mention of Krestovski.

"Continue!" he said as Dawlish paused, his flow of words halted by the sudden frown.

And then the worst part of all, almost as terrible to recollect as to endure. Dawlish paused, choked with horror and regret. He felt a hand on his shoulder, gentle, surprisingly comforting.

"Now you too understand." Barely concealed sadness in Topcliffe's voice. "Raison d'état, Dawlish, raison d'état."

And then, somehow composed, Dawlish told of the great ironclad's destruction. On then to the meeting with Polly, whose memory now seemed the most pathetic of all, and on to the recovery of the torpedo, the last gruelling journey and the *Orlov's* final plunge. A long silence followed after he finished.

"I made a mistake, a grave mistake." A terrible intensity in Topcliffe's tone. "I counted on the mines to dispose of the ironclads, but the timing was critical. Melville's mining party had sailed for the Delta in *Druid* even before we left Devonport for Killary. It was essential to know that the Russians were trapped like flies in a bottle. Once that was achieved, we couldn't just wait for them to emerge in their own good time. Their very existence was a threat."

"You couldn't wait, sir?"

His impatience had been my people's death sentence.

"We couldn't wait, Dawlish, and we had to be certain that they were destroyed. I had no hope for the success of your attack, none whatsoever, but I counted on it to panic the Russians towards the mine-belts. Once they were no more, we would have a free hand for massing the fleet at the Bosporus if it proves necessary."

"You didn't tell me, sir." He could not suppress his tone of recrimination.

"I underestimated your determination." Topcliffe looked Dawlish straight in the eye. "I know now that you would have pressed on just as resolutely even had you known about the mines."

"Not just me, sir. Every one of us. You selected better than you knew."

For Topcliffe had indeed underestimated.

It would have made no difference, not to me, not to my men, not to Polly. We would have pressed on in just the same way.

But I would have liked to have known.

*

An overheated bearing immobilised *Nomad's* engine for two days. Though the screw was hoisted, the funnel lowered and full sail spread, light and adverse winds slowed progress as she headed northwards and artificers slaved to replace the bearing. Topcliffe paced constantly, only his furrowed brows betraying how he fretted over the delay. Dawlish, his strength returning, spent much of the voyage working first on his formal report, and then on another, self-initiated, on ideas for improved tactical deployment of torpedo craft. That single night of Homeric action against the *Nevski* had yielded insights undreamed of in any navy but Britain's. And, in that service, he alone possessed them. That should stand him in good stead. Ambition was stirring again.

Egdean was recuperating well in the sick-berth, but still weak. He tried to rise when Dawlish first visited him there, but he dropped back. An attendant reproved him, apologised and settled him back on his cot. Dawlish sent the man away and then sat by the wounded seaman. There was an awkward silence, embarrassed, endless.

"I see that your reading's still a comfort, Egdean." Dawlish said at last. His eye had settled on a half-a-dozen past editions of *Ashore and Afloat* by the bedside, provided by some kindred soul from *Nomad's* lower deck.

"It's always a comfort, sir."

"And I trust they haven't been dosing you with rum?" A weak joke.

"No, sir." A ghost of a smile and Egdean gestured towards a borrowed Bible. "There's better medicines, sir."

And there was silence again until Dawlish voiced the unspoken thought.

"She couldn't have suffered," he said. "She died instantly."

What was always said about violent death, was seldom believed. Egdean knew better. The emptiness in his eyes told that he had recognised the infinity of despair, and of hope denied, that those last threshing, bloody moments had encompassed.

"And she loved you," Dawlish said. "She told me that. In her whole life it was only you who ever cared for her. And she died knowing it."

He turned away and moved towards the door, an officer again, leaving the enlisted man with his sorrow, his thoughts of what might have been and the bleak comfort of love remembered.

The familiarity of the swamp was at an end.

*

Nomad remained at Madeira for just three hours, enough for an officer to go ashore to send a telegram to London. Topcliffe showed it to Dawlish beforehand, a single one-word message.

Sybil.

"You can guess the recipient," Topcliffe said.

Dawlish laughed. A novel written by Beaconsfield some thirty years before when he was still plain Benjamin Disraeli. And a success.

Topcliffe was unwilling to send anything longer, even coded, from here. He did however wait for the return of the young officer with the answer to the question that he had been sent to ask the British consul.

Yes, a white yacht with a clipper bow had docked five days before and had remained just long enough to take on coal. And more than long enough to send a telegram.

The consul also sent a bundle of English newspapers on board, all out of date by at least a week. All told the same story. The Ottoman Army of the Balkans, against all odds, was blocking the Russian advance at a Bulgarian town called Plevna. Fortified with trenches and redoubts, the Turkish troops had already repulsed a massive assault. But all correspondents agreed that it could be but days before this last bastion would fall and release the Russians to forge on towards Constantinople.

The passage to Gibraltar was a fast one over smooth seas.

The captain's gig carried Topcliffe and Dawlish shoreward even as *Nomad* was dropping anchor beneath the great rock. Topcliffe brushed aside all formalities of reception and within half an hour he and Dawlish were standing in impatience by the telegraphist who was establishing contact with the Admiralty in London. Two armed Marines stood watch outside the door, denying access even to the Governor, who hovered there with his aide-de-camp. Topcliffe had engaged these gentlemen in no more conversation than was needed to confirm that the Turks were still holding Plevna. He made no comment but he shot a single significant glance towards Dawlish.

"The line's clear now, sir," the telegraphist said. "I can transmit your message."

A long one. Topcliffe had coded it himself.

And now the wait.

In London an Admiralty messenger would be scurrying down Whitehall to place the decoded message in a limp hand, almost that of an invalid. But a smile of quiet triumph, of joy suppressed at a deliverance that must remain secret, would be spreading over a wizened, clever face and a mind, sharp and ingenious, would even now be calculating how best to exploit this more detailed news.

The telegraphist shifted in his chair, awed by the proximity of the two tense and silent officers who stood waiting by the window, looking out across the anchorage or flicking through the most recent English newspapers.

It was almost an hour before the telegraph chattered into life again. Topcliffe sent the operator from the room., then said to Dawlish, "You're familiar with Playfairs, are you not?

Dawlish nodded. His beloved uncle had taught him that cipher system, simple but virtually unbreakable, during the last sad months he had spent with him with him in Pau.

"The key is Coningsby."

Another novel by the young Disraeli,

"You might like to decipher it, Dawlish."

It took two minutes. He read it out.

"Congratulations and thanks. Advise Dawlish of immediate promotion to commander, effective date *Nevski* sinking. Proceed to London forthwith."

No sender's name.

Promotion dearly bought. But the promotion he had hungered for.

Nightfall saw them both, in mufti now, dining in the single carriage of a privately chartered train that rushed northwards across the parched Spanish landscape.

Chapter 33

It was the same group that had met one evening a few weeks before. Only the venue, Downing Street, the Prime Minister's residence, was different.

Beaconsfield, Kegworth and Barnaby were gathered already. Corry had met Topcliffe and Dawlish, tired and travelworn, on arrival at Victoria Station. He had brought them straight here on this warm late-August afternoon.

Beaconsfield's eyes glittered in his wizened face as Dawlish told his story.

The drawing of the *Nevski* that had bought a French draughtsman's retirement lay spread on the table before them. The graceful S-curve of the tumblehome and the brutal strength of the barbettes now had a sinister quality that they had lacked before. Dawlish looked away, out through the open upper-floor windows towards the companies of troops drilling to barked commands on Horse Guards Parade.

Simple, disciplined men, he thought, loyal and brave.

As mine were.

He looked down on the drawing, fixed his glance on the midships barbette where Day and the others had been penned. He forced himself to drain all emotion from his voice when he described his first encounter with Krestovski.

Beaconsfield stiffened at the mention of the name. He held up a flannel-swathed, gout-stricken, hand to halt the narrative's flow.

"Krestovski?" he almost whispered. "Prince Vladimir Mikhailovich Krestovski?"

Dawlish nodded, remembering how Topcliffe had also reacted to the name. He pointed to the scar on his cheek.

"A man I shan't forget, sir." He could not disguise his loathing. "A cowardly blackguard who aped the graces of an English gentleman on the strength of a term or two at Oxford and who boasted of passing acquaintance with Her Majesty's family."

A bitter smile puckered Beaconsfield's face.

"I have a surprise for you, commander," he said, "but it can wait. Pray continue."

And then the story of the unending horror on the deck, more terrible, more inconceivable, when it was related beneath the decorated ceiling and the sparkling, unlit, chandelier, with the sun bright outside and bees busy in the blooms in the walled garden beneath the windows.

Silence when Dawlish paused. Barnaby was shaking his head in disgust and Kegworth's florid features were blanched. But Beaconsfield showed no emotion.

"You never considered accommodating Prince Krestovski?" he said at last.

"I considered it all through the day."

"And you know the truth now, Dawlish? That you were but the beater, not the hunter?"

"I want to forget about that, My Lord."

"Not a pleasant business," Barnaby said.

"But life should be more than pleasant," Beaconsfield's tone was cold. "An ox in a field has a pleasant life. Life is often conspiracy and extortion, gentlemen, and there's no help but to make the best of it. Pray continue, Commander Dawlish."

He described the penetration of the magazine and the destruction of the *Nevski*, the course of the cascading explosions through the giant hull indicated on the drawing by a pointing finger, the words incapable of conveying the terror and the horror. Barnaby was hungry for details of the ruptures and disintegration of the ship.

"Later," Beaconsfield's gouty hand stilled his queries. "You can discuss that with the commander later."

And then the meeting with Polly and the salvaging of *Beta's* torpedo, the brutal journey through the swamp to attack the *Orlov*.

All unnecessary, all futile.

Dawlish watched the faces of his listeners, wondered how they had regarded him on that far-off night in Kegworth's library. How many of them had been privy to the cynical manipulation to which he had been subjected? Beaconsfield and Topcliffe had planned to sacrifice him and his crews to panic the Russians into the mine-belts. The mild and solicitous Corry must have been party to it too. But had the benign-looking Barnaby, or the hospitable Kegworth, known of the deception?

But I'll swallow it. I'll have nothing for it if I don't. This is the way of the world and I've been no more than a child in it. Until now.

"A satisfactory outcome," Topcliffe said to Beaconsfield when Dawlish finished. "I trust you agree, My Lord?"

"I summoned Shuvalov, the Czar's ambassador, within an hour of your message from Madeira," Beaconsfield said. "I expected surprise, indeed I'd rather looked forward to his discomfort, but he seemed prepared for it already. I only understood why when I received your further report from Gibraltar."

The telegram despatched by the white yacht's captain from Madeira would have reached St. Petersburg in time for the ambassador in London to be alerted.

"We met alone," Beaconsfield said. "I advised him of the certain destruction of the ironclads. Shuvalov played his role well. He denied all knowledge of the vessels' existence and I left it at that. But I confirmed to him my resolve to concentrate our fleet at Constantinople in the event of the Muscovite hoards advancing so far. He offered no comment but I believe he appreciated that the shift in the naval balance had changed the situation. We parted on personally amicable terms."

"What now, My Lord?" Dawlish felt he had earned the right to ask.

"The Russians will no doubt make a few more spirited attempts to take . . . what's the place called?"

"Plevna, My Lord," Topcliffe prompted.

"That's it, Plevna. And they'll take it at whatever cost. With that fellow Skobelev in their ranks, how could they fail? And they'll press on. Honour will demand it. The war may drag on for another six or eight months. They may reach Constantinople. But if they'll threaten to take the city we'll send a powerful naval squadron there – as we can now afford to do – and we'll signal our willingness to enter the fray."

"It may not even come to that," Topcliffe said. "Tough fellows those Turks. They'll fight the Russians every step of the way and bleed their manpower reserves and their coffers."

"Better that way." Beaconsfield was nodding. "Better too that we assist it happening. But not openly."

"I've some thoughts on that, My Lord," Topcliffe said. "I'll have something to present to you in a few days."

"See Mr. Corry. He'll arrange an appointment."

Beaconsfield turned to Dawlish.

"I may have gained some little fame as a man of letters, more perhaps than I may win as First Minister, but I should never have ventured to lay before the public a tale as strange, as dramatic, as we have just heard." His tone was silky and Dawlish had the impression of a speech often used before and adapted to each new set of circumstances. "I speak for all here, and for that gracious lady whom I serve, when I thank you for your gallant action and congratulate you the courage of your loyal crews."

"A suggestion, My Lord?" Topcliffe spoke. "An ex-gratia payment of two hundred pounds to each of the bereaved families? As an addition to the pensions appropriate in such cases. And five hundred perhaps in the case of Lieutenant Day? On the condition, of course, of absolute confidentiality on the families' part."

Beaconsfield sighed, nodded assent.

"And that woman," he said. "Polly, you called her. Did she have relations?"

"No, My Lord. Miss Cringle had no relations."

Miss Cringle – she deserves that much courtesy in death.

"It may seem hard that there can be no public recognition of the services rendered," Beaconsfield said. "I regret that diplomatic conventions demand that we draw a decent veil over the Czar's duplicity and his shame at his frustration."

The meeting was at an end. Corry was helping Beaconsfield to his feet.

Nothing had been said of the sympathy of highly placed persons that Topcliffe had extended as bait in the Pall Mall club. Dawlish suspected now that he might never hear of it again. His promotion was probably the end of it.

"You'll be welcome at my place tonight, commander." Kegworth was shaking his hand with unfeigned warmth "In Piccadilly, you remember it? I'll see to it that you're collected. Topcliffe will be coming too. Just a small affair, Dawlish, a small affair – not many people are around at this time o' year, you know – but we'd be honoured were you to come."

Beaconsfield detained Dawlish before he left.

"I too will be present." His voice was low. "As will be another guest whom you'll be interested to meet. And one other thing, Dawlish. It hardly needs saying. None of this ever happened. You understand that, don't you? It never happened."

He understood.

And on the brief journey to the Charing Cross Hotel in the carriage that Kegworth provided, Dawlish remembered, and was ashamed, that in his moment of glory he had not pleaded more for the dependants of his butchered crews.

*

A telegram awaited Dawlish at the hotel, a response to his own hasty message that had announced his return from the West Indies. He tore it open.

He began to laugh.

The timing of his return had proved fortuitous, his father wrote. He wanted him to serve as groomsman at his wedding in eight days' time. He would have a step-mother. Miss Rowena Emery.

Topcliffe collected him at the hotel at half-past seven in a brougham bearing Lord Kegworth's arms on the door. The drive to the mansion at the far end of Piccadilly was a short one, but long enough for Topcliffe's offer, one of the sort for which Dawlish had hungered.

"Deputy to the Senior Instructor in *Vernon*. There'll be little instruction involved, there'll be more junior officers for that. You'd be responsible for new developments, testing, improving depth and direction-keeping, that sort of thing."

Fisher had held that position, Dawlish knew, a stepping stone to greater things. The youth, scarcely older than himself, whom he had first encountered in the mud before the Taku Forts in '59 was now captain of the large ironclad *Bellerophon*. Many spoke of him rising higher, much, much higher.

"I'd be honoured, sir," Dawlish said.

The navy's mine and torpedo school was housed in an old wooden fourth-rate, moored permanently at Portsmouth. The torpedo boded to transform the nature of naval warfare and senior Admiralty figures were always interested in activities there. That had done Fisher no harm and he himself could expect the same.

And most officers lived ashore. There would be an opportunity to spend a few years in a society in which he had almost become a stranger.

"When would I take up duty, sir?"

"No great rush, Commander, no great rush." Topcliffe sounded vague. "There'll be a few months' delay before the *Vernon* position becomes vacant. The present incumbent's wife is ill. Nothing mortal, Dawlish, but she needs nursing. A damn fine woman too. It would be inhumane to send her husband back to sea too soon."

"And half-pay until then, sir?" The prospect of a few months of idleness was tempting. There might be time to visit Switzerland and Italy.

"It would be a pity to keep you kicking your heels," Topcliffe said. "An active officer like yourself, commander, a man who thrives on responsibility."

Visions of Alpine valleys and Roman glories faded.

"There may be an opportunity, a possibility only, mark you, Dawlish. Something of short duration. But an unusual one. You'd like it. There's nothing concrete about it yet. We might speak next week if there is."

The brougham was slewing to the right and wheeling through the gates of the Kegworth mansion.

"Thank you, Morton," Topcliffe called up to the coachman when a waiting footman opened the door.

Up the steps and into a blaze of light and brilliance, flowers and music, women gorgeous in silk and diamonds, men no less superb in starched white and splendid black. Dawlish felt shabby in his own cheap finery, hastily acquired with the aid of the hotel concierge.

The announcement of their names provoked no stir. Topcliffe's might be familiar to some of the guests but Dawlish's was unknown.

Lord Kegworth, as ever, was effusive in his greeting.

"Commander Dawlish, my dear, the hero of the Anti-Slavery Patrol." He introduced him to his stout wife and Lady Agatha, his heavy, sheep-faced daughter. "The gentlemen who rescued those slaves on Pemba – Pemba, wasn't it, Dawlish, or was it Zanzibar? You've heard me mention the affair a dozen times, haven't you, my dears?"

Both ladies looked blank. It was obvious that they had never heard of him. Dawlish was relieved to be delivered into the clutches of a silk-clad crone whose main interest in life appeared to be conversion of the heathen. He endured ten minutes of her admiration of the Navy's slavery-suppression and of her donations to missionary societies. She would have given even more had her husband's ungrateful Irish tenants not been causing such mischief in recent months. Lord Lowhurst, poor man, was quite out of his head with concern about the rents.

The ambassadors of France, Italy and the United States had been announced but it was the arrival of the Prime Minister that allowed Dawlish to escape from the old harpy. Beaconsfield was ascending the staircase to the great reception room with the aid of an ebony cane and leaning on Montague Corry's arm. It difficult to accept that this delicate old man had been able, by a single ruthless stroke, to thwart Russia's growing might and somehow shore up the tottering Ottoman edifice.

The frail figure was at once surrounded by a group of admirers but Corry manoeuvred his way through them to seek Dawlish.

"He likes you, commander," he said. "He wants to talk to you."

Dawlish approached and Beaconsfield reached for his arm.

"You won't object if an old man leans on your strength, commander," he said. "I fear that power and position are but poor physics for age and decrepitude. Do but see me as far as the card-room. My old friend Kegworth will have had a table prepared for me there."

The throng opened to let them pass through. Beaconsfield drew Dawlish to sit by him.

"I tire easily," he said. "My best physicians at present are Doctor Solitude, Doctor Silence and Doctor Warmth"

"And two general practitioners, Doctor Regular Hours and Doctor Regular Meals," Corry added. Beaconsfield smiled. Dawlish had an impression of a familiar joke between them, often repeated.

"I fear that Her Majesty's interests ensure that those gentlemen's house calls are all too infrequent".

"But you have done great and difficult things, sir." Dawlish found it impossible not to admire this man.

"I took a motto in my youth," Beaconsfield said. "Forti Nihil Difiicile"

"To the brave, nothing is difficult," Dawlish had just enough Latin to understand it.

"It took me a lifetime to learn that it was untrue, though I suspect you've learned that already, commander. The brave overcome what's difficult. But it's never easy for them. And they suffer for it."

Beaconsfield leaned closer.

"A small gift will be delivered to your hotel tomorrow," he said. "A personal expression of thanks. I hope you're interested in literature, commander. Books are good companions, even if you don't ever open them. I thought you would welcome a signed edition of my novels, poor as they may be."

Dawlish was touched. "Nothing would please me more," he said.

"A paltry token." Beaconsfield's melancholy had passed, and his was smiling now. "I doubt if my literary fame will outlive me. It's been my misfortune that my talents had to shine in the century of much greater writers. But listen!"

There was a pause, during which the Prime Minister's eyes seemed to hood over, before the butler's voice from the top of the stairs announced the next guest.

"His Excellency, Prince Vladimir Mikhailovich Krestovski."

Dawlish started to his feet. Blood rushed to his head. Was it possible? Krestovski alive and here in London?

Beaconsfield caught him by the wrist and drew him back gently into his seat.

"I promised you a surprise," he said. "I didn't promise that it would be pleasant."

"That he should live!" The words slipped out, the anger too.

Beaconsfield looked straight into Dawlish's eyes. His gaze was unblinking and devoid of all emotion. His voice was flat. "Prince Vladimir arrived in London two days ago. He's the trusted friend of many of the highest – of the very highest, you understand? – in this realm. No better envoy could return to St. Petersburg to convince the Czar that his hand is played out."

"He's a murderous pervert of the worst kind, My Lord." Dawlish realised that the remark might well end his career, but he made it anyway.

"His personality, my dear commander, is quite beside the point. I suggest that you accompany me to meet him. If you would climb the greasy pole, Dawlish, then a lesson in dissimulation would not come amiss."

The voice held a cold authority that left Dawlish no option but to comply. He assisted Beaconsfield to his feet. They met Topcliffe by the entrance to the ballroom.

"We'll wish Prince Krestovski a safe return to St. Petersburg," Beaconsfield said. "I don't believe you know him, Topcliffe. You might like to make his acquaintance. A charming and accomplished gentleman."

"A pleasure indeed," Topcliffe bowed slightly. He shot a glance at Dawlish, whose face was now as impassive as the Beaconsfield's, then followed.

The music was louder here and couples were gliding across the ballroom floor. Krestovski's back was turned and he was exchanging pleasantries with the Kegworths. Several of the other guests also seemed to know him well. A ripple of laughter greeted one of his sallies but Kegworth signalled to him as Beaconsfield approached, and he looked around.

The sight of his face was some small compensation for the disappointment of knowing that he had survived. The beauty that had made Krestovski a man apart was gone forever – a white scar, livid at the edges, marked where the bottle had smashed into his face and where the hair had been burned from the left side of his head. On that side also the cheek was scarred, the mouth twisted down in a hideous rictus. The other side looked as if some beast had chewed it and then abandoned it to heal. The left hand was still bandaged and his stance seemed lop-sided. But the voice was as soft as ever.

"My dear Lord Beaconsfield!" He bowed from the waist. "A pleasant surprise indeed. It must be – let me see – four years since we met. At Lord Carnarvon's, was it not?"

"Surely nobody who was present could forget you, Your Excellency." The faintest trace of amusement on Beaconsfield's face.

"But now you must forgive my scarecrowish appearance!" Krestovski's attempt to smile was horrifying." I've been telling Lady Kegworth of my oafish misadventures – the little matter of an overturned spirit lamp. Nobody to blame but myself, but all's well that ends well."

Only then did he glance beyond Beaconsfield. His shock of recognition, immediately suppressed, was imperceptible to all but Dawlish.

"But, my word!" he said, with every indication of pleasure. "Can that be my old friend, Mr. Smith?"

The eyes turned on Dawlish were as friendly and sympathetic as when he had first stepped on board the *Nevski.* And again he caught a distinct whiff of eau-de-cologne. He forced himself to shake the hand extended to him. Krestovski's grip was firm.

"You must be confusing me with someone else, Your Excellency." Dawlish looked him straight in the eye. "Though I believe we have indeed met before. At Cowes Week, was it? Were you not a member of Prince Alfred's party?"

Krestovski shook his head, was still attempting to smile.

"Or was it at White's boatyard? Perhaps a prospective customer for one of Mr. White's fast pleasure craft? My name's Dawlish, by the way. Commander Nicholas Dawlish, Royal Navy."

"White's it must have been then," Krestovski said. He turned to Topcliffe. "And I do believe you must be Admiral Sir Richard Topcliffe, though we've never been introduced."

"Prince Krestovski makes light of his misfortune," Lady Kegworth linked her arm with his and took the uninjured hand in hers, "but the poor man suffered dreadfully on his expedition up the Amazon River!"

"An ornithological expedition," Lady Agatha said, but nobody took heed of her.

"I'm attempting to prevail on dear Vladimir to spend a few days with us before he returns to Russia," her mother said. "Perhaps you, Lord Beaconsfield, might be more persuasive than Agatha or I have been? Vladimir's always been quite a favourite with us even if he does now make jokes about what a lesser man might consider unmitigated misfortune."

"A small sacrifice on the altar of science, madam." The smile was again a repellent grin "And truth to tell, a small price for fleeing our Russian winter for warmer climes."

"Quite a remarkable coincidence," Dawlish failed to keep the cold fury from his voice. "I too am returned just recently. from warmer climes. And I too have suffered facial disfigurement while there." He raised his hand to the strawberry patch on his cheek. "Perhaps you are made of sterner stuff, Your Excellency, but small as it may seem, I count this mark no little thing. I'll carry the memory of what caused it to my grave."

Nobody spoke. The gentlemen looked uneasy. Lady Kegworth was looking at Dawlish with a mixture of distaste and contempt.

"I understand you're returning to St. Petersburg?" Beaconsfield broke the silence. "At a time of such regrettable strain between our nations, we're mutually fortunate to have men such as yourself to explain one to the other for the benefit of both."

"May such difficulties be of short duration," Krestovski said. "Aah – if only the energies of our peoples could be diverted into such peaceful channels as my recent scientific expedition, heavy as the cost has been for me personally. Is it too much to hope for such a golden age?"

"Dear Vladimir's sentiments do him much credit," said Lady Kegworth, "but he hasn't changed in that. We used to so welcome his visits when he was up at Magdalen with our son Oswald – did we not, my dear?"

Her husband said nothing. His was avoiding Dawlish's glance.

Krestovski might have simpered had his face permitted. "Dear old Oswald!" he said. "What pleasant memories you evoke, Lady Kegworth.

I trust he's well? At the Constantinople Embassy now, I understand, and invaluable no doubt to the ambassador."

"Only that knowledge makes his absence bearable," Lady Kegworth dabbed her eyes. "A mother feels such separations."

"A bite of supper might be acceptable?" Kegworth was embarrassed by his wife's emotion.

"If Vladimir would accompany me and tell me more of his fascinating adventures in Brazil, I'd be most flattered." She brightened, was almost coquettish. "And perhaps Lord Beaconsfield would join us so that I would be flanked by the united wisdoms of Albion and Muscovy?"

She gave Dawlish a look of withering contempt as she led her chosen guests away. Krestovski bowed to both naval officers as he left but it was impossible to know whether his twisted countenance bore a sneer or a smile.

Dawlish flushed with anger and humiliation. He half-turned as a woman spoke at his side.

"I'm so sorry Mamma was angry with you, commander. I did so want to speak to you myself."

Kegworth's daughter's myopic frown conveyed almost vulnerable sincerity and her voice was soft and pleasant.

"To me, Lady Agatha?"

"About mathematics and scientific things that a naval man must know about," she said. "They're my passion, you know. Unseemly for a lady, Mamma says, but Pappa's more understanding. And you must needs be a practical mathematician for your navigation – spherical trigonometry fascinates me. I may learn something of its application when I visit Oswald in Constantinople. With that dreadful war between the Turks and Russians, I can't go directly. I'll have to travel to Athens, and take a ship from there."

"Is that really desirable in the present circumstances, Lady Agatha?"

"Oswald's letters assure me that Constantinople will never be at risk. And my companion will be travelling with me. Miss Morton's much more practical than I am."

Dawlish felt touched by her naïve enthusiasm. But before he could respond she excused herself to follow her parents.

Topcliffe was still by his side. Looking past Dawlish at the dancing couples beyond, he said in a low voice devoid of all intonation: "It's a long road, and a dangerous one, to St. Petersburg." Then he recognised an acquaintance and advanced to meet him, hand outstretched.

And in that instant Dawlish realised that, regardless of consequences, there was just one action he could take if he was ever to respect himself again. Calm descended on him with his decision.

He glanced around the room, past the carefree revellers and beyond the glittering assembly of power and riches. His eyes came to rest on a low marble-topped table in the far corner. A small bronze statuette stood on it, next to a tall vase of flowers. He moved towards it, stopping once to take a glass of champagne from a passing flunkey's tray. Five minutes were lost when he was again detained by Lady Lowhurst. The ingratitude of her husband's Irish tenantry still outraged her.

There was an empty seat within a foot of the table. He introduced himself to the half-senile gentleman who slouched next to it, nursing a large tumbler of brandy and studying the ladies on the dance-floor with undisguised lasciviousness. He seemed glad of company, for the middle-aged daughter by his side seemed both embarrassed and exasperated by him.

"I'm eighty-nine, sir." He shouted with pride and with all the vehemence of the half-deaf. "And I stood in line with the 30th Foot at Waterloo! Would you credit that, sir? In the line that day! Damn few of us left, sir, damn few!"

"An honour, sir, to shake your hand then," Dawlish edged close to the table.

"You never heard the story of the duchess and the chimney sweep, did you, sir?"

And so, despite his daughter's blushing attempts to quieten him, he began to regale Dawlish with a series of salacious stories.

He pretended to listen avidly and, much to the disgust of the mortified lady, to laugh at each of the increasingly filthy jokes. The old satyr sniggered when she finally excused herself and left, blushing in fury.

"They're all so damn proper nowadays." He nudged Dawlish with his elbow. "Not like in those days, sir! There was a bit more life in the fillies then! We weren't all dancing at the Duchess's ball on the eve of Waterloo! We'd better things to do!"

Dawlish regarded the figurine from the corner of his eye. It was a miniature bronze reproduction of the Winged Victory of Samothrace, nine or ten inches tall.

Victory. A good omen.

The torso, skirt and base looked solid, though the wings could be a complication. It stood no more than eighteen inches from him. He waited until all eyes were directed towards the dancers and then, with a single movement, swept it up and pushed it into his trouser pocket.

The rheumy-eyed satyr next to him had noticed nothing and was already laughing to himself as he approached the climax of his latest tale.

". . . and at that moment who should come upon Her Ladyship but the butler and . . ."

Dawlish heard him out, feigned amusement, then excused himself. He headed for the entrance, but hung back as he saw that Beaconsfield was leaving. Corry had draped a fur-lined cloak across his shoulders and was easing him towards the door, while Kegworth and his wife hovered by attentively. There was no sign of Topcliffe.

A cry of "Lord Beaconsfield's carriage coming up!" sounded from outside and then the frail figure went out into the night.

Dawlish retreated and minutes later met Lord Kegworth by the ballroom entrance and complained, passing his hand across his brow, of an incapacitating headache. An early night was indicated. Would Lord Kegworth excuse him and convey his thanks for the evening to Her Ladyship? He almost overplayed his hand.

"Let my coachman bring you to your hotel," Kegworth said. "Morton will have you there in ten minutes."

In the end Dawlish managed to convince him that a walk through the night air would be the best remedy. Kegworth saw him down the front steps to the courtyard, hoping that he would be able to come to dinner later in the week.

"Don't be put off by my wife, Dawlish." He sounded sincere as they parted, "Her bark's worse than her bite – I learned that myself years ago. But a good woman, a good woman. And my daughter Agatha, she's a strange girl. Clever but strange. You might be able to talk her out of her notion of going to Constantinople."

Dawlish moved from the circle of light flooding from the mansion and beyond the cluster of carriages that waited patiently for the guests within. He pushed a few coins at the tattered beggars who descended on him from the darkness and crossed the street to the Green Park side. Beneath the cover of his enveloping cloak, he withdrew the statuette and tested its balance.

It felt heavy enough for its purpose.

As heavy as a bottle.

Chapter 34

Dawlish sauntered eastwards until a darkened doorway offered cover from which he could observe the Kegworth entrance. Ten minutes passed before a group descended the steps and departed westwards in a carriage. Krestovski did not appear to be among them. A little later a patrolling constable shone a bull's eye lantern into his face. Dawlish winked and told him that he was waiting for a certain lady to leave without her husband as he pushed a sovereign into his hand. The policeman seemed assured by his respectable garb and tone of authority. He understood the situation – he was a sporting man himself, he said – and he passed on.

It was after midnight now. Another carriage departed, then three gentlemen on foot who passed eastwards on the other side of the street, laughing, smoking cigars. There were several more departures but another half-hour passed before Dawlish's patience was rewarded.

A lop-sided figure emerged on the brightly-lit steps. He was in conversation with another gentleman and there was a third figure, a stout one, who looked like Kegworth. The stance of the half-maimed Krestovski was unmistakable. Dawlish endured an agony of apprehension for another five minutes, fearing that the presence of a companion might imply departure by carriage. To his relief, Kegworth at last shook hands and went inside while his two guests descended the steps, were lost to view for a moment behind the waiting carriages, and then went strolling eastwards along the northern side of Piccadilly. Dawlish shrunk further into the doorway and tilted his hat to throw his face in shadow but they passed on the opposite pavement without noticing him. He waited until they were twenty yards past him before he left the doorway and followed with soft footsteps.

Krestovski and his companion were in no hurry. They paused to light cigars and Dawlish slunk again into shadow to observe them. Snatches of conversation carried back to him. They were speaking English, not Russian, so Krestovski's companion might be just a chance acquaintance. Both men threw back their heads and laughed. They crossed the street at the Albany, close to Piccadilly Circus. The greater concentration of people here allowed Dawlish to come yet closer to his quarry while still remaining lost in the crowd. They were entering the Haymarket now, the area known as 'Babylon', and it was more densely thronged at midnight than at midday. Eyes locked on Krestovski's limping figure, Dawlish pushed himself through the bizarre mixture of ragged waifs, garishly painted and costumed harridans, cigar-smoking young bucks in evening dress and check-suited bruisers.

Several women pushed themselves at Dawlish but he smiled and shook his head and moved on past them. A legless beggar croaked out 'Hearts of Oak' against a wall. A rouged child, no more than twelve, clutched at his cloak and invited him to come with her in terms that would have disgusted a man o' war's lower deck. He prised her fingers free and followed Krestovski and his companion down the Haymarket, deaf to the child's parting obscenities.

Progress was difficult. A great press of humanity jostled down the footpaths on either side of the central thoroughfare, up and down which a steady stream of carriages moved, their occupants sometimes gesturing to women to enter. Dawlish found himself accosted by cheerful and brazen sluts, by whey-faced seamstresses, by gaudy hags old enough to be his mother.

Krestovski and his companion stopped halfway down the Haymarket, drawn into conversation with three flashily attired women. One laughed raucously as Krestovski's friend withdrew a flask from his pocket and raised it to his lips. Dawlish stepped in against the wall to watch, inviting in the process the shame-faced advances of a decent-looking girl in a plain grey dress.

She touched his arm timidly, as if afraid of being struck. "I don't do it often sir," she said, "and I'm clean – honest, I am, sir. It's only for my baby that I come here."

Dawlish had eyes only for Krestovski but the girl could give useful cover. He slipped one arm around her and gave her a sovereign. "Just stay with me a moment," he said. "Just hold me and keep talking."

The girl's bonnet gave ample cover for viewing the animated group. He approached within a few yards. Krestovski's companion had his arm about the waist of one of the women. She was laughing shrilly as he led her to the kerb and hailed a cab. Krestovski was engaged with the two other women, pushing them out from the shadows into the pool of light cast by a nearby gas-lamp. One of the women reached up playfully and tipped his hat backwards, revealing for the first time the extent of his disfigurement. She shrieked and pushed herself away with a coarse expression of disgust.

Krestovski's reaction was fast and vicious. Before the horrified woman could raise her arm in defence, he was bringing his cane up in a sweeping motion and cutting it across her face. She screamed and sank to her knees while Krestovski's companion hurried back to restrain him. Dawlish moved forward, impeded by the now-terrified girl who clung to him, then stopped to watch the tussle develop. Krestovski's friend was trying to remonstrate with him and the injured girl's companions were helping her to her feet. A menacing crowd was starting to gather. Krestovski, his face contorted to a mask of fury that was all the more dreadful for its scars, grappled with his companion and pushed him aside. He stood before the sobbing girl and pulled the cigar from between his clenched teeth. She realised too late that he was not finished with her. The glowing cigar was being ground into her cheek before she started to scream.

Krestovski pushed past her and into the group of horrified onlookers. In a moment he was lost in the throng and heading southwards. The bystanders were too surprised by the swiftness of his action to react immediately but when their shock had passed their anger focussed on his unfortunate companion. One of the women flung herself on him, tearing his face with her nails, and an enormous ruffian in a check suit and a billycock hat grabbed him from behind, holding him for another thug to pummel.

Dawlish fought free from the frightened girl who still held him. He moved swiftly around the knot of onlookers, frantically scanning the crowd ahead for some sign of Krestovski. Beneath his cloak he grasped the bronze figurine by the torso, his thumb braced on one outstretched wing. By the southern end of the Haymarket, where the crowd was thinning, he caught sight of a limping figure on the other side, unmistakable as Krestovski. He was pausing now and looking back, wary of pursuers. Reassured that there were none, he resumed his progress. Dawlish fell back a little before following. This area was too frequented for his purpose.

Trafalgar Square, was a pool of darkness dotted with islands of yellow light, deserted other than by destitutes sleeping on the benches. Bright pinpricks indicated where two policemen were scanning their faces with bullseye lanterns, rousing some and moving them on. Krestovski passed along the northern side with rapid steps, then crossed towards St. Martin's in the Fields. Dawlish followed.

A woman tried to accost Krestovski as he cut through Duncannon Street towards Charing Cross Station. Dawlish heard his snarl as he flung her sprawling in the gutter. She was picking herself up and hurling abuse after him when Dawlish passed her on the other side. He stepped into the shadows as Krestovski paused at the intersection with the Strand before crossing.

He tracked him at a safe distance. A few windows were still bright in the dark facade of the Charing Cross Hotel. He realised that there was a chance even now for him to turn aside from his purpose, for his bedroom there was but yards away. He knew that what he intended could put a rope around his neck but the memory of his tormented crewmen was bitter inside him, and he pressed on.

I want more than vengeance, more than retribution. I want justice.

There was light enough to see Krestovski moving along the eastern side of the railway station, down the ill-lit thoroughfare of Villiers Street. He seemed less furtive now, more confident that he had shaken off any pursuers from the Haymarket. There was no sign of life in this street that sloped towards the river other than the down-and-outs sleeping in doorways. Nearer the river, the sound of drunken singing came from a knot of wretches huddled around a meagre fire beneath the railway viaduct.

Krestovski crossed the street at the Embankment to stroll eastwards along the pavement at the riverside, past Cleopatra's Needle.

Dawlish kept pace in the shadows on the opposite side. He paused at a bench and, with cautious movements, removed his hat and cloak so as to be unencumbered. He laid them down on the seat and looked about. Nobody in sight. And any destitutes in the vicinity would be unlikely to intervene.

Krestovski had paused by a lantern and was looking out over the stone parapet at the river's edge, seemingly lost in thought. He had clamped another cigar between his teeth and was lighting it when Dawlish commenced his stealthy crossing of the street, his heart thumping, his hand that grasped the statuette trembling.

He was close, close enough to hear the swish of Krestovski's cloak as he waved the lucifer to extinguish it, when his foot slipped on a patch of loose gravel. Krestovski whipped around as he sprang at him with the figurine upraised. He had a fleeting impression of anger and surprise on the Russian's twisted features as he swung the crude weapon down, but the advantage had been lost and his victim was sidestepping. The statuette caught him a glancing blow on the shoulder but Dawlish went stumbling past him and fell on his knees against the parapet. He struggled to his feet with the Winged Victory still grasped in his right hand.

A wicked metallic whisper accompanied the sweeping motion with which Krestovski whipped a sword-blade from his ebony cane.

Dawlish paused, expecting his adversary to lunge at him, and so he was unprepared for the blade slashing horizontally at his head. Only a fraction of an inch separated his crown from the scything blade as he ducked. He must get inside Krestovski's guard and he flung himself forward as the sword was being drawn back for another swing. His head smashed into Krestovski's chest and his arms locked around his body, flinging him backwards.

They hit the pavement, Krestovski cushioning Dawlish's fall and the back of his head striking the ground. A clanking sound somewhere behind confirmed that the sword had been knocked from his grasp. Dawlish pulled his hands from behind Krestovski's back – there was a noise of ripping cloth as the figurine tore free - and he grappled with his left hand for the throat while he raised the right for a blow to the face.

His fingers were closing on Krestovski's neck when the Russian's rising knee caught him in the groin. The stabbing agony forced him to loosen his grip. Krestovski was twisting out from beneath him and Dawlish rolled over, half-blinded by pain. He tried to struggle to his knees and saw his enemy half-wriggling, half-crawling towards the sword by the wall.

He fought down his nausea and staggered to his feet. Krestovski made one last vain grasp for the blade before Dawlish's right boot dug deep into his side and doubled him up. Dawlish kicked again before flinging himself down with both knees on Krestovski's chest and gripping his left hand on his throat. He squeezed, saw the tongue protruding and heard choked gurgling from the open, lopsided mouth.

For the first time Dawlish saw those eyes, which had witnessed so much suffering unmoved, register terror, though only for a fleeting instant. The statuette came smashing down. Krestovski's body twisted and his hands groped weakly at Dawlish's hold on his neck. The second blow destroyed whatever semblance he still retained to anything human. Dawlish raised the figurine again and again, beating it into the scarlet mess before him. The writhing and shuddering stilled, then died beneath him.

He staggered to his feet, aghast at the horror before him. His hands and clothing were spattered with red. He clutched the wall for support, his chest heaving as he regained his breath. His grip on the lethal statuette relaxed and it clattered to the ground.

He never knew how long he remained there, panting, before the sound of footsteps caused him to spin around.

Topcliffe stood some twenty feet from him on the edge of the light cast by the street lamp. His face was in shadow and his expression could not be distinguished. Dawlish stared at him in numb silence.

"Dear me." Topcliffe's voice was heavy with mock concern. "I fear that the streets of London get more dangerous by the year. Can it be that our august visitor has had the misfortune to encounter a footpad?"

He advanced into the light and Dawlish saw that he was smiling. With the tip of his cane he flicked away a corner of Krestovski's cloak that had obscured the battered visage. He shook his head.

"The work of some gang of professional thugs, I'll warrant. And you, my dear, gallant Dawlish, went so bravely to the poor victim's aid. So quixotic! I regret that I was too far off to render some assistance myself."

He dropped to one knee and wrenched open the front of Krestovski's clothing. Reaching inside, he pulled out a wallet and pushed it into his own pocket. Then he began rifling the dead man's other pockets, shaking his head all the time. "The lawlessness of the capital is little less than a scandal," he said. "To think an honoured foreign visitor should be set upon in this way."

Topcliffe rolled the body over and extracted a notebook from the hip pocket. He flicked through it with an expression of satisfaction and put it in his own inner pocket before rolling Krestovski on his back again. His fingers closed on the watch chain.

"Strange that the ruffians should have omitted to take the watch," he said, "though of course they might not have realised its value. Solid gold I'd say, wouldn't you?"

He tore both watch and chain from the waistcoat, ripping the fabric, then pitched them into the darkness over the river.

"It seems the blackguards also forgot to help themselves to his ring. An emerald I think." He pulled it, encountered resistance, then dragged it from the finger with a jerk and hurled it too over the parapet. He rose, smiled at the still-dazed Dawlish and took his arm.

"Don't say anything, commander," he said. "You've had a bad shock through your gallant failure to save this gentleman's life. And I know that you're a modest hero. There's no need for your name to be associated with this business. It's fortunate that your hotel is near."

Dawlish tried to look him in the face but found that the eyes would not meet his. Topcliffe guided him to the kerb and raised one arm. Then a sound of hooves as two closed carriages emerged from the darkness by Hungerford Bridge. Something caught Topcliffe's eye at that moment. He stooped and picked up the blood-spattered statuette between finger and thumb. He pulled out his handkerchief and wrapped it in it.

"What strange habits even the most civilised of foreigners have," he said. "I fear the dear departed was taking a little souvenir from Lord Kegworth's. I'll see that it's returned unobtrusively so that the grieving relatives won't be embarrassed."

Topcliffe bundled Dawlish into the first carriage, which had now drawn alongside, then spoke to the unseen occupants of the second.

"The villains made off before I got here," Dawlish heard him say. "You'll see to it that the police are informed of a probably insoluble crime. Such a pity that the poor fellow came walking here alone."

He re-joined Dawlish and called out the name of the hotel to the driver. The carriage lurched into motion. Dawlish lay slumped in one corner, staring blankly through the window.

"Your hat and cloak are on the seat opposite," Topcliffe said. "I had them picked up before I joined you."

The carriage passed along the Embankment, disturbing the sleep of some beggars huddled on benches. It would mean nothing to them that the gateway to India was secure and the Sick Man of Europe reprieved.

Topcliffe leaned forward and tapped Dawlish on the knee.

"Make sure you have a good night's sleep, commander," he said "You may want to make an early start for your home in Shrewsbury. Get some rest there. I'll telegraph you when it's time to talk next week."

Probably again in the library of that Pall Mall club.

For he was Topcliffe's man now.

They were two of a kind.

THE END

(And what happened next is detailed in *Britannia's Wolf*)

A message from Antoine Vanner and a Historical Note

If you've enjoyed this book, I'd be most grateful if you were to submit a brief review to Amazon.com, to Amazon.co.uk or to Amazon.com.au. If you're reading on Kindle you'll be asked to rate the book by clicking on up to five stars. Such feedback is of incalculable importance to independent authors and will encourage me to keep chronicling the lives of Nicholas and Florence Dawlish.

If you'd like to leave a review, whether reading in paperback or in Kindle, then please go to the "*Britannia's Guile*" page on Amazon. Scroll down from the top and under the heading of "Customer Reviews" you'll see a big button that says "Write a customer review" – click that and you're ready to go into action. A sentence or two is enough, essentially what you'd tell a friend or family member about the book, but you may of course want to write more (and I'd be happy if you did since readers' feedback is of immense value to me!).

You can learn more about Nicholas Dawlish and his world on my website www.dawlishchronicles.com. You can read about his life, and how the individual books relate to events and actions during it, via www.dawlishchronicles.com/dawlish/

You may like to follow my weekly (sometimes twice-weekly) blog on www.dawlishchronicles.com/dawlish-blog in which articles appear that are based on my researches, but not used directly in my books. They range through the 1700 to 1930 period.

By subscribing to my mailing list, you will receive updates on my continuing writing as well as occasional free short-stories about the life of Nicholas Dawlish. Click on: www.bit.ly/2iaLzL7

Historical Note

In the mid-1870s the torpedo was a new weapon and as yet untried in war. The so-called "fish torpedo" that moved under its own power was the invention of a brilliant English engineer, Robert Whitehead (1823 – 1905), who set up a business in Fiume (now Rijeka, in Croatia) where his most important customer was the Austrian (later Austro-Hungarian) Navy. Whitehead was responsible for design of engines used in its warships, including some of those that gave a magnificent account of themselves in the Battle of Lissa, in 1866, against the Italians. This meant that, by the time he began to think about a new and revolutionary weapon, Whitehead had recognition as a talented engineer and not an impractical visionary.

The word "torpedo" had initially meant a moored mine and later an explosive device held at the end of a long spar and pushed against an enemy hull by crews in small boats. Intrepid Russian crews did score successes with the latter against Turkish vessels on the Danube in 1877 but tactic was all but suicidal. Whitehead's concept was one that would allow torpedoes to be launched from a distance, drive themselves at a set depth beneath the water's surface and hit enemy warships at their most vulnerable point: below the waterline.

The technical challenges were immense, demanding an effective pneumatic motor, sufficient compressed-air storage to drive it, and steering on as straight a course as possible. Whitehead's single most important innovation was the depth-maintenance mechanism, the details of which were to be guarded by such levels of confidentiality and security as to make it known as "The Whitehead Secret".

His prototype was ready for trial in 1866 but it took another four years of testing and modification to bring the weapon to a level that satisfied him. The speed was still low – some seven knots – and the torpedo was likely to be outrun by any moving target but the promise was there for devasting attacks on moored shipping. By 1870 Whitehead was sufficiently confident to offer his invention to the Royal Navy for testing. It is a tribute to the open-mindedness of the Admiralty that it was prepared to devote significant time and resources to a lengthy and rigorous programme for assessing the potential of this new and revolutionary weapon.

HMS *Oberon*, an iron paddle-sloop, was made available and provisions, designed by Whitehead, for launching torpedoes were built at her bows.

The trials took place in the Medway estuary, close to the Chatham naval base, in September and October 1870. Repeated launches of 14-inch and 16-inch torpedoes with dummy warheads, towards a net, proved their ability to maintain course. Meticulous records were maintained, including those by Lieutenant Arthur Wilson, who would later win the Victoria Cross and rise to Admiral of the Fleet. The torpedoes were retrieved at the end of each run, adjusted, and then launched again, showing in the process the ruggedness and reliability of the motors.

The culmination of the trials was live firing of a 16-inch weapon, armed with a 67-pound guncotton warhead, against a coal hulk, the former wooden corvette *Aigle*. This vessel was moored, but was defended by a weighted net suspended from spars along its side that extending to fourteen feet below the surface. Despite this protection, the torpedo, launched at a point-blank range of 136 yards, sank the hulk. When raised, the hole blown in its side was found to be twenty-feed long by ten feet deep.

The Royal Navy was convinced.

The torpedo had arrived. It would have a decisive impact on world history – and efforts to make it yet more lethal continue even today.

*

The confrontation between Russia and the Ottoman Empire, that led to war in 1877, had been triggered by events in Bulgaria in the previous year. In what was then a Ottoman province, the majority of the population was Christian and, for much of the time, lived in harmony with its Muslim neighbours. Despite attempts at modernisation, the Ottoman administration was generally inefficient, often corrupt, and always unhesitant to suppress disaffection by the most savage means. In the mid-1870s, growing nationalist feeling and resentment of Ottoman hegemony led to revolts in Bosnia, Herzegovina and Albania and to outright war with Serbia, which intervened on behalf of the rebels. Serbia was saved from defeat by the participation of Russian volunteers and hostilities were ended by the threat of Russian willingness to go to war over the issue.

In this period Russia had recovered from the disaster of the Crimean War of two decades previously. Significant legal, social and administrative reforms – including liberation of the serfs – had been implemented and more were in the offing. Military efficiency had been improved and vast territorial gains had been made in Central Asia, thanks to leaders of the calibre of General Mikhail Skobelev. Russia also saw herself as protector of Orthodox Christianity, regardless of where it was established. This view was very widely shared by members of the court, by much of society and by influential writers such as Dostoyevsky and Tolstoy. The latter had Anna Karenina's lover Vronsky volunteer to fight in Serbia after her death. Tchaikovsky composed his Slavonic March to help raise funds for medical support in Serbia. The combination of military might and idealistic thinking – not to mention her centuries-long ambition to secure access from the Black Sea to the Mediterranean – made Russia a very dangerous potential enemy for the Ottomans.

An uprising in Bulgaria against Ottoman rule in mid-1876 led to savage repression by both regular troops, "Bashi Bazook" irregulars and Bulgarian Muslims. Massacres such as that at the small town of Batak, often accompanied by torture and by widespread violation of women and girls, may have cost in excesses of thirty-thousand lives. Such massacres had been not uncommon in the Ottoman Empire in the past (and would culminate in the Armenian genocide in 1915) but had often been dismissed elsewhere as events in "a faraway country of which we know little". In 1876 however, the arrival of mass circulation newspapers and the ability of intrepid correspondents to report their findings, led to the details of theses atrocities becoming widely known internationally.

The key figure in publicising the massacres was the Irish-American journalist, Januarius MacGahan (1844 – 1878) who had previously covered Russian campaigns in Central Asia. Accompanied by the American consul-general in Constantinople, Eugene Schuyler (1840–1890), he visited Banak and other locations three months after the massacres. They found horrific, unburied, evidence of their scale and ferocity. MacGahan's reports in London's *Daily News*, corroborated by

Schuyler, and reprinted elsewhere in Europe and America, left nothing to the imagination. The outrage that followed was all but universal.

With a slide towards Russian intervention accelerating, the Ottomans had lost all moral authority and were unlikely to find any ally in the event of war – other than Britain.

Revulsion in Britain was as strong as elsewhere but was tempered by strategic considerations. A victory in a war with Turkey could give Russia access to the Eastern Mediterranean and thereby menace Britain's maritime links to India. Similar concerns had brought Britain into the Crimean War of 1854-56 as an Ottoman ally. Now, in 1877, regardless of the moral aspect, Britain's brilliant, pragmatic and ruthless prime minister, Benjamin Disraeli, Lord Beaconsfield, recognised that Britain would have to stand by Turkey if its total defeat seemed imminent. It was a hard decision, and one that encountered fierce opposition in Britain itself initially, but strategic considerations would trump all else. (And how this worked out in practice provides the background to the next novel in the *Dawlish Chronicles* series – *Britannia's Wolf*).

*

The French battleship *Admiral Duperré,* on the design of which that of *Alexander Nevski* is based, was the most powerful warship in the world for a brief period. Her innovations were to appear, frequently in more-exaggerated forms, in all subsequent French Battleships up to 1900. This often resulted in a bizarre "Steampunk" appearance).

French shipyards constructed warships for foreign navies in the late 19th Century. Copies of these ships were sometimes built thereafter in the yards of the purchasing country. The most notable example is the Russian five-ship *Borodino* Class, the first of which, the *Tsesarevich*, was built in France and the other four in St. Petersburg. Three of these vessels were to be sunk at the Battle of Tsushima in 1905, guns blazing to the last, and with only a score of survivors from the combined crews of some 2300 men.

Our Authors

Rick Spilman is the founder and manager of Old Salt Press, an independent publishing company that provides the umbrella for a number of authors who write nautical fiction. As well as keeping up a hugely popular blog, "Old Salt Blog", Rick has published three very successful nautical books — *Hell Around the Horn, The Shantyman*, and *Evening Gray, Morning Red*, plus a novella, *Bloody Rain. The Shantyman* won a Kirkus Reviews Indie Book of the Year award, and deservedly so. All four are absolutely first-class reading.

Alaric Bond, an English Old Salt Press author, is the producer of the hugely popular "Fighting Sail" series, set in the Napoleonic Era, the latest of which is *Seeds of War.* At time of writing, he is working on the fifteenth book in the series. He has also produced three stand-alone books, *The Guinea Boat, Turn a Blind Eye,* and *Hellfire Corner,* the latter being set in WW2.

Joan Druett became a maritime historian by accident. While exploring the tropical island of Rarotonga in the South Pacific, she slipped into the hole left by the roots of a large uprooted tree, and at the bottom discovered the centuries-old grave of a whaling wife. Because of this, Joan became a noted expert in the history of women at sea, leading to ten novels and 17 works of nonfiction, including the bestselling *Island of the Lost.*

Linda Collison is American and has written the Patricia Macpherson nautical adventures series, the first being *Barbados Bound*, the next two books being *Surgeon's Mate* and *Rhode Island Rendezvous.* Linda has also published other works independently, including biting satires under the *'Knife and Gun Club'* banner, and *Redfeather*, which was a finalist in Foreword's Book of the Year Award. A fourth book published with Old

Salt Press is *Water Ghosts*, a haunting tale that was a number one Amazon bestseller in the Young Adult category.

Seymour Hamilton is Canadian and the author of The *Astreya Trilogy*. His work, though maritime, is very reminiscent of Tolkien's carefully wrought fantasy worlds. He also set *Angel's Share*, which was beautifully illustrated by Shirley MacKenzie, in the *Astreya* world.

The list also features V. E. Ulett, the nom-de-plume of a very successful Californian writer who normally specializes in steampunk adventures. Her three maritime novels, are published under the Old Salt Press colophon: *Captain Blackwell's Prize, Blackwell's Paradise,* and *Blackwell's Homecoming.*

And there is also Antoine Vanner – author of the *Dawlish Chronicles* series of historical naval adventures set in the late 19th Century. Ten books in the series so far, and still counting!

Visit: oldsaltpress.com/about-old-salt-press

Printed in Great Britain
by Amazon

16731074R00169